Praise for Lucy Dillon

'A book you'll read into the wee hours, full of warmth, love and bravery.'

Lucy Robinson on *One Small Act of Kindness*

'A brilliant book . . . clever and deeply moving. I'll be passing it on to all my friends.'

Sophie Kinsella on *A Hundred Pieces of Me*

'A thoughtful, romantic, bittersweet story'

Sunday Mirror on *A Hundred Pieces of Me*

'A totally feelgood novel about the importance of living life to the full'

Sun on *A Hundred Pieces of Me*

'Lucy Dillon's voice is gentle and kind throughout . . . perceptive and well handled.'

Red on *The Secret of Happy Ever After*

'Witty, heart-warming and a very real tale of loss and redemption'

Stylist on *Walking Back to Happiness*

'I loved this book! Heartwarming, real and entertaining'

Katie Fforde on *Lost Dogs and Lonely Hearts*

'A charming, heartwarming, entertaining read'

Glamour on *The Ballroom Class*

Lucy Dillon

all I ever wanted

HODDER

First published in Great Britain in 2016 by Hodder & Stoughton
An Hachette UK company

A CIP catalogue record for this title is available from the British Library

Paperback ISBN 978 1 444 79604 9
eBook ISBN 978 1 444 79605 6

Typeset in Plantin Light by Hewer Text UK Ltd, Edinburgh
Printed and bound by CPI Group (UK) Ltd, Croydon, CR0 4YY

Hodder & Stoughton policy is to use papers that are natural, renewable
and recyclable products and made from wood grown in sustainable
forests. The logging and manufacturing processes are expected to
conform to the environmental regulations of the country of origin.

Hodder & Stoughton Ltd
Carmelite House
50 Victoria Embankment
London EC4Y 0DZ

www.hodder.co.uk

For Scott, a Happy Ever After man,
right down to the Border Terrier.

Prologue

Nancy clutched her bag of caramelised nuts and gazed out at the lights dancing between the buildings on either side of Oxford Street, glittering in the dark sky like gold and silver stars, while hundreds of thousands of people hurried along the pavements beneath them. They were very high up on the bus, and she was glad they weren't down in the middle of the crowds. Everyone moved so fast, rushing into the shops, pushing and shoving. They'd nearly lost Joel at the bus stop, and Daddy had shouted and said something that had made Mummy shout too.

She glanced over to her big brother to check he was still there. He was. Joel was waving at the crowds like he was the Queen, just like he did when they went on the bus at home in Bristol. He was practising, he said, for when he was famous.

Nancy and Mummy were on one front seat on the top deck of the big red bus while Joel and Daddy were squashed onto the other side. Joel was perched on the edge of his seat, waving and pretending to fall off every time the bus went round a corner.

Nancy thought Joel was being funny, but Daddy didn't. Even though they were on their way to see Santa, the highlight of what had been one magical thing after another, Daddy was

1

in a bad mood. He'd been in a bad mood since they'd arrived.

'That policeman's waving back at me!' Joel announced in delight. 'Look! The policeman's waving!'

Daddy grabbed Joel's arm. 'Stop that, Joel! This isn't the time or the place to be acting up.' He glared at Mummy over Joel's bobble hat. His eyes were red, and not kind. 'Bloody Oxford Circus. At Christmas. Madness.'

'It's fun!' Mummy hugged Nancy. 'You'll remember your trip to see Santa Claus forever, won't you, Fancy Nancy?'

She nodded, unable to stop looking at Daddy's cross face. When he was cross, he didn't look like his normal self, and it made her feel strange inside, as if he was someone she didn't know. Now he pressed his lips tight together, then got out his phone.

Nancy was gripped by a sudden panic. What if Santa thought Daddy was cross because she and Joel had been naughty? What if he thought they didn't deserve any presents? Her tummy felt churny.

Mummy leaned over and lifted the earflap of her hat to whisper in her ear. 'Don't forget, you've still got one more wish!'

Nancy's favourite book was about a magic cat who granted wishes. Her second favourite book was about a little girl and her mummy seeing the sights of London. Mummy had brought a special cat that she kept in her squashy handbag, and said that she and Joel could have one wish each for every one of the things they saw from the London book. So far, they'd seen Big Ben, the big wheel, and ten black taxis.

'Up to three wishes a day,' Daddy had interrupted, but Nancy didn't need to be told not to be greedy. She knew from the cat book that if you were greedy or selfish with your wishes, bad things happened. You had to be *very* careful.

'Oh my God I'm going to faaaaaaalll!' yelled Joel, dramatically.

'Joel!' Daddy yanked him back by his hood. 'Behave, or we'll skip Hamleys and go straight home.'

Nancy's panic increased. Santa knew they were coming – Mummy had confirmed it. If they didn't arrive because Joel had been naughty, what would he think?

Mummy leaned over and pulled Joel onto their seat, sliding Nancy onto her knee to make room. She put her arms around them both but Nancy couldn't enjoy the cuddle when Daddy was glaring at Mummy from the other side of the bus. Would he tell Santa? Was that why he'd got his phone out? Was he sending Santa a text? She felt sick.

'Settle down, Joel. You've got one more wish too,' said Mummy. 'What's it going to be?'

'I wish . . . I wish . . .' Joel's voice was too loud, and people were looking round at them. 'I WISH . . .'

Nancy wanted to say, 'Be quiet, Joel', but her head felt jumbled up.

'Joel!' It was Daddy's scariest voice, the quiet hissy one.

Mummy put her hand gently over Joel's mouth, but she leaned over and kissed him on the bobble of his hat. Nancy saw, to her panic, that Mummy's eyes were shiny wet, and when she blinked her lashes made dark smears. Maybe she was worried about Santa too.

I wish Daddy would go away somewhere so me and Joel and Mummy could go see Santa on our own, thought Nancy, and immediately a dark feeling spread over her, that she'd done something very wrong.

3

Before she could take it back and wish for something kinder, the bus shuddered and stopped, and people started to stand up, blocking the aisle with their damp coats and shopping bags, shuffling impatiently towards the stairs. The bus felt unfriendly all of a sudden, and not as much fun.

Nancy's stomach flipped over.

'Regent Street!' announced Daddy and stood up, bending his head so as not to hit it on the low roof. Nancy turned to see the people in the seat behind had stood up, and the people behind them, and when she turned back, Daddy's dark blue coat had vanished. He'd gone! Just a wall of blank-faced strangers in front of her, and the dark, sparkly sky on the other side of the window behind her.

'Quick, quick, you two,' said Mummy, picking up her bag, and Joel's bag, and Nancy's Union Jack backpack, but Nancy was frozen to the seat.

It was already happening! Daddy had gone! What if the bus started moving before they could get off? They might never find him! She'd wished for him to go away, and it was happening!

'Come on, Nancy!' Mummy stretched out her hand, but Nancy pushed past, her legs wanting to run so hard she was scared they'd go without her, running off down the bus leaving her body behind.

'Nancy!' Mummy was calling, but Nancy wriggled through the passengers, not listening to them shouting and grumbling at her. All she could think about was Daddy, finding Daddy, hanging onto his hand and stopping him disappearing. *She hadn't meant it! She hadn't really meant it! He could tell Santa what he liked as long as the scary crowds didn't eat him up.*

He wasn't at the bottom of the stairs. He wasn't by the door. He'd gone. Nancy pushed past the people standing by the yellow poles and jumped off the deck of the bus onto the crowded pavement. She could smell toasted nuts and cinnamon and Christmas but all she could taste in her mouth was the nasty taste of sick that she'd had when she and Joel had flu.

Big gulping sobs burst out of her chest.

London wasn't magical at all. It was scary. Everything was loud and strange. Shops were hot, then freezing cold. The food was different. And Daddy didn't look like Daddy here. Mummy seemed different too. They didn't talk, they got cross about things they never got cross about at home. Nancy *wished wished wished* she could be back in Bristol, in their house at the end of the street, with the green fireplace and the black cat next door. She wanted to feel her Daddy's hand holding hers, Mummy holding the other, so much she wanted to cry. But she'd had her three wishes. There were none left to fix this.

Then she saw him standing in a shop doorway, checking his phone.

Relief shocked her. Had *she* wished him back? Could she do that now? Was London listening to her wishes? It made her feel wobbly, the thought too big to fit inside her head.

'Daddy!' she sobbed, and ran towards him. A bike on the pavement swerved, the rider swore, Nancy barely noticed.

He looked up, just as she launched herself at his legs and staggered under the force of her grip.

'Careful, Nancy,' he said, and his voice was so familiar that Nancy blanked out everything else. Everything apart from the smell of his coat, and the feel of his arms around her.

'Don't go, Daddy,' she cried. 'Don't go!'

'I won't, Nancy,' he said, but his voice sounded very far away.

Chapter one

As Patrick opened his notebook of issues to raise in mediation, Caitlin dug her fingernails into her palms and tried to remember where it was she'd read that it was always the little things you fall in love with that make you want to stab your partner to death with a fork in the end.

Patrick was still handsome, with his strong cheekbones and thick brown hair that grew faster than hers; he was still energetic and annoyingly refreshed-looking for someone apparently racked with distress at being separated from his wife and kids. (Possibly *because* of the extra sleep he was getting, Caitlin thought, waspishly.) He still smelled of coffee and aftershave, still politely opened the bloody door to their mediation session for her, was still wearing the jellybean cufflinks Joel and Nancy had given him for Christmas, but all that was obliterated by his relentless, tedious, *enraging* control freakery, which she'd initially mistaken for old-fashioned gallantry.

Divorce and separation, Caitlin decided, brought out the worst in control freaks. Even more so than marriage.

'Just to recap on the allowances?' Patrick tapped a page with his pen. 'I'm not sure these figures my wi—' His face froze for a split second, revealing a sudden flash of vulnerability, then it was gone, bustled away with some facts. 'These figures *Caitlin*'s produced seem off. I've looked at the weekly food bills, for instance, and they just don't add up.' He paused. 'Literally.'

Caitlin stared at the cactus on the mediator's desk. Patrick had loved referring to her as his wife; he used to smile goofily as he said it, as if he couldn't quite believe his luck. That was Patrick though, her knight in shining armour, the only driver to stop behind her lifeless Renault on the windswept hard shoulder of the M25, six years ago now. She'd been hyperventilating with panic with a huge-eyed Joel strapped in his seat behind her as the motorway traffic zoomed past, shaking their little car, while her phone refused to find signal. Patrick had knocked on the window, and she should have been scared, but something in his face was so honest, so openly concerned for a woman stranded with a young boy, that Caitlin had sensed deep inside that she was safe. Patrick walked to the emergency call box in the pouring rain (he had appropriate wet-weather gear; she didn't), and waited with them till help arrived. Awkwardly at first, but when the AA van's headlights broke the cocooning darkness, she'd found herself slipping her hand into Patrick's, silently thanking him, and he hadn't let it go.

And then, of course, after a few thoughtful dates had turned into a charmingly courtly relationship, he'd gone on to save Caitlin in all sorts of other ways. She'd let things get into a mess. The house, her finances, her life. But nothing was too annoying for Patrick to smooth out. Nothing was too broken in their little house that he couldn't sit down and fix it. He hated disorder, hated unfairness, did his own PPI claim forms, rescued spiders from the bath with his bare hands. A modern knight. Caitlin – with her fatherless child, and her 'wasted' degree, and her totally depleted cupboard of self-esteem – was overjoyed to be rescued.

7

But that same methodical calmness felt like water torture now their marriage was broken to the point where even Patrick had given up on it. As he carried on speaking, Caitlin boggled at his ability to separate all the causes and faults into piles, ready for assessment by the mediator, in the same way he laid out the components of their first IKEA wardrobe so not a screw or washer would be lost. A set of final straws here, a stack of rational sums there. Nice and neat, and final, no sticky emotion messing up the conclusion.

And that was the difference between the two of them, Caitlin reflected, as Patrick moved his laser-beam attention to tax credits. She'd approached their separation like *she* used to tackle an IKEA wardrobe before they'd met: i.e., no careful consultation of expert instructions, just rushing straight into the task in hand, followed by self-inflicted pain, frustration, and then tears. Tears, and wine, and hours reading online separation guides that might as well have been written in Swedish. Worst of all was that guilty ache that, through her own carelessness, she'd managed to lose the tiny, precious Allen key to Patrick's heart.

Once, Patrick had thought she was perfect. Now he could barely look her in the eye, and the happy, supportive, *safe* relationship she'd longed for all her life was in bits.

Caitlin sank back into the plastic chair. Maybe she and Patrick were just too different to work, long-term. Even now, while Patrick and the mediator were talking, she couldn't stop part of her brain rejoicing that finally she could stack the dishwasher as she saw fit, or dye a blonde streak into her hair without getting the 'oh, really?' eyebrow. She'd cope. She'd coped before. The real problem was how to stop it shattering the lives of the two bewildered bystanders in the middle of the drama, neither of whom deserved to be dragged into their parents' mess.

Joel and Nancy's anxious faces cut through Caitlin's secret idea for a very discreet tattoo, and she flinched. But it was better for them, surely, not to be trapped between two squabbling adults?

'We don't need to finalise any financial agreements in this first session,' said Andrea the mediator. Her voice was pleasant, but her expression made it clear that she wasn't going to waste any of their allotted hour on point-scoring. 'Top priority is working out arrangements regarding the children. And we're talking about . . .' She glanced down at her notes. 'Joel, who I see is ten, and Nancy, who is four.'

'Four and a half next month,' said Caitlin. 'Five on September the tenth.' She smiled at Andrea; she looked like a mum – she understood that this was really the only part of the mediation that mattered. Not money. Not who got the car. 'I can't believe she's going to be starting school in September! My little pickle.'

'*Our* little pickle,' Patrick pointed out, and Caitlin crossed her legs to stop herself reacting. Yes, she should have said *our*. Patrick always tripped her up like that, seeing hurt where she hadn't meant any. But: she was the one who fed the kids, understood their funny, ever-evolving language, anticipated their tears, their tiredness, their smiles, their hunger. She was the one whose life revolved around their sleep, their nits, their endless questions, the moods that roared from love to frustration, their constantly reaching hands. Patrick always laughed drily and said he was just the one who paid for them. Which, neatly, made them *both* feel bad.

'I want to share parenting,' Patrick added. 'It's important to me to maintain as much contact as possible.'

Caitlin couldn't stop herself shooting him some side-eye at that. Patrick worked so hard he barely saw them even before the break-up. She fought down the urge to ask Patrick to name any three of Nancy's favourite teddies, knowing he couldn't. He didn't even know she ranked them. In an order that changed weekly.

'What?' Patrick turned to her, and raised his eyebrows; Caitlin noticed fresh flecks of silver in his dark sideburns. 'Are you saying you don't want that too? For the children to see both of us?'

'Of course not!' God, he was annoying. 'Why on earth would I be saying that?'

Patrick's silent accusation hung in the air. It was uncharacteristically mean of him. *He doesn't even like me any more*, thought Caitlin, miserably. *That's what happens when you get put on a pedestal – there'll always be a point where you fall off.*

'It's good that you want to share responsibility.' Andrea picked up a pen to make notes. 'What are the current living arrangements? Caitlin, you're still in the family home in Bristol?'

She nodded. 'Yes, it's my house.'

'Now who's making a point?' Patrick shot back. 'It's *our* house.'

Caitlin refused to rise to that. 'It was my gran's house, she left it to me in her will. I've lived there since Joel was born. Patrick moved in when we got married, and he left in January. When he got his new job.'

'It's not a new job, it's the same job in a different place,' said Patrick.

Andrea jotted something down on her pad. 'And where are you living now, Patrick?'

Ha! Go on, thought Caitlin. *Tell her.*

There was a short pause while Patrick framed his answer in the best possible light. 'I'm currently looking for a property – I was moved up to Newcastle by my company at the beginning of this year.'

Five Monday mornings ago. It occurred to Caitlin that it was Valentine's Day soon, and something in her chest caved in. Always at least a dozen roses, and some sweet, thoughtful notes hidden in her coat pockets, or tucked in her purse. Not this year. Never again.

'Three hundred miles away,' she said instead, to fill the aching gap. 'You think it's reasonable for Joel and Nancy to do a six-hundred-mile round trip every week?'

'What? And you think it's reasonable to refuse to move with your husband when he gets a chance to improve the whole family's situation, because you *like your sitting room*?' He said it in that 'I am at the end of my considerable patience' tone that made Caitlin clench her fists.

She turned to him on her chair, so he could see how pissed off she was, in her eyes if not in her words. 'Since we're deciding what's reasonable, no, I don't think it's reasonable to apply for a job at the other end of the country, without even telling your family.'

'I didn't apply for it! I was sent there by head office – it's part of my responsibility!' Patrick threw his hands up. 'What was I supposed to do? Tell them I can't go because my wife cares more about her original fireplace than me? That's not how these things work, Caitlin. You don't always get a choice.'

Caitlin bit her lip. It wasn't just about the fireplace, he knew that. And yet it *was*. That fireplace was where her shattered world had been put back together by her gran when everything fell apart after university; where she'd nursed both her children, and sat with Patrick watching him gaze into Nancy's sleeping face, shell-shocked by the force of his own love. The coal fire burning in the grate made her feel secure and happy. Like Patrick used to. And no, she hadn't wanted to leave it. It wasn't the reason, but it was the final straw. A symbolic straw.

She turned back to Andrea, determined to stay dignified.

'Not having a mortgage makes a significant difference to us financially. The kids have their own rooms. Joel's at a great school, which Nancy'll be starting in September, and there's a playground next door. And it's near my *job*, because I have a job too, even though it doesn't pay as much as Patrick's and . . .' Caitlin made herself say the real truth since Patrick seemed to refuse to hear it. 'I didn't feel our relationship would survive the move. We were barely talking. I didn't want to uproot the kids only to have to bring them back again.'

Patrick fixed her with his clear, straight-into-her-head look. The one that made her want to babble anything, just to get him to stop . . . *looking*. 'Is that the only reason you didn't want to leave Bristol? Be honest, Caitlin.'

Caitlin stared at him, baffled. 'I *honestly* don't know what you're talking about.'

This wasn't the first time Patrick had said something like that, but he wouldn't explain what he was getting at. She'd tried, but he'd stonewalled her, as if she *should* know. OK, so things had been rocky for a while. What sleep-deprived, over-worked, under-sexed parents don't get irritated and snappy with each other? But somewhere along the line, 'rocky' had solidified into stony silence. The love hadn't vanished completely: at the start of December they'd managed a night out for Caitlin's birthday, and it was as if they both remembered why they'd fallen in love in the first place. She squeezed into her spotty circle skirt, Patrick came home early from work, and for the first time in months, he slipped his hand into hers as they walked into town. Caitlin caught sight of herself in a shop window, dark corkscrew curls and scarlet lips, an hourglass bombshell out on a date with a good-looking man, and her heart had lifted as if it was attached to a million balloons. In the pub, after a few ciders and her Comedy Store-worthy re-enactment of Joel's school play, Patrick had laughed the way he used to. He looked a decade younger, happier. They'd walked home slowly, ignoring the babysitter's calls, and Caitlin had pulled him close under a streetlight and kissed him. *Thank God*, she'd thought with relief, as his hand reached for her waist inside her winter jacket, *it's going to be fine*.

But the following week had been horrible. She'd been late back from her weekly Zumba class, which always made Patrick twitchy, and that in turn made Caitlin defensive – he worried about her being out alone on dark nights, but she hated feeling 'monitored'. Joel picked up nits; the tumble drier broke down, out of warranty because she'd forgotten to register it. Then Patrick's manager phoned about the job. They'd disagreed. First politely, then – with Joel and Nancy out of earshot in bed – the discussion had got a bit heated. By the time she and Patrick had taken the kids to London for their Christmas surprise, they'd both said too much, yet not enough. Worse than squabbling, there'd been silence. A brick wall of resentment on both sides. When Patrick brought it up again, Caitlin realised he hadn't listened to a single reason she'd given him – or else he didn't care.

And then, after New Year, Patrick announced he had to make a decision and Caitlin, caught between Nancy's tantrum and Joel's bookbag, more or less told him to put his job first, since he would anyway. He was still giving her that baleful 'you've done something' look, but Caitlin genuinely didn't know what she'd done. Other than not be the ideal woman Patrick had always wanted to believe she was.

Shame flooded her.

'Caitlin?' Andrea prompted her. 'You look as if you want to say something. About the shared parenting?'

She tried to focus on what was important now. 'I don't want Joel and Nancy to feel this is their fault – we don't want them to be affected any more than they have to be. Joel's . . . Well, Joel has no memory of his biological father because he's never been in his life . . .' She trailed off, because even after ten years she still hadn't found an ideal way of explaining it.

It was Patrick who leaped in. 'Joel's called me Dad since he was four. I hope he considers me his father. As far as I'm concerned I've always loved him and Nancy exactly the same. *Exactly* the same.'

'Of course you have.' In her mind's eye, Caitlin saw the moment on the roaring motorway when Patrick had lifted a wailing Joel out of his car seat into the recovery vehicle, and Joel's tears had dried instantly. She'd known, right then. Joel had too. Here was a good man, and she wasn't on her own any more. And yet he'd changed his mind. Not about Joel, or Nancy, but about her. About *them*.

'It's clear you're both very committed to their happiness.' Andrea's tone was conciliatory. 'That's a great start. So, let's find a middle ground for these weekends. Are there grand-parents who might enjoy hosting contact?'

'Sadly, no – my father died when I was very young, and my mother is in a care home.' The vulnerable Patrick vanished; he was managerial again. Caitlin reached for her cold coffee and wished it were a glass of wine.

I'm going to have a really cold, really good glass of wine when I get home, she thought. Her mouth watered at the idea of it. Once Joel had gone to bed. Now Patrick wasn't around to sigh disapprovingly at the bottle.

'Caitlin?'

'My parents are the other way, in North London.'

'OK.' Andrea turned back to Patrick. 'Any other relatives? Aunts, uncles? Godparents, perhaps? Family friends?'

Caitlin was surprised to hear Patrick clear his throat. 'I was about to suggest my sister,' he said. 'She lives in Longhampton – that's not too far to travel for the weekend. About seventy miles.'

'Eva?' It came out more dramatically than Caitlin meant it to, but even so. *Eva?*

'Yes, Eva.' Patrick sounded surprised. 'Why react like that?'

'I'm reacting *like that* because the poor woman's just been widowed!' Patrick could be incredibly dense about other people's emotional needs. 'Do you honestly think sending Joel and Nancy to stay with a woman who's still grieving is appropriate for any of us?'

'It's two years since Mick died,' said Patrick, reasonably. 'And she's not the sort of woman to spend the rest of her life wearing black and refusing to go out.'

'How would we know? We never see her.' Two years, though. Ouch. The last time they'd seen Eva was at Mick's funeral. Caitlin had genuinely meant to call her sister-in-law more regularly, but months sped past with playdates and shopping and basic family admin, and Eva was often away on holiday. Even then, she wasn't someone Caitlin could easily pick up the phone and chat to. Eva was everything she wasn't. She'd run her own company. She knew celebrities. She had two dogs and no family, and that seemed to suit her fine. Caitlin never knew what to talk to Eva about, so their conversations always seemed to end up being polite explorations of the weather.

And that amazing house. Even now, Caitlin felt grubby thinking about it. 'And it's not as if Eva's exactly set up for children, is it? Her house is all white. White sofas, white carpets, white . . . everything.'

And glass. Glass as far as the eye could see, without a single smear. Beautiful, but not exactly fun for two exuberant kids.

'I don't see what her carpets have to do with anything.' Patrick shook his head as if she was being irrational. 'She's their aunt. She's their family. I'm sure she'll want to help us out.'

Caitlin seized on that. 'Have you even asked her?'

Patrick's expression flickered. 'Yes.'

'No, you haven't.'

Andrea stepped in. 'Ah well, we shouldn't make firm arrangements until we're happy that they stand a chance of working.'

'My sister is being very supportive in what's a painful time for everyone,' said Patrick, and Caitlin knew he was making it up as he went along, because he could draft meaningless management responses like this in his sleep. She'd be surprised if he'd even spoken to Eva since the Christmas duty call.

Another thought nipped at her imagination. 'What about Eva's dogs?'

'What about them?' Patrick turned in his chair.

'If they're not used to children, they might be territorial.

You read terrible things about dogs that aren't used to children suddenly turning nasty. Even nice ones.' A Jack Russell fitting that exact description had taken a small but painful lump out of Caitlin's own calf as a child. It had left her very vigilant around supposedly placid dogs. The thought of Joel trying to rope Eva's unwilling pets into some improvised musical, or Nancy trying to cuddle them too hard, like she squeezed her rows of soft toys . . . She felt a chill across her skin.

'What kind of dogs does your sister have?' Andrea asked Patrick, calmly.

'Pugs. They're a pair of fat *pugs*, for God's sake, not rabid Rottweilers. They're more likely to be scared of Joel sitting on them than anything else.'

'Why do you always minimise my concerns?' Caitlin demanded.

'I don't! I just don't understand why you fixate on the irrelevant concerns and let big ones go. What's the problem with the kids being at Eva's?' Again, the look. The accusing, hurt look.

She shook her head, mute with defeat. There wasn't a reason. Apart from, *I don't want you to take my children away from me.*

Patrick's mouth was a tight line. 'Anyway, you get the weekend off. Isn't that what you wanted? You're always complaining about how you have no time to be yourself. No *space*. Make up your mind.'

Oh, now I remember why we're separating, thought Caitlin, balling her fists. *Now I remember.*

Andrea pushed a box of tissues across the desk and Caitlin realised she must look tearful. 'Maybe you could visit with the children on your own, before the first contact weekend? It would normalise the situation for Joel and Nancy, and you could put your own mind at rest about any further arrangements you need to put in place.'

'I should be there too,' said Patrick.

'Of course.' Andrea looked weary now. *How exhausting,* thought Caitlin, *having to listen to couples squabbling like toddlers over the biggest bit of cake, hour after hour after bloody hour.* 'It's vital the visit is a positive, encouraging experience for Nancy and Joel.'

'Can you be happy with that?' He turned, an eyebrow raised. This was how all conversations with Patrick seemed to end up. Like being dragged along under a train you originally wanted to get on. When had he changed? She wondered. Would this new man lift a wailing toddler from a broken-down car? Would he bring a first date present of jump-leads, oil, emergency triangle, as well as tulips?

Andrea was eyeing her. Caitlin steeled herself. Eva might not even say yes. She probably wouldn't want Joel and Nancy running riot in her pristine white-carpeted house. She might not even be living there. She might have gone to wherever that other holiday home of Mick's was – Provence, or San Tropez. Somewhere linen-suity, where everyone drank gin and tonic and knew Cliff Richard.

'Fine,' she said. 'Call Eva and see if she's got a weekend free for us to visit.'

'I'll ring her this afternoon,' said Patrick. 'Then we can move things on.'

'Great!' Andrea sounded relieved. 'So we've got a positive to take away from today's session. Well done, both of you.'

'Do we have time to deal with some of those points I raised about monthly budgets?' asked Patrick. 'While I'm here?'

Caitlin glanced up at the clock. There were only five minutes left. It felt like they'd been in there hours.

'No,' said Andrea, firmly. 'Let's stop while we're ahead.'

Chapter two

For all his mining roots and soap-and-water attitude to grooming, Michael Quinn – Hollywood actor, television star, famous Yorkshireman – had loved his clothes. Eva stood in front of the wardrobe that ran the length of Mick's custom-built dressing room, raised a hand to slide the door back, then let it fall. She knew what was inside, and she knew what she had to do. She just couldn't bear to do it.

Disposing of Mick's personal belongings was a task she'd been putting off for months. When the wooden hangers moved and a trace of his familiar cologne drifted out, for a second Eva imagined he was behind her, that he'd just been in another room all this time. Mick's clothes were *him*, his life laid out in colourful chapters: the casual cords and country shirts she'd bought nearest the front, then the designer jackets from the celebrity years before they were married, then at the back, a glimpse of the paisley silks and velvets of two lifetimes ago, when Mick had staggered out of 3 a.m. Soho lock-ins while she'd been . . . well, a baby. Eva had started with those clothes, since they didn't mean anything to her, but the pockets were full of questions she'd never have the answer to: loose change, matchbooks from a jazz club, scraps of paper with 071 London numbers, faded taxi receipts. Eva's heart twisted inside her chest, knowing she'd never be able to ask where the club had been, who he'd seen there; whose number this was, whose business card. Seven years hadn't been long enough to scratch the surface of decades' worth of anecdotes; it tormented Eva that total strangers had memories from Mick's life she'd never even know about.

She rested her forehead against the wardrobe door and inhaled his smell. Not a glorious second-chance life together then, as they'd both hoped. Just a short, happy interlude. Eva no longer woke up crying, and now went days without feeling bereft, but this final task brought what she'd lost rushing back. Who else was going to do it, though? For all that fame he'd enjoyed, Mick had no other family, just two ex-wives and a son he hadn't seen in ten years. This was her home, with or without him, and the last thing Mick had told her, the last thing he'd told anyone before he closed those mischievous blue eyes, pale like faded denim, was, *Don't stop living because I've gone, my darling.*

Easy for *him* to say that.

Eva raised her head to psych herself up, and was startled by the middle-aged woman she saw in the mirrored door. Mick preferred her 'natural', and she'd been baby-faced enough to get away without much make-up ten years ago, but suddenly, since her last birthday, she'd started avoiding mirrors. She looked tired. She felt tired too. Eva squinted critically. Heartbreak had sharpened her slim face into angles, hollowing her cheekbones, emphasising her long nose. She could see white threads in her brown hair, a frown line like her dad's between her eyes. Her eyes, at least, were still OK. Like the sea, Mick had always said, very changeable – sometimes Mediterranean blue-green, sometimes a colder North Sea grey, when she was annoyed.

Eva pulled her fringe to one side, then the other, to see if it helped. It hid the frown line, but made her look disconcertingly like her mum.

Claws skittered on the wooden stairs, and from the quick tippety-tapping Eva knew that it was Bumble, the boy pug, hunting her down. The pugs had been asleep in the kitchen, resting after their morning stroll down the lane behind the house. Bee, his fatter, peachier, bossier sister, would be asleep until lunchtime, but Bumble needed to monitor his remaining human. It was nice to feel needed, but being the sole focus of canine adoration made Eva feel inwardly claustrophobic.

'Hello, Bumble,' she said without turning round.

The little pug slid to a halt by the wardrobe, sat down with a plop and a huff, and regarded her with the quizzical wrinkles he'd had since he was a puppy. Bee didn't suffer from the same perma-anxiety; she was confident in her loveability. That was how Eva instructed people to tell the two nearly identical fawn pugs apart: 'Does it look worried? Bumble. Is it trying to get on your knee? Bee.'

Eva removed two hideous white Miami Vice jackets from the rails – some Longhampton teenagers would be making quite an entrance to this year's prom, thanks to Mick – and slipped her hand into the pockets to check for rogue memories. Nothing. Good.

'What do you reckon?' she said, folding the jackets up. 'Do you think we should give Mick's wedding suit to the charity shop where we met?' Eva never called Mick 'Daddy' to the dogs, although he'd jovially referred to her as 'Mum'. 'Would that be a nice ironic twist? I don't think I'm likely to meet another celeb in there. Although you never know.'

Bumble's wrinkles unfolded into a smile at the sound of her voice and his pink tongue lolled. He loved being spoken to. So did Bee. Mick had used the willing pugs as his own ventriloquist's dummies, and since he'd died, their world had fallen abruptly silent. For weeks after the funeral, Bumble and, more touchingly, independent Bee had searched for him, their floppy ears twitching for the voice they'd got so used to hearing all the time. Eva couldn't bear their confusion, tilting their soft heads to pick up her voice, as if they'd gone deaf without knowing.

'Maybe we'll just start with the clothes I don't remember,' she said, conscious of the silence where Mick would have provided Bumble with a lugubrious opinion, and she stuffed two silk dress shirts in with the suits. And a cummerbund, two red bow ties and a silk scarf.

It came so naturally to Mick, as an actor, that sometimes Eva forgot the dogs couldn't actually talk. Bumble had a camp Northern whine that veered into an Alan Bennett impression at times; Bee spoke like a sitcom Brummie housewife who'd won the Pools. It was Mick's doggy improv at one of their Christmas parties that had landed him the voice-over for Barney the Baker, the mischievous Black Country pieman – his last job that had earned Mick more than his entire LA career in repeat fees alone. 'It's all down to moi,' Bee often 'told' visitors. 'Oi am Daddy's pension provider, ow yes.'

Eva stood motionless, holding a paisley dinner jacket. The last time he'd worn it he'd won a BAFTA, for Best Children's Entertainment series. 'I owe everything to two pugs and an IT goddess in flat shoes,' he'd said, and blown Eva, sitting at their star-studded table, a winky kiss. The jacket still bore a smudge of candlewax from the club afterwards, and the memory exploded inside her like a camera flash, vivid, and now a bit surreal.

Bumble let out a groan and sank onto the rug, his eyes still watching her face.

'Sorry, Bumble,' she said, more to let him hear her voice than anything, and felt foolish. 'I don't like it being so quiet either.'

Without Mick's raucous laugh, his sporadic singing, his ever-changing moods, his daily 'Eva? Eeeeva?' yells, it felt empty. The wood absorbed every noise, sucking it in and flattening the air. She tried to talk to the dogs as much as Mick had, but without the voices. Really, the three of them were in the same boat: masterless and a bit lost in their own house.

She pushed two more hideous waistcoats into the charity bag. Eva didn't know the Mick who'd chosen them. Maybe Cheryl, or Una had bought them. 'I know it's boring with just me,' she added.

The phone rang in the bedroom next door, and the pug's ears twitched hopefully. Only three people ever rang Eva's landline. Roger, Mick's best friend and solicitor of many years; Kim, his agent who persisted in trying to get Eva to do interviews about Life With Michael Quinn, even now; or her friend Anna, who managed the bookshop in town, and was the kindest person Eva had met, in a town where even the nurses at the vet's had sent a sympathy card to the pugs. Since Christmas Anna had been waging a gentle 'time to start living again' campaign. Some days Eva was more receptive to it than others.

The ringing stopped, then started again. Eva sighed, and went through into the master bedroom, Bumble at her heels. The phone was on Mick's side of the bed nearest the door, his silver bowl of cufflinks still next to it; another thing she couldn't bear to move.

Her shoulders tightened as she picked up the receiver.

'Hello?' No name, no number – privacy rules. The nightmarish days after Mick's death, when the phone had rung constantly with reporters and 'friends' she barely knew, had made Eva even cagier than before.

The voice on the other end wasn't one she was expecting.

'Eva, it's Patrick.'

'Paddy! Hello!' Eva couldn't hide her surprise; her brother hadn't called her in weeks. But then she hadn't called him either. 'Are you ringing from the car?'

'Yes, of course.' Patrick usually called her from his car; he was the national sales manager for a chain of pet supermarkets and spent his life speeding from one end of the country to the other in order to troubleshoot guinea-pig-related problems. On the rare occasions he rang his sister, usually a duty call about their mother who lived in her own twilight world in a nursing home near where they'd grown up in Berkshire, it felt to Eva as if it was a strategy to make two junctions of a motorway more time-efficient. 'I'm just on my way home.'

'Wouldn't it be better if you called me when you got there? So you can concentrate on our conversation, rather than the M40?'

'I'm not on the M40, I'm on the M1. And anyway, I'm not . . .' He paused. 'I'm not going back to Bristol.'

'What?' Eva had been wandering around the bedroom, but something in his voice made her sink down at the dressing-table stool. Bumble slumped too, on anxiety alert. 'Is everything all right?'

'Not really. Caitlin and I have split up. I'm moving up to Newcastle. Well, strictly speaking, I *have* moved up to Newcastle.'

'What? When did this happen?' Eva stood up, then sat down again, shocked.

'Just after New Year. A few weeks ago.'

'Oh God. I'm so sorry. What came first, the job or the split?'

Patrick sighed. 'The job. Well, no. The job caused the split but it had been coming for a while. Basically, the northern sales manager walked out, and I've got to handle her region till they find a replacement, on top of my own workload. I couldn't do it from Bristol, so head office offered to relocate me, plus a big bonus if I can get the area to hit target. To be honest, I thought it was a great opportunity for us. New house, more money, fresh start – something we could do together. But Cait flat out refused to consider moving, and we argued, and . . . stuff came out. Neither of us has been happy. Like I say, the final nail.'

Eva was lost for words. None of this made sense. She'd always thought Patrick was the marrying-for-life type. And he *adored* Caitlin. His wedding speech, in which he sweetly thanked his new wife for turning his dull life from black and white into colour, starting with his new red socks, made everyone at the reception cry. 'I thought you two were blissfully happy?'

'Apparently not. Apparently, Caitlin was . . .' He sounded wounded. 'Look, I don't want to talk about it. What's done's done. The main thing is we're trying to make this as civilised as possible.'

Which meant there *was* something. Poor Patrick, thought Eva, shocked. Well, poor Caitlin, really. Poor everyone.

Eva had never quite understood how her cautious, logical brother had ended up with a livewire like Caitlin, in her DMs and her purple tights and her ribbons that trailed after her like a jellyfish. Privately, Eva thought that Nancy, aged four, wore more adult ensembles than her mother, not that she ever said that out loud. Which wasn't to say Eva didn't like Caitlin: the few times Eva had met her, she'd been warm and friendly, and funny in a slightly exhausting kind of way – and Patrick had loved her. Patrick made decisions carefully and was rarely wrong, so there must have been something about Caitlin's spontaneous sparkiness that clicked in his soul.

But that was love. It hit you when you least expected, with the people you least expected. She of all people was proof of that.

Eva raked a hand through her hair. 'I don't know what to say, Paddy. I'm sorry. Why didn't you tell me sooner?'

'You've had your own problems. I wasn't going to add to them.'

'This isn't a *problem*. This is . . . you.' The trouble was, they weren't close, she and Patrick. Their family dynamic had never been particularly touchy-feely, even though Eva had looked after Patrick a lot during their childhood. Months could go past without her setting eyes on her brother, despite him living relatively close. It didn't seem to matter. They spoke on the phone, if Patrick had a junction he needed to fill. 'How are the children taking it?'

'We've told them that I've got a job up north and I'll be working away for a while.'

'And they're fine with that?' she asked, incredulously.

'I doubt they notice I've gone.' There was a splinter of heartbreak in his voice. 'Caitlin's probably pleased she can get them into bed earlier instead of waiting up for me.'

'Oh, Paddy,' she said. 'I'm so sorry. Are you sure it's . . .'

'Yes. Don't. It's over.' And he let out a sigh that shocked Eva out of the platitude she'd been about to offer. It was a shapeless grief she recognised. Too much despair to fit into old words.

In the silence, Eva heard Patrick's sat nav directing him across the next junction, a bossy female voice taking charge. For a second she felt intensely sorry for him, being ordered from one work crisis to the next by a disembodied voice. But then Patrick liked a timetable. He'd always made to-do lists, even as a small boy. He got it from their mother, who in turn, had her need to be efficient honed by their dad's rigid domestic order requirements.

'So what happens next?' Practicality was what Patrick needed, not sympathy. 'Have you discussed when you'll be seeing the children?'

'Yeah, that's the thing. I need to ask a favour.'

'Anything. Do you have a good lawyer? Roger doesn't handle divorces, but I'm sure he knows a really great . . .'

'No! We're trying to keep lawyers out of it.' Patrick sounded almost affronted. 'We've got a mediator helping us in the short term. I want to see the kids as much as I can, but apparently my new place is too far to travel for weekend contact. So I wondered if I could bring Nancy and Joel to yours for our visits?'

She frowned. 'To Longhampton?'

'Yes. Longhampton. Unless you've got a secret property portfolio you didn't tell me about?'

He was trying to be funny but Eva wasn't prepared for the recoil she felt: she'd been expecting a request to pay for the solicitor, or maybe even a loan for a house deposit: Patrick worked hard but didn't earn a huge amount. But this . . . Other people in Mick's house.

Not just other people, either – children. Baby voices, unpredictable balls of energy in her home, shattering the calm routine she and the pugs had got into. The idea of change made Eva's stomach knot. Joel and Nancy were family, with the same blood and quirks and features (well, she corrected herself, Nancy was, not that that mattered), but she didn't really know them, and they didn't really know her, and the whole 'divorced dad' experience would be frosted with their unhappiness and Patrick's unhappiness, and her own unhappiness.

No no no no no.

Bumble looked up at her from the rug, his anxiety doubled by the sudden waves of tension coming off Eva.

'It'd only be every other weekend,' Patrick went on. 'It'd give you a chance to get to know them better.' He added the last in a cheerful voice that made Eva glare at the phone. Was there an implication there that she should have got to know them *before*? It wasn't like she hadn't sent regular birthday, Christmas and holiday presents, all guided by the internet since neither Patrick nor Caitlin ever gave her any clues about what they liked.

'And for them to get to know you better too,' he added, a beat too late.

'What did Caitlin say about this?' she asked, mildly.

'Caitlin thinks it's a great idea. You're their aunt. And it's a beautiful house, lovely garden, plenty of space to run around.'

'Patrick, you don't know what this house is like, you've barely been here. It could be full of ceremonial knives for all you know.' Eva tried to keep her tone light. Parents had a way of making her feel hypersensitive to the dangers of her unchild-proofed home: hot tea, carelessly placed bags, swear words. Even the time she'd given Mick's great-godson her bunch of keys to play with, the toddler's mother had giggled nervously, and removed them from his grip 'before he hurt himself'.

Patrick, though, seemed unconcerned. 'I didn't notice any knives last time we came.'

'Didn't you? They were on the glass coffee table. By Mick's air rifle.'

'Ha ha. Very droll.'

Eva moved a photo of Mick's parents from one side of the antique dressing table to the other, and wrestled with the stubborn resistance pushing up inside her. She didn't like the sensation, but at the same time, she couldn't stop it.

Then she caught another glimpse of herself in the mirror. Her whole face was rigid with refusal, like their dad's. The familiarity of it made Eva feel cold.

'I'm sorry,' she said. 'If this is going to help sort things out, then I'd be happy to have you. Have you got any dates yet?'

The relief in Patrick's voice was palpable. 'Caitlin was hoping we could all come round one weekend, as a trial run. Maybe the weekend after next? Whenever you can fit us in.' He paused. 'I appreciate this, Eva. I . . . really miss them.'

Eva's heart caught at the hesitation: Patrick would never have said any of this if they were in the same room – it'd be far too emotional.

'So, how was Monaco?' He sounded quite cheerful now he'd got the main business sorted.

'Monaco?' Eva had to think quickly: she'd got out of Christmas at the Reardons by pretending she'd been invited to stay with Mick's old friends in Monaco. She'd told Mick's old friends that she was going to stay with Patrick. Eva didn't want to be a sad widowed ghost of Christmases past, or a strange auntie crashing the jolly family present-fest. In the end, she,

Bumble and Bee spent Christmas Day watching archaeology documentaries and drinking Baileys. It wasn't that bad.

'It was very nice, thanks.' It was true. Monaco was very nice. She'd loved it, the last three times she'd been.

I probably won't go to Monaco again now, she thought, and felt a bit weird, as if she'd never actually been at all. Quite a lot of her married memories were starting to feel like that: as if they'd happened to someone else.

'You could have come to us, you know,' said Patrick. 'We don't do cocktails before dinner but you were still welcome.'

Bumble rolled over onto his back, his flawless tummy offered up for love, and Eva leaned over to stroke it. 'Patrick, it sounds as if you had quite enough going on this Christmas without me there too.'

'Fair enough. But we were thinking of you.'

'Thanks.'

'And the kids loved their presents.'

'Great!' Eva tried to remember what she'd sent them, but was shrewd enough to know that Patrick had forgotten too.

The line beeped, indicating a call waiting, and Patrick snapped into work mode.

'Eva, that's the Sunderland store,' he said. 'I'm going to have to go. Sorry. I'm working stupid hours trying to sort out the mess Jenny Scholes left.'

'More stupid than usual?'

'Stupid even for me.' He sounded tired. 'But I don't have a choice. You know what it's like. When your boss is making decisions based on numbers, and you're the one dealing with the *people*.'

'You'll make time to talk properly soon, though?' she said. 'We need to catch up before this . . . visit.' Even though Eva was squeamish about prising personal information out of her brother, this time it was unavoidable – she needed to know why he and Caitlin had split, whose fault it was, what was really behind it . . .

Do I need to know that, though? This was as bad as the 'fans' Kim kept telling her wanted to know about her marriage. You were allowed to keep some things private.

'Sure. I'll text you when I know dates,' Patrick was saying. 'It'll probably be a Saturday.'

'Give me enough warning, so I can get all the ceremonial knives put into storage, and you'll have to let me know what I need to . . .'

But Patrick was talking over her, as if she was another office call. 'Sorry, Eva, I've got to go – thanks a million for this. I'll be in touch. Cheers, bye.'

'. . . get in for Joel and Nancy,' Eva finished, to thin air.

Upside down on the sheepskin rug, Bumble gazed at her as if he was reading something ominous in her expression. He rolled back onto his side, and sat up, his liquid brown eyes pleading to fulfil his sole task in life. To be her companion. To follow her around. To love her.

What have I just done? thought Eva, twisting her fingers in the phone cord. Something had shifted. The weeks had been sliding by, one into the other until whole months had vanished, but now suddenly, the air was static with something else. A definite date stabbed into the peaceful monotony that shrouded her life like dust sheets. A date when things would change, tipping her into the next phase of her life: disruption, challenge, new voices, the broken edges of someone else's marriage.

She looked at the phone, uncertainly. Should she call Caitlin, tell her she knew, and she was sorry? Maybe she'd be glad of an ear?

Eva hesitated. Or would that put her in the same bracket as the women who'd written to her, via Kim, to tell her that they were sorry for her loss – well-meaning old dears who'd nevertheless managed to make Eva want to scream that they didn't know her, or Mick, or what their marriage had been like, much less how empty her life was now. If Caitlin had wanted to confide in her, surely she'd have called first? And what would she say? What if Caitlin was *pleased* about the separation? What if Patrick had done something unforgivable? Or Caitlin had?

Eva's skin crawled at the awkwardness of that conversation.

I'll wait till I hear again from Patrick, she thought, and put the phone back in its cradle.

Chapter three

'**W**e're going to be late!' Joel yelled from the foot of the stairs. 'Late! Late! Late! *Late*! Late! Late! Late!'

He had taken to singing his *late*s in rising arpeggios like an opera singer warming up. He was quite capable of going through his entire range, if the irritation factor got Caitlin moving faster. It usually did. Lisa and Steve next door also seemed to get out of the house more quickly these days, if the sound of their slamming door was anything to go by.

'Stop singing. And we're not going to be late!' Upstairs in the bathroom Caitlin stepped around her gyrating daughter, and rubbed a clear space in the steamy mirror with her sleeve. She aimed the mascara at the piggy dots where until recently her eyes had been. It was hard to be accurate with make-up when a four-year-old was insisting on grooving round the bathroom as if possessed by Jamiroquai. 'I need to put some make-up on.'

'Why?' Nancy paused, her finger pointing in the air.

'Because I'm leaving this house, and I don't want people to know what I really look like.'

There was a pause, while Nancy processed this, then Joel started another 'Late! Late! Late!' a semitone higher than before. It was loud enough to be heard over the Scissor Sisters, Nancy's current morning-music of choice.

'Mummy? Why don't you want people to know what you look like?' asked Nancy. She had stopped dancing, temporarily, and was watching Caitlin with undisguised interest. The concentration in her blue eyes reminded Caitlin of Patrick. Nancy had huge eyes, round and otherworldly, like a pixie's. It had to be his genes: Caitlin knew she wasn't capable of passing on concentration that intense.

'Because I don't want them to know I spend my nights fighting crime in Bristol as Spiderwoman. Which is why I look so knackered.' She pulled a fish face, and swept blusher where her cheekbones were supposed to be. So much for the heartbreak diet.

'You're beautiful, Mummy.'

'Thank you, darling.'

'You have hair like . . . like a big black sheep.'

'Um, thanks.' Caitlin abandoned the blusher and inspected the spot that had started rising under the surface of the skin on her nose, in a place it'd be impossible to squeeze. For God's sake. Spots at thirty-two. It wasn't fair.

That was what stress did for her instead of the more useful weight loss. Spots and eyebags, both even more obvious when you were paler than the average Goth. Conscious of the time ticking by, Caitlin dabbed as much concealer over the spot as she could, then swiped the rest over the purple circles under her eyes. Once upon a time, she'd genuinely considered a career in art – maybe trompe l'oeil painting, or set design. Now, repairing her knackered face was as close as she got to wielding a brush. Between looking after the kids and spending all hours on the internet trying to work out what she was going to do next, Caitlin had forgotten what a good night's sleep felt like, much less what you did with glitter.

35

'Mum! Dad's timetable says we should have left the house twelve minutes ago!' Joel bellowed up the stairs.

'Well, we're not going on Dad's timetable, are we?' Caitlin yelled back.

'Why not?'

'Because Dad isn't here to implement it.'

'Why not?'

'Because he's . . .' Caitlin stopped herself, and shoved her make-up back in the tatty bag she'd had since college. Lisa and Steve didn't need to hear all this. The walls, despite being Victorian and solid, were not soundproof. She went out onto the landing and peered down the stairs.

Joel was swinging on the bottom newel, already in his school coat, buttoned around his neck like a cape, with his bookbag over his shoulder.

'Because Dad's working up in Newcastle on a special job,' she said, less loudly. 'And since he doesn't have to drop you at school to be in work for a certain time, we don't have to go exactly by the timetable.'

'But we're always late,' Joel protested. 'I don't want to be late, we're starting Romans this morning.'

'We're not going to be late. I promise.'

Caitlin turned back into the bathroom, where Nancy was looking at her oddly.

'You OK, Fancy Nancy?' she asked.

'When's Daddy coming back from Newcastle?' Nancy's heart-shaped face was very still, and her eyes bored into Caitlin's soul.

Caitlin felt cold. She'd been dreading this moment. Caitlin had hoped that Nancy, like Joel, would just go with it. But Nancy wasn't like that. She was more like Patrick.

'He doesn't know yet,' she said lightly, as if it wasn't a big deal. She and Patrick had decided not to tell the kids until they knew themselves what was happening. 'He's got an important job to do, and because he's so good at it, he needs to be there a lot. Have you had breakfast yet? And are you finished getting dressed?'

'No.' Nancy had started to dress herself while Caitlin was dealing with Joel's half-finished homework. She'd chosen woolly tights like Caitlin's, but had topped them with a tutu made of pink net flower petals and her Christmas jumper, with a fluffy snowman on the front. *Eyes like Daddy,* thought Caitlin, *fashion sense like Mummy.*

It was already quarter past eight. Where did the mornings go? Not that she was going to crack and use Patrick's morning timetable. It was laminated and held on the fridge with a magnet – another of his 'helpful' parenting gestures that her mother Lynne thought was marvellous, but which Caitlin didn't find as useful as Patrick actually *being there* to make the porridge and find the PE kit.

'We need to get a move on.' Caitlin leaned towards the stairs. 'Joel? Put some toast in the toaster for Nancy, please.' She made an 'arms up' gesture to Nancy who obediently obliged. Underneath the snowman sweater was the *Frozen* T-shirt Patrick had bought for her in London, on the first day of their Christmas trip: the brief moment when everything had been going swimmingly, and the Reardon family was full of the festive spirit.

Princess Elsa smiled up from Nancy's chest and Caitlin's heart clenched. Nancy wore the T-shirt every day under everything. Caitlin suspected it was her way of keeping Patrick in the house. She often wanted to sleep in it, even though she had

Frozen pyjamas. Now the children were both crawling into her bed at night, filling the space Patrick had left, Caitlin knew Nancy sometimes pulled it on, secretly, and the extra warmth of the little bodies curled up with her was offset by the chill in her heart when the T-shirt silently reminded her what was missing.

'Isn't it time this went in the wash?' she asked.

Nancy shook her head. 'Want to wear it.'

'Maybe Daddy can find you another in Newcastle?'

Nancy fixed Caitlin with the gaze that Caitlin's mother Lynne called her 'been here before' look. It freaked them all out. 'It won't be the same. This is my Christmas one.'

'Cat? Caaaat!' Joel shrieked into the garden, underneath the bathroom window, in a voice so piercing Caitlin could almost see the clouds of imaginary birds taking off from the trees in shock.

She leaned out of the window and bellowed, 'Oi, Joel! Quietly!' then turned back to Nancy. It was twenty past eight now. 'OK, fine. But this is an inside skirt. How about your tartan skirt today?'

'Don't want to wear the kilt.' Nancy twirled on one toe and the net floated up. 'The kilt doesn't do this.'

'You can't wear it to nursery.' Caitlin admired Nancy's determination, but it tested her every single day. Sometimes she felt as if she was being trained by a much higher, more evolved mind, in the body of a small and preternaturally articulate girl. 'It's March,' she argued, pointing at the window and the still-sullen morning sky. 'Fairy clothes are too cold for March. You need your kilt!'

Nancy folded her arms, and Caitlin struggled to keep her expression patient. This was so unlike Nancy. Normally she

38

was ready to leave way before Joel – she loved nursery, and chattered about it all the way there, all the way home, all the way up to bedtime. This morning she seemed to be delaying on purpose.

Where did this fit into Patrick's timetable? Caitlin wondered, waspishly. Oh no. It didn't. Patrick didn't put up with any 'faffing about' with clothes; on the days he'd been in charge (Monday, and Saturday), he put the kids' outfits out on the bed the night before and didn't brook any discussion about what was worn. Caitlin often braced herself for the screams of debate from under her warm duvet, but they never came. Weirdly enough.

'Come on, Nancy,' Caitlin heard herself begging. 'Please. I don't want us to be late for Joel's school. We need to go. Kilt, now.'

'No.' The small chin lifted.

Then Caitlin had a brainwave. There was a book about this. Nancy could usually be talked round by whatever happened in a book; if it was in a book, then it was the gospel truth. 'What would the little girl with the cold blue toes do? She'd put on her warm clothes, wouldn't she?' She smiled encouragingly. 'To turn her toes pink again?'

Nancy's chin dropped a notch and Caitlin saw her eyes engage, then slide sideways. 'No,' she said, in a smaller, babyish voice.

'What?' This had never happened before. 'Oh, come on. You don't want your toes to turn blue like Betty's, do you? It happened in the book – it might happen in real life!'

Nancy's eyes darkened but before she could answer, the sound of thundering footsteps rattled the wooden staircase, and Joel burst through the door with a plate of toast.

'Hurry *up*,' he urged, shoving the toast towards Nancy. He'd buttered it lavishly and applied a thick layer of Nutella, Nancy's favourite. There was also a thick layer of Nutella around his own mouth. Caitlin ignored that and focused instead on how well Joel took care of his little sister. He'd always looked after her, but since Patrick had moved out, she'd noticed it even more. Checking Nancy's laces, taking her hand when they got near a road. It made Caitlin feel so proud, as if maybe the first four years of Joel's life, when she'd been bringing him up on her own, hadn't been quite the disaster her mother liked to imply.

Nancy was sitting cross-legged on the loo like a sulky elf.

'You can't wear that skirt, Nancy,' Joel pointed out, matter-of-factly. 'It's freezing outside. There's all frost on the garden, and we've got to walk to school.' He let out a dramatic sigh towards Caitlin. 'Why can't we go in the car?'

'Because everything's so near,' said Caitlin, breezily. 'That's the beauty of this house! That's why Granny Joan loved it. It's *convenient*. There's a new word.'

Granny Joan had actually loved it because when she'd bought it, in 1983, it was all she could afford as a middle-aged widow without much cash, but back then Clifton Village hadn't been quite what it was now.

'Did Granny Joan go to my school?' Joel leaned on the door frame and helped himself to a slice of toast. Clearly he didn't mind being late, if there was Nutella.

'No, she went to school in London,' said Caitlin. 'In Highgate.'

'When? In Victorian times?'

While they were speaking, Nancy did a final twirl, grabbing a slice of toast from the plate as she passed, and skipped out of the bathroom.

'No! In . . .' Caitlin did some rapid maths. Her grandmother had died seven years ago, aged eighty-two, after a very merry widowhood; she'd been the only one of the family not to clutch their pearls in horror when Caitlin had gone to Glastonbury the summer she graduated from university and returned, unwittingly, already on the road to her new life as a single mum. 'Much worse happened in the sixties,' she'd told Caitlin, clearing the spare room for her and her hastily acquired collection of second-hand baby gear. 'It's as if your mother's generation think we found them under gooseberry bushes.'

'When?' Joel raised his eyebrows. Granny Joan was a mixture of Florence Nightingale, Emmeline Pankhurst and any other historical figure to him, depending on what they were doing at school.

'She went to school in London during the war,' said Caitlin.

'The Boer War?'

'No. The Second one. With the air raids. And the rationing.'

'So why did you live here with Granny Joan, and not actual Granny and Grandad?'

'Because Granny was . . . um, she was working, and she couldn't give me the help I needed with you as a baby, and Granny Joan could.' Caitlin had told Joel this story so many times, but he liked hearing it; she occasionally reminded herself that she could start dropping in details as he got old enough to appreciate the subtle nuances of moving in with your grandmother while your own mother 'came to terms with the situation', packing your belongings into the nearly-new VW Polo you'd been given for getting straight As at A-level, complete with Happy Ad in the local paper. No Happy Ad for her subsequent new arrival. Or even for her History of Art degree, which had been where it all went wrong, apparently. Because doing Engineering or Modern Languages stopped you getting pregnant by accident.

'And then Granny Joan gave you the house when she died. On her deathbed!' Joel loved a gory detail. 'So we could live in it.'

Caitlin stroked his hair. Despite the spikes it was still puppy-soft: the last bit of Joel's babyhood she was clinging on to.

'Exactly. She wanted us to be happy in her house. And then I met Dad, and then he came to live here with us, and then Nancy came along.'

'And now it's just you and me again,' he went on. 'And Nancy.' He tried to smile, but Caitlin could see he was dragging the corners of his mouth upwards. The 'see it at the back of the hall' smile they taught them in the school drama group – he was doing it to make her feel better. Her throat went dry, and she caught his small hands in hers. They were ink-stained, from his homework attempts.

'Joel . . .'

She gazed into his worried face. *I should tell him,* she thought. *I should just rip off the plaster and say, 'Dad's never coming back', but how? How do you do that? And anyway,* she reasoned, *Patrick needs to be here when we do that. He's the one who started all this.*

Caitlin struggled to tell either of her kids anything bad, from the genuine lifespan of goldfish to plane crashes, and this was way beyond her. The books made parental separation sound simple to explain to children, but not when they were *your* children, your own eyes looking out of perfect, hopeful faces. She wanted to say, 'I'm so sorry, it was our fault, not yours', but she knew that wasn't what they'd hear, and something in her shrank from revealing her failure to two little souls who needed to believe Mummy and Daddy were strong enough to protect them from everything bad in the world.

Granny Joan, I wish you were here, she thought, gripping Joel's hands, trying not to let her fear show. Joan didn't see failures, she merely shrugged at the way life sometimes took you down an unexpected path. Joan was the only one who didn't talk about Caitlin 'starting again', because she was the only one who, frankly, didn't see why she needed to. Caitlin missed her granny, never more than now. The thought of leaving her, and her house . . . Too much.

Joel reached out and touched her lips, where they too were now forced upwards in an unconvincingly bright smile.

'Don't be sad, Mummy,' he whispered, and it took every ounce of Caitlin's self-control not to cry. He'd stopped calling her Mummy before Christmas as part of his new ten-year-old 'maturity', but since their trip to London, he'd started again. She forced the smile upwards.

What would Joan say? *Look for the positives*. And there were positives to single-parenting. She could make her own rules. She didn't have to wrangle with Patrick over discipline. They were free to have Nutella for breakfast, lunch and tea if they wanted. She had another chance to find happiness. And that could only be good for her children, right?

'Well?'

Nancy had appeared at the bathroom door, hands on hips, now wearing her red kilt. And another Christmas jumper over the top.

'*I'm* ready to go,' she announced, in an accusing tone. 'Are you ready, Mummy?'

Caitlin checked her watch: she'd only started wearing one since Patrick moved out. It was half past eight. They were going to be late, even though the school was just down the road.

But, she argued, here's a chance to turn this into a positive: they won't be this young again, let's have an adventure instead!

She showed Joel her wrist and he squinted at the watch: he'd just learned to tell the time.

'Oh dear, half past eight,' said Joel, then arpeggioed, 'Late, late. Half past eight. Cait is late.'

'Why don't we all skip work today?' She opened her eyes wide. 'Why don't we get on the bus and . . . go to the zoo? Hey? Let's have a running away day! A fun day!'

Joel sighed. 'But it's Romans, Mummy. And Nancy's got a forest day.'

'Oh. Have you?' Caitlin had totally forgotten about the forest day. 'You were going to wear your fairy tutu to the forest day? In March?'

'It's what fairies wear in the forest,' said Nancy, barely suppressing her 'durrrr'. 'Like in the flower fairy books.'

They gazed at her, with Patrick's eyes. One through nature, the other through nurture.

'Fine,' said Caitlin, with a sigh. 'I suppose we'd better go to school, then.'

Once Joel had been released into the playground, a red-hooded marble pinging into a pinball machine of running, yelling children, Caitlin and Nancy walked around the corner to the nursery. Caitlin walked; Nancy skipped, hopping and mouthing morning greetings to the birds and the white cat who sat on the wall by number 15, waiting for her.

While they were walking, Caitlin's phone buzzed – it was her mother Lynne ringing from her office for one of her regular 'catch-ups', i.e., list of queries and well-intended suggestions regarding efficient child-rearing – but Caitlin rejected the call, and instead watched Nancy, drinking in every detail of her bouncing earflaps and fluttering fingers.

She wouldn't have this for long, she thought, with an ache. In September, Nancy would be starting reception class at Joel's school, leaving Caitlin with extra hours for herself, but without these special moments with her babies who were more like little adults every day. Nancy and Joel were funny together, a real double act, but Joel's dramatic nature meant Nancy found it harder and harder to get a word in edgeways. Caitlin knew she'd miss their morning conversations, just Mummy and Nancy, when Nancy shared the intriguing world inside her colourful mind.

'Shall I tell you what I'm doing today, Nancy?' Caitlin called. They did this every morning – Nancy would ask about the cakes in the café where she worked, in great detail, and the regular customers, and the staff.

Nancy finished bouncing her hand along the wall, turned back and nodded.

'I will be serving sandwiches, and I will be frothing frappuccinos,' said Caitlin, but stopped when her phone buzzed again. Lynne's number and photo – dark eyes, wire-rimmed glasses, neat grey bob – reappeared on the screen. Caitlin's heart sank. Had her mother telepathically detected trouble with Patrick? Lynne had a knack for that. Part of her job was sensing trouble before it started. Caitlin decided to call back later. When she had more coffee on board, and her wits about her.

'And . . .' Caitlin carried on, 'I might be cutting cucumbers. I will definitely be sizzling sausages. And grilling gherkins.'

She paused, waiting for Nancy to say, 'Urgh-kins, not gherkins!' as she usually did, but Nancy had reached the white cat and was engrossed in its big pink ears.

'I'll definitely be carrying cakes.' Caitlin stopped behind her and placed a gentle kiss on the top of her head. 'Would you like me to see if there's any cake spare at the end of the day?'

Nancy nodded so hard the cat slid off the wall.

'What colour cake?' Caitlin squeezed the small mittened hand that reached up for hers, tucked in her own red glove, and they carried on walking. 'Carrot or yellow?'

Nancy stopped and indicated for Caitlin to bend down.

'Carrot!' she whispered, right into her ear, quite seriously, as if it was a secret.

'OK,' said Caitlin. It was a bit odd that Nancy wasn't singing but maybe she was playing a game. Lynne had tried to teach them to play Charades at Christmas and Joel, who was up for anything that involved throwing himself around and acting, had become obsessed with it, and frequently mimed what he wanted, for hours at a stretch. Nancy often copied Joel, without totally understanding what it was she was copying.

But it was unusual for her not to *sing*, Caitlin thought, as Nancy skipped ahead, flaps bouncing on her hat. Generally, Nancy's attention swooped around like a pigeon, her sweet, high voice running on and on without a break as one new wonder after another presented itself to her. Every day she said something that left Caitlin amazed that she'd created this clever creature, who saw things in funny, fresh ways, and produced words out of nowhere without being taught them. With Nancy, everything felt so easy. Joel had been a worried child, slow to speak (ha! hard to imagine now) but Nancy's endless, sparkly chatter made Caitlin feel as if she wasn't quite such a useless mother after all.

The shadow descended on her. *I've got to tell them about Patrick soon,* she thought. *Together. We'll have to tell them together.*

'Is that your wish for the day, the carrot cake?' They were near the nursery now, and Caitlin bent down and squeezed Nancy's hand. 'You can have another one, if you want.'

But instead of leaping on the extra wish – a variant on the game they'd played in London – she shook her head, swinging her hat flaps.

'Go on. Maybe you could wish for . . . snow?'

Nancy's brow furrowed.

'Oh, OK.' Surprised by the reaction, Caitlin straightened up, and saw Shelley the nursery leader in the playground. She waved at her. 'Look. There's Shelley! She's got a hat with flaps like yours! Nancy?'

Nancy was staring at the ground, scraping at a spot on the pavement with the toe of her black patent shoe.

'Careful, Nancy, you'll scuff your shoes.' Caitlin gave her hand a tug. Patrick hadn't agreed with patent leather as an appropriate choice for an active four-year-old but Caitlin could remember how obsessed she'd been by her own shiny shoes at Nancy's age, and had told a small white lie: that they didn't have any others in Nancy's size in more boring, practical materials.

Nancy didn't respond.

'Nancy? Are you ready to go in? I've got to go now.'

Without speaking, Nancy threw herself into Caitlin's arms and hugged her tightly, burying her face into her coat. Caitlin hugged her back and swung her around from side to side, so her feet lifted off the ground – something that normally made Nancy squeal with delight. This morning, there was no squeal and when Caitlin put her down, Nancy's heart-shaped face was serious. Like a Botticelli cherub, Caitlin thought, her heart contracting.

Nancy beckoned her down so her mouth was level with Caitlin's ear. 'Will you be here for me at home time?'

'Of course, Fancy Nancy,' said Caitlin. Was something up? 'With cake. Promise.'

Nancy pressed her lips together. 'I love you, Mummy.' Then she ran inside, taking a ragged scrap of Caitlin's heart with her to add to the other goodbye moments that Caitlin was collaging in her heart.

Caitlin pulled a happy expression on her face and waved, then she turned back to the main road, walking quickly as her usual morning feeling swept over her: sadness at leaving Nancy behind, mixed with guilty relief that the adult part of her day was finally starting, free of unanswerable questions and the distant sound of breakages and squabbles.

Right, she thought, *what do I need to do today?* It was at this point, daily, that Caitlin had to suppress a powerful desire to light a cigarette, just because she could. She didn't, though.

One, check weekend arrangements for taking the kids to Eva's.

I hope she's taking the pugs to a sitter, thought Caitlin, then felt bad. Would it be unreasonable to ask a widow to take her only companions to a kennels? Probably. And it would give

Patrick more ammunition to make out she didn't want to co-operate.

She swung her bag, imagining how tense it was going to be, keeping an eye on both children while making conversation with Patrick *and* Eva. Neither of them were small-talkers, and Eva's house was the sort of minimalist designer dream that her kids could wreck in under an hour. She found the houses of childfree people stressful, not because of uncovered sockets and ornaments, but because of the sharp intakes of breath when juice was poured, or kids acted like kids and ran around a bit.

There'd probably be a piano somewhere too, thought Caitlin, her heart sinking the more she thought about it. Old-school actors like Mick always had pianos, didn't they, covered in framed photos, but never played? Keeping Joel off it would be nigh on impossible. He'd found YouTube footage of Freddie Mercury playing a piano while standing on it, and . . . *Oh God.*

And then she would have to sit down with Patrick and work out how to tell the kids they were splitting up. Properly.

Patrick's face flashed up in Caitlin's mind – that look he'd given her as he'd left the mediation session to go back to Newcastle, struggling to contain his disappointment, with her, with himself, with everything. They couldn't have spent another day in each other's company, but in a weird way, the absence of Patrick was more noticeable than she'd anticipated, given the hours he'd worked. The house felt wrong without him: vulnerable, and unguarded. Her bed too big, her sofa too empty. Their wedding photos were still on the wall, because taking them down would signal to the kids – and to herself – that it was definitely over.

But it is over, Caitlin told herself, hoisting her bag over one shoulder. *You can't live with someone who insists on believing you're perfect. No one is. Constantly walking on eggshells so as not to let Patrick down . . . that was never going to work, no matter how hard you'd tried to live up to his rose-tinted version of Us.*

She gazed ahead, suddenly weighed down again with all the things she could have done differently. Maybe the really incredible thing was how long Patrick had doggedly insisted she *was* everything he thought.

The street with Caitlin's café at the end was busy with office workers heading out for the day, a few older people strolling to the shops in pairs. She passed a woman carrying a takeaway cup from Sadie's Kitchen and upped her pace.

Six shops down, outside the off licence, Caitlin stopped to redo her pink lipstick in the wing mirror of a delivery lorry when something – someone – caught her eye. She froze, the lipstick halfway to her mouth.

Was that him? Running down the other side of the road, in dark shorts and red trainers?

She straightened, nearly catching her chin on the wing mirror, but he'd gone past, and she could only see the back of his head, blonde curls crushed by a floppy beanie hat. Long legs, ending in strong runner's calves. But the stride was famil- iar – long and effortless, one she'd seen thousands of times, a technique she could pick out from a hundred other joggers.

It was him. Lee. Caitlin felt as if an invisible hand had grabbed her and lifted her upwards. Because now she was standing on the brink of infinite possibility, and the roads were suddenly open, in every direction.

The man paused at the kerb and looked twice to check for traffic, but even though he glanced in her direction, he didn't spot her. Then he ran over the road, and around the corner. Seconds after he'd vanished from sight, Caitlin still felt suspended, and breathless.

It hadn't hit her until now. But everything was going to change. Everything *had* to change. And for once, she was going to start seeing that as a Good Thing.

Chapter four

Eva finally identified the bad feeling that had been torment-ing her since she arrived at Paddington station when she stepped out of the taxi on Piccadilly and spotted herself in a coffee-shop window. It was her oldest fear: she was wearing the wrong clothes.

She stared at her middle-aged reflection in dismay. Why? Why had she worn her *parka* to a lunch appointment in London? Because, her brain pointed out unhelpfully, in Longhampton it was edgy, in a Scandinavian detective way. In Longhampton anything that wasn't a fleece was edgy. She didn't have an excuse for these jeans, though. When had the world stopped wearing skinny jeans? And when had she started to look so . . . scrawny in them? Worse than that, there was nothing she could do about it, because it was already ten to one, and Roger would be at Mick's usual table at the Wolseley, making calls and working his way through the bread basket.

Through the coffee-shop window Eva could see office workers queuing for lunchtime cappuccinos and they were all better dressed than she was. Purposeful, filling their clothes with confidence. The massive irony was that she'd overseen a viral advert that played out exactly like this for StartWithShoes. com just before she resigned: horrified woman defrumps herself outside a party using only StartWithShoes's reassuringly prescriptive website and a credit card. '*Click, click, chic.*' It had ended with a kiss – and a pencil skirt, and a blow-dry. Mind you, that had been ten years ago. Who knew what you needed now? Full Botox and a . . . ? A . . . ?

And a what? Eva realised she had no idea.

She glanced half-heartedly down Piccadilly towards the shops of Knightsbridge, and knew she wouldn't know what 'must-have piece' to grab even if she *did* have time to run down there. Somewhere in the last few years, she and Fashion had parted company on any meaningful level; subscription copies of *Vogue*, *US Vogue* and *Porter* still thudded onto the mat, but Eva never got round to reading them. The truth was, she'd stopped needing to care about directions and trends: Mick loved her whatever she wore, and black clothes and pug hair didn't mix. She still had clothes, *gorgeous* clothes, but they belonged to a city girl with a hot desk office and gym membership. Eva wasn't sure who she was now. Not a businesswoman. Not a wife. Not a mother. Not . . . anything in particular.

She took a deep breath and straightened her spine. Roger was a heartily traditional solicitor in his early seventies. He didn't know the difference between a parka and Prada. And maybe some fashion editor, somewhere in East London, was wearing a parka just like this. But in a subversive way, with orange brogues and a bowler hat. Maybe she was ahead of the trend.

'Hey, Becky! Becky!'

Something was moving in the window's reflection: a man waving on the other side of the street, by Starbucks. A black cab passed, blocking him from view, and a Routemaster bus, but when they passed, there he was, still waving goofily. He was dressed for a colder day than it was, in a grey duffle coat.

It was all right for blokes, thought Eva. They could wear anything, for as long as they liked, and everyone said, 'Ah, quirky'.

She wavered, wondering if she had time for an espresso to kick her brain into action, and heard him yell 'Becky! Over here!' again. This time she couldn't help turning round. He had thick sandy hair brushed in a floppy quiff and old-fashioned glasses like Morrissey, and Eva could make out a broad smile, visible even across four lanes of London traffic. *Poor Becky,* she thought, *I bet she's hiding behind a postbox.* Tourists were turning to stare at him, wondering if he was all right.

It was five to one, too late for coffee. *Time to face the music,* thought Eva, and decided to make one last attempt to salvage her look with a statement lip. Lip gloss and its magical image-polishing effect had come to Eva's aid after a few red-eye flights before now. It showed you hadn't given up completely.

Eva tucked herself into the corner of the coffee-shop front-age, took her compact out and was going for a second layer of gloss when she felt two hands clap on her shoulders. She spun round in alarm, one hand flying instantly to her bag. Her hair stuck to her tacky lips and she struggled to get away, bumping herself into the plate-glass window.

'Ooof!' She caught the surprised eye of a girl in a navy suit stirring sugar into an espresso on the other side as her shoulder rebounded off the window. The only good thing about the parka was its padding.

'Becky! Are you ignoring me? Or have you got your head-phones in?' It was him, the man, so close to her Eva could see the freckles on his nose. He wasn't as young as she'd thought from across the street – maybe late thirties – and as she shoved him away, he lost his balance, and a cartoonish expression of shock froze on his face when he realised his mistake.

'What the hell are you doing?' she yelled. 'Get off!'

'Gosh! I'm so sorry!' The man's eyes opened wide and he lurched backwards, barging into a passing couple of women heading towards the restaurant. They were tall, blonde and carried Bond Street bags, the sort of women Eva had dealt with all day, every day for ten years, and despite her own shock, she winced on his behalf at the daggers they shot him as they stalked around his flailing form.

'Wait! Sorry! Sorry! Oh God, sorry,' he said, first to them, then to her, twisting and turning in confusion, unsure where to start apologising first. His face was bright red, and he stumbled again to avoid a tourist coming the other way. 'I don't know what to say, I thought you were . . .'

'Becky,' said Eva. Her heart was still hammering, but his slapstick staggering was too gormless for her to feel threatened. 'I'm not Becky.'

'No, I can see that now. I'm so sorry!' He took his glasses off and rubbed them with a hanky. 'Sorry, I lost my usual specs, these are my old ones, not that that's any excuse . . .' He put them back on and peered straight at her. His eyes were gentle; round and brown with unruly eyebrows edging under his frames. The eyebrows were almost joined together with mortification. 'It was your *coat*. One of my students has one the same, I was absolutely convinced you were her. What a pillock.'

Eva hadn't heard the word *pillock* in ages. It was one of the non-swear words her parents had used in front of her and Patrick, unaware that they had the full range between them.

'I like your furry hood – it's . . . Eskimo-ish.' He gestured round his head, then added, 'You're not hurt, are you? I really didn't mean to grab you like that. Please don't sue me for assault!' He stretched out a hand without thinking, and then snatched it back, self-conscious. 'Sorry, sorry.'

'No harm done.' Eva raised an eyebrow. 'Have you lost a Becky?'

'Sort of. Well, she's supposed to be hard at work researching at the British Film Institute Archive right now, but then again, so am I.' He smiled, an apologetic, crumpled smile, then frowned. 'Oh. You've got a sort of . . .' He made a gesture towards her face, as if he was going to touch it but didn't want to make the situation worse. 'No, there. By your . . . mouth.'

Eva put a hand to her face and felt gloss. Smeary gloss. 'Is it all over my face?'

'Yes. Sorry. Here.' He offered her his hanky. 'It's clean.'

She didn't have a hanky of her own so she took it. It smelled of fresh laundry, nicer than she'd expected. 'Thanks.'

Eva turned to the window to check her reflection; on the other side of the glass, in the coffee shop, several people were now peering at them. They abruptly pretended to take a sudden interest in their drinks.

She wiped her face. Well, at least she now had something to tell Anna. Anna was constantly on at her, in her kindly way, to strike up conversation with random men, 'just to get back in the swing of things'. But then Anna firmly believed real people met the love of their life in art galleries. She would *adore* the idea of being manhandled outside a Piccadilly restaurant by a geeky teacher in a duffle coat who was skiving off his own field trip. Anna read far too many books for her own good.

Eva turned back to see the man was squinting at her. Actually, geeky was mean. He wasn't bad-looking. Maybe it was the quiff. But it was an indie-boy, cricket-playing, tea-drinking quiff, not a rocker's one. Cliff, not Elvis. 'Listen, I hope I'm not making even more of a berk of myself,' he began, 'but *do* I know you from somewhere?'

'No, I don't think so.' At that, Eva's defences shot up. People did sometimes recognise her from the rare times she'd been photographed with Mick – that wasn't something she wanted to go into now. She straightened her parka with as much dignity as it warranted. 'But, thanks a million for mistaking me for a student, that's made my day.'

'Becky's a *mature* student,' he added, then corrected himself. 'By which I mean, she's thirty.' He winced, and corrected himself again. 'But still very beautiful. Argh, not *but*, I don't mean . . .'

Eva raised a hand. 'I'd stop there.'

The man covered his face, groaned, then said from behind his fingers, 'I swear to you, I'm not normally this clumsy.'

'Verbally? Or physically?'

'Both.' He removed his glasses, rubbed his eyes, and then looked directly at Eva. The eyes looked younger, unframed with the specs. Twinklier. 'Actually, to be honest with you, I am. I'm clumsy. Can I buy you a coffee to apologise?'

'So you can pour it down my front? I don't think so.' Eva paused, unwilling to let the conversation end. 'Anyway, I'm late for a lunch appointment. But I hope you track Becky down soon.'

'So do I.' He paused, then added drily, with perfect timing, 'She's got all the tickets for tonight's performance.'

The moment hung on the air, hooked on a tentative smile from each of them, and Eva had the sudden tingling certainty that if she *hadn't* had a lunch appointment, she'd have said yes to the apology coffee, even if he had spilled it. A shiny, fluorescent bubble floated up in her chest, something new, something totally different that could lead her down an uncharted path if she let it. She let it hover there, shocked that it had appeared at all. Then it popped and was gone.

And she was due for lunch with her late husband's solicitor and best friend.

The tingle remained, humming high in her chest, trickling along her skin. Eva couldn't remember the last time she'd felt like this.

Oh, wait. She could. When she'd bumped into Mick in the charity shop, over the binbag of Cheryl's clothes he was throwing away to make room for his new start.

Mick. Her Mick. *The love of her life.*

Eva flashed a tight quick smile and said her polite goodbye, trying not to meet the man's brown eyes, then turned on the heel of her deeply unfashionable boots, and marched into the Wolseley.

Roger Ransome was wedged into Mick's old corner table, surrounded by papers, an empty wine glass by his side. He was in the middle of a phone conversation, squeezing his forehead with one hand, a familiar expression of weary patience on his lined face.

When he looked up and saw Eva, he finished the call with a few words, and his baggy eyes brightened with delight, so much that Eva momentarily forgot she was dressed like someone's dogsitter. 'My darling!' he said, getting to his feet and making the china cups rattle on the table. 'How lovely to see you.' And when he folded her into his cologne-and-proper-shave embrace, Eva felt as if the world might not be such a dark place after all.

Roger, Mick's friend from primary school, self-made celebrity lawyer and reliable dispenser of expensive if foolproof advice, made Eva feel better about everything. He always had done. The only moments of comfort Eva had had in Mick's awful last days had been when Roger's Jag had roared up outside, every other day at six, and his leonine bulk had emerged, followed by his ancient briefcase and overcoat. The suffocating darkness had retreated in the hour Roger spent dealing with every problem Eva laid, despairing, in front of him; when he left, it engulfed her and the pugs again.

He held her at arm's length, inspecting her. 'How've you been, Eva? We've barely seen you lately. Lorraine's worried about you. You didn't come to the Christmas party!'

'Sorry, I was away. And I'm fine, honestly.' Eva settled herself in the seat, not meeting his eye. 'Fine' was the answer that came out automatically. How she really was – lethargic yet twitchy, lonely yet resistant to company – was too difficult to explain, and in any case, she wasn't sure she knew herself exactly what was up with her. Just that she'd finally accepted that something had ended, but she couldn't seem to get started again.

'Well, it's good to see you now,' he said. 'Mick would be livid if he knew how long it's been since I last took you out for lunch. Have you changed your mobile?'

'No.' She shoved her bag under her chair and smiled. 'I'm often out. With the dogs. Or . . . gardening.'

Roger looked at her for a long beat, and as ever, Eva wondered what he was thinking. *It's probably my clothes,* she thought. That was the kind of thing Roger would spot; the wrong clothes. Signs of someone not quite themselves.

'Have I got lip gloss on my cheek?' she asked, suddenly. 'I bumped into someone on the way in. Don't worry, I haven't started to let myself go completely . . .'

Roger laughed. 'I was just thinking of the last time we were all here. Happy days. But let's eat,' he said, rubbing his large hands. 'I can't talk on an empty stomach, and you look like you need a square meal.'

They ate – Roger checking the notes in his diary about what his heart-friendly diet plan would allow, then ignoring them – and Eva began to relax. It was bittersweet to be back in one of Mick's old haunts; it reminded her of the many long nights they'd had here, the blurry taxi rides home, the laughter, the frisson of sitting with witty people topping each other's stories. A world of familiar faces that had seemed strange at first, then become completely normal. Well, almost.

When the coffee arrived, Roger tipped his head, the pink-ness of his scalp offset around the temples with fluffy white hair. It gave him the air of a Roman god in a pinstripe suit. He pressed his lips together, as if he was considering the right words. 'Now, listen,' he said. 'I don't want to make either of us cry, but we need to talk about Mick.'

'I knew it would be about Mick,' said Eva. 'When you said you needed to discuss it in person, not over the phone? Is it something to do with the will?'

'In a way. It's nothing awful, don't worry. It's . . . something you might actually be interested in. You remember I had to come to the house a few days before Mick died.'

Eva nodded. 'I'll never be able to thank you enough for doing that. I can't remember most of what happened after we got out of the car from the airport. I mean, I remember the ambulance but . . .' She'd told the story so many times, but just repeating details she'd been told. It was a blur. Holiday, collapse, blue lights, scans, sympathetic but matter-of-fact doctors, home, then . . . Mick was gone. All in the space of ten days. It had felt as if time was telescoping, and she needed to stuff as many last details into her head as she could. As a result, she only recalled pointless details – the line of wilting bouquets from friends, stacked in their boxes by the door, the smell of the hospital bed sheets, the phone ringing and ringing.

'Eva, it was the least I could do.' Roger reached over the table and took her hand. 'I just wish I could have done more afterwards. Those bloody vultures. But when you live a life like Mick's, it sells papers. I mean, three wives! And four careers!'

She blinked. That wasn't the Mick she'd been married to. Roger had protected her from the worst, throwing out injunctions and pulling every string he could, but it hadn't stopped the more lurid stories in the papers, none of which were true. Well, as far as she knew.

'He hasn't left some mad thing in his will that I have to do, has he?' Eva made herself press on. Her stomach was beginning to sink: she'd always thought Mick's will was too simple, with no Poirot-style 'gather the family together' drawing-room reading requirement. 'I did wonder if maybe you'd talked Mick out of some dramatic twist. Are Una and Cheryl contesting the house?'

'No, no, that's yours, darling. Definitely yours.' Roger tapped his fingers. 'It's something entirely separate, although it does involve them too, I'm afraid. You're aware Mick kept a diary?'

'He said he needed to write down his best stories in case he got Alzheimer's, like my mum. Or if he needed some money for his old age.'

Don't want the bastards getting off scot-free if I lose my marbles, do I, love? Got to get it all down in black and white so they can't deny it . . .

He'd said it so often. Eva was starting to lose the exact memory of Mick's face, but his voice was still sharp in her mind. Warm and whisky-edged, flat vowels and unexpected chuckles.

'Mick gave me the diaries that night. Whole stack of 'em.' Roger shook his head in disbelief. 'I should have known the man would write like he talked – never bloody stopped! He asked me to hold on to them for safekeeping, further instructions to follow.'

So that had been what Roger had been carrying out to his car in packing boxes. Eva had assumed it was legal paperwork – contracts, investments, accounts that needed a quick polish before probate. But the boxes were Mick's private thoughts, and he'd given them to his lawyer. Why hadn't he given them to *her*? 'What do you mean, further instructions?'

'He never mentioned anything to you?'

'No. Well, he left me with a list of things he wanted me to do after his death, but the diaries weren't on it.'

'What did he ask you to do?' Roger paused. 'If that's not too personal a question?'

She shrugged, not wanting to think about the list she'd found in Mick's handwriting, the words fumbled with morphine, in case it made her cry again. 'Oh, to live life. To find someone to make me happy. To look after the pugs. To travel. The usual things.'

'And how's that going?' he asked gently.

'I'm looking after the pugs.'

'And have you found anyone to make you happy?'

Eva shook her head. 'Roger . . .'

'I'm sorry.' Roger smiled apologetically. 'Mick asked me to wait two years – to let the dust settle, as he put it. Then I was to let you, and Una and Cheryl, know that the three of you were bequeathed these diaries, to be divided up into the years in which you were married to him.'

'Ha!' The laugh burst out of her. 'Like a three-part mini series. That's so him.'

'Indeed. With Mick as the star. It divides up fairly equally,' Roger added, with a lawyer's precision. 'I know he was married to Cheryl the longest, but there are about the same number of volumes for each of you. I say, volumes – they're mainly exercise books.'

'From what I can gather, he and Cheryl were too busy flying back and forth to America to do much writing of diaries.'

Roger peered over his glasses. 'Yes, well, all that money didn't squander itself, you know. They put quite a lot of effort into burning through that cash.'

Cheryl and Mick's marriage had more or less been identical on and off-screen: they met playing archetypal Brits in a glossy American legal drama series, had a whirlwind romance on set, then set about losing lots of money buying sports bars. Cheryl made millions starring in another soap opera and promoting whitening toothpaste, while Mick lost money making a film about an amateur football team, then both of them had hurled what was left of their fortune at lawyers getting divorced.

Not that Eva had anything against Cheryl; she'd only met her for the second time at the funeral. Ditto Una, the first wife. The childhood sweetheart, hairdresser now queen of her own salon chain and mother of Mick's only son, Tyson. As far as Eva knew, most of Mick's Una Years had been spent touring the bedsits of Britain in rep theatre productions and occasionally modelling cardigans for knitting patterns while she cut hair and changed Tyson's nappies. Eva had never let herself think too hard about Mick's life Before Her; he told her repeatedly that he felt life had started when they'd met. His 'real' life, when he wasn't trying to be someone else.

'So, what exactly are we meant to do with these diaries?' Eva wasn't sure what she felt. Did she really want to read Mick's private thoughts? 'Read them? Burn them?'

'Here's the thing.' Roger tapped his coffee spoon against the thick tablecloth. 'Mick was approached several times about publishing his memoirs while he was alive, but he didn't feel he could be honest *and* fair. People want the gossip, you know how it is. The stories. The wild shenanigans with his old drinking buddies.'

'My four decades of celebrity hangovers, by Michael Quinn,' said Eva, dully.

'He led a colourful life, did our Michael.'

Until he married me, thought Eva. *Then it went into peaceful black and white.* 'But Mick always said diaries are private. I mean, I know he joked about them being his nest egg but I don't think he'd *seriously* want other people to read them, would he?'

Roger shrugged. 'But who was he writing them for then? He must have known someone would read them one day. Does anyone write a diary, thinking they'll be the only one to read it?'

'I'm sure he wrote them for himself.' Eva shrank at the thought of strangers prying into Mick's private thoughts, his memories, *their* history. *Her* life. 'Maybe they were just to remind him of stories. He always said he was going to write a novel.'

'You should know what actors are like by now, Eva.' Roger looked wry. 'If a tree falls in the forest and no one says *oh well done darling*, did it fall at all?'

She slumped back in her chair. This wasn't what she'd expected. The defensive feelings returned, a need to throw a wall up around their life from nosy onlookers who had no right to peer in. 'Did Mick leave explicit instructions that we *have* to publish them, though? Really? Even if there are things in there that I don't want people to read?'

'The instructions he left were that you three – you, Una, and Cheryl – were to read the diaries between you, then decide. You all have to agree. Whether you go ahead with publication is up to you, but Mick had already put a few plans together. He'd been in touch with an old pal at a publisher's, and they'd found a freelance editor they liked to knock the diaries into shape. Mick was very smug about that, I might add, getting an academic to edit his *memoirs*. A professor, if you will. The publishers are very keen to go ahead. And if you girls were happy to proceed, then the advance was to be split equally.' Roger paused. 'It's a fair chunk of money we're talking about. Not that that makes any difference, I'm sure.'

It didn't. Eva stared across the table, trying to picture her husband's face when he'd planned this. Gleeful, probably. At the drama. 'And did he spend a lot of time thinking about that?'

'About what?'

'About me and Una and Cheryl in a room discussing him? And whether we were happy to reveal all manner of personal stuff about ourselves?' She turned her hands over. This whole conversation was surreal. 'We don't know each other. Mick was well aware of that. I don't want to discuss my marriage with two women I've barely met, let alone the rest of the world.

And what do they say? Surely Una won't want to drag up those memories about Tyson's rehab again. Mick was *incredibly* touchy about Tyson. What if Una disagrees with what he's written? What if any of us do?'

'I've long since given up predicting what Una Quinn will or won't want.' Roger's diplomatic mask slipped for an instant but he caught himself. 'Anyway. One step at a time. I suggest you read your diaries first. See what you think.'

Eva took a long sip of the wine in front of her. To her surprise, the glass was almost empty. She put it down carefully on the table, at the centre of her place setting. 'No,' she said. 'I can tell you that now. I don't want to read Mick's diaries. I don't want anyone else to read them either. I want my memories of our marriage to stay exactly as they are, and for the public's view of Mick to stay the same too. And I don't particularly want to have a meeting with the other . . . former Mrs Quinns to discuss it.'

Roger regarded her strained expression with familiar compassion. 'It's entirely up to you, Eva, but if you'll let an old codger offer you some advice, it's always best to know, rather than to guess,' he said. 'Mick wanted to wait two years so you'd be able to look back and remember the good times. Be proud of him, and his writing. I doubt he'll have said anything in these diaries that he wouldn't have told you himself. He made sure they'd be edited properly, by someone with an interest in his *work*. Did Mick ever let you down about anything else?'

Eva stared at Roger over the tablecloth, and felt the stirring of an emotion she'd forgotten: a stubbornness about being told what to do. It surprised her.

'Because you were the only one he didn't let down,' Roger added.

As far as you know, thought Eva, but said, instead, 'Have you already sent Una's and Cheryl's?'

'When I get back to the office.' Roger paused. 'I wasn't as keen to have lunch with them, funnily enough. Cheryl will only eat grains and certain brands of mineral water, and Una loves reminding me I used to have a fine head of hair she learned to perm on. Operative words being, *used to.*'

Eva responded with the expected smile and let the silence stretch, knowing while she didn't say yes or no, she still had the option of both. *Weird,* she thought. *For the first time, this is* me *and Roger having a meeting here, not me joining 'the boys' for coffee after a long lunch. First time I've had a business meeting in years and it's about Mick.*

'Tell you what,' said Roger, as if struck by a sudden idea, 'are you busy for the rest of this afternoon? Planning to hit the shops?'

Eva shook her head.

'Well, why don't we have another glass of something and you join me for my next meeting.' Roger checked his watch. 'That editor chap I mentioned's dropping by at three so we can discuss a few matters. Well, him *or* her, I shouldn't assume! Alex is the name I've got on this email. Don't like to make assumptions, in these PC times!'

'I don't know,' said Eva. But the thought of the shops wasn't as tempting as it had once been, and the pugs were probably having a better time up at the kennels than they would do mooching around with her.

'You probably *should* stay, make sure I ask the right questions! After all, you're the expert when it comes to job interviews.' Roger sat back in his chair, and regarded her over the top of his glasses. 'You can pretend to be my colleague if you don't want to reveal your true identity . . .'

That swung it for Eva. She didn't want to meet anyone dressed as she was, much less someone who'd be forming an opinion about her and her husband and her marriage. The clumsy but charming stranger in the street – specifically his eyes – kept popping into her mind, and that was awkward enough. Those feelings. Eva wasn't sure what they were, or if she wanted to have them. She began to gather her things. 'Thanks, Roger, but I think I need to process this first.'

'Of course. I understand.' He signalled to the waiter for more coffee. 'I'll bare my teeth with this Alex on your behalf, and have the diaries sent over as soon as. And Eva?'

She stopped surreptitiously checking her phone for messages from the dogsitter, and looked up.

'I say this as a friend, not as your solicitor.' Roger's tone was gentle. Concerned. 'Mick was a great one for *the moment*. Never seeing endings, just chances for new things. He wouldn't want your life to stop, just because he's gone. After all, didn't he always say he saved his best shot at happiness for last?'

She nodded mutely.

'Don't stop living,' he said. 'Mick'd be sad to think you weren't off shopping, at the very least. Buy yourself some frivolous new shoes.'

Eva forced out a watery smile. Even Roger seemed to forget she'd once had access to more shoes than he and Mick had had Cuban cigars. Shoes didn't interest her any more. They only reminded her that she no longer understood them. 'I'll go home via Harvey Nichols,' she lied.

'Good girl,' said Roger.

Chapter five

'**M**um, that man in the tractor is waving at you,' Joel announced, as Caitlin screeched to a halt, and only just swung the car into the unsignposted turning to Eva's village. Behind her, the red tractor's horn blared and Caitlin made a gesture out of the window that – in an ideal world – she wouldn't have made in front of Joel and Nancy.

'Don't tell Dad,' she warned them as she pulled her arm back in. The sleeve of her jumper was covered in burrs. It had been hard enough to know what to wear to the house of a celebrity widow, without now turning up looking like she'd literally been dragged through a hedge backwards. 'That was a special driving signal. For tractors.'

'No, it wasn't,' said Joel.

'Let's pretend it was.'

There was a deep sigh next to her. 'I don't think I like this house,' Joel announced.

'How do you know?' Caitlin frowned across at him. 'We haven't even got there yet.'

'I just know.' He gave a theatrical shudder. 'Why is it so . . . secret? Why isn't it on a road, like a normal house?'

'Because Auntie Eva and . . . and Uncle Michael wanted to be private.'

Uncle Michael sounded weird. One, because he'd only met

Joel twice and Nancy once, and two, because he was Michael Quinn. It was like saying Uncle Sean Connery. Uncle Roger Moore. Although there was the small matter of Uncle Michael also being Barney the Baker. Caitlin had reminded Joel not to mention Barney the Baker, and he'd rolled his eyes and pointed out he hadn't watched that for *years*.

'I think it's spooky,' said Joel, definitively. 'I reserve the right to be freaked out.'

'You reserve the right?' Where was he getting this stuff from? Patrick? Television? Joel didn't watch television much; his own dramatic monologues were more interesting.

Caitlin glanced at Nancy in the rear-view mirror, cocooned in her car seat. She was sitting still, staring intently out of the window, as if she might have to find her way back via a trail of breadcrumbs. Her face was pale above her favourite red jumper. Caitlin didn't like seeing Nancy so quiet. It was strange not to have her voice chirping away from the back. Was it because Patrick was going to be there? Was she already dreading saying goodbye?

We have to tell them, thought Caitlin. *Today.*

'What do you reckon, Fancy Nancy?' she asked, cheerily. 'Do you think it's going to be a magical house? I know there'll be lots of flowers.'

'How do you know that?' Joel demanded.

'I've been there. There are flowers from all over the world. The garden's beautiful.'

Caitlin had Googled Eva's house, partly so she could forestall any awkward questions Joel might have, and partly because, yes, she needed to remind herself about any ponds or wells. Funnily enough, it hadn't been a showbiz website that had come up with the goods, but an architecture site: the designer who'd built The Quarry for Michael Quinn and his then-wife Cheryl Murray had been well known, and there were photos of the 'ground-breaking' structure and 'futuristic' use of glass, and 'imaginative garden architecture'. It just looked like a ski chalet to Caitlin: all sloping lines and lots of pine and glass and big windows. It wasn't the sort of house you'd expect to find on the outskirts of an unambitious Midlands market town. It was incredible they'd managed to get planning permission for it, let alone found builders who could deal with that much glass.

There were also several photos of Cheryl and Michael. Caitlin could tell, from the body language you'd expect from an ex-model, that Cheryl was much keener on being photographed in the house than Michael. As well as the obligatory shot of them arm-in-arm on the lawn, with two black pugs in front of them, she found more than a few of Cheryl on her own, throwing poses that mirrored the house's angles and showing off her long, tanned legs and dead-straight blonde hair. There was only one of Michael, sitting in his study with a pile of books and three crystal whisky decanters, empty. He wore a cardigan.

That must have been the beginning of the end for Cheryl, Caitlin had thought, feeling a bit like a stalker. You couldn't raise hell in a zip-up cardigan.

There were no photos of Eva and Michael in the house, even though that's where the pair of them had lived all their married life. But by then Michael had become very keen on privacy, and Eva wasn't exactly a party animal.

'Why's it called The Quarry?' Joel asked. 'Is it built on a mine?'

'No, it's called that because Uncle Michael's name was Quinn, and the lady he was married to then was called Murray. So Qu- and -urray. Quarry.'

'Cool!' Joel seemed pleased at the logic.

Caitlin glanced back at Nancy. The nearer they got, the quieter she'd become. Nancy had chatted a bit when they left, choosing the soundtrack they were going to sing along to – Joel holding up the CDs, splayed like a gameshow host – but her sentences had shortened with every mile. Caitlin's chest tightened in sympathy, and she could hear her voice getting jollier as she tried her hardest to keep Nancy in the conversation.

'But Mum, it should be The Quirry,' argued Joel. 'The Quirry. Qui- and -urray. They've got it wrong. Does Auntie Eva know?'

'Quarry is fine.'

'I should tell her. She should know.'

'I don't think it really matters now . . .'

'But the Murray lady, she's not there, is she? Auntie Eva is. She needs to change it back. Her name was Reardon, wasn't it, like ours? So it should be called . . .' His brow furrowed. Both Joel and Nancy might as well have see-through foreheads, thought Caitlin; you could see their brains working. 'The Queardon! I'm going to tell her.'

'Bloody hell . . . Joel, please don't do that.'

'Oh no, wait. *He's* not there any more, is he, Uncle Michael?' Joel's face darkened, and dropped his voice. 'He's died.' He looked almost pleased at the macabre detail. 'What happened to the Murray lady? Did she die too?'

Caitlin took a deep breath. This was the part she'd been rehearsing in her head. The complicated family arrangements of Michael Quinn: the first wife in Yorkshire, the second wife who'd lived in this house, the one child (as far as she knew), the final wife. Although maybe this might be a way into their own awkward divorce conversation later.

'Cheryl and Michael split up,' she began, carefully. 'They loved each other, but then they fell out of love, and decided it would make everyone happier if they didn't live in the same house . . .'

Joel wasn't scared of direct questions. 'So where does Cheryl live now?'

'Um, London, I think.'

'Mum? You know something? Strictly speaking, it should be called The Reardon! Now Uncle Michael's dead and it's just Auntie Eva living there.'

In a way, Caitlin thought, it was good that he didn't seem too troubled by the *principle* of divorce. 'Joel, we need to be sensitive about Auntie Eva's feelings.' She peered at the hedge for a sign. Had they gone too far down this lane? Patrick's instructions said they'd probably miss the sign first time. It was almost like he expected her to get lost without him there telling her where to go.

Well, not almost. He *did* expect it. But she didn't need rescuing from now on. From now on, she was looking after herself and her babies. Like she had been doing before he even came on the scene.

There was the sign. *The Quarry*. Caitlin slammed on the brakes.

'So, remember, let's have our indoor voices, no opening any cupboards, and don't ask any questions about Uncle Michael or Barney the Baker,' she said, turning down the drive. 'Just . . . just tell Auntie Eva what you're doing at school. And don't touch the dogs unless there are at least two adults supervising.'

Joel flung himself back in his seat with a heavy sigh. 'I don't think I'm going to like this house.'

'I think you will,' said Caitlin. 'It's extremely dramatic. Like you.'

She glanced in the rear-view mirror.

Nancy's mouth was firmly closed.

Eva watched from her bedroom as the car made its way down the drive, and her stomach churned.

It was ridiculous to be so nervous, but she was. She'd hoped Patrick would get here before Caitlin, so he could fill her in on things she should know but he hadn't arrived. He'd said he'd be there before lunch, 'to check there are no child-safety issues', but there was no sign of him, and he wasn't replying to texts. Eva reminded herself that the silver lining to this was that now she and Caitlin would have a valid reason to shrug their shoulders and agree that this wasn't going to be a great idea. One thing they could bond over, at least.

Bumble and Bee knew someone was coming. They'd spotted the tidying-up signs, just as they knew the 'cleaner coming' signs and the 'going to the vet's' signs, but, in stark contrast to Eva and Bumble's anxiety, Bee was sitting on the window seat, tongue stuck out in happy anticipation of an audience.

Bumble was curled up in his cupboard just off to the side of the main bedroom. The dogs' 'room' was the edge of one of the triangles that made up the house, with a small window letting in shafts of light onto their padded beds; despite the sloping roof making it impossible for an adult to stand up in there, the architect had optimistically designated it 'a shoe closet'. It was the right size for Bumble and Bee's basket, and meant they could sleep in the bedroom (Mick's preference) but not on the bed (Eva's line in the sand).

Eva lifted chunky Bee off the window seat and she made a complaining half-yap, half-purr of protest.

'Don't give me that,' said Eva, enjoying the suede-y mass of her body. It was one of the things she liked about the pugs: their solidness. She deposited her next to Bumble. 'You two stay in here and chat for an hour or so. Don't want you scaring the children. Or their mother.'

Bee gazed up at her, the deep wrinkles making her big black eyes even more emotional. *Don't deproive me of my right to entertain,* she seemed to say in her Brummie drawl. *Oi just want to be their friend.*

Eva shook herself. It was very, very hard to get out of the habit of hearing Mick's Pug Voices in her head when she looked at them.

Bee's plaintive, kohl-ringed eyes locked on hers. *Where are yow going?*

'I'm going downstairs. I'll come and get you soon. Please don't bark,' she said, and left the room.

Eva could hear Bumble's squeak of protest as Bee made her self comfortable on top of him in their basket, and focused her thoughts instead on Joel and Nancy.

Come on, Eva, she told her self. *Two children and a woman ten years your junior. All family. What are you actually nervous about?*

She didn't have an answer to that, which only made the nervousness worse.

Caitlin arranged herself between Joel and Nancy on the doorstep, holding each one by the hand. It was a charming tableau of happy families, she hoped; or did it look as if she was stopping them running away? Stopping *herself* running away, more like. Her heart was pounding and she wished she'd spent a bit longer drying her hair.

Not that she wanted to impress Patrick.

'Be nice,' she said. 'And if Dad asks, you've been doing your homework.'

'Of course we'll be nice.' Joel looked outraged. 'Why did you say that? When are we ever not nice?'

She noted he didn't query the homework.

'You know what I mean.' Caitlin squeezed Nancy's hand but there was no answering squeeze. Her hand felt tiny in Caitlin's. She'd never known Nancy to be shy, but perhaps the combination of the new house, and the unfamiliar aunt, and the promise of seeing Daddy was a lot for a little girl to process.

Too much, she thought, hating herself. *Too much.*

'Would you like to ring the doorbell, Nancy?' she said, pointing at the elaborate button. It looked like the launcher to a space rocket. 'I'll lift you up if you want?'

'No! *I* want to ring the bell!' Joel lunged for it, and before Caitlin could stop him, he'd jammed his finger on the button, letting out a loud peal somewhere inside.

'That's enough,' said Caitlin after a few seconds, but Joel was relishing the drama of the chimes inside too much. They were majestic chimes, amplified somewhere.

'Joel!' She glared at him, and reluctantly, he removed his finger from the button.

'I'm trying to like the house,' he objected. 'So far, this is the first part I've liked. The rest of it is creepy. It's like a supersize doll's house or something.'

The door was opening, and Caitlin only had time to glower before it swung back to reveal her sister-in-law, smiling as if she wasn't quite sure whether she was pleased to see them or not.

'Hi, Eva!' Caitlin went to kiss her, her usual instinct, but then extended a hand instead. Just in case.

Her first thought on seeing Eva was, blimey, who knew she had weight to lose? When Caitlin had first met Eva, at a slightly awkward 'getting to know you' dinner organised by Patrick in an expensive London restaurant, she'd been intimidated by Eva's Parisian style, something Caitlin had never seen in real life, despite being familiar with it as a concept in fashion magazines. She'd seemed effortlessly confident, slender and chic in cropped cigarette trousers and gold pumps. Caitlin had sneaked off to the loo after the starters and removed fifty per cent of her jewellery, and still felt overdressed. Today, though, Eva looked plain skinny, and she was wearing what looked worryingly like *slacks* with a loose silk shirt. Her hair was still in a long bob, but there were silvery threads where Caitlin remembered a perfect blow-dry like a glossy chestnut. She had a sudden mental image of the female duck Joel had had to draw for class one week, all brown and beaky and drab.

Sympathy overwhelmed Caitlin's own nerves. *This is what grief looks like,* she thought, *it's a sort of hunger,* and impulsively, she leaned forward and hugged Eva. 'It's lovely to see you. It's been too long.'

Whatever Eva said was lost in Caitlin's bosom, but when she emerged there was a spark of warmth in her hazel eyes and a reluctant smile. Caitlin saw her gaze flicker down towards Nancy, clinging to Caitlin's hand, then to Joel. What was it that crossed Eva's face? What had Patrick said about them? About her?

There was a movement to Caitlin's left.

77

'My name is Joseph Magnus Reardon!' Joel stepped forward and made an elaborate bow, doffing an imaginary hat. 'At your service!'

Oh Joel, no, please, thought Caitlin. *Don't be wacky.* 'Joel,' she warned and made a 'dial it down' gesture.

'Pleased to meet you.' Joel took Eva's hand and kissed it with a generous smacking noise. 'May I present my sister, Nancy Diana?' He stepped in front of Caitlin, and swept an arm towards Nancy, who, to Caitlin's relief, offered her hand, at Joel's prompting.

'Hello, Nancy. I'm Auntie Eva. Or you can call me Eva, if you prefer?' Eva shook Nancy's hand and glanced up at Caitlin when she didn't reply. Her eyes were suddenly more alive, an unspoken question in them.

Nancy coughed, and Caitlin thought she heard her say hello, but she couldn't be sure.

Out of the corner of her eye, she saw Joel nudge Nancy's shoulder; a silent reassurance that brought a lump to her throat. He'd be doing that so much from now on. Now she wasn't going to be there to reassure her baby girl on these weekends with Dad.

Caitlin heard Joel's dramatic intake of breath, ready to introduce her next, and said, quickly, 'Joel, you don't need to introduce me. Eva! What a wonderful house!'

'Thank you,' said Eva.

'Yes,' said Joel, 'but did you realise it should be called . . .'

'We're so glad to be here!' Caitlin stepped forward before Joel could finish his sentence. 'It's really kind of you to invite us.'

'My pleasure, it's lovely to see you. Do come in . . .' Eva opened the door wider.

'Shoes off, you two!' said Caitlin, just in case Eva was a 'shoes off inside' sort of person. 'Sorry, I don't know how they've managed to get their shoes muddy already . . .'

'No need to worry about that,' said Eva. 'It's the country-side. Can't keep the mud out.'

Caitlin wasn't taking any chances. 'Shoes off anyway! It'll be less noisy, running around.' She hoped that was warning enough, to everyone.

'Is Dad here?' asked Joel, his eyes darting around the hallway.

If Patrick had been there, they'd have seen him at once. The house was open plan beyond the porch, with strong lines sweeping up to the panelled wood of the vaulted ceiling, the beams arcing above them like a church. Everything was pale, or wooden. Cream carpets. Bronze bowls on floating shelves. Glass tables. Low, squashy pale leather sofas. Lots and lots of wood, and glass, and framed photographs.

God, thought Caitlin. *Imagine the havoc Joel and Nancy could wreak in here with a pack of crayons. It's like a giant pad of blank paper.*

'Not yet,' Eva began, but Joel's attention had already skipped on.

'Wow! It's like Noah's Ark!' He pointed to the staircase, and the mezzanine sitting area hovering over the main room, with more big sofas covered in sheepskin rugs. 'Look! Dead sheep!'

'It's beautiful,' said Caitlin, because it was. Neat and archi-tectural and tidy in a way only achievable without two kids running riot around the place, leaving their toys and drawings and socks scattered about, sabotaging all attempts at minimal-ism. She felt a momentary grip of jealousy, then reminded herself that Eva's house was this tidy because Eva lived here *alone*.

'Yes, it is pretty amazing.' Eva spoke without any sort of boastfulness; presumably she'd had to describe it lots of times. 'Mick designed it himself, with Arnold Halliday. It was a holiday home, really – that was the inspiration. He wanted something to remind him of skiing with his friends in Gstaad and . . . well . . .' She gestured towards the big open fireplace, with the foamy cream sheepskin in front of it. Her face was wry. 'Can I get you a cup of tea? Coffee?'

'Coffee would be great. It does feel like a holiday home,' said Caitlin, following her through to the kitchen-diner. Half her brain was on Joel, and what he might do or say next. 'I don't mean that in a bad way . . . I mean, it's very relaxing.'

What she meant was, like no one actually lives here.

'Thank you,' said Eva, and Caitlin knew she'd heard the real meaning.

'Nancy!' she called, to break the awkwardness, 'come over here and tell Auntie Eva if you'd like a drink.'

Nancy stepped shyly towards them, and Caitlin put a hand on her forehead: was she ill? It wasn't like her to be so quiet. But Nancy's forehead was cool and smooth. She made an 'are you all right?' face at her, but Nancy just gazed at her. Silently.

'You'll have to show Auntie Eva your dancing later,' she said. But she wanted to ask, don't you want to skip round this room, sing from that balcony, twirl in those curtains? All the things you'd normally do?

Nancy said nothing, but just stared at her with her round eyes, as if her thoughts were too big for her head.

Caitlin forced out a smile. We've *done this,* she thought. *We've made her wary and quiet by shoving her into a new situation even we don't know the rules for.*

'She's very quiet,' said Eva, turning back from the marble counter, covered in stainless steel appliances of various kinds.

'Just shy.' Caitlin pulled Nancy towards her legs, comforting her. Maybe if Eva put the radio on, or some music to break the silence, the kids would relax. 'Lots to take in. Do you want a drink, sweetheart?'

Nancy shook her head.

'Have you got dogs?' Joel had reappeared with a pink lead. He held it triumphantly, like Poirot discovering a key piece of evidence.

Eva glanced at Caitlin. 'Yes, but they're in their room. Your daddy . . .' She hesitated over the word; it marked how little she knew them, Caitlin thought, that she didn't even know how the kids referred to their parents. 'Daddy said that Mummy is allergic to dogs, so they're staying upstairs. Out of the way.'

'They've got their own room? Cool!' said Joel.

'I'm not actually allergic,' said Caitlin. That was Patrick again, over-correcting. 'More phobic. I had a bad experience with a neighbour's dog when I was a child. It got through the hedge and jumped on me. I was only tiny . . . Joel. Stop earwigging.'

Caitlin didn't want to transfer her own edginess around dogs onto Joel and Nancy, but it was hard not to, especially as Joel seemed to be a magnet for the slobbery things. Every time she and Patrick had taken the kids out for a walk, dogs of all shapes and sizes would home in on them, dragging their owners over, and every time, Patrick would explain she was 'allergic' ('It sounds less flaky than that you just don't like them').

'I'm not earwigging.' Joel twisted his mouth. 'What else am I supposed to do?'

'Didn't you bring a book to read?'

'I've read it.' Joel liked reading but he liked listening to adult conversations more. Not that their conversation would be exactly scintillating, thought Caitlin. The tension was making her talk in a posher voice, one she didn't recognise. She and Eva were clearly both waiting for Patrick to arrive to take charge, and she wondered what he'd told his sister about their separation. About her. About him. His version, of course.

She fought back a strong urge to blurt out 'heworkedinsanehoursandtoldmeIwasperfectsooftenIstarted-tofeelparanoidIwaslettinghimdownthenIdidlethimdownbuthe-won'ttellmehowandthenheleft'.

'Why don't you run around the garden, Joel?' Eva suggested. 'Explore a bit? There are some nice cows on the other side of the fence – if you're very gentle they let you stroke their noses.'

'Don't touch the cows, Joel.' Caitlin couldn't stop herself. 'Just look, all right? And no shouting at them.'

Joel gazed at her. 'OK.' He turned and ran off. Nancy had sat down on the sofa, and was gazing into space.

'I've texted Patrick,' said Eva, as if she could read Caitlin's mind. 'No reply. He might be stuck in a jam somewhere?'

'I would guess he's been called to sort something out and he's turned his phone off.' Caitlin took the cup of coffee Eva was offering. It was white porcelain, fine as a goose feather. She was very glad Joel wasn't around to demand his own cup.

'Patrick says this new role is very demanding,' said Eva, as if that made it permissible to stand up his two children, his wife and his sister, all of whom had gathered in this house at his behest. 'He was interrupted three times when we last spoke.'

'He can make one call to let us know he's delayed.' She tried a wry look. 'We both know he can use a phone.'

There was a moment's pause, then Eva rolled her eyes in unexpected solidarity.

'Good job he can,' she said. 'We'd never know what was going on otherwise.'

An awkward, if friendly, silence descended and Caitlin's mind went blank. There were two enormous conversational elephants in the room, in the shape of their missing husbands. It should have bonded them, but instead she felt tongue-tied. What took precedence? A dead, loving husband, or a living, estranged one? Who was the worse off?

Her eye fell on a photo of Eva and Michael in evening dress, with John Nettles and Lulu, and another question shot across her mind: *what on earth did you and Michael Quinn have in common?*

'So . . . how was the journey?' Eva asked, and Caitlin made herself recount the whole tedious journey: the diversion around Worcester, the possibility of coming by train next time (next time! Ha!), the parking near their house.

And then, just as she was racking her brains for one more thing to say about the M5, three things happened at once.

The door opened, and Patrick yelled, 'Sorry I'm late, here now!' and at the sound of his voice a rush of irritation and relief and something else swept across Caitlin like a storm cloud.

Nancy leaped off the sofa to race down the hallway, where she flung herself into her father's arms, without uttering a word.

And there was a loud crash from the conservatory, followed by Joel yelling, 'I'm soooooo soooorrrrrrrreeeeee!'

A cavalcade of yapping broke out upstairs. Caitlin saw Eva's face freeze, then she bit her lip and turned away, and Caitlin couldn't work out which of the three had caused the reaction.

The breakage, she thought. *Probably whatever it is Joel's smashed. And she doesn't even realise that that's the easiest thing to mend.*

Chapter six

Bumble and Bee's daily constitutional took an hour, minimum: forty minutes for the walk, twenty minutes for the conversation with admiring passers-by. The two pugs in their jaunty tartan coats were as famous in their own right in Longhampton as Mick had been, probably more so with a particular type of dog walker. When they stepped out with their handsome friend Pongo the Dalmatian, Eva and Pongo's owner, Anna, might as well be invisible.

Still, it gave the pugs the attention they craved, and gave Eva and Anna a chance to talk. Even if most of that time was spent hauling Pongo out of bins and away from toddlers with ice creams.

'I still can't believe you went up to London, had lunch, and came straight back,' said Anna, barely concealing her envy. 'You didn't even pop into an art gallery while you were there? Or . . . a nice bookshop?'

'An art gallery? Why would . . . ? Oh. This is where I'm supposed to bump into eligible young men, right?' Eva shot her a side look.

Anna lifted her hands, in a 'why not?' gesture, and for a split second, Eva considered telling her about the duffle coat man outside the Wolseley, but then decided not to. It would confuse the issue about the diaries. That was what she wanted to focus on today. Mick's diaries, and what she should do about them.

'No, funnily enough. I didn't. I had enough to think about. And I just wanted to come home.'

'Ah. That's nice, *home.*' Anna beamed. She had a very wholesome, milkmaid-ish smile. 'You normally say that about London. Longhampton's finally won you over!'

Eva had to nod. True. This was home now. The quiet town's yellow-and-red spring flowerbeds and looping Victorian ironwork borders and the bandstand. But it felt different today. Everything did. Waking up in her bed felt different; looking at the pugs snoring in their basket felt different. It was the diaries. It was that fear that opening them might reveal Mick's view of their marriage didn't match hers.

'But it's exciting,' Anna went on. 'I might be stocking Mick's memoirs in the shop!'

'Maybe. Maybe not.' She winced. 'I couldn't stop staring at those celebrity biographies at the station. I kept thinking, would I get my own index? **Quinn, Eva**, *meeting with, marriage to, conversations about multivitamins with.* Then I thought, what if I only get half a page in the index and Cheryl gets three? What if my marriage isn't interesting enough to warrant more than a few pages? Should I be relieved, or pissed off?'

Eva was joking, but at the same time . . . she wasn't.

'Don't think like that, Eva.' Anna stopped walking. Her round face showed concern, but at the same time, excitement lit up her eyes. 'Look, I didn't know Mick well, but he was a fantastic story-teller. I'd love to read his memoirs. I bet they're fascinating.'

'In what way, fascinating, though?' Eva knew she sounded paranoid; she couldn't help it. 'What if . . . they're all factual and dull? What if they're bitchy, or if they're just not him?'

'They won't be.'

'How do you know? I haven't even read them yet. And they won't be published at all if the three of us don't agree. Roger hinted that there'll probably be some personal stuff about Cheryl, or Una – do I want to read that?'

'You've been fine until now, knowing he had other marriages.'

'But . . .' Eva struggled to put the wriggling feeling into words. '*Then* it didn't matter. I had him, and our life together was just starting. Now . . .' The darkness closed in her chest and she felt her defiance rise, even with Anna. It wasn't just grief for Mick, it was more selfish than that. It was their future she grieved for, *her* future, the plans they'd made for a life of travel and experiences and possibilities, unfettered by school runs or annual leave. The trade-off for the other opportunities of life most of her friends enjoyed.

Anna touched her arm. 'Well, Mick won't have anything bad to say about you. He adored you. And if he wants to spill the beans about Una and Cheryl, so what? There was a reason they were both exes.'

It wasn't that. Anna was right, but it wasn't that.

'You can't unread things once you've read them.' Eva watched the pugs trotting together, charging towards some disinterested pigeons. 'I don't know if I want to discover something new, some secret Mick didn't tell me, without being able to ask him to put it into context. I want to remember Mick – and me – exactly as we were.'

Anna slipped a hand round her waist as they carried on walking. 'But until you read the diaries, you'll only imagine the worst. And you said yourself, you're starting to move on again – won't this be a good way to draw a line? By making sure he's represented in the best way?'

'Maybe.'

'Well, look, I don't want to lecture. Change the subject. How did it go at the weekend with Joel and Nancy? Did they like the cakes?'

Eva stared ahead down the path and, in her mind, touched the memories of the weekend gingerly. Ouch. 'It was . . . fine.'

'Only fine? No tears? Nothing got broken?'

'Not many tears. Just when the kids had to say goodbye to Patrick. And only one thing got broken – one of Mick's awards. I should have moved it, my fault. But . . .' How to put it into words? That it wasn't what she'd secretly hoped? 'It didn't feel like anyone was having much fun,' she admitted.

'Well, come on. Who would, first visit in a new place? They must be so confused.'

'I think we all were.' Eva said. 'Nancy didn't say a single word. She looked terrified.'

'Give it time. I know when I first started seeing Phil, I thought I could be the perfect stepmother if I only put in enough effort. Waltzing in like a cross between Mary Poppins and Maria from *The Sound of Music*. Making everything better with bedtime stories.' Anna waved her arms around, mocking her own enthusiasm. 'I was *very* naïve, Eva. Way too keen. You've got to let children sniff you out.'

'Like dogs?' Eva was joking, but Anna wasn't.

'Just like dogs.'

They watched as Bumble and Bee were approached by two twin girls, hands outstretched in delight, their faces mirroring the joy on the dogs' wrinkly masks. No words were spoken, but complete communication in coos, squeals and wagging tails.

'It'll be fine,' Anna reassured her. 'Look at me now, a stepgranny before I'm forty!'

'And if it's not fine?'

The cheery reassurance slipped a notch, and Eva saw a glimpse of Anna's secret determination. 'Then I've got a million self-help books I can lend you on the topic.'

Eva was leading the pugs round from the garage to the back of The Quarry when she saw someone standing on the front step. A man.

It had started to drizzle, and he'd whipped his glasses off to dry the raindrops while he was waiting for someone to answer the door, and now he turned round, shoving them hastily back on and nearly poking himself in the eye. It was a clumsy manoeuvre that rang a bell in Eva's head, and a funny light feeling started to rise in her like mist.

No, she thought, spotting the duffle-coat toggles as he turned around. *No, surely not.*

It was him. The man from Piccadilly. The mist in her chest abruptly turned to a chill; how had he tracked her down? How did he know where she lived? Was he a journalist? The pugs weren't so stunned – they charged ahead, rocking backwards and forwards on their short legs as they bounced around him. Bee barked imperiously, Bumble sniffed and whimpered. But their tails were wagging as they swarmed around his legs, and he seemed discombobulated but not scared.

'Hello!' he began with a polite smile. 'I'm looking for Mrs Quinn? I'm Alexander . . .' He extended a hand, and then realisation dawned as she pulled back her hood. 'Blimey. It's you.'

Clearly he didn't expect to see her. He didn't know who she was. Or did he? Journalists had turned up before, after Mick died, pretending to be charity collectors, lost hikers, anything to get a nose inside the house . . .

'Hello,' said Eva, drily. 'It's not-Becky. Did the different coat confuse you? Same coat, different colour, you notice.'

'No! I'm glad you have more than one coat.' He ran a hand awkwardly through his hair. 'I like . . . aubergine. Would I be right in thinking that you're Eva Quinn?'

'I am. Who's asking?' Bee was bouncing around his trousered ankles with glee, rubbing her flat face against the corduroy. 'Hey, madam! Leave!' Eva grabbed Bee by the harness and picked her up, draping her on her shoulder. Bee snorted with disapproval, then settled for glaring at the intruder at his own head height. Reassured by Bee's solid protection, Eva heard herself add, 'Sorry, she loves cords, something about the texture.'

'Maybe it's the wrinkles? They match her face.' He smiled, not completely relaxed, and extended a hand. 'I'm Alexander Montagu, I'm editing your husband's diaries. Sorry, no, correction, I *hope* to be. I didn't mean to surprise you like this. Roger was going to phone last week to let you know I'd be coming.'

There had been several missed calls from Roger since their meeting, but Eva hadn't returned them, not until she'd decided what she actually thought about his proposal. She'd never not returned calls, but it was an easy habit to get into. 'I've had a hectic few days.' She lied.

There was a moment's hesitation, then she reached out and shook Alexander's hand. It was warm and dry, and quite soft. Eva made herself concentrate on the thoughts in her head, not the sensations of his fingers around hers.

So this was the academic Mick had been so chuffed to engage, she noted. Alexander Montagu looked more like a student who'd never quite left university than a professor. But then most of the professors she'd met had been ancient and fussy, and none of them had nearly bowled her over, leaving her weirdly flustered in the street with their Ealing Comedy swear words and big hankies.

His hanky was still in her handbag. She pushed that aside.

'Hello, Alexander,' she said, and he replied, immediately.

'Alex, please. Not even my students have to call me Alexander.'

Eva ploughed on with a question, ignoring the hopeful smile in his eyes. 'Was that why you were on Piccadilly last week?'

'Yes. I'm afraid you caught me checking out the meeting place ahead of time.' Bumble had ventured from behind her legs and was sniffing around Alex's ankles, cautiously, but with some interest. 'Which makes it all the more embarrassing that I didn't recognise you. I knew your face was familiar, I just couldn't place it.'

'Why would you?' Eva shrugged. 'I'm not the famous one.' There was only one official photograph of her with Mick, and she was all too aware how she'd changed from the bride posing in a Stella McCartney trouser suit for 'just one photo' outside Chelsea Registry Office. The best hair and make-up in the business could render you unrecognisable even to yourself.

Alexander made a demurring noise, then stumbled as Bumble pushed against his leg, nearly sending him off balance.

'Oof. Sorry, sorry, dog!'

'Bumble,' said Eva. 'And this is Bee.'

'Hello,' he said, to each of them. He glanced up at Eva, and confessed, 'I never know how to talk to dogs. I have a cat.'

'Called?'

'Burton. After Richard Burton. He's a bit of a one.' He bent to stroke Bumble's ear. 'Out all night, yowls constantly. In Welsh, I assume.'

They'd started to chat as if it was entirely normal to have bumped into each other again on her doorstep, but then Eva noticed the battered laptop bag on Alex's shoulder, the box by his feet, and the bubble of flirtation that had started to rise again in her chest popped. The diaries were in there. Mick's thoughts, Mick's secrets. It was a simple packing box, nothing special, but this one held something alive: memories. Secrets. The past. Her future.

Her heart twisted. *Mick.*

'Are those the diaries in there?' she asked and he nodded.

Eva drew a deep breath. The sooner they started talking about Mick, the better. Mick, her husband. Mick, and his legacy. Mick, Mick, Mick. 'You'd better come in,' she said.

Alexander perched on the edge of the L-shaped sofa, a cup and saucer balanced on his hand. Eva sat in a chair opposite, but the pugs were stationed on the far end of the L, nearest the fireplace, observing him in unison with their huge black marble eyes. Two chunky hardbacks ('my previous editing projects', both contemporaries of Mick's) he'd brought for her to read were on the coffee table, but the box of diaries remained in the hall, on the chair by the telephone.

Even so, Mick was in there with them, and Eva felt a sense of relief that he was.

'I didn't have the pleasure of meeting your husband in person, though we did speak several times on the phone.' Alex seemed more formal once he'd removed his duffle coat to reveal a proper shirt and grey jumper. 'Roger mentioned that you weren't very keen on the idea of publishing the diaries – I can understand that. So he suggested that rather than have the books just turn up on your doorstep, I could drop them off and talk you through how it all works.'

'So instead *you* turned up on my doorstep,' she observed.

Alex looked awkward. 'I did ask Roger to make sure it was all right. I didn't want to intrude . . .'

Roger wasn't daft, thought Eva. He knew she would find a good reason not to open the box without personal encouragement. Politeness was her Achilles heel. 'Have you read them yet?'

Alex shook his head. 'It's all dependent on a nod from you, and the, er, other . . . Michael's previous wives. Have you spoken with them?'

'I don't even have their phone numbers.' Eva poured her own coffee. 'It's not like a club. We don't hang out and compare war stories.'

'Of course not.'

Eva turned her cup round, so the handle was level with the lily pad pattern on the saucer. It was Spode: a wedding present, from a film director she'd never met. 'If you haven't read them, how do you know they're worth publishing?'

'Because if your husband wrote the way he talked, they'll be impossible to put down.' Alex gave up trying to hold his cup without spilling and set it on the table. He leaned forward, and his earnest brown gaze locked with hers. Eva sensed he was trying to rein in a puppyish excitement. 'I teach Film Studies at the University of Warwick – my personal interest is actors who moved between film and stage and television in the sixties, seventies and early eighties. Popular actors, I guess you'd call them. Usually dismissed as lightweight, and underrated by critics, but never out of work – you don't end up with a CV like Michael's unless you've got talent, plus an ability to adapt. I think – well, I know, from the conversations I had with him – that Michael wrote incisively about screen work versus television, changing production values, how he prepared for it, what he liked and didn't like. That's my interest in these diaries, to be honest. Michael's professional experiences, and how they reflect a period in the industry that's often overlooked. He'd be the first to say he was no Olivier, sure, and he never pretended to be, but he was *there*. And he saw it all, and unlike a lot of his contemporaries, he wrote it all down.'

Alex sat back, dislodging a pug-embroidered scatter cushion onto the floor. He struggled to make it look intentional.

'Sorry. Roger should have warned you I'm a bit of a film nerd when I get going.'

Eva couldn't help being flattered on Mick's behalf; so many people just remembered him for the years he'd done on *Without Prejudice*, when he'd barked half his lines from his trademark Ferrari and delivered the others while shooting his cuffs in the courtroom set. Alexander had suddenly revealed a serious air that she hadn't expected. He seemed interested in Mick's skill, not just the hell-raising and the gossip, and she felt herself begin to soften.

'He loved acting,' she said. 'He enjoyed being challenged. That's why he couldn't ever retire completely.'

'Indeed. And,' Alex's eyes twinkled, 'he lived a very interesting life off-screen outside that, let's be honest.'

'Oh.' Eva sat back too, disappointed. She tried to hide it with a blasé boredom. 'You know, Alex, I'm so tired of the whole "inner demons" business. That's what people are going to want to read, isn't it? No matter how fascinating his observations on film practice are. And I don't honestly feel anyone has a *right* to know the offstage Mick. Other than those who actually knew him.'

'Isn't that up to him, though?' Alex asked. 'He wrote the diaries. He intended them to be published.'

'But I'm the one he's left with the final say-so,' she shot back. 'And if you want a quick decision, it's no. I don't even want to read them myself. It might be about Mick's work for you, but it's our life being exposed. And I can't detach like that.'

Eva hadn't meant to come out with such an abrupt statement of intent but there it was. She sat back and stared at her folded hands. Her gold wedding ring, under her antique engagement ring. And on her other hand, the eternity ring that Mick had given her out of the blue one day. *For the eternity I spent looking for you, and didn't even know.*

There was a long pause, broken only by Bumble's sniffing.

'Fair enough.' Alex picked up his cup; there was no ring, Eva noted, then wondered why on earth she'd even looked. 'All I can say is since neither of us know exactly what's *in* the diaries, maybe we should reserve judgement until you've read them? Then discuss the pros and cons?' He paused, then looked at her, hopefully. 'This is very unprofessional of me, and I do apologise, but I really would *love* to read them. They say all actors are in sales, but Michael really sold those diaries to me. He knew exactly what he wanted to do, how he wanted them presented.'

Mick's voice suddenly echoed in Eva's head – *Fancy a professor saying that, eh?* – and Eva couldn't speak. Saying a hard no to a man who seemed genuinely interested in Mick's art was difficult. It wasn't all about her, she argued. Mick obviously felt passionate about this last project; he'd trusted her to see it through.

'I must say,' Alex went on, cheerily, 'as a bit of a props obsessive, it's rather exciting to see his shield from *The Man in Africa*.' He gestured towards the hall where a multi-coloured piece of wall art hung above the long window.

Eva had sat through *The Man in Africa*, Mick's second Hollywood movie, very early on in their relationship; she hadn't realised that was a prop from the film. Until now.

'Good,' she said.

'So, did you and Michael always live here?' Alex went on, sipping his coffee. 'If you don't mind me asking? Did you meet in London?'

Eva raised an eyebrow. 'Surely you've read that story? We met in a bookshop.'

That was the version of their meeting that the press had evolved from the less-glamorous reality – the charity shop turned into a bookshop, the bin bags of Cheryl's cast-offs discreetly Photoshopped out of the picture, Eva recast as a lowly bookseller spotted by a star, not a businesswoman on gardening leave.

Eva had never cared that it wasn't the truth. It kept the real version private for her and Mick.

'The bookshop in the town?'

She nodded.

'And you were working there. Selling books.' He leaned forward again, elbows on his knees, and beamed at her. 'Like in *Notting Hill*? How appropriate! Had you always been a bookseller?'

Eva considered Alex more carefully. His sharp eyes had probably already registered the fact that there were no books at all downstairs in The Quarry. She liked light fiction, nothing too serious, and although Mick's study was lined with books, that's where they'd stayed. A *lot* of them were about wine.

'No,' she said. 'It was just a . . . temporary job.'

'I see.' Alex smiled, amiably. 'Wow, though. How did you feel when Michael Quinn walked in? What was he buying?'

'Are you interviewing me?'

'No, I'm just interested.' Alex looked directly at her. Not at the framed photos, or the awards, but at her, as if she was the most interesting thing in the room. 'It must have been pretty surreal. A Hollywood star chatting to you about the latest paperbacks one minute, then asking you out for a drink?'

'It wasn't a drink, we had tea. Michael was sober when I met him. We went to the café a couple of doors down for a pot of tea. He had Lavinia with him – that was his pug at the time – and I was surprised they'd let us in with her, but they did.' Eva stopped: she'd just meant to defend Mick, as was her habit, but the whole memory popped out of her mouth, before she realised what she was saying.

'Maybe they were letting Michael Quinn in?' Alex suggested.

That hadn't occurred to Eva before. She hadn't properly recognised Mick then, not being much of a film buff.

'Maybe,' she said, then added, 'Lavinia was *terribly* charismatic, though,' and he smiled.

In the real version, Mick had tipped Cheryl's bin bags onto the floor, and the shop manager had gone into a panic, possibly caused by the epilepsy-inducing colour clash that ensued. There was lamé and diamanté and thousand-dollar couture all over the lino. Cheryl had the fashion sense of a billionaire magpie. Eva had stepped in to help, because the manager was clearly ready to price the Chanel jackets and D&G power suits at a pound a time, and, gardening leave or not, Eva's business instincts simply couldn't let that happen. And then of course, there'd been that little joke, the conspiratorial double act that had sealed their flirtation . . .

Alex carried on smiling at her, clearly interested, and a switch flipped inside Eva. The story of how she and Mick met was so much more typical of the gentle, funny man she wanted Alex to know.

'OK, it wasn't a bookshop,' she confessed. 'It was a charity shop. And I wasn't working there, I was just browsing. He was making a very generous donation – about fifty grand's worth of designer clothes that he'd just cleared out of Cheryl's wardrobe. They'd been divorced a year or so, but this place was their holiday home at the time, so she hadn't been back to collect them and he lost patience. The manager wasn't sure who he was, because you don't expect to see famous people in a local charity shop, do you? So Mick . . . Michael somehow made the manager believe they were his dresses. That he was a reformed transvestite.'

Mick said later he hadn't intended to make a performance out of it. He'd come in trying to be low-key, in a raw, hungover mood, but he'd caught Eva's eye, and that had made Eva quip, deadpan, that he must have great legs to wear skirts that short, and it went from there. It had been their first in-joke. Mick complaining how Armani sizes were much smaller than they used to be; Eva agreeing that sequins could be ageing. And all the while, the shop manager squinting with her glasses whipped off in vanity, trying to work out whether he was Ian McShane or not.

Eva's heart did a slow loop-the-loop in her chest, as the scene played out in her mind for the millionth time. It had changed her life. That click. That sudden surge of desire through her veins at this confident man's command of the situation, of her and the shop manager, the naked charisma in that handsome face when he winked over the tatty paperback stand. He knew he was attractive, he led her into that impromptu double act as gracefully as a ballroom dancing champion guiding a shy beginner round the floor until she felt like Ginger Rogers.

Alex had asked how she'd felt. As if she was dreaming. As if her world had suddenly gone into Wizard of Oz Technicolor, louder, brighter, sharper. But she'd felt scared, too. Fearful, even, of what she should say, who she should be, what this man wanted and whether she *was* the woman he thought she was.

No one's ever asked me how I felt, Eva realised. And if they did, I'd only have trotted out some anodyne 'so in love' response. I'd forgotten I was scared. I was scared of falling in love with a man who could make me feel so helpless.

Alex sat back, fascinated. 'A reformed transvestite? Is this the ultimate scoop?'

'No! He wasn't. Obviously. I worked in fashion, so I couldn't let the shop manager price up these couture dresses for a quid each. I think he liked the fact that I wasn't star-struck. I was more impressed with the gear, to tell you the truth. We got chatting, and he suggested we went for a cup of tea and . . .' She lifted her shoulders and smiled. 'That was that.'

'So what were *you* doing there? You don't sound local.'

Eva wasn't really concentrating on being stern any more; Alex was so easy to talk to. 'I'm not. I was taking a year off. I'd just sold the internet company that I'd started, and I had a no-compete clause for a year. I should have been in Italy, learning Italian, but the villa fell through so I wound up here, in my accountant's holiday cottage.'

'You had an internet business?'

Was Alex being disingenuous? He should have known that. But he sounded curious. 'A fashion website. You wouldn't have heard of it – this was fifteen years ago.' She started to shake her head, but Alex prompted her to go on. 'I just got very lucky. Some people did, at the start of the dotcom boom.'

'Tell me. I'm interested.'

'Well . . . My boyfriend at university was reading Computer Science and he wrote a program to help me get dressed more quickly in the morning. It catalogued clothes, put them into outfits . . . Just a joke, because I was always late for lectures because I never knew what to wear. I had to start with the shoes, hence the name. But my friends used it for swapping clothes, then Simeon and I had this idea to develop it, so you could make a virtual wardrobe online, work out what items you were missing, and then create links to online retailers – this was when internet shopping was still relatively new.'

'That sounds amazing.'

'It was just one of those ideas you can't believe no one else has had.' Eva topped up her cold coffee. It felt weird talking about StartWithShoes; it had seemed so straightforward at the time but now she marvelled at her own insouciant confidence.

'I got investors involved, did the marketing myself, while Simeon ran the tech side. It grew, and we ran with it, and we were just getting out of our depth when someone offered us a stupid amount of money for the business, so we cashed out. Our initial engine is the basis for some major fashion retailers. It was quite a glamorous time, for a few years. For a girl who could never find a black top.'

'Wow,' said Alex. 'So you were the perfect person for Michael to meet with his bag of recycling. Why did you tell reporters you met in a bookshop?'

'I didn't. I just didn't correct them when they said we did. What difference does it make?'

'For a biographer it makes a huge difference. It's the truth.' He pushed his glasses up his nose. 'It's always interesting when people don't bother to correct mistakes. About themselves.'

Eva crossed her legs, annoyed with herself; she liked Alex, but she'd let out more than she meant to.

'Speaking of which,' she said. 'I still have several bags of clothes I need to take down to that very shop. I don't mean to be rude but . . .'

'No, no!' He jumped up. 'I've taken up way too much of your day as it is. You've been very kind.'

'Shall I take that cup from you . . . before you smash it, drop it or tip it over my sofa?' she asked innocently, and he looked horrified for a second, then caught her eye.

'Are you teasing me?' he asked.

She nodded, and he handed her the cup – carefully – and flashed a rueful glance from behind his glasses.

They walked through the house, and Eva could tell Alex was trying not to stare too hard at the photographs on display. At the front door, he turned to her. It had stopped raining, and the sun had come out, making the drops of rain on the cobwebs around the doorstep bay trees glisten.

'If I ask you one thing, it's to read the diaries before you make a final decision.' His expression was serious. 'If you gave your approval, we'd go through them together, highlight key sections, and anything you didn't want to share would never see the light of day. My role, as editor, would be to capture Mick's voice. His own voice, not the lines he spoke as an actor. That's what he asked me to do – to give him a final stage.'

Mick's voice. It came through so strongly in every line. Eva put her hand on the doorframe. 'I'll try to find time.'

'Ah. Time,' said Alex. 'The publishers need a decision from you, and Cheryl and Una, in four weeks. Obviously they've got a production schedule in mind, and ... well, you know deadlines.'

She inclined her head.

'Call me if you have any questions, and I'll be in touch,' he said, and then tentatively, he held out a hand for her to shake.

This was the second time they'd shaken hands, thought Eva, feeling Alex's fingers wrap around hers. In theatrical circles, they'd be on to kisses-on-the-cheek by now. But the solemnity of the handshake seemed strangely fitting. As if they were agreeing a deal they hadn't been aware they were making.

'Thanks so much for the coffee. Bye bye!' he added, and Eva realised he was waving at the pugs, who'd followed them silently to the front door, and were now standing behind her, seeing out the guest. Or maybe seeing *off* the guest.

She watched as Alex retrieved a bicycle she hadn't previously noticed by the hedge, and closed the door as he wobbled back down towards the railway station, his briefcase slung over his back, not wanting to see him crash into anything. She had a feeling he might. Then, unable to stop herself, she peered through the glass to make sure he made it safely down the drive, and onto the road.

Chapter seven

Waitressing in a Bristol café hadn't been high on Caitlin's careers wishlist, but it turned out, to her mother's despair, to be her favourite of the many part-time jobs she'd had since Joel was born. Lynne kept encouraging her 'not to give up on your potential!', but the hours at Sadie's Kitchen fitted in with Joel and Nancy's routine (give or take a few skin-of-the-teeth after school pick-ups), and cleaning, feeding and micromanaging her children had given Caitlin such a rock-solid catering skill-set that she could have done her shifts in her sleep.

Plus, she got to talk to adults. Until she started to spend all day with toddlers, Caitlin had never realised what a treat that would be.

Sadie's Kitchen – there was no Sadie; the owner, platinum-blonde business tiger Joanne, thought it sounded 'more retro' – was twenty-three minutes' fast walk from her house, in the middle of a village high street of estate agents, solicitors and other coffee shops. It was a functional black floor/chalkboard walls kind of café, with a personality that morphed according to the time of day. In the mornings, the grill kept up a stream of bacon sandwiches for bleary-eyed suits; from ten, the tables filled with coffee morning mums; then at lunchtime the office workers came back for baguettes; then everything went quiet in the afternoon. That was when Joanne was trying to lure what she called 'the afternoon tea brigade' in, with fancy cakes.

The best thing about waitressing, for Caitlin, was that it gave you time to think when you needed to think, and kept your brain occupied with small, easily achievable tasks when you didn't want to. This Monday, she had plenty to run through in her head: viz, the weekend contact visit at Eva's, and how she felt it had gone.

And even more importantly, how she and Patrick were going to get round to telling Joel and Nancy why they were putting them through this. Another opportunity had slipped by, and Caitlin was determined that they *both* had to shoulder what was going to be the worst moment of everyone's lives.

She slapped some bacon into rolls for the two estate agents who came in at exactly one o'clock each lunchtime, and cringed again at the mental image of Eva's face when Joel had announced he'd broken 'some glass thing'. (An award, it turned out, for Michael's run in some West End theatre production of *The Witches of Eastwick*. Bloody, hell. Bloody *bloody* hell.)

'Ketchup?' She waved the bottle at the estate agents, both on their phones. Eva had been gracious, for which Caitlin was grateful – but she'd given Joel a lecture about taking care of people's property when they got home. He'd been practising receiving an Oscar, apparently. It had 'slipped'. But even with Eva clearing up the mess and assuring a mortified Joel it was fine, Caitlin hadn't been able to relax again. The Quarry wasn't a relaxing house, and Eva fluttered about the whole time, on edge. Understandably so, Caitlin reminded herself; Eva had been living a retired person's life for ten years, and she was barely forty. But there was something so stiff about her. So anxious. Nancy had barely said a word, and Nancy hadn't been fazed by any adult, including some borderline dodgy Father Christmases, since she was old enough to stand.

Caitlin squirted ketchup crossly. Poor Eva. Patrick had clearly strong-armed her into it. When they left, she hadn't looked relieved, as Caitlin expected (well, maybe a bit relieved). Eva had looked . . . sad. Scared and sad and kind of small, standing on the doorstep of that big empty house. Like the housekeeper, not the owner.

Caitlin pushed aside some troubling feelings she'd had about Patrick and focused on his rudeness. He should have been there early. Preparing the house. Preparing his sister. Making things easy for *his children*. Not turning up late, claiming he'd been dragged into work . . . He wanted the contact. The least he could do was make a difficult experience as smooth as possible for everyone else. What had happened to him? Where had the thoughtful, helpful Patrick she'd met gone?

Was someone else taking up all his time now? Her throat tightened.

'Caitlin?'

She swung round. 'What?'

Scarlett, the other waitress, nodded at the bacon rolls. They were covered in ketchup. So was the counter. The estate agents had spots of ketchup on their ties. Their expressions were more afraid than angry.

'Oh God.' Caitlin put down the bottle and wiped her forehead with the back of her hand. 'I'm so sorry. Sorry. Sorry.'

They backed away, refusing her offer of napkins.

When they'd left, Scarlett opened her eyes wide, and Caitlin lifted a warning finger. Scarlett's relationships lasted only slightly longer than Nancy's library loans. She was unlikely to get this. 'Don't even ask.'

Welsh Mary the cook nudged Scarlett aside with a tray of fresh sausages. She slammed them down on the counter and said, 'Contact weekend, wasn't it? How'd it go?'

Mary remembered everything. Even things Caitlin didn't remember telling anyone. But then she did, by her own admission, have quite loud phone conversations, and the café phone was right by Mary's cooking station.

'Fine,' she repeated.

'Fine?' Mary shoved up her sleeves, revealing a red dragon curled around a leek. When she crossed her arms, the dragon bulged, menacingly, as did the leek. 'I've been there, love,' she said. 'Bloody nightmare, contact weekends. So's Joanne. The stories she could tell about her ex . . .' She paused, inviting Caitlin to elaborate.

'Well.' Caitlin cracked. She had to tell someone. It wasn't like she could tell her mother; Lynne would pounce on it and insert herself firmly into the situation like a cross between Kofi Annan and the SAS. 'Joel broke an award, Nancy sat on Patrick's knee like a ventriloquist's dummy, my sister-in-law declined to tell any juicy showbiz stories, despite my best efforts for you lot, and I had to go for a walk around the garden because I'd run out of conversation.'

'You ran out of conversation?' Joanne had appeared from the back, and let out a bark of laughter. 'Where were you? A Trappist monastery?'

Caitlin squirmed at the audience that had formed: Scarlett, Mary and now Joanne too. Soon the customers would be joining in. 'Longhampton.'

'Longhampton?' said Joanne, with a curl of her lip. 'Well, that'd explain it. Still, take it from someone who's been there, got the T-shirt – it gets better. Once you get past the argy-bargy, think of it as two days' holiday a fortnight. You can get a lot done in a weekend. Speaking of which,' she added, with a wink, 'you missed your man this morning.'

'Who do you mean?' Heat flamed into her cheeks. What did Joanne know?

Joanne poked her in the ribs. 'Stan Lawson! The sausage sandwich man. He asked for you. "Where's my curly top?" he said.'

'Oh.' Stan Lawson was the postman. He was fifty, bald, and always asked Caitlin for 'extra sauce' with a leer.

'Who did you think I meant?' Joanne peered at her. 'You've gone very red. Oooh! Something we should know?'

'No!' said Caitlin. She had a face that blushed too easily. Pale skin, again. 'I'm just very hot. I'm standing near the hot plate. Is no one going to serve this customer?'

Joanne laughed knowingly, but out of the corner of her eye, Caitlin could see Mary glancing at her and she had to move quickly to stop the blush spreading any further.

The lunchtime rush kept Caitlin busy and by half two, her prepared speech to Patrick had only got as far as, 'We need to talk to the children together at their next weekend because . . .' She kept coming back to her instinctive desire to tuck both Joel and Nancy under her arms and run far, far away from the whole mess.

Her guilty thoughts were interrupted by Scarlett, holding out the café phone.

'It's for you?' Scarlett wiggled the receiver. 'School? Or nursery or something?'

'Which school?' Caitlin wiped her hands on the apron and

swung her way quickly between the empty tables. 'Joel's or Nancy's?'

'Didn't say. Just that she had to speak to you, like, now.'

Caitlin held her hand out for the phone, aware that 'she', on the other end, could hear all this. Scarlett looked as if she was going to hang around to listen in, so Caitlin pointed at the uncleared tables and made a 'help me out?' face.

Scarlett made a face back, but sloped off nonetheless. Caitlin turned towards the wall. It was one thing discussing Patrick's shortcomings with the others, but the kids were private.

'Hello!' she said, brightly. 'Caitlin speaking.'

'Hello, Caitlin, it's Mrs Yardley.'

That meant Nancy. Mrs Yardley was the nursery manager at Busy Bees, the nursery Nancy went to; her granddaughter Shelley owned it, and was very nice, but Mrs Yardley had been a school secretary for years and liked to keep things on a strictly no-first-names basis.

'Is everything all right?'

'I just wanted to advise that Shelley wanted to have a word with yourself at pick-up this afternoon, so if you could allocate an extra fifteen to twenty minutes, that would be ideal.'

'What about?' Caitlin felt her heart speed up. 'Is there a problem? Is Nancy hurt?'

'No, nothing like that. But I'll leave that for Shelley to discuss.' Her voice was kind. That set alarm bells off.

'Is Nancy all right?' Caitlin's head buzzed with all the things that might be wrong. Was it the fees? They went out on direct debit from the joint account and she never checked it; that was Patrick's area, finances. Or had he stopped it? He couldn't be that mean, surely?

Was it something to do with the weekend? Had she said something about going to Eva's? Was she sad? Caitlin hated the thought of Nancy being sad, at nursery. She *loved* nursery. She'd never once cried, not even on her first day. A memory of the nativity play, just a few months ago, filled her mind: Nancy singing as loud as she could in her tinsel halo and specially made wings that she'd worn home, straining to see Mummy and Daddy in the audience, then unleashing that smile that had made Caitlin's arms ache to hold her baby girl tightly and never ever let her grow up from that moment . . .

Caitlin realised she couldn't speak because she would cry if she opened her mouth.

'Service? Hello!'

She spun round. A taxi driver was standing at the counter, tapping a baguette against the glass top. Then he tapped his watch with it.

Caitlin's legs felt weak. *This is where it starts for real,* she thought. This weekend was Joel and Nancy realising something's definitely wrong with Mummy and Daddy. *We can't pretend much longer; we're going to have to have the talk.*

She had to force herself to smile. 'Be right with you, mate. So, fine,' she said, to Mrs Yardley, 'I'll see Shelley at ten to three, then?'

'Very good. There's no need to worry,' she replied, but in a tone that made Caitlin worry even more.

Caitlin spotted Nancy through the French windows as she hurried across the playground outside the nursery: she was sitting in the reading corner on the pink beanbag, her usual spot, her strawberry blonde head bent over a book, fringe falling in her face, thumb tucked in her mouth.

Caitlin stopped for a moment, just to imprint it on her memory. So many times a day, she longed to stop the clock.

Nancy couldn't read on her own yet, but she wasn't far off it, and Caitlin often wondered what it must feel like to be teetering on the brink of understanding: a little bird poised on the edge of the nest, ready to leap into the air and find power in her wings, taking her to places she hadn't imagined. She loved to watch the concentration in Nancy's eyes when they read in bed, understanding moving across her face like wind sweeping invisibly over cornfields. Time seemed to be speeding past, and the familiar books were Nancy's first steps towards the day when she wouldn't need Caitlin at all, not just for unpicking hard words.

Patrick didn't think Nancy was reading, just that she, like him, had a good memory. 'She's *learned* those books,' he reminded Caitlin, when she floated downstairs bursting with pride at their advanced child. 'Come on. How many times has she heard them? Hundreds? Don't get carried away.'

Patrick's rationality felt like a double dig, diminishing Nancy *and* her, and he'd stared at her over the dining table, covered in papers and emails from work, as if she was being ridiculous. Caitlin had deliberately looked past him, at the bookshelf filled with the books she'd bought since their marriage. Not one of them was Patrick's. He hadn't, Caitlin realised, brought a single book home since he'd moved into her house. Not even one for Joe or Nancy.

'She's just a normal little girl, and I don't want you to put unnecessary pressure on her,' he'd said, calmly.

'Reading isn't *pressure*. It's magical, watching our baby turn into her own person!'

'Really?' He'd paused. 'Maybe I miss the magical stuff, while I'm out at work.'

And without warning, that night, for the first time, Caitlin had thought, *I don't know you any more.* She could tell, from his dismayed expression, that Patrick was thinking much the same thing.

The memory burst through her mind then vanished, like a lightning strike. For the second time that day, Caitlin realised she was on the verge of tears. It had been so good once, she and Patrick. And now it was ruined, and gone.

Deep breaths, she told herself. The nursery window was open and she focused on Shelley in the classroom, chatting away to some of the other children waiting for their parents. She could hear Shelley telling them about a trip the nursery was going on, to a park with ducks; *That'll be what she wants to talk to me about,* Caitlin thought. *Some permissions thing. Nothing bad. And I can tell her about Patrick, face to face.*

She pulled herself together, forced a smile onto her face and walked inside, into the dayroom. It was a happy space, with big airy windows and handprint flowers around each wall. The children were grouped by age, as flowers: Nancy, about to leave, was a daisy, but she'd enjoyed being a sunflower the most. Sunflowers were 'the happiest of the flowers', according to her. Caitlin loved the way Nancy gave everything a personality: flowers, cats, houses – she cared about all their feelings.

As soon as Caitlin walked in, Nancy dropped the book that had been on her knee and ran over, giving her the same tight hug she'd given Patrick when he'd arrived at Eva's.

'Hello, Fancy Nance,' said Eva, kissing the top of her silky head. 'Are you ready to come home?'

She expected her to ask about the cake – every day, Nancy checked whether Caitlin had managed to sneak some cake away – but there was no question. Just a quick nuzzle and then a tighter hug.

She's tired, thought Caitlin. *A lot to take in.*

'Our bookworm,' said Shelley affectionately. 'We always know where to find Nancy, don't we? With our books!'

Nancy looked up at Caitlin, her arms still tightly wrapped around her legs, but she still didn't say anything. Her blue eyes seemed even bigger than normal in her heart-shaped face.

'Nancy? Why don't you go and have a story with Kath while I have a chat with your mum?' Shelley didn't seem to be reacting to Nancy's quietness, and waved to the classroom assistant, who was putting a small boy into a jacket he didn't seem very keen on. 'Kath? Time for a quick Bing?'

'I've always got time for a quick Bing!' Kath held out a hand. 'Nancy? Do you want to come and pick the book?'

Nancy glanced at Caitlin, who smiled encouragingly, then darted off to the other side of the room.

'She's tired,' Caitlin heard herself saying. 'It was a long weekend for her. Lots of travelling. We went to Longhampton, to visit Patrick's sister. She doesn't know her, and I supposed she's still processing that . . .'

Why am I making excuses? she wondered. *I've got to tell Shelley the truth; she needs to know.* And yet telling people made it real.

This isn't about you, Caitlin told herself, fiercely, but the shame wouldn't go away.

'Ah. OK.' Shelley nodded. 'Is there anything else going on at home? Any changes? I don't mean to be nosy but . . .'

'Has Nancy said something?' She panicked. 'Well, the reason we were there, was a bit . . . Well, Patrick's working in Newcastle and . . .' *Tell the truth, Caitlin.* She steeled herself. 'We're separating. He's moved up there and he's only seeing the kids every other weekend at the moment. At his sister's. We're working out the details, so we haven't told them what's happening in so many words but we will be very soon.'

'Oh dear. I'm sorry to hear that. But thank you for telling me.'

'I was going to come in anyway to let you know, because obviously Joel and Nancy are our main priority, well, our *only* priority! But Nancy . . .' Caitlin ground to a halt, hot with shame. 'Has she said something?'

'Not exactly.' Shelley looked wry. 'Well, no – exactly the opposite, funnily enough. She hasn't said *anything* for the past few days.'

Oh God. It *was* Nancy. It wasn't the school trip. Caitlin's heart dropped like a stone in her chest. She'd seen Shelley talking gently to other parents before, and felt sorry for them. Now my child has a problem. *I've* given my child a problem.

'I don't want to make too much of it . . .' Shelley lowered her voice. 'But we noticed a change in Nancy after she came back from her Christmas holiday. She's been very quiet in herself, still playing but not really as verbal as normal, but it's just been more noticeable today because we've been doing some language play and— Hey!' She patted Caitlin's arm. 'No need to look so worried!'

'I don't understand. What do you mean – she's not verbal? She isn't talking? Nancy's such a chatterbox . . .'

'I know! I thought she might be a bit under the weather – you know what it's like, always something going round! – but

Kath noticed too, that she's not joining in the way she usually does. She's our best singer, is Nancy.' Shelley's kind face was concerned. 'But it makes sense, given what you've just told me. Poor little thing. Poor you too. How is she at home?'

'Fine. She was a bit quiet on the way back from her auntie's – Patrick had to go straight back to Newcastle, and the kids were upset, obviously – but last night she and Joel were playing on their karaoke machine as normal.' The noise had been horrendous, but Caitlin hadn't had the heart to stop them – she was glad to see them behaving like normal kids again, after their subdued journey home, as if Eva's house had already sucked some of the life out of them.

Or *was* it both of them singing? Was it Joel making enough noise for two?

'Karaoke? Well, that's good.' Shelley tried to sound encouraging.

'When you say she's a lot quieter, what do you mean? Isn't she joining in?' Caitlin's mind raced for reasons. 'Is it . . . Has she fallen out with her friends? Might that be it?'

'No! No, she's joining in fine. No problem there.' Shelley looked across to the reading corner, where Nancy was perched on Kath's knee. Kath was reading; Nancy was sucking her thumb. 'Still bossing the play shop and the kitchen, don't worry! She's just . . .' She frowned, searching for the right words. 'She doesn't seem to have any trouble communicating, but she's not using words when we ask her directly. We don't push her, of course, but I wanted to mention it to you so we can stop it becoming a thing.'

'A *thing*?'

'Sometimes little ones go through phases of not talking, we've had it before. Usually the bilingual kids, but not always.

We try to ignore it, and they usually start again soon enough. Maybe she's just trying to process what's happening? But you know how much we love Nancy here, and if she's unhappy about something then I want her to feel she can talk to us if she wants.'

'There's nothing she's too scared to talk about if that's what you mean!' It came out louder than Caitlin intended but the implication shocked her. 'Patrick's not leaving because . . . it's not like I've kicked him out because of any . . .' It was too horrible to say.

'Of course not!' Shelley touched her arm, but Caitlin knew she'd been thinking it. Withdrawn children, too scared to speak. It added up to something horrible.

'Caitlin, I wasn't accusing you of anything! I only wanted to mention it – if she's chatting away normally at home then maybe it's something we need to look at here.' Shelley's eyes were fixed on her face. 'Now I know things are a wee bit complicated at home we can make sure that's handled carefully here too. OK?'

'OK.' Caitlin's head was filled with yelling voices, but everything else felt very still. Her only instinct was to cuddle Nancy up in her arms and protect her, but you couldn't protect anyone from sadness, could you? That had been one of the first things she'd learned about parenthood, that she'd throw herself in front of any car, bus, rampaging lion for her babies, but the types of pain she most wanted to protect them from were invisible, out of her control, and those were the things that kept her awake at night.

'Tomorrow's another day,' said Shelley, cheerfully. 'You're not our first mum to come in and tell us what you've just told us, Caitlin, and you won't be the last. Promise.'

Caitlin managed a weak smile. First the café girls, now Shelley.

'And between us . . .' Shelley pressed her lips together in a sort of solidarity gesture. 'Take care of yourself too, won't you? Tough times.'

'Thanks.' It came out as a croak.

'Great! You take Nancy home, and we'll see you in the morning. Nancy? Would you like to take that Bing book home with you to read with Mummy at bedtime?'

Over in the reading corner, Nancy looked up, grinned and nodded. But she didn't speak. A prickly chill went over Caitlin's heart.

'That's brilliant. Are you ready to go? Where's your coat?' Shelley kept up the stream of happy chat but there was no response from Nancy other than her obedient smile, a nod of her head and the constant motion of her watchful blue eyes.

Chapter eight

The diaries stayed on the chair by the door where Alex Montagu had left them. They'd been there for four days, and the sticky label was still intact across the top, holding the two flaps of the box together and keeping several years of private, secret thoughts inside. Unpredictable thoughts, like bees slumbering in a winter hive. Each time Eva walked past the front door she hesitated, reached forward, then found something else to do first.

The pugs didn't like the box either. Bumble sniffed the air around it and looked anxious, as if Mick might be in there. Bee took up guard by the chair, glaring at Eva if she came near. The energy in the house had changed. In the two years since Mick's death, Eva had got used to being there on her own, with the dogs, but now it was as if a door she'd never noticed had opened, and something had slipped back into her life, watching her, waiting for her to turn round and confront it.

No, she thought. *Not something. It was Mick.* It felt as if Mick was back in their home, but she couldn't touch him, she couldn't kiss him, she couldn't talk to him. All she could do was hear his voice, and miss him. Like the Barney the Baker DVDs but worse, because this time his disembodied voice wasn't just joking about magic pies and Flo the Dough – he would be talking about *them*.

The box was still unopened a few days later when a padded bag arrived in the post, bundled together with Eva's subscription copy of *Vogue*, some bills and the new issue of *Longhampton Matters*, the town's magazine and monthly round-up of jumble sale opportunities.

As usual, the pugs responded to the arrival of post by charging to the front door barking, and Eva struggled to rescue the bag before Bee shredded it. It didn't weigh much. Her name and address were written in a hand she didn't recognise: small capitals in a blue fountain pen that had smudged in the rain.

Inside the bag was a red exercise book with a cream correspondence card paperclipped to the front. *Professor Alexander Montagu.*

Many apologies, [read the note.] *This notebook was returned to me from Cheryl Murray, as it had been erroneously included in her portion of the diaries. I apologise for the oversight, and hope you hadn't been wondering about any unexplained gap during this era of your marriage! Very much looking forward to hearing your thoughts and, of course, I'm always available to discuss any questions you might have about publication or editing. Thank you once again for making time to see me – PTO >>.*

She turned over the card, and in a more informal scribble, Alex had added, *Thought you might be interested in the attached, from our archive collection. It's Michael on the set of* The Man In Africa *– different times, eh!*

Eva looked in the bag: a photograph had detached itself from the paperclip. She tipped it out and yes, there was a young and lavishly sideburned Mick relaxing between takes, surrounded by chatting extras in tribal dress smoking cigarettes and holding cans of lager. A seventies Land Rover was clearly visible in the background, the shield propped up against the front wheel.

Eva glanced up – yes, that was the shield. Mick's shield, now on her wall, there in the photo. It looked better in black and white too.

She was touched that Alex had remembered. The odd thing was, she didn't feel . . . anything much about the photo itself. It was Mick, on a film set. She felt more connected to the shield than the cocky-looking young man in the linen suit.

She put it down, and picked up the notebook, plain and innocuous, and without thinking, opened it.

The first words Eva read could have been spoken in Mick's voice:

I've known Tim Herald for twenty-one years now and, bloody hell, he doesn't get better with age. The man is the opposite of Stilton. Eva, of course, patron saint of diplomacy, told me she thinks Tim's 'one of a kind'. Yes, thank Christ. If there were two of him, even Noah wouldn't let him on board.

Adrenalin rushed through Eva's veins. The familiar loop and scrawl of Mick's cursive handwriting filled the pages with the same energy that his conversation filled a room: there were no crossings out, but lines were sprinkled with exclamations marks, capitals and underlinings, the same way his conversation was punctuated with hand gestures, short barks of laughter and winks.

The diary started with no preamble in April 2008.

Spoke to Terry Newton about the cartoon baker proposal. Easy enough gig – voice-overs for twelve episodes to begin with, no acting required. A little start-up production co but Roger says Terry's investing and he's a Yorkshireman after my own heart – short arms, deep pockets. Kim's not sold, she keeps going on about this HBO Western she's nearly got in the bag, according to her, but Roger thinks Barney the Baker's good news – his grandkids are mad keen on the books, and there are lots of 'em. No shame in a nice retirement gig – as Ringo Starr's been telling anyone who'd listen for years.

Barney the Baker. So that was how it happened. Eva remembered Mick coming home from a lunch with Terry, a mate from way back, all shifty because he'd promised her they'd go on their year trip across the States and suddenly 'a job' had come up and it had been postponed. Huh. She remembered the Western too, the one Kim had wanted him to read for. Mick wrote exactly what he'd said to her.

To be honest, I can't get up the energy for the US work any more. It's such an arse-ache, with customs and losing the same ten pounds over and over for the cameras. And actors are no fun these days. All on diets, swearing off bread or anything white, all chugging pomegranate juice for their prostates and going jogging. Jogging! God save

me from getting old. Anyway, we've got enough
cash, me and Eva, and I'd rather be at home with
her and the puggles and the garden. Jesus. There's
a thing I never thought I'd write – wanting to be at
home with the wife and the garden. But it's true.
What more happiness is there in life than being
surrounded by love and your own roses?

The tenderness leaped off the page; it made Eva's breath
catch in her chest. She'd always wanted to believe Mick loved
his domestic life with her. And he did. He said here he did. She
felt the ruffle of his hand on her hair. *Daft bird.* Why had she
worried that he wouldn't? Instead of closing the book and
hiding it under the unopened box, she skimmed on, hungry
for more detail but holding her breath against stumbling on
something less comforting.

Speaking of which, Eva came home this eve from
town with a new jacket. Funny blue thing, like our
old school blazer. I expect it's fashionable. She
asked me what I thought – like an old git like me
would know! – but bless her heart for asking. Told
her she could wear a flour-sack and she'd still be a
stunner. Think she thought I was joking. Can never
remember how unPC you're allowed to be with the
younger generation – my compliments are all of the
older vintage, but E's too sweet to complain.

Blue jacket? Eva frowned, trying to remember which one
he'd meant. She'd stopped buying clothes: most days revolved
around walking the dogs, then maybe walking to the pub.

She flipped back to check the date. May 20th, 2008. Then she remembered: a navy Hugo Boss jacket. She'd bought it in London, on a rare solo trip back to see her business advisor and sign the last papers relating to the company. It had been chillier than she'd expected in the city, and she'd nipped into Selfridges for a jacket. Eva remembered the effort she'd made not to reach for a practical one, instead picking something sharp and tailored to get her brain working back in business gears. Even then she'd sensed her old life slipping away from her, but it only made her glow inside. It had never really felt like hers. And she was giving it up for a far more warm, and enriching existence – a shared life that would *mean* something.

Eva closed her eyes, searching in her heart for that 'coming home' feeling she'd had when she turned her house key in the lock, and heard the pugs skittering down the hall, and Mick singing to himself in the kitchen. The slim cut of the jacket had suddenly felt constricting. Mick had appeared, flour on his hands, and he'd commented on it; Eva had felt his eyes taking in the difference in her so, self-consciously, she'd modelled it down the hall, mimicking the dead-eyed slouch she used to see so often on catwalks. He'd laughed, the pugs had barked and barked at her weird behaviour and when she took it off and hung it in the wardrobe Eva already knew she'd never wear it again. It wasn't who she was. And she didn't care.

Not that Mick had written any of that down. That was her memory. The last line on the page read:

I know I'm a jammy sod, more than I deserve, but the day I met that woman was the luckiest of my life.

Eva bit her lip. That memory had nearly slipped away, but Mick had brought it back: not just the jacket but the sense of belonging she'd felt when she stepped into his arms. That feeling of having come home. That memory was only just clinging at the very edge of her remembering.

She turned the page, only letting her eye go to the end of one sentence at a time, inching her way down the lines.

Thought about asking E her opinion on Barney Baker and kids' programmes in general but didn't want to spoil the mood. Not her thing. Not our thing, I guess. Best left.

Abruptly the glow faded. What did that mean? Eva stared at Mick's words. ***Not her thing. Not our thing***. What wasn't? Cartoon bakers? Discussing work? But she knew that wasn't it. Children's programmes. Was that not her thing? Is that what he thought?

What do you mean? she wanted to ask, but Mick wasn't there. He'd never be there. She would never know exactly what he meant by that.

The phone rang, and she wondered if it was Alex, calling to see if she'd kept her promise and started to read. She realised she had, without thinking.

Eva reached for the phone, keeping her thumb in the exercise book, but it was Patrick, calling from his car, en route from one meeting to another as usual.

'Is this a good time?' He always said that, a hangover from when he'd called her at work and she could never talk. Patrick still talked on anyway, regardless.

Eva took a deep breath and tried to centre herself. She put

the exercise book down on the sideboard, next to a photograph of Mick posing in a black beret with Bumble and Bee on his lap: his sixty-second birthday at a villa in the South of France. Bee was encased in a stripy T-shirt, Bumble was frowning. Mick, his arm stretched along the loveseat where she'd been sitting, winked rakishly. At her, behind the camera. In the picture, yet out of it.

She turned away. 'Of course!' Bee was nosing around in the bag by the door, old ties and jumpers waiting to go to the charity shop. Bumble stood by, looking up at her like a community policeman, not quite sure if he was authorised to report the misdemeanour. Eva decided to ignore it for the time being.

'Brilliant!' said Patrick. 'Listen, I'm just ringing to confirm arrangements for next weekend. For me and the kids.'

'Next weekend! Already!' Eva didn't want Patrick to think she wasn't being helpful about his contact time – this one, she'd decided, with the help of a few books Anna had given her, was going to go better that the last. 'Great. What's the plan?'

'Right, so Caitlin's texted to say she'll be dropping them off with you at nine o'clock on Saturday morning, and she'll come back for them on Sunday at three.'

'Sunday? They're sleeping here overnight?'

'Yes. Well, obviously. Last weekend was just a trial run. Sorry, didn't I make that clear? We agreed with the mediator that I'd have every other weekend, and holidays.' Patrick sounded apologetic. 'I want to work up to having them from Friday after school until Sunday evening, but it's going to take some negotiation with work to get away in reasonable time on Friday. Is that going to be a problem?'

'No, not at all. It'll be lovely to have everyone stay but you're sure . . .' How did you phrase this? 'You're sure Joel and Nancy want to come?'

'Yes! Why do you say that?'

'Because . . .' Eva habitually edged her way around observations regarding children. Like plumbing or politics, she had opinions but didn't always feel qualified to deliver them. 'It didn't seem to be a lot of fun for them? Nancy was so quiet, and Joel . . .'

'Can I apologise again for Joel breaking that award? He shouldn't have been messing around with it. He's going to write you a letter to say sorry.'

'He doesn't need to do that. It's fine, honestly.' Joel's fearful expression was stuck in Eva's mind like a splinter from the glass: ashamed-scared, like Bumble the time he peed in Mick's suitcase. 'I'm sorry if I over-reacted. I just . . . remembered the night Mick won that award. It was the night after we got back from our honeymoon.' Her eyes had locked with Joel's, and she'd wanted to reach across that adult–child chasm between them, to tell him the pain she felt wasn't what he thought he'd caused, but she hadn't known how.

That gnawed at her more than losing the award did.

But Patrick was talking. 'No, Caitlin agrees, Joel needs to apologise. He was being silly – we're trying to nip this showing-off phase he's going through in the bud. It's just attention-seeking, probably our fault, of course, but even so . . .'

'Well, showing-off didn't do Mick any harm in the long run.'

Patrick had the grace to laugh. Briefly. 'In the long run. Joel needs to focus less on winning imaginary Oscars and more on his maths. For the time being, anyway.'

Attention-seeking. Poor Joel. Eva wound the phone cord around her finger. 'Paddy, I'm sorry if this is out of line, but have you told Joel and Nancy you're getting a divorce yet? It's just that I didn't know what to say when they were here. To the children, or to Caitlin, for that matter. You were going to arrive early and brief me.'

There was a long silence on the other end. The sat nav lady warned about stationary traffic ahead.

'No,' said Patrick, eventually. 'We haven't told them yet.'

'When are you going to?'

'Soon. I know, I know . . . But it's so important we don't mess it up. It needs to be the right moment. And Cait and I have to do it together, somewhere the kids won't be permanently traumatised, in words that makes them understand it's not their fault . . .'

'Really?' When was the right time to tell children bad news? Patrick had been about the same age as Nancy when their dad *died*; no choice there. Eva's mental image of Joel was replaced with Patrick at the same age, playing endless board games in the front room of their old house with their mum. Whatever the game, he refused to take any risks until he had 'a strategy'. Half Eva's teenage life seemed to have been spent in grinding rounds of Monopoly, which Patrick always won – eventually. 'I know it's hard, and you want to get it right, but the longer you leave it . . .'

'I don't want to jump the gun. It's a big thing. Let's adjust to us being apart . . .'

'Let *who* adjust?' said Eva.

'Well, all of us.'

Eva guessed this was about Caitlin. Patrick didn't want to give up on Caitlin, as well as his kids. 'Are you hoping Cait's going to realise what she's missing, if you give her a few months of putting her own bins out?'

There was another pause. 'It's not just that. But yes.'

'Surely that's all the more reason to get things out in the open? Caitlin needs to face the reality of what divorce means – it's not a game.'

'It's more complicated.'

Eva stared at the photograph of Mick and the pugs. *Do I offer advice?* she wondered. *Me, with just the one serious relationship under my belt?* She and Patrick had always chatted easily about business, a topic where they both felt secure to bounce ideas off each other and agree to disagree without any bad feeling, but they'd never waded into the treacherous waters of emotional advice – not when Mick died, not even when their mum wandered off in her nightie for the third time, and they had to move her into the home. Neither of them were very good at it; emotions hadn't been part of their family vocabulary, and neither of them had had much romantic experience to fall back on.

But Patrick was her brother. They were all the other had now, and the weekend had stirred up a few memories for Eva. Like Joel's crumpled expression when he thought no one was watching. The effort of pretending he was fine because the adults wanted him to be fine. And Nancy, with her big liquid eyes who saw everything and said nothing. It brought back feelings Eva had shoved to the back of her mind years and years before, when she was somewhere between the two.

Eva girded herself, and said, 'Why exactly did Caitlin ask you for a divorce? Just tell me.'

The answer surprised her.

'She didn't,' said Patrick. 'I asked her.'

'What? Why?'

'Because she wasn't happy. And I didn't want her to stay with me if she wasn't happy.' She heard him swallow. 'What we had was too special to end up like that.'

'Seriously, Patrick, has something happened? Was there someone else?' Eva didn't even know who she was referring to.

'I don't want to talk about it,' said Patrick, and in her mind Eva could see that bullish look on his face, the dark frown that appeared when she and her mum tried to persuade him to sell Monopoly utilities against his will. It was only possible to see that little boy Patrick over the phone, in the shadows of his voice. In person, he was resolutely adult. 'Can we get back to the children? Please?'

'But it's *about* them.' Eva threw caution to the wind. 'Don't take this the wrong way, but watching Joel and Nancy together the other weekend . . . at times, they reminded me a lot of you and me. The way Joel was helping Nancy with her book but earwigging the grown-ups at the same time? I know there's a bigger gap with us, but it just struck me – I understood a lot more about what was going on than Mum and Dad thought I did.'

'How do you mean?'

'Oh, you know. When they argued in the kitchen with the radio on, then pretended everything was fine. Dad giving Mum the silent treatment. The pair of them being scarily polite, and the smell of Mum smoking at the bottom of the garden. You know.'

'I *don't* know. I remember us all listening to *The Archers* omnibus on Sundays, and roast beef and that custard Mum made, but never any rows.'

Eva stared at her reflection in the mirror in the hall, the African shield looming on the wall behind her. Why was she telling Patrick this now? Maybe it was a mistake. It wasn't a road she wanted to go too far down herself. But she'd started, and if she couldn't talk to her niece and nephew, then at least she could try to help them this way. 'OK, maybe you were too young to notice. But I always knew when Dad was giving Mum a hard time about something because Radio Four would be blasting out of the kitchen and she'd send me into the garden to clean out the rabbits. I don't know what they were rowing about, but the point is I *knew* something was up.'

And I wondered if it was something we'd done. Or I'd done.

'Caitlin and I aren't like that. We've never argued. Definitely not in front of the kids.'

'I'm not saying you do. Just that kids sense bad atmospheres and blame . . .'

'Why do you always try to make out Mum and Dad argued, anyway? I think you're just remembering one bad incident as if it happened all the time.' Patrick had very fixed views about their parents. He had their wedding photo, the one item he'd wanted from their old house: the happy couple posing outside the church, Dad in his suit, freshly graduated from medical school, Mum like a perfect doll at his side, her jet-black beehive sprinkled with confetti, clutching a paper horseshoe. In his head, Eva suspected, that was how they remained, rather than the prematurely old lady their mum had turned into, disorientated by dementia, and their tetchy, often absent dad.

'I'm not saying it *was* always like that, just that they thought they were hiding their arguments, but I could tell.'

'I only have happy memories of Dad,' he went on. 'And Mum. I know Dad worked long hours too, but we had fun, didn't we? It's only now I'm getting to his age that I can understand just how much pressure he was under at the surgery . . .'

Eva didn't reply. Patrick loved talking about what a great role model Dad had been, how respected and decent, even more so 'now he was a dad himself'. She stared into the mirror over the telephone table, and her reflection glared back at her, a collage of family photographs in one face. Dad's sharp nose, Mum's big, emotional eyes. Dark circles and crows' feet, model's own. Ironically, the only trace of the gawky teenage Eva was in her eyebrows, still plucked to fine arches the same way they'd been since 1985, the year their dad died. Patrick had been five, she'd been thirteen and too enthusiastic with the tweezers. How much of this could he really remember? *Really* remember, not borrow from the version of their dad Mum liked to talk about when he was safely deceased and unable to contradict her version of events?

But then Nancy was nearly five, and *she* looked as if she was taking it all in – every adult flinch, every pointed silence. As for Joel . . .

'So, next weekend,' said Eva, knowing she was cutting across her brother, but at a loss as to how she could steer them back to a subject she wasn't even sure she should be raising. 'Caitlin will drop Joel and Nancy off on Saturday, but you'll be here beforehand?'

'I'll try,' said Patrick.

'And you'll think about speaking to them then? I don't want to stick my oar in, but . . .'

'Yes, Eva! I get it.' He paused then said, in a more gentle tone, 'I get it.'

'Good.'

This was the longest conversation they'd had about their childhood for years, she thought. It was one of their longest conversations about anything personal, full stop.

'You don't mind, do you?' he asked, suddenly. 'Having me and the kids to stay?'

'Why would I?'

'It's not . . .' Patrick hesitated, long enough for Eva to guess he was trying to find the right words for an uncomfortable question, then he bottled whatever he was going to ask. 'It's not, I mean, it's not disrupting your social life, ha ha!'

'No,' said Eva. 'It's not.' She picked up the exercise book from the sideboard, and the photograph of Mick on set fell out. She tucked it into the frame of the birthday portrait with the pugs. Two Micks, one young, one old. One hers, one Una's.

'We'll speak before then.' Patrick's voice had gone back into 'rounding off the meeting' mode. 'And thanks, Eva. You're a great big sis.'

'What else are big sisters for?' she replied, but he only laughed, and rang off.

'They're for looking after their little brothers,' said Eva's mother's voice in Eva's head, as she avoided her own reflection in the mirror, and swept back into the sitting room, Mick's exercise book in her hand.

Chapter nine

Caitlin had to hand it to the newly appointed head teacher at Joel's primary school: Mrs Douglas was nothing if not ambitious. There was barely a fund-raising opportunity that Mrs Douglas didn't leap on with a big smile and an All Parents Mail Out, and usually an invitation to assorted press to come and cover the occasion for the local paper.

This weekend was the school's latest attempt to get into the Guinness Book of Records – for the most under-elevens singing and dancing to 'Happy' at the same time, a feat that appealed to Joel on multiple levels. They were originally going to sing 'The Bare Necessities', he informed her, but apparently someone else had done that first, with about eight thousand people. Not even Mrs Douglas could raise eight thousand people in the middle of March.

Caitlin's mother Lynne phoned while they were walking over to the park where the record-attempt was taking place, and Joel had seized the opportunity to explain the whole event, i.e., his first step on the road to stardom, to a fresh pair of ears. Caitlin let him ramble on – served her mother right, she'd *asked* – so she could try to coax some words out of Nancy who was walking along by her side, clutching her book about the wishing cat, but saying nothing.

No made-up songs about trees. No pointing at birds. Just a

tight squeeze of Caitlin's hand whenever Caitlin asked her a question.

Since her chat with Shelley at the nursery, Caitlin found herself watching Nancy like a hawk, noticing every nod or smile where a word should have been. Nancy wasn't totally silent at home but Caitlin could see a pattern forming: minimum speaking in the house, vanishing into absolute silence outside. For once, Dr Google had been fairly reassuring – it was a common enough phase, as Shelley had said, especially for children negotiating complex emotional changes – but the lack of joy in Nancy's pixie face broke Caitlin's heart. The sheen had gone, and it was something they'd done. How could she possibly tell Nancy she and her daddy were getting divorced? Would she ever speak again?

Caitlin felt as if someone was pressing the air out of her chest.

'. . . I'm going to be in front!' Joel finished. 'You want to speak to Mum now?' He looked up at her, and Caitlin hastily rearranged her face. 'Yes, OK. Bye, Granny Lynne.' He shoved the phone in her direction and resumed practising his dance steps, humming as he went.

'Hi, Mum,' she said.

'Hello, Caitlin.' Lynne sounded shell-shocked. 'When did Joel learn to breathe through his ears?'

'Be grateful you only had to imagine the routine that goes with it.'

'Well, it sounds wonderful. I *wish* you'd told me about this earlier, Caitlin. Your father and I would have loved to be with you. We always seem to miss out on the kids' big days . . .'

Caitlin made her best non-commital agreeing noise. Lynne was always complaining about missing out on 'big days' but she rarely left London. She didn't have time. She still worked a five-day week as HR director of a big consultancy firm, then packed her weekends with extra volunteering and mentoring of teenage girls. Almost as if, Caitlin thought, she was trying to make up for the unsatisfactory job she'd made of her own teenage daughter. Lynne did phone a lot, though, usually with instructions and suggestions about how Caitlin might maintain 'Mum's house'. Caitlin took roughly fifty per cent of the calls, and blamed the local mobile signal more than was fair. She also sent Lynne a lot of videos from her phone, which she secretly hoarded herself, watching and re-watching her babies growing up frighteningly fast.

'Next time!' she said, brightly. 'There'll definitely be a next time.'

'Joel says Patrick's missing out too. Is he still up in Newcastle?'

Lynne had got the same 'Patrick is working up in Newcastle on a temporary contract' story as the kids. For the time being. The prospect of explaining how Caitlin had broken up with the man Lynne frequently referred to as 'my dream son-in-law' wasn't something she was looking forward to. Patrick was exactly the sort of man Lynne had always hoped she'd marry, rather than the long-haired types she'd gone for in the past – she'd actually overheard her mum saying, 'Yes, we're so *relieved*!' to her godmother at their wedding, as if the liability that was Caitlin was now in safe hands.

'Yes, he is.' She checked the children weren't listening in. Nancy wasn't, but Joel was pretending to be interested in his thumbs. His ears, however, were virtually rotating like satellite dishes.

'Oh, poor Patrick. They're certainly getting their money's worth from him, aren't they? Has he checked his contract? It doesn't seem fair that he's missing out on weekends . . .'

'Well, he'd be the first to admit he was never a huge fan of music performances.' Caitlin struggled with tact, in front of little ears. 'But I'll film it on my mobile. I'll email it to you.'

'No, on my phone,' Joel piped up, giving himself away. 'The phone Dad gave me for Christmas.'

'I heard that,' said Lynne. 'Isn't Joel a bit young for a phone?'

'He's ten,' said Caitlin. 'Apparently that's old enough for all sorts.'

They were nearly at the park now, joining the back of the crowd of parents and grandparents heading towards the main road.

'Anyway, Mum,' she said, 'I have to go, we're almost there . . .'

'Are you ready to cross?'

Caitlin turned her head to see Joel holding his hand out to Nancy, deliberately looking left, then right. Teaching her the right thing to do, picking up where Patrick had left off.

Joel had all the good bits of Patrick, she thought with a pang, even though he wasn't his. Joel cared, he liked things to be right, and fair. Patrick had instilled that in him. It was her job to keep it like that, and not let it turn into the sort of need to be in charge that could end up driving people away, scared by their own imperfection, instead of keeping them close.

'Send me the video and we'll speak in the week!' said Lynne, as if she was adding it to her planner, and Caitlin ended the call, grateful that no further questions had been asked.

While they waited in the queue to get in, Caitlin racked her brains to think of ways to surprise Nancy into speaking. That was all it'd take. A surprise. A fun surprise.

'How about . . .' she said. 'How about we go for ice cream after this?'

'Ice cream? In March?' Joel stopped trailing his hand along the railings, to look outraged.

'Why not?'

'It's wrong! That's like . . . eating Christmas pudding in July.'

'Why can't you eat Christmas pudding in July?'

'You can't!' Joel's eyebrows vanished under his hat. 'Anyway, we haven't had lunch.'

'We can have ice cream for lunch.'

'What?' He mimed 'mind blown'. 'You *can't* have ice cream for lunch.'

'We can do whatever we want.' Caitlin swung her unicorn bag. It was the one Patrick had hated. She used it every day now. 'It's Saturday!'

'Mum, you've gone mad,' said Joel.

'Whatever,' said Caitlin. 'Do you fancy an ice cream, Nancy?'

Nancy nodded, smiling with her lips pressed together.

'If you insist,' sighed Joel, filling the gap. 'It'll be good for my throat.'

'Nancy? I can't hear you!' Caitlin persisted, but a shadow passed across Nancy's face. She looked badgered, and Caitlin recoiled. Then Joel grabbed her hand, singing, 'Are you coming to the park, Nancy? Are you coming to sing with me?' and she had to leave it.

The record attempt was only one part of a bigger school fundraiser, and the park was full of cake stalls, face-painting and other reasons to hand over cash.

Joel wasn't allowed to have his face painted (official record-breaking photographs), but Nancy took Caitlin's hand and dragged her towards the queue, snaking back around the bottle stall and the human fruit machine.

Caitlin let her, thinking Nancy'd have to tell the face painter what she wanted. That was definitely worth the three quid involved.

They stood, Joel hopping from foot to foot, narrating the events in a tone that Caitlin had long since learned to tune out, while she scanned the crowds for one of the other mums who might be up for a collection swap, to give her longer hours at the café. Patrick leaving had made that quite difficult too.

And then she saw Lee. Same grey beanie crushing the same dark blonde curls, same vintage Nirvana sweatshirt he wore out running on chilly autumn nights. Same half-smile surrounded by faint golden stubble. He was chatting to another long-haired bloke with a guitar, and carrying three tambourines up one arm and maracas in his other hand.

This time it was definitely him. He laughed, and Caitlin felt the hairs on the back of her neck stand up.

Lee. Jogging Man's name was Lee. Caitlin didn't know his surname. But she knew he was Scottish, that he took three sugars in his tea, and he ran four miles on Mondays, Wednesdays and Thursdays past the park bench she spent an hour sitting on twice a week, and he may or may not have taken his place in the Bristol 10k by now. That's what he'd been training for when he tripped over a loose dog about ten metres from Caitlin's feet the previous April, sprawling in a heap of muscular thigh and short shorts in front of her.

Up until then Caitlin had been enjoying the Jogging Man's laps in the same way she enjoyed the other scenery that wasn't the four walls of her house: the teen goths, the sunsets, the seagulls, the silence. Patrick thought she was at Zumba. In actual fact, Caitlin was drinking one can of pre-mixed gin and tonic and eating a Twix. Sometimes, for a treat, she had one cigarette. She'd had to learn Zumba moves off the internet to show to Joel when he demanded she teach him too. Yes, it was a tiny deception, but who did it hurt? Having one hour in her routine where only she knew what she was doing, and nobody asked her a single question, had been like an airhole in Caitlin's 'Mum? Mum? Mum? Mum?' existence.

And then Jogging Man had fallen over, and they'd spoken for the first time after weeks of silently acknowledging each other, as you did in parks, and the airhole had cracked, letting in a dangerous blast of fresh air.

His name was Lee, he told her through gritted teeth, as she helped him limp to the park café to sort out his bleeding knees, and he was running the 10k for his mum, who was recovering from kidney disease. He was listening to Def Leppard: 'Don't tell anyone, please!' And then he'd offered her a cup of tea to say thanks, and Caitlin had thought, well, why not?

The conversation had started easily, and got easier. They'd chatted about running, Bristol in general, the book she was reading. 'You're always reading,' Lee had said, and Caitlin was flattered he'd noticed – and glad he hadn't noticed she'd been carrying the same book for weeks. As they chatted, she could feel the first flickers and pops of flirtation snapping over the plastic ketchup containers. Lee was Caitlin's 'old', pre-Patrick type – the easy-come, easy-go muso sort – and from the way his grey eyes mirrored his smile when she made a joke, Caitlin could tell he liked her too. But it was just talking, and that was all she wanted. When they left, there was a moment, a juicy three-second silence, then Caitlin pushed some hair out of her eyes and he spotted her wedding ring, then closed his mouth with a wry look. A door clicked shut. One that kept her safe, but shut out another life behind it, and Caitlin had walked home feeling half-numb, half-relieved.

They'd never spoken again after that, but they'd watched out for each other: she'd always waved and Lee always grinned back. It was enough for Caitlin to daydream as Lee loped around the running paths, rearranging the facts she knew about this attractive stranger like bright beads on a secret thread in her imagination.

And now he was here, crossed over into her real life. Caitlin watched as he wandered over to where a band was setting up, presumably to accompany the school children. It appeared in her head like a thought balloon: *I can talk to him now. There's absolutely no reason why I can't march up to him and say, Hi, Lee, how's the running, because even if people do see me, I'm free to talk to whoever I want.*

Do it, urged a voice in her head. *Do it now, before the singing starts.*

Caitlin glanced at the face paint queue. It was moving at its usual glacial rate, thanks to the number of complicated butter-fly requests. There'd be at least a twenty-minute wait before they got anywhere near the front, and even then, Nancy's detailed specifications would make Kim Kardashian's make-up look slapdash.

I've got time to say hi, she thought. In fact, it'd be ideal – *I can just say, hello, hello, nice to see you, my son's singing, oops, I've got to get back to the queue, good luck.* It wasn't about Lee as much as taking that first step, to prove that her life would go on after Patrick. She *could* do what she wanted.

Joel was fiddling with his phone, probably filming some-thing, and Nancy was staring intently at the children ahead of her in the queue as if she could move them by force of will. Caitlin made a decision.

'Joel, can you wait with Nancy for two minutes? I just need to go and say hello to someone. Hand?' She fished in her pocket for cash and dropped three pound coins into Joel's open palm. 'Stay here. And make sure the paints rub off this time, OK? Remember panda-gate.'

'No pandas,' he confirmed. 'Or leopards.'

'Good. I'll only be over there,' she said, gesturing to the stage but he was already making mystic waves with his phone; Patrick had installed a compass app that Joel found endlessly intriguing.

With one quick backward look, and before she could think too hard, Caitlin marched over to Lee.

She touched him on the arm, and he turned around. There was a brief moment of recognition, then he grinned.

'Hey! The girl with the book!' He was even better-looking close up; his lashes were unusually long, both upper and lower. 'How are you?'

'Good! I'm good, thanks.' *God, I sound breathless,* thought Caitlin. *That's because you are,* said a voice in her head. *Just breathe. This is just a normal thing. Talking to someone you've met once in a park. It's not a big deal.*

'It's Katie, right?' he added. 'Sorry, I'm hopeless with names.'

She'd only told him once. 'Caitlin. Cait. Either.' She was strangely pleased he'd remembered, and rushed on to hide her delight. 'How funny seeing you here! I didn't realise you had kids at St Bede's!'

She knew he didn't; she'd have met him before if he had, surely. Surely?

'I don't.' He nodded towards the pile of musical equipment. 'Long story, but my mate Danny's going out with Rosie, who's a teaching assistant at the school, and she roped him in. He made us come too.' He dropped his voice to a pretend-intimate undertone. 'Think he was a bit worried about turning up unaccompanied to a children's event. Didn't want to look dodgy.'

'Ha ha ha ha!' Caitlin racked her brains for something witty, but nothing would come out. Her head was fuzzy with a sort of lurchy top-of-a-rollercoaster sensation. Normally she could talk to anyone – her tips in the café were legendary – but this was different. This was taking her back to a Caitlin she'd almost forgotten existed.

'So, what are you doing here?' he asked, conversationally. 'Have you got a record breaker in the family?'

'Yup. My son, Joel, will be attempting to drown out the band with his musical stylings.'

'Oh! Joel?' An amused expression crinkled Lee's eyes. He didn't say, 'But you seem far too young to have kids at this school', as a few of the chancier dads had done at PTA events. Caitlin gave Lee extra credit for that, then wondered if it meant he didn't see her . . . like that. She pushed that thought away.

'The soundcheck boy?'

'Sorry?'

'Rosie said one of the boys asked if there'd be a soundcheck before the performance. So we're doing one. You must be very proud,' he added, as Caitlin groaned. 'He seems to know his stuff.'

'Oh, I am. I'm also very resigned to the fact that I may end up as a bit player on his reality show in about ten years' time.' She raised her palms. 'Maybe not even ten years' time. Sometimes I wonder if I'm actually starring in it now, but I don't know I'm being filmed.'

Lee laughed, deep and easily, and butterflies swarmed Caitlin's chest.

Stop it, she told herself. *Don't get carried away. Come on.*

'I feel like I should say that we don't *just* play kids' record-breaking attempts,' said Lee. 'Just in case you were thinking that's our niche.'

'Oh? What kind of music do you play?'

'Ha! That depends who thinks they're in charge that night. If I tell you our lead singer reckons he's the Bristol Bowie but our lead guitarist writes songs about his cat, that kind of sums us up.'

'And you?'

'I'm the drummer,' he said, deadpan. 'I don't have opinions. But I do like Led Zeppelin. And Justin Bieber.'

'Ha ha! Who doesn't? Do you play round here?' Caitlin knew she was getting to the end of her 'two minutes' but the queue didn't seem to be moving and Joel would probably relish the responsibility – just for a minute or two more.

'Indeed we do.' Lee pulled off the beanie and ruffled a hand through the teddy-bear blonde curls. 'We've got a gig next weekend – although at this rate there'll be more of us on stage than in the audience. Danny was supposed to be getting Rosie to knock off some fliers for us on the school photocopier, but she hasn't had time, and there's a real chance no one'll turn up.'

'Come on, you've got a captive audience here!' She gestured to the crowds. 'Tell them you're playing songs about a cat and you'll be packed out.'

He grinned. 'I've heard the noise this lot can make. Frankly, half of them are louder than us.'

'So when is it?' Caitlin smiled, pleased at how genuinely grateful he seemed by her interest.

'Seriously? Saturday, all day. It's a beer festival in town, but don't panic' – he raised his hand – 'I've been assured it won't all be beards and real ale. We're on at five, which, to be honest, is hardly the headline slot but at least it gives you time to sneak out and do something else after.'

'With all that real ale around? Surely not.' Caitlin tucked it away in her head. 'I'm not busy this weekend. I might look in.'

'Yeah? I'll look out for you.' He smiled again, but before the moment could develop, someone tugged on her sleeve.

'Mum! Mum!'

Caitlin turned to see Joel. His face was white. 'What is it?'

'Just . . . come now.' Joel glanced at Lee, then at Caitlin. He hopped from foot to foot.

'I'll let you go,' said Lee, and winked. 'Good luck, mate. See you at the soundcheck, eh?'

Normally Joel would have latched straight on to a musician, asking him questions and pestering him about his amplifiers, but he dragged Caitlin away so fast she feared for his bladder.

'What's up? Is Nancy getting her face done?' asked Caitlin. 'Didn't you have enough money? Do you need the loo?'

'No. I don't know where Nancy is.' Joel's eyes were huge. 'A lady from school gave her a balloon but she let go and it floated away, and she started crying, so I went to get it. I *told* her to stay there, and I tried to catch it, but the wind kept blowing it, and then it went over the railings and into the street, and you said not to go out of the park ever without you so I turned round to tell Nancy that we'd have to let it go, but she wasn't there! And there was a big crowd around the face painting and I couldn't see her!'

'So then what did you do?' Caitlin's chest caved in. *It'll be fine,* she told herself. *How far can she have gone? There are teachers everywhere. It'll be fine.*

'I looked for her. I asked the face-painting lady where she'd gone but she couldn't remember which little girl she was because she'd done so many butterflies.'

'So then what?' Caitlin felt nauseous with fear: it wasn't Joel's fault for losing Nancy, she'd given him too much to be in charge of. He seemed so grown up, but he was only ten.

'I couldn't see you either! You'd moved!' he said accusingly. 'And everyone's wearing jackets like yours!'

Frantic, Caitlin scanned the crowds for Nancy's pink coat with its furry hood. 'Don't worry, Joel, there are lots of mums here. They'll make sure she's OK.'

You only needed one, said the voice in her head. One credible mum person leading a little girl by the hand, promising to take her to her mummy, leading her off God knows where . . .

Acid rose in her throat and she started walking on jittery legs towards the face painting.

'I phoned you!' Joel was nearly crying. His breathing had got very fast and high. 'I phoned you on your phone but you didn't *answer*!'

Caitlin yanked her phone out of her pocket. There were four missed calls from Joel. How hadn't she heard them? Then she remembered the bossy signs at the gate – ***Please turn your phone to silent for the performance!!*** – and Joel reminding her.

As she held it, Patrick's face flashed up, frozen in a holiday snap on a beach. He looked unusually carefree, possibly because he wasn't wearing a tie.

Oh . . . bollocks, thought Caitlin. *Bollocks, bollocks, bollocks.* Patrick had a sixth sense for things going wrong. Even three hundred miles away he knew when she'd screwed up.

She rejected the call, and focused on Joel. 'Right, where did you last see her?'

'Who was that?' He looked hunted.

'Dad. Doesn't matter, we can speak to him later.'

'But I . . .'

'Dad can wait. We need to find Nancy. She'll be here some-where.' Caitlin made herself sound more confident than she felt. 'She won't have gone far.'

He grabbed the back of her coat as she walked away. 'But she can't tell anyone who she is!'

Something in Joel's voice brought her up short. As if he knew something she didn't, some bigger thing he was trying to tell her. Caitlin stopped and turned. 'What do you mean, *can't?*'

'I don't know.' He squirmed. 'Sometimes Nancy can't talk.'

'Of course she can. She talks to you,' said Caitlin, impa-tiently. Now wasn't the time for Joel's dramatics.

'Sort of.'

'And me.' *But not always,* added the insinuating voice in her head. *Not the way she used to. And why is that?*

'What if a policeman asks her what her name is and she can't tell him?' Joel's face was contorted with guilt, and suddenly very young. 'I'm sorry, Mum. I'm sorry!'

'Let's not panic, Joel. Nancy's a clever girl.' Caitlin grabbed his hands. 'She'll just be feeding the ducks. Come on, let's go and find her.'

Nancy wasn't feeding the ducks. She wasn't by the face painting, and she wasn't by the cake stall, the first place Caitlin imagined she'd have headed. Suddenly the park seemed full of identical butterfly-faced girls in pink parkas and none of them were Nancy, and Caitlin's lungs didn't seem able to take in enough air to breathe properly as she ran round the park, hunting desperately for her.

Mrs Douglas was very understanding. 'Happens to the best of us,' she said, before commandeering the stage to make the missing child announcement.

But it didn't, thought Caitlin, wobbling with adrenalin as she tried to summon a smile to ward off the sympathetic glances from the other parents. How could she have let this happen? It only took a second. Chilling visions of Nancy bundled in a car, Nancy ashen-faced and silent dragged by the hand . . .

Joel tugged her sleeve as she was describing Nancy's outfit to a community support officer and trying not to cry. 'What?'

'Dad's ringing me on my phone.'

'We'll call him back later. Don't tell him about this,' Caitlin muttered, aware of the CSO listening in. Brilliant. Secrets from Dad. Another black mark. 'He'll only worry. And there's nothing he can do. I can sort this.'

'But . . .'

'Joel! Please. We can sort this,' she added, 'together.'

Joel's eyebrows tilted with stress.

'Mrs Reardon? I think I've got someone who's missing a mummy.'

Caitlin spun round and relief swept through her with such force that she gasped out loud. One of the mums from Joel's class was leading Nancy by her small hand. Even under her silver and gold face paint, Nancy looked pale, as if she were holding her breath. Next to her, Joel made a choking noise.

'Nancy!' Caitlin swept her up in her arms and hugged her so tightly she could feel Nancy's heart banging in her chest. 'Where did you go? We were so worried!'

'She was by the stage,' said the woman (Lily's mum? Isaac's mum? Caitlin couldn't remember her name but she'd never forget the expression on her face). 'We couldn't get a word out of her. You've obviously trained her well about stranger danger.'

'Yes!' Caitlin grabbed on to the excuse. 'Not that you're a stranger as such, but you know . . .'

She felt Nancy's legs grip around her waist, her sharp nose burrowing into her neck, and to her horror, Caitlin realised Nancy was still soundless – no whispered 'Mummy!' in her ear, no 'I'm sorry!', no 'I was only playing, it was an accident'. Instead, she trembled in silence as if no words were big enough to explain how she felt.

Caitlin rocked her from side to side, stroking her hair and making soothing noises, while Joel regarded them both with a glum expression. Like a dog waiting to be punished, Caitlin thought. She reached out a hand and laid it on his head. .

'Not your fault, sweetheart,' she said. 'Mine, for leaving you in charge. And it's all sorted now. No harm done.'

Except there was. Nancy clearly had a problem, and it was putting her in danger. Shelley hadn't been exaggerating: Nancy really wouldn't speak in public. *Couldn't*. The true ramifications suddenly rolled out in front of Caitlin: this meant Nancy couldn't ask to go to the loo at nursery. Or tell Shelley if someone was mean to her. Or if someone was hurting her. Her heart turned to ice in her chest. Her baby was so vulnerable in the big world anyway, and this silence made her completely defenceless.

'Mum,' said Joel. 'I want to go home.'

Caitlin tried to make her expression normal. 'No! You haven't done your singing!' She ruffled his hair. 'Come on, Joel, there's going to be a soundcheck, just for you!'

'I want to go home,' Joel repeated, staring at his red wellies. 'Please.'

'No ice cream for lunch?'

He shook his head.

Caitlin hitched Nancy up on her hip and wished she had better answers. Patrick had a way of dealing with incidents like this that made the children believe the world was back in the right order now Dad had dealt with it. Even Granny Lynne had a bossy authority she suspected they secretly liked. She didn't. She never had done.

But you wanted it like this, she told herself. *Independence. You've got to find your own way of handling the bad stuff, now.*

'Well, I want ice cream for lunch.' Things would look better inside the ice cream parlour. For her, at least. She held out her hand to Joel. 'Come on, Joel. Then we'll have karaoke at home.'

He looked at her, mistrustfully, and Caitlin had the sense that something had changed. Something she couldn't fix.

'Please?' she said.

Eventually, he took her hand. 'OK,' he said, and they left the park, to the distant thud and parp of Lee's band tuning up and several hundred under-elevens practising their 'happy's.

Chapter ten

Eva sat very still at Mick's study desk, resting her elbows on the worn leather, and ran her eyes over the words in his diary in the hope that they might stop hurting her if she just stared at them long enough. Over and over, until the hollow ache in her chest filled in again. Till they didn't mean anything any more.

> *I often wonder what kind of kids Eva and I would have had.*

She flinched, made herself read it again. It still hurt. Again. She had a flashback to sponging out wine spills the morning after one of Mick's famous Twelfth Night parties. Salt, luke-warm water, tea towel, patting, more water, patting over and over, until the scarlet speech-bubble splashes in the carpet faded out – a skill that, it turned out, had always impressed her husband. Not that he'd told her so; she'd read it the previous day, in his diary.

> November 6th, 2013: *I watched Eva this morning dealing with her accountant, telling him about some investment opportunity she wants him to set up, then she sat back, changed the expression on*

her face like other women change their shoes, and came downstairs to sort out the wine stain from last night. She fixes things, does Eva. She walks through this house leaving peace and order in her wake, along with Chanel No. 5 and perfect square piles of magazines. God bless whoever sent her my way, but I'm in awe of my wife.

Ha. She rubbed her thumbs into her temples. Wasn't that what she was doing now? Running her eye over the lines of handwriting, pressing them into herself, leaning her brain into them to blot out the meaning. Trying to make the ugly stain vanish off her memories.

But the startling truth of Mick's words didn't fade. It was his familiar handwriting, but it felt as if a stranger had written it. A throwaway comment so personal, and so important, and *so utterly central* to their marriage – and if Alex hadn't made her read these diaries she would never have known. Mick would never have told her.

December 2nd, 2013 – was an innocuous enough entry, sandwiched in between an account of driving to the garden centre to choose a Christmas tree, and some catty comments about the *recently debagged* eyes of a fellow Yorkshireman who'd just done a *shambolic* guest run in *Eastenders*.

Tyson's birthday. He's made it to 45, no thanks to me and Una. Would brothers or sisters have helped the lad? Maybe. Probably. I often wonder what kind of kids Eva and I would have had. Magnificent rascals, I think. Her brain, her lovely long legs, our combined charm, hers subtle and mine shameless, my bloody-mindedness. Pity parenthood wasn't in our stars. That DNA could have made a prime minister! Or a criminal mastermind, at the very least – heaven help us. A shame.

The loops of Mick's handwriting blurred in front of Eva's startled eyes. There was no possibility this was for effect. Mick always told the truth to these diaries: she'd spotted a few unembarrassed admissions that he wouldn't have made outside them. In Mick's public life, she'd played along with some of what he called 'accepted truths' like the story of their meeting, or the more rambunctious drinking years yarns, but here, he was honest.

She made herself read the line again. *I often wonder what kind of kids Eva and I would have had.* There: one small, tender, pitiless sentence that cut her heart to shreds.

Because Eva *had* wondered about their children. A lot. And she'd never wondered to Mick, because he'd made it clear he didn't wonder at all. Didn't want to wonder. Or so he'd told her.

She leaned on the desk and covered her eyes with her cool palms, and saw his face.

They'd had The Conversation early on. Mick had taken her out for dinner about three months into their relationship, yet another place where everyone seemed to know him, and when the coffee and brandies arrived, he'd coughed and said, 'Now then, love, something we need to get on the table'. Children, he'd told her firmly, weren't on the agenda. Not at his age; not with his lifestyle. As Mick spoke, his confident posture had turned vulnerable, as if he was bracing himself for her walking out, and Eva felt honoured by his honesty: 'You'd make a terrific mother, Eva,' he'd said as the restaurant emptied, threading his strong, tanned fingers through hers. 'So if that's important to you, go now, and find someone who'll give you some babies. Before I fall any more in love with you.'

Love. The first time he'd said the word. Eva had chosen him. Of course she had. She'd wanted Mick and his hearty, head-back guffaw, his wicked eyes and his Catherine-wheel mind, not a possible baby with a possible man like the bland City types she'd been set up with by her happily married friends. How could she be happier than she was now? Eva hadn't heard her biological clock ticking, and she assumed she would have done, by thirty-five, if it was ticking at all. No one, not even her own mother, had ever said: Eva, you'd make a great mum. Well, no one apart from Mick, and when he said it, she heard a very different message underneath.

'You're all I want,' she'd said, without needing to think.

Mick proposed weeks later, on holiday in Italy, with a diamond ring that had once belonged to a Russian princess: it fitted her perfectly. It was a night that Eva never believed would happen to her – the champagne bottle bobbing in the lake, the fiery sunset, her hiccups of surprise. Perfect, grown-up romance. And they never spoke about children again, out of respect to each other's decision, or so she'd thought.

Parenthood wasn't in our stars, he'd written. *Our,* as if he knew her mind too.

Eva reeled at the unexpected resentment roaring up inside her. *I didn't* not *want children,* she wanted to yell at Mick. *I just didn't want them* more *than you. And I thought I had you for another twenty, maybe thirty years, another half-lifetime together.*

She stared at the page, stunned by the force of her own reaction. All the time Mick was privately wondering about the children they'd chosen not to have – and assuming she didn't care either way. That she didn't want his baby. Their baby. *Any baby*. If she'd known that . . .

Eva stared at her husband's handwriting, alive on the page with his familiar shrugs and flourishes, and felt as if the walls of her life were turning around, behind her chair, to make a very different room from the one she thought she was in. If he'd changed his mind, why hadn't he said? How much had Mick actually thought about the decision she'd made? Had he ever thought properly about the sacrifice she'd made, choosing him over motherhood? Or did his arrogance assume it wasn't even a sacrifice?

But then, nagged a persistent voice, how much had *she* thought about it? It had seemed almost a compliment at the time, Mick asking after a few months whether she wanted to spend the rest of her life with him, but now it seemed crazy, demanding a decision like that on the basis of a few dinners and nights away. How could you possibly speak on behalf of your forty-five-year-old self when you were thirty-five, drunk on a love that you thought would never happen to you?

Eva groaned, and under the desk, Bumble stirred and grunted until she rested her bare foot on his back to reassure him.

She'd never let herself think too hard about the baby she might have had, only when she was drunk or very hormonal, but now it skipped around her head, pressing its small hands up against the back of her eyelids: a golden-skinned, long-haired boy-girl. Mick's lashes. Her nose. The blonde curls she'd seen in his baby photos, her wide eyes. A happy, affectionate cocktail of their genes, a breathing proof of their love, reflecting them the same way Eva caught glimpses of Patrick and Caitlin in Nancy and Joel, or her own parents in herself. A ribbon of inherited traits and quirks, unfurling down generations, changing and growing.

She ground the heel of her palms into her eyes, but the child carried on dancing around, just out of her field of view, and the reality of the situation slowly hardened into fact – it was too late. Not just for her to have Mick's child, but for her to have *any* children. She'd never know what her genetic kaleidoscope would have created. She was a dead end. Unattached to the rest of the universe. Drifting, alone, the guy ropes of her father gone and her mother slowly fraying, and no children to anchor her to the future.

The hollowness in Eva's chest increased until she felt as if she were so light she could float away. The final traces of grief for her lost love that had clouded her mind for the last few months cleared without warning, leaving her the rest of her own life in focus. Her future.

I'm not going to have a baby, she realised. *I'm not going to be a mother.*

Eva hadn't expected the shock to be so physical. Tears coursed down her face, and she wiped clumsily at her eyes with the side of her fingers. *Stop it, stop it.* But she couldn't stop it: this grief was coming from a different place, one beyond her rational control.

Patrick had something she'd never have. Caitlin did. Mick had. Everyone around her, in a club she was never going to join now.

The clock in the hall chimed nine o'clock, and she cursed herself for even opening the diaries today, of all days. Caitlin was arriving with Joel and Nancy in an hour – she'd only sat down with the exercise book because Alex Montagu had emailed, asking if he could ring her on Monday to discuss 'some matters arising'. Eva knew he'd expect her to have read them, when in fact she'd only just opened the box and started to flick through this first exercise book so she could tell him no, and have some reasons ready.

Eva pinched the bridge of her nose tightly; *breathe in, breathe out*. She'd never been the odd one out before. But everyone she'd been at college with was a mother. She knew that because she'd slowly lost touch with all of them, once they'd moved out of London in search of a bigger garden, or given up work for 'the important years', or just stopped seeing her because they only had so much time and they preferred spending it with other mums. The kinder ones had exaggerated their envy of her lie-ins and spontaneous holidays; she'd exaggerated her Carrie Bradshaw life to keep up her end of the game – and if her old friends wanted to assume Eva's internet business was her baby, that felt less humiliating than them feeling sorry for her because unlike them, she simply had never met anyone she loved enough to want to start a family with.

Now she *was* different. Outside that experience, looking in, through thick glass.

'Eva, get a *grip*,' she muttered with such force that even Bee dropped down from her viewing position at the study window to see what the problem was. Bumble emerged from beneath the desk and put his paws up on her chair, tilting his head.

Eva stared at the pugs. The pugs stared back at her. Bumble's pink tongue lolled out with concern, and his eyes bulged with the effort of transmitting his love through doggy thought waves alone.

Oh God, she thought. *Who can I talk to without sounding utterly, utterly stupid?*

Anna. Of course. Anna would understand: she didn't have children. They'd only ever touched on the topic carefully, sparked off by Eva's comment about how much she hated politicians' 'speaking as a parent' comments after an atrocity, but Eva sensed Anna's feelings were complicated. Phil, her husband, had three girls with his first wife, and he'd drawn the line at another baby: that hadn't been Anna's plan either, but like Eva, it had been her *choice*. She mothered, but she wasn't a mother, and she'd bemoaned, in her gentle way, the complicated shades of grey between childless and childfree.

Eva shoved the exercise book back into the box, and hunted for her mobile. It had just gone nine, the bookshop would be open, and Anna would be behind the counter, talking customers into buying poetry books they didn't know they needed. They could meet that afternoon, she thought – a great excuse to escape the chaos the house for an hour.

But before she could dial, the front doorbell rang, and the pugs shot off towards the hall, barking and bouncing.

Patrick, thought Eva, rubbing mascara smears from under her eyes. *He's early this time. Good. He can get things ready for Joel and Nancy, and I can go for a walk and gather myself a bit.*

But it wasn't Patrick on the doorstep. It was Caitlin, with Joel and Nancy either side of her: Joel the spitting image of Caitlin, and Nancy, a tiny replica of her dad.

'*Good* morning!' said Caitlin, bestowing her broadest, toothiest fertility goddess smile.

Eva felt an invisible hand shove her, right in the centre of her chest. 'Um, hello,' she managed.

Two things struck Eva through her fug of emotion: Joel was wearing a cape and clutching a cake tin, and Caitlin's dark mane, which was usually wild and curly like Kate Bush's, was sleek. She was also wearing a well-filled pair of skinny jeans and a leather jacket instead of her more familiar long droopy skirt and DMs.

It wasn't what Eva had been expecting. The previous time, Caitlin had seemed on edge from the moment she arrived, and had barely let the kids out of her sight, other than for the short period in which Joel had got loose. With a first ever overnight stay on the cards that night, Eva had braced herself for tears and a long, painful goodbye on the doorstep, but Caitlin was a whole hour early and looked positively cheerful.

'Hey, Eva!' said Joel before anyone could speak. He presented the tin as if it were on a ceremonial cushion. 'I've got a sorry present for you. It's cake. I hope you like cake. We made it. It's got Smarties on, but not the orange ones.' He dropped his voice, 'They're Nancy's favourites, for future reference.'

Caitlin nudged him with her hip. '*Auntie* Eva. And I thought we were going to save the cake until we got inside?' She gave him an '. . . and?' look. 'With the apology?'

'I might drop the tin,' Joel pointed out. 'And I need to get my last sorry in first, in case I do anything else I need to say sorry for. But I'm really sorry for breaking Uncle Michael's award. I've written you a letter. In the tin.'

Eva dragged out a smile; she didn't want Joel to think she was upset because they were here. 'Well, cake is always welcome, but there's nothing to say sorry for, Joel! Patrick's . . . your dad's not here yet. Did I get the times wrong? I thought you were arriving at ten?'

Eva knew she sounded awkward. She felt awkward. A quick glance at Nancy threatened to set off the irrational tears again: she was a beautiful child, with Caitlin's peachy cheeks, fine eyebrows like her grandmother's, Patrick's concentration, her small fingers curled around her mother's safe hand for reassurance.

Caitlin's eyes softened and she leaned forward. 'Eva, are you all . . . ?' she started, but Eva nodded hard.

'Fine,' she said. 'Fine, yes.'

Caitlin didn't seem convinced. 'We're a little early. Is that all right?' She made to step forward, then added, 'Unless we're interrupting something?'

'Of course not. Come on in.' Eva waved them inside.

As the Reardons clattered their way down the hall towards the kitchen, bumping overnight bags against the wall, the human racket made Eva's head ache. She followed them, ignoring the whining of the pugs behind the sitting-room door. She hadn't had breakfast and neither had they; none of them liked their routines disrupted.

Eva heard Caitlin hissing at Joel not to touch something, and entered the kitchen with a smile fixed on her face. Patrick would be here soon. He'd take charge. She only had to keep this up for half an hour or so.

'Would you like a coffee and something to eat until Patrick gets here?' she asked Caitlin, then added to Joel, 'Shall I take that cake tin, Joel?'

Joel was clinging to it as though afraid to put it down on the granite worktop. He shot a side look at his mother.

'Give Auntie Eva the tin, you klutz,' said Caitlin, easily. 'And then sit up on that stool where you can't break anything. You too, Nancy. Let me help you up.'

Nancy's eyes were fixed on the floor, long lashes brushing against the soft curve of her cheek, as Caitlin hoisted her onto the stool. She seemed weightless.

'Would you like some milk, Nancy?' Eva asked. 'Or some fresh orange?'

There was no response; only a faint dipping of the head that could have been yes or no. Eva wondered if she was doing something wrong.

'She doesn't like orange,' Joel informed her. He swished his cape out from underneath him on the stool. 'But if you have some warm milk, that'd be perfect.'

'Let Nancy speak for herself – you're not her interpreter. Nancy's going through a shy phase,' Caitlin explained. 'Which isn't helped by not being able to get a word in edgeways with Mr Chatty here.'

'I always know what she wants,' said Joel, ignoring his mother's playful tug on his cape. 'Even if she doesn't say anything, I can tell.'

'Telepathy? What a great skill to have,' said Eva, brightly.

'That means mind-reading,' Caitlin explained when Joel looked non-plussed, and Eva felt a bit stupid.

'Tea? Coffee, Caitlin?' she asked over her shoulder. 'Patrick won't be long.'

'That's so kind, but if it's all the same with you, Eva, I'll make a move,' said Caitlin, hitching her bag back up her shoulder, the same massive satchel she always toted about.

'Don't you want to see Dad?' asked Joel, too casually for it to be casual. 'You can tell him about my audition. I'm going to audition to be in a play, Auntie Eva! And Mum, you said you'd talk to him about my phone . . .'

Nancy looked up, clearly not expecting her mother to leave so soon either. The round eyes were shiny all of a sudden.

Eva held her breath. Was this when the drama would kick off? Caitlin and Patrick obviously hadn't told them about the divorce – she could tell from the way Caitlin wasn't meeting her eye now. She felt annoyed with the pair of them.

'You can tell him yourself, sweetie. It's not that I don't *want* to see Dad,' said Caitlin. 'But I've got lots to do today – I need to get back to Bristol.'

'Anything fun?' asked Eva, then realised how that would sound. Accusatory. Nosy even?

Caitlin adjusted Nancy's collar, where it had twisted in on itself. 'I'm going to a festival,' she said. 'Just a little one, beer and some bands. But I've got some things I need to do first. So I'll say goodbye now, and leave you two to your breakfast! Be good for Auntie Eva – I'll ring you at bedtime to say goodnight!'

She opened her arms to descend on Joel and Nancy with noisy kisses, and Eva could detect a thread of tension in her expression, as if the cheerfulness was harder to maintain now.

Please don't cry, she thought, making all the right cheery noises herself, as Caitlin bustled down the hall and out towards the car, followed by her two small ducklings.

'Bye bye! See you soon!' she called, and then the door closed, and she was gone.

Eva turned round to see Joel and Nancy both staring at her, expectantly. Behind the sitting-room door, Bumble started up his howl-grunt of bewilderment, the one he employed when he'd been ignored for more than five minutes.

'So,' said Eva and tried to look as if she knew what she was doing. Her mind had never felt as blank as it did now, with two pairs of curious eyes trained on her, waiting for the grown-up to tell them what was going to happen next.

Joel patted her arm.

'Mum says we're not supposed to ask for Barney the Baker on DVD,' he said confidingly. 'So we won't. I like your coffee-maker machine, it's bigger than the one at Mum's work. Can I have a go on it?'

'Yes,' said Eva, then thought about the health-and-safety aspects of that request, and said, 'No.' Then she thought about how long this morning was going to be if she kept saying no to every request Joel made, and said, 'Why don't you go and get the cups out? I'll show you how to make a cappuccino.'

Joel gave her two thumbs up, and barrelled back into the kitchen, singing a song Eva didn't recognise. It sounded like an End of Act One number – Mick would have known.

Nancy was still gazing curiously at the sitting-room door, where Bee had joined Bumble in his grunty protest. Eva didn't want to let them out just yet: she wasn't sure what mood Bee particularly would be in before breakfast, especially if everyone else was tucking into croissants.

'We'll have our breakfast first, then we'll give Bumble and Bee theirs,' she said. 'Bumble likes toast. He'd eat yours if he could. He's partial to a bit of toast. With jam. On special occasions.'

As she spoke, she realised she'd inadvertently slipped into Mick's lugubrious Bumble voice, and Nancy looked up, her interest suddenly engaged, and stared straight into Eva's face. There was something resigned, but not sad, about the little girl's expression, and Eva felt her whole soul contract and expand inside with the urge to protect her, combined with a fear of getting it wrong, of somehow making things worse.

Without thinking, she held out her hand. Almost the same way the dog trainer had told her to let a strange dog sniff her out.

There was a moment's silence, then slowly Nancy reached out and put her hand into Eva's. Her fingers closed around her aunt's, and squeezed just hard enough to say thank you, without words.

There was a connection. Eva blinked back the tears that sprang without warning into her eyes, and smiled.

Nancy smiled back, and looked as if she was trying not to cry too.

Driving back to Bristol without the children in the back of the car made Caitlin feel dangerously light-headed.

Two emotions were surging up and down in her, one after the other, making her grip the steering wheel tightly. The first, and most powerful, was the guilt she'd felt leaving Joel and Nancy behind with Eva. Caitlin couldn't get their brave, scared faces out of her mind. She'd tried to be as upbeat as she could when she arrived, so they'd take their cue from her and see the weekend as a fun minibreak with Dad, but the second she turned to walk away, her whole body had been flooded by a fierce urge to run back and grab them. It had been worse than Joel's first day at nursery. Admittedly that had been harder for her than Joel too; he'd galloped into the playground shouting 'helloooooo!' to his bewildered new playmates, while a gulping Caitlin had had to be prised away from the nursery doors and taken for a coffee by another parent.

It was wrong, leaving them behind. It went against every single thing she'd done over the past ten years. Poor Eva already looked stressed, as if she was sitting an exam she didn't expect to pass. But what else could she do? It was what they'd agreed. And they needed to see their dad.

The other emotion, slinking up behind the first like a bad friend, was a sense of freedom so unfamiliar to Caitlin that it made an occasional smile pop up on her face. She knew the excitement bubbling inside her was selfish, embarrassingly so, but for the first time in ten years, for the first time *since she was at university*, she could do whatever she wanted, wherever she wanted, for as long as she wanted. Anything!

Well, until five o'clock on Sunday afternoon.

Still, Caitlin reckoned, slipping into the overtaking lane on the bypass with a joyful burst of acceleration, that was at least one very long, uninterrupted bath. Maybe two! And whatever she felt like for supper, even curry or one of the many icky food stuffs neither Joel nor Nancy would consider. There was maybe time to read a book! And, of course, a date, of sorts.

Her stomach flipped over at that thought. Not a date. A gig, where she may or may not get to chat with Lee. Didn't she have to fill the hours that the kids were away? That's what the girls in the café had said. 'Keep yourself busy, hon. Don't let yourself think too hard and it'll be Sunday before you know it.'

Joel had been very solicitous about what she could do to fill the time until she came to collect them. She'd told them she had to do an extra birthday-party shift at the café that afternoon, and then see a friend the following morning.

'I've made you some ideas,' he'd said the night before, pressing a carefully written list into her hand. He did it while Nancy was deliberating over which four stuffed toys she should 'take on holiday' in her pink weekend bag. Caitlin caught Joel's quick, cautious glance over at his sister, checking she didn't see the list or pick up the idea that Mummy needed help, and his caution stung her heart.

Joel's suggestions included 'watch a box set', 'go for a walk' and 'do dancing in the sitting room'.

'Thanks, Joely.' Caitlin had kissed his head. He was fresh out of the bath. 'I'll save the dancing for when you're back. It's more fun when you two are here to dance with me.'

His face had fallen at that, so she'd quickly added, 'You know what? I'll do stuff you and Nancy *don't* like! Like . . . Cleaning. Or ironing.'

It was a joke, because Caitlin never ironed, but Joel's brown eyes darkened with concern. 'Don't do cleaning, Mum. Do something nice.'

'Good idea. I might go out,' she said casually, just to see if the kids minded her having a social life that didn't involve soft-play centres or Nando's.

The idea didn't seem to faze Joel. Possibly because he couldn't actually imagine it. 'With your friends?'

'Yes.' Caitlin had a strange stepping-onto-ice sensation as she said it, and decided not to tell him exactly what she had planned. 'I'll probably go to see a film. One you and Nancy wouldn't like.'

'One with kissing in it?'

'Yup, lots of kissing. And no songs.'

Joel had beckoned her down to his level, so he could tell her something without Nancy overhearing. 'Please don't worry about us,' he'd whispered into her ear. 'We'll be fine with Dad.'

He smelled of the biscuits he'd had instead of supper, and the first, very faint tang of boy-ness. And then Caitlin had felt like crying.

Her throat closed up again with tears as she approached the roundabout at the Longhampton ring road, and she drove all the way around it twice, each time wavering about whether she should head back to Eva's house to call the whole weekend off. This weekend would be the longest time she had ever been apart from them. Even Nancy's birth had been at home, downstairs by the fire in the birthing pool Patrick hadn't wanted her to have in case something went wrong.

Nothing had gone wrong, though. Nancy had arrived with a crescent-moon lick of brown hair, crying like a tiny chick, and Patrick had held their perfect, starfish-fingered baby with an awe that had made Caitlin euphoric with love for them both. Dangerously euphoric, like every moment after that would never be as good.

The car was too quiet. Caitlin realised she'd been listening to the radio for nearly ten minutes now without the 'Mum?' 'What?' 'Mum?' 'What?' 'Mum?' 'WHAT?' routine interrupting the travel news or the weather forecast. Even the silence felt reproachful, as if she'd forgotten something vital.

She jabbed at the radio and decided that the first song that came on would make the decision for her.

It was 'Freedom' by George Michael.

Caitlin gripped the steering wheel, and cut across a honking car to take the turning signed for the M5 and Bristol.

Chapter eleven

'So, what would you like on your toast?' asked Eva, when she'd reinstalled Joel and Nancy on the kitchen stools at her breakfast bar. They looked like miniature game show contestants, staring back at her with expectant gazes that bored into her uncannily like Caitlin's. Both were waiting for her to say something, but her mind had gone blank. Adults, Eva could deal with – they threw you conversational bones to get things going. Children didn't.

Eva's cheeks tightened with the effort of smiling confidently. She wasn't sure whether she should plough ahead and feed them without Patrick supervising, but didn't know what else to do. Caitlin hadn't left instructions about what they could or couldn't eat (or should or shouldn't), and she had an uncomfortable memory of one of Mick's friends regaling them with a story about how he'd opened a bag of peanuts on a flight to Florida and made the child next to him swell up 'like a basketball'.

And underneath this, a distant throb of pain was pulsing in her chest, for the diaries. The diaries that she half wanted to throw away, half needed to get back to.

'Joel?' she asked, in a higher pitch than she intended. 'You *do* eat toast, don't you?'

'Yes, definitely. Have you got peanut butter?' Joel enquired, counting off on his fingers. 'Marmalade? Raspberry jam?

Cashew butter? That's like peanut butter but with cashews and it's very expensive so Mum says we have to have it *sparingly* on toast,' he added with a flourish. '*Sparingly*.'

'Fine, I've got all those,' said Eva, shuffling the rows of jars. The cupboards needed a good clear out. 'Apart from maybe the cashew butter. What would *you* like, Nancy? Marmite? Honey? I don't suppose you'd like Gentleman's Relish . . .'

'I'll try it!' offered Joel.

'No, don't,' said Eva. 'It's foul.'

'So why've you got it in your cupboard?'

Good question, thought Eva, peering at the sell-by date. *Use by December 2009. Oh dear.* 'Because Mick liked it. Only at Christmas, for some reason.'

'Uncle Michael,' said Joel to Nancy in a stage whisper, without taking his eyes off Eva, checking he'd got it right. 'You won't remember him. You only met him when you were a baby. He's . . .' He dropped his voice. 'Gone to heaven.'

Eva opened her mouth, then paused – was it really the time to open up that conversation? – but the moment was saved by a sudden light in Nancy's eyes. She'd seen something that clearly made her very happy indeed. Eva spun round: what was it?

Nutella. Moving the jars had revealed some Nutella hidden behind the massed ranks of jams.

'Would you like chocolate spread on your toast?' she asked. Nancy nodded happily.

'Nancy *adores* Nutella,' said Joel. 'She'd like butter first, then Nutella on top.'

'I'm sure Nancy can tell me what she wants herself,' said Eva calmly. 'Girls are perfectly capable of speaking for themselves in this house.'

'She can't,' said Joel, through a large bite of marmalade-y toast.

'There's no need to be shy here.' Eva picked up two slices of bread and turned to look directly at Nancy. 'Brown or white, Nancy? Or half of each?'

Nancy pointed at the white slice, then dropped her eyes.

'Nancy's not *shy*. She just can't talk sometimes. Where are your dogs?' Joel reached for the marmalade and started applying more to his remaining half slice.

'They're in the sitting room. They're going to stay there while we eat breakfast.'

'Then what?'

'I don't know. I might take them for a walk in town while you do something fun with your dad.' Eva cut the Nutella'd toast into four triangles and pushed them across the counter. 'Here you go, Nancy.'

Nancy smiled, revealing small white teeth, and Joel said, 'Thank you!' so fast it almost sounded as if it had come out of her mouth.

'You don't need to say thank you for her.' Eva could see something was going on, but she didn't know quite what. 'I'm sure she was about to say it herself.'

'I'm saying it for her, because she doesn't want to be rude.' Joel put his knife down and looked straight at Eva. His eyes were disconcertingly honest. 'Some people think Nancy's rude because she won't answer them and say please and thank you, but they don't understand that she can't speak.' He glanced sideways at his sister, and an expression of concern shadowed his face. 'I can't be there all the time, though. I'll be at a different school next year. We'll have to work out a way for then. Maybe a recording on her phone, or a special card, or something.'

Eva screwed the lid back on the Nutella. She wasn't sure what to make of that. Caitlin had mentioned a 'shy phase' – that she understood, she'd been shy herself. But not being *able* to talk?

'Does Mummy know about this?' she asked.

If there was a real problem, wouldn't Caitlin have warned her? Patrick certainly hadn't mentioned anything.

'Mum? Yup.'

Mum, fine, that's me corrected, thought Eva. 'And Dad?'

'Dunno.' Joel folded his toast into his mouth and said, 'When's Dad coming?'

'Soon,' said Eva. 'Do you want to text him, to see where he is?'

'Can I have a go on your coffee machine first?' He beamed with delight. 'Dad's bound to say no, so please can we do it now?'

Eva squinted at her nephew. For a child who wasn't technically a blood relation, he was displaying a lot of family traits.

When Caitlin arrived at the beer festival hall, it was already half full of people holding pints of real ale and chatting to one another. Gangs of friends, couples on dates, older foursomes, a few families, one or two kids running around – a very varied crowd, but definitely no other single women in jeans they hadn't worn for three years and their one 'non-mum' handbag.

Usually, not knowing a soul didn't bother Caitlin, but this afternoon she felt self-conscious, aware of every detail of herself. Her too-tight jeans, for a start. She'd tried on so many clothes in half an hour at home that she'd had to make herself stop and remind herself this wasn't a date. Or at least, it was a date with *herself*.

She ordered a bottle of cider at the bar and drank it while a folk band played an acoustic set on the stage behind her. Caitlin swayed, enjoying the live music, if not the songs about plague and rural infidelity, but restless thoughts began to spring up in her mind like weeds. There was no sign of Lee – but why would there be? Had she got it wrong? Was Lee just being polite inviting her?

Would he be surprised she'd turned up?

Should she even be enjoying herself without the kids?

What was Patrick doing with them?

Would Patrick tell them about the divorce without her being there?

What if Lee's band was crap?

Should she have asked Scarlett from work to come with her? Just for moral support?

The *no* came very sharply inside her head, surprising her. This was a moment just for her. Something she needed to do on her own. This was a chance to explore who she was now, aged thirty-one, at the start of a new life. This Caitlin was someone who went to new things on her own, who didn't wait for permission or approval from anyone.

The song finished, the crowd clapped, and Caitlin looked down at the empty bottle in her hand.

I'm going to have another, she thought, as the folkies embarked on another song about potato blight. *Why not?*

Caitlin had finished her second cider by the time The Glebes charged onto the stage at five, and the crowd that had gathered

to see them was several times the size Lee had modestly anticipated. Some were even wearing band T-shirts.

She tucked herself into a corner in front of a pillar, where
she had a clear view of Lee up on the stage. He wasn't the
focus of attention – the lead singer was bouncing around in
leather trousers, making it hard for the audience to see anything
other than his imminent wardrobe malfunction – but the way
Lee leaned back behind his drum kit, his blonde hair shaking
with each rise and fall of his strong shoulders, made him look
far more rock star than his mate.

Caitlin leaned back on the pillar and relaxed, letting the beat
thud into her body while the crowd surged around her like a
wave. It didn't matter that The Glebes weren't brilliant. The
fact that she was there was all that mattered. She'd almost
forgotten how much she loved live music, and being part of a
shared moment. The first thing she'd done at university was to
start saving up for her Glastonbury ticket, despite Lynne's
protests that driving lessons would be more useful, and she'd
worked two bar jobs to pay for her three-festival-a-year habit.

All that had stopped with Nancy, obviously. It should have
stopped with Joel, but Granny Joan had sent Caitlin out on
some nights off in Bristol when he was a baby; she understood
Caitlin's need to be twenty-two, as well as a new mum. But
Patrick didn't like the same kind of music as Caitlin – he 'didn't
mind it', which should have told her everything – and though
he'd tried to enjoy what she enjoyed, he'd looked so uncomfortable in his polo shirt at the two gigs she'd taken him to in
their early days that she'd noticed all the irritating things she
usually managed to ignore, and they'd been too knackered
with Nancy's sleep refusal to try again. She sang in the car, she
sang with the kids – that was enough.

Now, though, the memories of more abandoned times rushed back, and Caitlin felt a physical lightness she hadn't felt in years. The set went past too quickly, and then Lee's band kicked into their closing number, a metal cover of Uptown Funk, and euphoria fizzed through her body. *I'm getting back to who I was before*, she thought, startled by the energy rush.

She closed her eyes and let the music lift her up until it felt as if the bass was pulsing the blood through her veins, not her heart. In that moment she didn't have to worry about Joel, or Nancy, or what she should be feeling or doing or cleaning or fixing. She could just be here, herself, feeling the music. It would end, and she'd go back, but just for now, Caitlin was just Caitlin again, in a cider-flavoured bubble of freedom and happiness.

Caitlin Reardon smiled at no one and lifted her arms over her head to dance.

And then it was over, the band bowed and bounced off stage, and the crowd flocked back to the bar, and she was left alone, by her pillar. Like Cinderella, but at six, not midnight, and with jeans that now felt restrictive and lipstick that had probably worn off along with the cider.

Caitlin wondered if maybe she should just go home, quit while she was ahead. Get an early night, take advantage of an empty bathroom and all the hot water. But a faint glow lingered: what she secretly longed for was for Lee to come over, his hair damp and straggly, to say he'd seen her, and thank her for coming.

Calm down, she thought, horrified at her own teenager-iness. *Three ciders, and this happens? Maybe you should go home, before you make a total tit of yourself.*

But before she could decide either way, a side door opened, and there was Lee, striding into the hall. He looked the same as he had done on stage, not suddenly reduced to boring normality, and from the broad smile that suddenly lit up his face when he saw Caitlin, he *did* seem pleased that she'd turned up as promised.

'Hey!' he said, pointing at her. 'You came! Did you like it?'

'Where was the song about the cat? I was waiting for it!' She'd been aiming for breezy, but the words burst out of Caitlin's mouth, too loud for the emptying hall. 'You were all so great! Why were you worried no one would come?' She knew she was gabbling but she couldn't stop herself. The moment was carrying her along.

'Thanks!' Pleased, Lee rubbed a hand through his damp hair, and Caitlin's eyes drank in the strong fingers, the lean underside of his triceps with the flash of dark blonde arm hair as his sleeve fell back. 'It went way better than normal, to be fair. Generally Noah falls off the stage. Or splits his trousers or something stupid.' He grinned affably and gestured towards the bar at the back of the hall. 'You must be a lucky charm. Can I get you a drink?'

'No, let me . . .'

'You're fine.' Lee waved his wrist full of fluorescent entry bands. 'We're not getting paid much but we're allowed to abuse these as much as we like. What are you drinking?' He nodded at her empty bottle. 'Is that cider?'

'Er, yes, please.'

Lee grinned. 'Bit of a rebel, aren't you? Cider at a beer festival?'

'Beer makes me burp,' said Caitlin without thinking, and immediately wished she hadn't. But Lee just laughed, looking right into her eyes as if she'd said something hilarious. 'Me, too.'

They were standing so close in the crush for the bar that she could feel the heat of his body through her T-shirt as it pressed against her arm. Lee smelled of Lynx and fresh sweat, a laddish kind of smell, another blast from the past, unfamiliar but familiar. It was still just a polite drink, nothing more, but something was bubbling away between them now, and it was so long since she'd done this sort of 'let's have a drink' thing that Caitlin wasn't even sure whether she'd spot the signs any more.

They reached the front, and Lee was served quickly. He turned round with the drinks, passing hers over the heads of the crowd, and Caitlin noticed he'd just got two – for him, and her. She'd assumed he'd been sent to get beers for the rest of the band, but if he had, clearly he'd changed his mind. She tried to keep her face as normal as possible as he motioned her over to a clear space in the corner, under a poster for the local Real Ale society. On the stage, another acoustic band was setting up, and noise levels were rising again.

'How's the reading going?' he asked over the top of his pint, then sank a grateful swig. Caitlin noted the sexy way he drank, as if he'd ploughed all his energy into the performance, and needed to replenish himself. The brush of his dark lashes as he closed his eyes in appreciation of the cold beer.

'Reading?' She had to think for a nanosecond: she'd told Lee, in the park café that night, that she spent exactly one hour, two nights a week sitting on a park bench, reading for her book group. Not hiding from the relentless energy of her children and the relentless micromanaging of a husband who came in from work and refused to talk, but still stuck to-do lists on the fridge with branded magnets from work.

'Oh, that? It's . . . good. Thanks.'

'I haven't seen you in the park for a while – I wondered if maybe you'd finally finished the book?' He raised his eyebrows, and Caitlin knew he'd noticed it'd been the same book, week after week. It gave her a wriggling sensation in the pit of her stomach. So he *had* been looking, taking in the details of her the same way she'd collected new observations about him from the other side of the path. A yellow running vest, a haircut, a bandage on his leg. Bright beads on her secret necklace, noted in her head, then hidden away until next time.

'Oh, I left the book group. It got very competitive, not really my thing. Actually, I thought I might start running,' she said, casually. 'You know, get fit, meet new people. Fresh air?'

He grinned – and not in a 'Ha! Really?' way, which was kind of him, Caitlin thought. 'Great idea. We have a beginners' running club at the gym I work at – I can get you details if you want?'

'Brilliant.' He worked at a *gym*. Brilliant.

They made common-ground small talk for a while – the hazards of the park, running, the race he'd entered – and then slowly branched out, finding things in common. Lee told her about the band and the power struggles between the cat-song-writing guitarist and the eyeliner obsessive singer. Caitlin made him laugh about the café. She didn't *not* talk about Joel and Nancy, but for once she made a conscious effort to talk about herself. It felt strange, but nice, and there were no breaks in the conversation, apart from Lee's second trip to the bar. He seemed to hurry back too, with crisps this time, 'to save queuing'.

They'd been talking for nearly an hour, when three long-haired men approached their corner through the packed bar, and stopped in front of them.

'Hey, man.' Caitlin didn't recognise the lead singer at first, not with his glasses on. And a checked shirt where the black vest had been. 'We're heading down to the Anchor in an hour. Danny's getting the gear into the van. You coming?'

'Is it that time already? God, it is. Where's it gone?' Lee checked his watch, then turned to Caitlin. 'Do you know the Anchor? It's got great beer on tap. And good craic, to be fair.'

'No, I've never been.' Was he asking her out? She hadn't explicitly said she was single. Had he glanced at her hand to check for a wedding ring – which wasn't there, and hadn't been since the day Patrick informed her that their marriage was over. *You're massively over-thinking this, Caitlin.*

'Ah, you'd love it, especially if you're into your live music. We usually end up jamming there – there's a kind of session atmosphere on a Saturday.' Lee's grey eyes were looking straight at her. Looking into her, inviting something to happen. 'Come down, if you're not doing anything later?'

In her head, Caitlin was thinking, *Oh, better not, I barely know him, he's just being polite*, but she heard a voice that sounded a lot like her own say, 'Why not?'

Why not? There was no one to get back to at home. No tea to cook, no bedtime stories to read. She knew where the pub was, she could get a taxi home. For a moment Caitlin teetered on the edge of safety, but something pushed her on. *What else are you going to do?* she asked herself. *You need to have some fun. Meet people. Get out there. Didn't you used to be more interesting than this?*

That did it.

'Great!' said Lee, and his eyes crinkled sexily at the corners. 'See you down there, then.'

'But only if I get to hear the cat song,' she added.

He looked blank, then the penny dropped and he winked, making Caitlin's stomach lurch dangerously in a way it hadn't for at least ten years.

'She *said* she'd ring before bed.' Patrick's face was thunderous in the shadows of the hall, and he'd dropped his voice so Joel and Nancy couldn't hear. The children were curled up together in the L of Eva's sofa, having 'one last go' on Patrick's iPad. 'She *promised* them. I don't care about her letting me down, it's them.'

'Caitlin knows when bedtime is.' Eva had bought fluffy new towels, washed and warmed in the drier for their baths; she clutched them to her chest. 'She's maybe run out of battery, or fallen asleep. Don't make a big deal about it.'

She glanced into the sitting room. Nancy and Joel's heads were bent together over the iPad, and though Eva couldn't hear any sound coming from them, she assumed they were whispering together from Joel's giggles. It made Eva feel better to see Nancy smile, even if she wasn't talking. Bumble was on the other end of the sofa, legs tucked underneath his body until he looked like a fat white sandwich loaf, watching Nancy, his new object of adoration. Bee, meanwhile, was asleep on Mick's leather armchair, snoring.

Patrick wiped a hand down his face. He looked shattered: he'd arrived talking on his mobile and it had rung several times an hour, despite it being Saturday. He'd whirled them round town, into ice cream parlours and round the park, but even when he was being an impressively fun dad, the phone was never off. 'I know Caitlin's spontaneous, and that's fine, but I never had her down as *selfish*. Not like this. It's so important to be consistent with children. Mum never broke a promise to me. Neither did Dad. That's what you build your trust on, your parents.'

Eva smiled tightly. The eight years between her and Patrick sometimes seemed a lot longer. 'Dad broke a few promises in his time, believe me.'

'Like what?'

'Like when he never came to any of my sports days? He swore every year he'd be there next time, and he never ever made it.'

Patrick made a dismissive noise. 'But knowing Dad, he would have tried. You can't just skip out of surgery. I'm talking about promises you should be able to keep, like phone calls.'

'You and Caitlin always made it to sports day, though, didn't you? Joel told me you saw him winning his sack race last year. And that you were third in the fathers' race.' Eva glanced across at her brother. Watching him with Joel and Nancy was sweeter than she'd expected, and more poignant too; he was relaxed, almost goofy, with them in a way he just wasn't with adults. Whereas their dad had been . . . An old memory sent a cold shadow over her heart. Not like that at all. But Patrick didn't have those memories.

'Anyway, it's not like there's a law that says you have to parent exactly like your own parents did,' she said gently. 'You're doing an incredible job.'

But Patrick was gazing at the children, not really listening to her. 'No parent is perfect, you learn that soon enough. I just want to give my kids security. The knowledge that they're loved, by people they can rely on. I feel like we've already screwed that up.'

'You haven't.' At least he said 'we', thought Eva. He wasn't blaming it all on Caitlin. 'In any case, it's not bad for children to see that you and Caitlin are human beings too. Everyone makes mistakes.'

'Mistakes are fine. Being unreliable . . . isn't. Kids need to be able to trust. It's bad enough when adults let other adults down.' He paused, painfully. 'When people you love turn out to be something they're not.'

'Paddy? Are you talking about Caitlin?'

He didn't answer. The silence stretched out between them.

'Look. We didn't have a conventional two-parent childhood, did we?' she pointed out. 'And we're OK.'

'That's different. Dad *died*, he didn't leave us. And Mum kept him alive, by talking about him, being so proud of him.' Patrick folded his arms in the half-darkness and Eva could make out the defiant jut of his jaw. Just like Dad's. 'If anyone at work asks me who my role model is, I say my father. Great doctor, strong father, talented sportsman. All-round good bloke.'

Eva hugged the towels tighter. She didn't want to deal with this, not tonight. It felt like the day had been going on forever.

Instead she said, 'Maybe Caitlin doesn't want to ring because of Nancy not speaking? Maybe she doesn't want to put pressure on her to use the phone.'

Patrick turned his head sharply. 'Sorry?'

'Oh. Just something Joel said.' Eva felt her face redden. Had she betrayed a confidence?

'What?'

'Well, Caitlin mentioned Nancy was going through a quiet phase, and then Joel told me Nancy didn't like speaking in public. *Couldn't* speak, as he put it.'

'I didn't know any of that.' Patrick seemed shocked. 'When did she tell you this?'

'Just this morning. It's probably just . . . shyness. I was like Nancy when I was little – always preferred to be reading a book than talking to someone.' Eva tried to sound upbeat. 'Still do, most of the time.'

'*Couldn't* speak?' His brow wrinkled. 'That sounds . . . Is there something I should know about?'

Their voices were rising, and Eva touched his arm to make him aware that they could be overheard. 'Shh. No, I don't think so. She's just . . . Well, there's a lot for her to take in. Didn't you notice this afternoon, when we went for a walk with her and Joel and the dogs?'

Patrick didn't reply at once, and Eva realised he'd spent most of the walk on his phone, trying to resolve a stock crisis in Preston. She hadn't even been listening hard, and still felt she knew more about traffic problems on the M6 than anyone outside the AA needed to.

His crestfallen expression told her how that made him feel, that she'd noticed, with her total lack of parenting skills, and he hadn't. *Oh, Patrick,* she thought. *You're more like Dad than you even know. Maybe we both are.* The idea made her feel dank inside.

'Deal with it in the morning.' She pushed the towels into his arms. 'Bath first. Here, nice warm towels for everyone. Caitlin left some bedtime story books . . .'

'I brought bedtime story books,' said Patrick, defensively. 'We're reading Charlie and the Chocolate Factory.'

'Great!' Eva felt herself slipping into an old pattern, solving problems before they came up. 'Shall I start running the bath? The room's ready – I've put them in together, next to you. I'm sure by the time they're in bed, Caitlin'll have called.'

'Mmm.' Patrick seemed lost in his thoughts, and Eva realised that no matter how much her brother leapfrogged her in life, as well as in height, he'd always be the boy she hugged to sleep when he cried. The boy who seemed to have a very different family, despite sharing exactly the same parents.

Chapter twelve

Eva was woken in the morning by the sound of her phone's email alert. She groped for her mobile on the bedside table. Her alarm hadn't gone off: it was that early.

Downstairs, someone was making breakfast. Rather, one person was making breakfast while another person sang a song that went, 'Let it go, let it go . . .' over and over again. Eva couldn't make out the rest of the words. The singer stuck mainly to the 'let it go' part.

She squinted at the screen. The email was from Alex Montagu. The subject was 'Clips.'

Hello, Eva. Just a couple of things . . . First, just checking the diary I sent in the post last week arrived safely? I was in a rush to get it to you, and forgot to add that Cheryl Murray was at pains to stress she hadn't opened it. In fact, she wrote me 2 (two) long emails talking about 'karma' and 'the responsibility of the sisterhood', and asked me to confirm that she would never trespass on your right to heart space while you make your decision re publication. (Not sure what that means.) I'm sorry, I should have reassured you on that point. I didn't open it either. Not so much for karmic reasons, as professional ones. I hope that goes without saying. I also hope you're

enjoying (?) reading the rest of the box now that's whet-
ted your appetite?

FYI. Cheryl has decided her karmic responsibility is to
publish her section of Mick's diaries.

Secondly, and unrelated, did I leave a bicycle clip at your
house? I've lost one. I only mention it because various
friends have found them in their houses over the years and
panicked that some vital piece of household machinery has
disintegrated. One friend replaced her hoover. No rush if
you do – I hope we'll meet again soon, and I can collect it
then.

Best, AM

Eva lay back on the pillows. She could hear Alex's voice in
the email: soft and self-deprecating. It felt intimate, reading his
words in bed. Was he really at his desk at seven on a Sunday
morning? Was he in bed too? She shook the image away, and
since she didn't know when she'd next get a chance to reply
with the kids in the house, typed back:

Thanks. To be honest, it hadn't occurred to me about
Cheryl reading 'my' diary. Not sure how I feel re that –
suppose I can't complain when millions could be reading it
soon enough.

Will look out for bicycle clip. Did you really cycle all the
way from the University of Warwick with that box on your
bike? Impressed.

Best, EQ

Her email style was a business one: short and to the point.
Not chatty and long, like his. She was re-reading it, enjoying

the way she could see him saying the words, when his reply
pinged straight back.

> That's very stoic of you! And no, I didn't cycle all the
> way – I took the train, and cycled from the station. Cycling
> isn't my eco statement, in case you were wondering; I'm
> simply not one of nature's drivers. I fear I may have demon-
> strated that on Piccadilly last month. Imagine that co-ordi-
> nation, in a car!
>
> Crashingly, A

Eva laughed out loud.

Then her eye fell on the box of diaries, moved out of harm's
way from the hall. Was it wrong to laugh, in bed, with her
husband's biographer? A bit.

I'll read the other diaries when the kids have gone, she
decided. And then I'll tell him no.

If Eva had wanted to slip away to do her own thing on
Sunday while the Reardons enjoyed some quality family time,
she soon found out they had other ideas.

First she had to make elaborate coffees for everyone, then
she had to watch Joel show Patrick how he could do it too, then
listen to Joel's 'three best' songs from *Les Misérables*, then
scramble eggs according to her mum's recipe, then load the
dishwasher, then be shown a better way to load the dishwasher
by Patrick . . . On and on, to a constant hum of commentary
from Joel, with interruptions from Patrick.

Nancy said nothing, but she was part of it all. She sat with
Bumble on her feet, smiling, nodding, and sharing her toast
with Bee. Her eyes were so expressive that Eva would have
forgotten she wasn't speaking unless Patrick hadn't persisted

in trying to make her talk, asking questions until Eva's chest knotted on Nancy's behalf.

Eventually she excused herself to check the phone in the hall for messages, hoping Caitlin had left some sort of communication to head off Patrick's seething mood.

There was the usual recorded spam about PPI, a 'just checking you're OK' call from Roger, a missed call . . .

'Oh!' Eva jumped.

Patrick was standing behind her, looming large in his weekend polo shirt. 'Nothing from Caitlin?'

'This might be her.' Eva checked the last message. 'Eleven forty-two p.m. Did you hear the phone ring?'

'I was out like a light.'

'Same here.' Eva couldn't remember feeling more exhausted, just from concentrating on not letting anything get broken. She listened to Caitlin's garbled message; she sounded a bit pissed. 'Um . . . Caitlin's phone's dead, she didn't have your number, she's calling as soon as she got home,' she reported. 'She's very sorry, she'll ring in the morning.'

Patrick checked his watch ostentatiously. It was nearly ten.

'What was she doing ringing at nearly midnight? Didn't she worry about waking us?'

Eva shrugged. 'Maybe she lost track of time. Don't make it into a big thing. Not in front of the kids. Especially . . . hello, Joel! How can I help you?'

Joel had picked up Patrick's gift for silently gliding into place. This morning, his cape had been replaced with spangly braces. Eva had no idea how he'd got them on.

'Auntie Eva? Can we make up a *play* with the dogs in? With songs!' He beamed, eagerly. 'Can you play the piano for me?'

'Let's do something quiet, while your breakfast settles,' said Patrick, herding Joel back into the kitchen. 'Did you bring your pens? He's great at drawing pictures,' he added, putting the bag with the art supplies on the kitchen counter. 'Nancy? Tell Auntie Eva about the octopus you drew at nursery, the one Shelley pinned on the wall? Nancy?'

Nancy didn't speak, but instead started to arrange the pens in rainbow order, her lower lip jutted out in concentration as she looked anywhere but at them.

Her bowed head gave Eva a nip of recognition: she could remember that same awkwardness when asked to do anything in public as a child too. She'd done it – sung the song, recited the poem – but only by pretending she was someone else. As she got older, she'd just got better at pretending. Someone brisker, someone more self-possessed. Clothes helped a lot. She'd even pretended she and Simeon were an item for years after they'd called it a day. Too long, probably, but it was part of the company schtick: the girl who never knew what to wear, and the boyfriend who sorted out her wardrobe.

Mick had seen through it, all the way through to the shy girl who gritted her teeth and did the tap dance anyway. But then he was used to pretending to be other people.

'Nancy doesn't have to do anything she doesn't want to,' she blurted, and Patrick gave her a strange look.

'She can be polite to her auntie.' He looked around the room for drawing ideas, and spotted Eva's Oyster card, left on the sideboard from her last trip to see Roger in town. 'Oh, look, Nancy! Auntie Eva's been to London too. Why don't you draw her a nice picture of our trip to London before Christmas?'

'Good idea!' said Eva. 'Where did you go? Can you draw me a picture of . . . Big Ben?'

Nancy's smile, which had begun to unfold on her face as she touched the pens, abruptly froze. Eva saw; Patrick didn't, and he pushed on.

'You could draw the London Eye? Or the black taxi we went in?' He looked up at Eva, as if he wanted her to know they *had* had a good time. 'That was one of Nancy's special wishes – we played a game where the kids had one wish for every thing they spotted from Nancy's book. Nancy wished for a ride on a big red bus, didn't you? One that went down Oxford Street, where we saw Santa and the Christmas lights. What else did you wish for?'

The pinch of concentration deepened between Nancy's eyes, and Eva felt her anxiety. It trembled in the air.

'I *love* buses,' she said, willing Nancy to look up and see her auntie there, understanding. 'I like sitting at the top, right at the front. Did you ring the bell to make it stop?'

'Nancy?' Patrick's voice had an edge of impatience. 'Auntie Eva's talking to you.'

Nancy finally glanced up at Eva, her eyes wide in a silent appeal. What was she trying to say? Eva felt the same yearning to understand that she did when Bumble pushed his flat face into her hand some nights, clearly trying to communicate something vital. She only had his wrinkled face to read, and he only had the strange human grunts she made back at him.

I want to help, Nancy, she thought, uselessly. *But I don't know how.*

'She can't talk, Dad,' said Joel. 'She's not being rude.'

Patrick put his hands on his hips. 'What do you mean, she can't talk?'

'I don't know. But she can't talk. Don't make her.'

'Of course she can talk! She's just being stubborn. Nancy?'

Nancy's head bowed further, hiding her face with her hair, and to her horror, Eva thought she might be crying.

Eva changed tack, not wanting Nancy to feel even more trapped. 'Why don't you draw Bumble?' she said, crouching down next to her chair. 'He sits nice and still. Shall I start you off? Pugs are easy to draw. Here, I'll show you.'

Nancy's small hand hesitated, then pushed a pencil towards her. A ripple ran across Eva's heart, like an insect skimming invisibly over the pond. 'And then you can draw Bee,' she continued, 'but you might have to write which is which because they're very alike, aren't they? Can you tell the difference? I bet you can.'

She had no idea whether Nancy could or not, but she nodded, the curtain of hair shaking softly. Eva began drawing Bumble's round face, his button eyes, conscious of the concentration focused on her.

'Great idea!' Patrick recovered, and seemed relieved. He checked his watch, then frowned and retrieved his phone from his back pocket.

Don't do that, thought Eva, but didn't know how to say it without pulling more attention to it. Was he going to ring Caitlin? Couldn't it wait? Couldn't he see Joel fidgeting with the need to be noticed?

'I'm going to draw Bumble,' Joel announced. 'But an action kind of Bumble. Like a superhero. Superpug! Super puuuuuug!'

'That sounds more like Bee to me,' said Eva. 'She's definitely one for a costume, don't you think?'

Patrick frowned at his phone. 'I can't wait to see them. Eva, I've got to take this – do you mind keeping an eye on these two for ten minutes?' He seemed flustered. 'Then I'll take them into town for a look round and some lunch. We'll get out of your hair.'

'It's fine.' Eva had planned to walk down to the bookshop, maybe see Anna, but it could wait. Nancy was leaning on her, watching where her pencil was going and the soft weight of the child's body, her breath heavy with concentration, gave Eva a feeling of closeness that she'd never experienced before. It was uncomplicated and trusting, the way the pugs slumped into her arms when they were puppies.

Bumble lay next to Eva's feet, observing them both.

'Bumble likes helping,' said Joel, and Eva had the funny sensation that he was saying the words while Nancy thought them.

Patrick's call took half an hour. Eva watched him pacing up and down the garden outside the kitchen window, his hands waving and clenching.

When he finally came in, she left the children drawing the dogs and went to see what the problem was. Whether it had been Caitlin on the phone, for a start.

'Don't,' he said, before she could speak. 'Don't even ask.'

'Fine.' *Had it been work?* For the first time, Eva wondered if maybe a mysterious third party in her brother's break-up was actually on *his* side. 'What was all that about?'

'What was what about?'

'Nancy. Didn't you see how upset she looked when you talked about London?'

Patrick lifted his shoulders, baffled. 'Yes, but . . . It can't have been that. Nothing *bad* happened. Cait and I took the kids for two nights before Christmas to see the lights. We went because of that book of Nancy's, *A Trip to London*. You got it for her, didn't you? For her birthday?'

Eva nodded. Anna had recommended it. She'd flicked through it before she wrapped it up, unsure whether it was suitable for a four-year-old, but it was a fun London she remembered, jazzy in fifties jaunty shapes and colours, not the stressful air-conditioned prison it had become.

'They loved it,' Patrick went on. 'We went on the river boat, on the London Eye, down Oxford Street on a bus to see Santa . . .' He trailed off, his eyes distant.

'And?'

He seemed to pull himself together. 'And nothing. That was it.'

'Well, it must have been something. You saw how she reacted. No police cars? Nothing scary? No creepy Santa telling her to keep secrets?'

'Definitely not a creepy Santa – we went to Hamleys. And no scares that I remember. But you never know with kids, do you?'

'No,' said Eva. 'I don't know.'

'My pug has gone wrong!' announced a voice from the kitchen. 'I need help!'

'You soon will.' Patrick patted her arm. 'Welcome to parenthood.'

The shrill ringtone sliced through Caitlin's fuzzy head and she sat up, then immediately regretted it, especially when the ringing stopped as soon as she was upright. She reached for the phone, with only one thought in her mind: *I was supposed to call Joel and Nancy first thing.* Was this Patrick pre-empting her? She squinted at the screen.

Missed call: Mum.

Great. She'd had a long text the previous day. **How are you coping without the kids? Do you need some suggestions about filling the time? Maybe you could use these weekends to think about retraining? Call me!**

Caitlin groaned and flopped back on the pillows, feeling nauseous. She couldn't phone the kids yet, not feeling like this. She hadn't even drunk that much, plus she'd lined her stomach with a solid supper before joining Lee and his mates at the Irish pub. Still, at least she could sleep it off without anyone bouncing on the bed and demanding breakfast. That was a silver lining.

The last time she'd had a hangover was at Patrick's Christmas party, two years ago. Caitlin had been over-excited by the prospect of going out and had thrown back five glasses of prosecco before the dinner even started. The following year Patrick muttered something about budget cuts and sandwiches in the local pub – which didn't make sense since their head office was in a business park outside Newcastle – but either way, spouses weren't invited. She'd had a shameful feeling she hadn't lived up to the version of herself he'd been telling his colleagues.

Nancy, nagged a voice in her head. *Nancy. Is Nancy all right?*

Caitlin grabbed her mobile, but before she could decide whose phone to call, it rang again. This time it was Scarlett from the café. Caitlin hadn't thrown caution to the wind completely; she'd made sure someone knew where she was going.

'So?' Scarlett sounded way too perky for a Sunday morning. 'How was the date?'

'It wasn't a date. It was just a . . .' How to describe it? It had started to feel like a date, towards the end. 'It was a gig.'

'Yeah, yeah. How was the date?'

Beneath the grinding mess of her hangover, Caitlin felt a faint, fizzing excitement. 'It was good. I watched Lee's band, and then we had a drink and we chatted, then we went to a pub and just hung out. And then I came home.'

She closed her eyes, trying to re-order the evening in her head. The simple fact was that it had been the best night out she'd had in years. Lee's face swam up through the fog: long blonde hair falling over his forehead, his grey eyes fixed on hers as she talked, that unspoken crackle of connection. There had been moments when she'd caught him looking at her, and she'd felt almost panicky with the possibilities.

Scarlett sounded impressed. 'Woah! And?'

'And what?'

'And? Did you, you know . . . ?'

'No, we didn't anything. I got a taxi back, and crashed into bed. On my own.'

'Boooooo.'

'Stop it, Scarlett. I'm not looking for another relationship.'

'Who said anything about another relationship!' Cackling down the line. 'Best way to get over one man is to get under another, that's what my mum always said.'

'Your *mum* said that?'

'Ha! You haven't met my mum.'

Caitlin rolled over; she felt clammy and grubby. 'Oof. I've got to drive up to Longhampton to get the kids in . . .' She took her phone away from her ear to check the time. She'd said five o'clock to Patrick, which meant leaving here at . . . three? It was nearly eleven. She couldn't remember sleeping this long since university. Another forgotten luxury. *I need to phone them*, she thought. 'About four hours.'

'Well, as long as you're OK. You were meant to call me last night, you doughnut. Let me know you were home.'

'I know. My phone died – I forgot to charge it – then of course I didn't know anyone's numbers . . .'

'Yeah, yeah,' said Scarlett. 'Has he texted you yet? Ready for round two?'

'No! I'm telling you, it's not like that.'

'Not even to check you got home all right?'

'No.' In a way, Caitlin was *glad* Lee hadn't. It was a Patrick thing to do: checking. He always said he couldn't sleep if he didn't know she was home safe. It was lovely at first, to be cared for so much, but it was the kind of surveillance Caitlin wasn't going to miss.

Scarlett cackled again. 'Well, I want all the goss tomorrow, right, lover?'

'Right.' Caitlin hung up, and sank back into the pillows.

Would Lee phone? Or text? Did she want him to? Excitement churned in her stomach, along with guilt and nerves and cider. Of course she did.

When Caitlin pulled into the drive outside Eva's ski palace at half past five, having bombed up the motorway to compensate for her unplanned three-hour power-nap, Joel and Nancy's faces were at the window, waiting for her, and an overwhelming warmth swept through her body.

She hadn't thought she'd missed them, but she had. So much. *So* much.

The faces vanished, and she knew they were running to the front door to meet her. It opened, and there was Eva, looking slightly less calm than usual, and Patrick, with what Scarlett would have called 'a right face on him'.

This is about me not calling last night, thought Caitlin. *Well, sod it. I spoke to them this morning.* The kids hardly looked traumatised. And if she had called he'd only have moaned about intruding on 'his' time.

Eva welcomed her in, and offered her tea, and then tactfully withdrew to take the kids upstairs to check for any forgotten items.

Patrick didn't waste any time. 'You promised you'd call before bed.'

'I know. I'm sorry. My phone died, and then I realised I didn't actually have your number to use someone else's.' Caitlin knew she was in the wrong, but could feel herself getting defensive. That was Patrick: he expected her to be perfect, then when she was *human,* she felt bad. 'I rang this morning, didn't I? I thought it was better not to distract them while they were spending time with you. Did you have a nice weekend?'

His expression was stony. 'Yes. We did. But that's another thing I need to talk to you about.' Patrick glanced at the door, and she knew what it would be about. Either Nancy's quietness or Joel's over-active behaviour.

Caitlin put her teacup down in readiness. 'Go on.'

'It's something Joel said to Eva earlier. He said Nancy couldn't speak. What's that about?'

Ugh. Patrick's 'line-managing' tone, the one that felt as if he was accusing her of deliberate negligence. She'd bristled the same way when he used to ask why Joel couldn't just be quiet now and again, or whether Nancy was a bit short for her age, as if Caitlin had deliberately stopped Nancy growing, or force-fed Joel musical soundtracks. Patrick didn't get that kids were *what they were.* And if he'd got home from work a bit earlier and done some actual child-rearing, she used to moan to the girls in the café, he could have asked them himself.

'What's what about?' she asked.

Patrick made the frustrated noise that always only escalated matters. 'Don't be dense. Has Nancy got a problem? Has something happened to upset her?' He paused. 'Did you tell her we were getting a divorce?'

Caitlin turned to look at Patrick properly. The frown lines had deepened around his eyes. It wasn't just because he was frowning at her, although he was; they seemed a permanent addition to his face. There were more flecks of silver in his dark hair, and he radiated weariness. Every time she saw Patrick now, he seemed a little bit less familiar, more like an acquaintance from college, an old workmate. It seemed bizarre to think she'd once floated round Paris with this impatient, annoyed man; swooned as he whispered how much he loved her into her ear while they watched New Year's Eve fireworks; rolled up her jeans and splashed in the icy cold sea with him, then let him warm her with his kisses in the car. Frozen feet, hot mouths, cold hands slipped under Patrick's big winter coat.

Caitlin felt a sudden mourning for that lost happiness. It was behind them. Gone, receding into the distance. Now they were just two adults, trying to negotiate the management of two small human beings, with no obligation to be anything other than polite to each other. Her chest ached, not for Patrick but for the confidence she'd once had that this was forever. Again. Hope dashed, again.

'Caitlin, focus. They'll be down in a minute.' Patrick's gaze was impatient, and there was none of the old indulgence in his voice. No *sweetheart*, no *darling*. 'What's going on? I'm Nancy's *dad*. I can't believe you didn't tell me.'

She sighed, not wanting to unleash Patrick's strategy-planning on a delicate situation. But he was her father. He did have a right to know. 'Nancy's going through a phase of not speaking at nursery,' she said. 'Shelley says it's not unusual at that age. Nancy's good at communicating without words and they're very attentive to her. She's managing fine.'

'And when did this start?' Patrick looked stricken.

'Last week?' It was longer, Caitlin knew. She hadn't told him. A part of her hadn't wanted to; after all, Nancy was fine, if very, very quiet, at home.

You didn't want him to know, she thought, and the coldness inside *her* was a nasty surprise.

'And is she talking at home?'

'Yes, of course she is.'

But she's not singing, added a voice. *Not dancing. Not lifting her face up to feel the sun when no one's looking. Not shoving her nose into flowers to smell the fairies.* Caitlin's heart ached.

'She hasn't been singing, though,' she added, suddenly needing to share that with someone who'd understand how scary it was. How heartbreaking.

Patrick's expression fell. 'No singing?'

Caitlin shook her head. Then she asked the question she didn't really want to know the answer to. 'Hasn't she been talking here?'

He ran a hand through his hair, frustrated that he didn't have an instant solution. It made him look more like the old Patrick. 'A word or two, but always whispering, only when we're on our own. She's been really clingy. I assumed she was going down with something, or she was upset about being here. Maybe worried about the dogs, not wanting to surprise them.'

'Maybe. Maybe that's all it is.' Caitlin grabbed the explanation. 'She's only a baby still – she's adjusting. Give her some space. Let's not start throwing labels around.'

Caitlin knew she'd made a mis-step. Patrick never ever let things go, once he'd got his teeth into them. Not when it concerned his family.

'Labels? Caitlin, this could be a serious problem . . . What have you done about it so far? Does she need her hearing tested? What did the GP suggest?'

'I haven't been to the—' she started to say, and Patrick's face darkened.

'What? You haven't even taken her to the doctor?'

'It's a *phase*. Kids go through phases. I've checked on the internet and—'

'Oh, well, if you've checked on the internet.' He ran a hand through his hair again, but this time it was fiercer. 'That's fine. Because that's where *all* the doctors hang out, on the internet. Not, say, at the surgery at the end of your own street.'

'Do you have any idea how hard it is to get an appointment at that place? You have to wait weeks, unless your leg's hanging by a thread.' Caitlin glared at him. Why was she saying this? Of course she was going to take Nancy to the doctor. 'I checked *on the internet,* which is incidentally what most parents do first, and refusing to speak isn't an uncommon reaction to a—'

'I want you to take her to the surgery,' he said. 'This week. Promise me you'll get her seen by someone who knows what they're talking about.'

'Are you telling me I'm not looking after my daughter properly?'

'*Your* daughter?'

'What's going on?' Eva appeared at the sound of raised voices. Caitlin wondered if voices had ever been raised in Eva's house. Probably not. Mick just *projected, darling*.

'We're discussing Nancy not talking.' Patrick turned to her. 'Can you tell Caitlin what you witnessed?'

Eva looked embarrassed. '*Witnessed*. Paddy. You're making it sound like I was at a crime scene. All I saw was a little girl being shy in front of new people. Don't be so dramatic. It doesn't help anyone. She's been charming company, Caitlin,' she added. 'As has Joel.'

Caitlin warmed to her sister-in-law. She'd never heard anyone put Patrick in his box before. And it was nice to hear Joel being called 'charming company'.

'Where is she now?' He turned and called up the stairs. 'Nancy? Nancy, are you ready to go?'

'Please don't shout. I think she's in the kitchen, saying good-bye to the pugs,' said Eva.

'I'll go and see.' Caitlin picked up her teacup. 'Thanks for the tea – I'll pop this in the dishwasher.'

'On the side's fine.' Eva gave her a quick smile. Caitlin real-ised Eva didn't have dishwasher-friendly tea sets. Of course not.

She caught a ghost of a glance pass between Eva and Patrick as she went down the hall to the open kitchen. Joel was at the breakfast bar picking up cake crumbs with a carefully-wetted finger, but there was no sign of her daughter.

'Where's Nancy?' she asked, and he nodded, crumbily, towards the French windows that led out onto Eva's picture-postcard country garden.

There was a huge wicker dog basket by the doors, and curled up in it was a chubby fawn pug wrapped in the arms of her daughter. Each had their head buried in the other, so Nancy's hair and the pug's coat blended into one honey-coloured lump. Nancy's delicate hand was stroking the pug's back with great care, and she seemed to be whispering in its ear.

Something caught in Caitlin's throat. No. Was it? Nancy talking?

'Nancy wanted to say goodbye to Bumble,' Joel explained. 'We've done amazing pictures of Bumble and Bee.'

There was a movement behind her. Patrick and Eva had followed her in.

'That's nice,' said Eva, with a delighted smile. 'Bumble's got a new friend.'

Caitlin glanced at Patrick. Had he caught the whispering, the smiling? Because his expression wasn't anywhere near as happy as his sister's.

Chapter thirteen

'**M**y name's Dora. Dora, like the Explorer!' Dr Lang leaned forward and held out her hand with a toothy smile. 'And I'm fifty-three. How old are you, Nancy?'

Caitlin glanced across at Nancy, sitting with her hands clamped under her legs on the chair next to the doctor's, and waited for her to speak. If it had been up to her, Caitlin would have given it another week or so before hauling Nancy to the doctor. In fact, knowing appointments were booked up in advance, she'd put 'call GP' on her to-do list for the week, but on the way to school on Monday morning, her mobile had rung. It was Patrick. He'd done what he always did, and taken over.

'I've managed to persuade them to see Nancy today,' he informed Caitlin. 'They agreed to squeeze her in at two forty, so can you get her there for half past?'

Joel had been in the middle of reminding Caitlin and Nancy about his latest plans to become a West End musical star via some audition the school was hosting for a local theatre. Caitlin had only had half an ear on the monologue, because she was trying to trick Nancy into speaking outdoors while mentally running through the fridge for tonight's supper, and he slammed his hands on his hips when she stopped walking to deal with Patrick's call.

'Jeez, Mum!' he said. 'What do I have to *do*!'

All I Ever Wanted

Caitlin recognised both the words and the intonation as her own, and gave Joel an 'in a moment' look while she turned her attention to Patrick.

'Did you request an emergency appointment?' She knew Patrick was good at negotiation but she was the one who'd have to face the dragon of a receptionist if she turned up without a child on actual fire. 'They get really arsey if you book emergency appointments for non-essential stuff.'

'Caitlin, our daughter can't talk! I'd call that an emergency, wouldn't you? Anyway, the receptionist agreed with me, hence the appointment today.'

Typical Patrick, she thought. He had to be right. He couldn't stand the idea that it might be just as helpful to give Nancy space and not stress her out by making her think she *had* a problem.

Caitlin hated the implication that she didn't care enough. She wanted to tell Patrick that Nancy needed love, and security, and reassurance, and she'd get through this phase, but both kids were standing right next to her – how could she put into words that his taking over like this undermined *her* ability to keep them safe? Anyway, Patrick wasn't listening. It was Monday morning; he had an exec meeting in Gateshead at nine; having sorted out their lives, he had to go.

'Nancy?' Dr Lang repeated. 'How old are you?'

Nancy hesitated, held up four fingers, then replaced her hand under her legs. Her feet in their pink Converse swung back and forth, and outside in the waiting room, a baby howled. Then another baby joined in.

'Oooh, I didn't see that,' Dr Lang pretended to look in the wrong direction. 'Are you ... ten? No? Are you ... a hundred and twelve? No? OK.' She leaned forward and cupped a hand to her ear. 'Can you whisper how old you are?'

Nancy gazed up from under her sandy lashes, and gave Dr Lang the funny smile Caitlin had noticed she'd given Shelley at nursery: a tight, polite smile that seemed precarious. Then she shook her head, hard.

Dr Lang glanced sideways at Caitlin.

'Come on, missus.' Caitlin tried to sound relaxed. 'It's not a trick! You're going to be five in September but right now you're ... ?'

Nancy's head dropped again and her straight hair fell over her face so only the point of her nose was visible. The white toes of her shoes stopped swinging completely. It was as loud a 'no' as she could have shouted. Nancy wasn't a rude child, or an obstinate one. This wasn't her, not at all.

'Nancy?' Caitlin suppressed the panic that had been growing since they'd walked into the surgery. 'You remember Dr Lang! She had the magic cream that stopped you itching last summer. Just tell Dr Lang how old you are, and we can ...'

What? We can go home? We can stop worrying about you? We can pretend nothing's wrong, when clearly something is?

A hand touched her arm, warning her to stop pushing. Dr Lang was taking over. Caitlin had a sharp recollection of her mother telling her that she'd been completely fearless – until she had children. Then fear could creep up on you at any moment, freeze you with its paralysing grip.

At the time Caitlin had scoffed at the idea of pant-suited troubleshooter Lynne Hardy being scared of anything. She'd scoffed at being scared herself – after all, she'd struggled through four years as a single parent before she met Patrick. But now she got it.

Something was controlling Nancy, some fear or emotion she couldn't see or mend or suffer instead, and it made Caitlin want to run round the room screaming.

'You know what, Nancy?' said Dr Lang, conversationally. 'I think it'd be fun if you went to sit with Karen in our reception. She might even let you press some buttons on our switchboard! Would you like that?'

Nancy's head lifted, her blue eyes sharpening with interest, and to Caitlin's relief she nodded.

'Great! Let's give her a buzz.' Dr Lang flicked her intercom, spoke to the receptionist, and Karen appeared at the door, looking a lot less like a bouncer than she sounded on the phone whenever Caitlin tried to get an appointment.

'Have I got a helper?' she said, holding out a hand towards Nancy. 'Come on, you!'

Nancy looked anxiously to Caitlin for approval. Caitlin smiled but her mind was spinning. Patrick had secured a gold-dust emergency appointment. Karen was being friendly. Patrick had an incredibly persuasive phone manner but maybe this was worse than she thought.

What have I missed? Am I a terrible mother? Is this something that triggers Social Services involvement?

'Go on!' Caitlin tried to make it sound like an adventure. 'I'll be out in one minute.'

Nancy's expression tensed and Caitlin's heart clenched with the realisation that she couldn't say, *I don't want to go, Mummy*. She could only agree, and go along with what everyone else wanted. Like Eva's boggly-eyed pugs. Picked up, put down, led around – silent and submissive because of whatever it was that was keeping her quiet.

Caitlin tried hard not to let panic show in her face as she waved Nancy goodbye.

As soon as the door shut, Dr Lang swung back to her screen, and started making notes with a disconcerting urgency.

'So, good – there are no comprehension problems, no hearing issues ... Definitely no speech issues. Last time I saw Nancy was about a year ago, wasn't it? When Joel got the pen stuck up his nose? And she was extremely articulate then. Very keen to tell me what else Joel might have up there.' The keyboard clattered.

They'd been in there five minutes, and Caitlin knew this surgery operated a strict ten-minute appointment slot. She had an urge to pull the clock off the wall, to freeze time, just to give Dr Lang long enough to work out what was wrong.

Patrick would be so much better at this, she thought, unhappily. He'd have notes, reminders, to help diagnose the issue. Instead, her head was jumbled with scraps of panic and flashes of Nancy's hunted eyes and the paragraphs she'd skimmed on the internet. Skimmed for sections that backed up her own need to believe there *was* no problem.

'How long's Nancy been like this?' asked Dr Lang. 'Unable to speak?'

'I'm not sure. She's been quiet at home recently, but I thought she was just ... going through one of those processing phases. She always has her head in a book, and Joel makes enough noise for two, at least.'

'So someone else made you aware there was a problem?'

'Yes. Her nursery. I was called in a few weeks ago, and the manager told me that Nancy had stopped talking.'

'Not talking to the grown-ups? Does she speak to her friends there? The other children?'

'Shelley says she doesn't talk to anyone. I mean, she *communicates*, just not with words. She makes her wishes known, as they put it. I checked with Shelley about any bullying or distress there, and there's nothing like that. Nancy's very popular.'

'Have you been with her when she's refused to talk?'

Caitlin nodded. 'There was an incident the weekend before last – she wandered off in a park, and couldn't speak to the adults who found her.' The words stuck in her throat; *I should have said something then*, she thought. 'I've told her not to speak to strangers. I thought it was just that.'

Dr Lang made a *hmm* noise and typed. 'OK. And at home? She speaks to her brother? And her dad? All normal there?'

'Yes,' Caitlin started, then stopped. *Normal.* Nothing was normal any more, not for Nancy. Suddenly Caitlin felt as if she was being diagnosed, not Nancy. As if she was part of the problem.

Dr Lang swivelled on her chair, hearing the silence.

'No, it's not really normal,' Caitlin confessed. 'Her dad and I separated after Christmas. He moved out in January. To Newcastle.'

'Oh,' said Dr Lang.

'It's an amicable separation,' she added quickly. 'No shouting, nothing to upset the kids. We were really careful about that. We've kept it as civilised as possible. Patrick and I just came to the mutual conclusion that our relationship had run its course. We don't want to live together, but we're both committed to *parenting* together. He sees the kids every other weekend. He's a good dad.'

That was true, he was. He just wasn't a very good husband. Caitlin bit her lip. Or maybe she wasn't a very good wife. Well, not the wife he wanted her to be, anyway. Up there on her pedestal, being the perfect mother just like his mum, while he got on with being the perfect dad. But she'd warned him from day one that she'd let him down. He was the one who insisted she never could.

'We get on much better now,' she said miserably. 'Better to have two happy parents separately than model unhappiness to the children.'

Dr Lang made a non-judgemental noise. 'But Nancy speaks to her dad?'

'I'm not sure.'

Her fingers hovered over the keys. 'You're not sure?'

'Patrick has his contact time at his sister's in Longhampton. Nancy was very quiet when I collected them on Sunday, but I assumed that was because things were a bit overwhelming.' Caitlin thought of Nancy's face, buried in the dog's wrinkled coat. Hiding. She ached. 'Everything's very new. They don't know their aunt very well, Eva hasn't got kids herself. It's a big house, with dogs. We're all . . . finding our way.'

'So it was Patrick who told you Nancy wasn't speaking there? He seemed very worried about the situation, according to Karen.' Dr Lang pulled a face. 'She took the call this morning. Wouldn't take no for an answer.'

'He worries about little things more than me. No, that's wrong, he doesn't worry *more*, he just needs to feel he's dealing with it. He's a manager.' Caitlin flashed a wan smile, conscious that she wasn't showing herself in as diligent a light as Patrick. 'I was planning on bringing her in if it didn't improve, but Nancy's been fine at home, so I . . .' That wasn't great, was it? *Fine with me, so I didn't make the effort.* Caitlin hated herself.

'You thought it was a phase. That's fair enough. You know her best. But Nancy's happy around her dad? Generally? No secrets she's been asked to keep? Nothing she wouldn't want to tell you about?'

It was a casual question, but Dr Lang didn't turn back to make notes. Instead she observed Caitlin's face, and the query in her eyes made Caitlin's blood run cold.

What? Did she think Nancy had been abused? By Patrick? A dark space opened up in Caitlin's chest. What was she suggesting? Patrick had his flaws but he'd never . . . Her brain wouldn't even picture it.

'No! Of course not. He adores her, she's a real daddy's girl. He's . . . No, there's absolutely nothing like that. Nothing.'

Dr Lang looked sympathetic. 'The trouble is, we don't always know what a child finds traumatic. Things that seem perfectly logical or normal to us, can be quite scary for a child trying to create their own rules. Has he asked her to keep any secrets? Have you?'

'No! Never. We don't have secrets in our house,' said Caitlin.

'Good. But sometimes children see things, or hear things, and an adult says, "Don't tell your mother . . ." They're not sure what it is they're meant to have seen or heard, so make a blanket rule.' Dr Lang shrugged. 'We've all done it. I stupidly once said little piggies have big ears to my husband, and my son refused to sleep with Piglet in his room for months. He thought Piglet could hear everything. Took us a while to work that one out!'

It was an attempt to lighten the mood but Caitlin didn't feel like smiling. A wave of tears was choking up her throat. What careless comment had she made, that Nancy was so scared?

'I'm not an expert in paediatrics, but what I'm seeing is a little girl who's anxious,' Dr Lang went on. 'It's a common coping mechanism. Children are happy to speak at home, or to certain people, but find it too stressful to communicate in other, more public, situations. Generally, selective mutism – being able to speak in some situations, but not in others – isn't officially diagnosed until children are school age. When does Nancy start? September?'

Caitlin nodded. The thought of Nancy marooned in the much bigger primary school, away from Shelley's careful eye, made her panicky.

'So we need to get on and tackle this – the big problem starts if the not-speaking becomes a habit.' Dr Lang spun round to her computer and started typing again. 'So! What I'm going to do is to refer you to the speech and language therapist at the hospital. She'll work with Nancy and give you an action plan to help.'

'She won't be made to feel like she's . . . like she's got a problem?'

'No, no. Don't worry, it's more like a play session.' Dr Lang smiled. 'Anyway, these things take a few weeks and maybe the situation may have begun to resolve itself by then. Once the new routine with her dad, and the contact weekends settles down. You never know.'

'You never know,' said Caitlin, and crossed her fingers. She felt like suddenly she knew too much.

Patrick called at exactly four o'clock, as Joel and Nancy were sitting in the café eating carrot cake that Joanne had deemed 'left over' while Caitlin wiped tables round them.

In order to make up for missing two hours of her afternoon shift, Caitlin had agreed to come in and help with the weekly kitchen clean-up after the café closed at five. Nancy hadn't said anything about the doctor's appointment and Joel had picked up where he'd left off that morning, outlining the convenient stairway to international stardom that had opened up to him, via some regional musical theatre production that needed extrovert ten-year-old boys, for some reason.

'. . . and they're going to pick three boys to sing the role of Gavroche in . . .'

'Joel, let me get this, it's Dad on the phone,' said Caitlin, and Joel left his mouth hanging open pointedly. 'I'm sorry,' she added. 'Three boys, I get it – hold that thought. Hi, Patrick.'

'Hi. How did it go at the doctor's?' he asked, without any preamble. He was calling from the car, as usual.

Joel still had his mouth open, pointedly. I've got very literal children, thought Caitlin. She mimed for him to close his mouth, then immediately worried about what Dr Lang had said about that.

'It went fine.' Nancy was watching her now, with wide eyes. 'Nancy had a lovely time playing with the buttons on the switchboard, didn't you?'

Nancy nodded.

'And what did the doctor say?' Patrick persisted. 'Was she worried? Is it serious?'

'She said that Nancy played with the switchboard so well that she's going to let us go up to the big hospital and play with some more people up there!'

'Caitlin, stop talking in riddles . . . Is Nancy with you?'

'Of course she is, I've just collected Joel from school. We're in the café. I'm not supposed to be on my phone – can I call you back?'

'I'm out later, supplier dinner. Tell me now. So did the doctor say what's causing it?'

Caitlin rolled her eyes and motioned for Scarlett to keep an eye on their table while she slipped outside. Even so, she watched through the plate-glass window, making sure the children could see her. She plastered on a bright smile so they wouldn't assume she was talking to Dad about anything remotely stressful. The effort made her jaw ache.

'The doctor said it's anxiety,' she said in a low voice, through the manic grin. 'She's referring Nancy to the specialist. She's going to assess her, and advise us how to support her till she gets over it.'

'And that was it? When will she be seen? Do I need to be there?'

'I don't know when, you don't get an instant appointment.'

'Why not? This is serious. Give me the number, I'll get things moving faster.'

Caitlin pulled her cardigan more tightly around her; it was cold. 'Patrick, will you back off? I'm doing everything that needs to be done. The doctor more or less told me that it's stress-related – probably down to our divorce. Or something she's seen. Maybe with you, since she talks fine at home.'

Caitlin didn't know why it came out like that but it did, and there was a silence at Patrick's end. She could hear the swish of his wiper blades. It was raining where he was.

At least I never thought he was cheating on me all those nights he was away, she thought. *Unless he got the other woman to impersonate a TomTom sat nav.*

'Something she's seen? What do you mean by that?'

'I don't know. Something she doesn't want to talk about.' Patrick began to protest and Caitlin talked over him. 'Can you think of anything? Have you asked her to keep any secrets? Did she see you doing anything that might have upset her? Something you haven't told me about?'

Her voice was rising. She didn't know why these words were spewing out of her; a horrible desire to transfer some of the shame she'd felt in Dr Lang's room had taken over. It was the not knowing, she thought. Not knowing what was distressing Nancy made the possibilities so much more terrifying, especially when they meant she didn't know her own husband either.

'I don't understand, of course not . . .' Patrick sounded confused. Then his voice took on a harder edge. 'What the hell are you accusing me of?'

'I don't know,' said Caitlin. 'What might upset a little girl so much she doesn't want to talk?'

There was a sharp intake of breath. 'Caitlin! I can't believe you'd even *say* that.'

She didn't answer. She stared instead into the café, at her son and her daughter sitting round the table. Joel was whispering into Nancy's ear, drawing something on her sketch pad, and Nancy was smiling, directing her gaze elsewhere, hiding her interactions so only Joel could see.

This is a tipping point, Caitlin thought with sudden clarity. *Up until now Patrick and I have managed to behave as if this is a civilised resolution of a bad situation. Any personal resentment swallowed for the sake of the kids. But what's happened to Nancy has to have a reason, and that reason is something* we've *done. One of us has done something to cause this. And now the gloves are going to come off, because obviously both of us think the other's capable of doing something really shocking. We just haven't said it yet.*

A shiver ran over her skin that was nothing to do with the air outside. Patrick had recovered himself enough to start yelling at her.

'And you think you're blameless in all this?' he demanded. 'You're absolutely sure about that? You're absolutely sure?'

'I've done nothing to upset Nancy.'

Patrick made a tutting noise. 'I've got to go, another call coming in. I'll call you later, OK?'

'I thought you had a supplier dinner?' *Now you want to talk,* observed a mean voice in her head. *Now you know something's up.*

'I do. I'll call you after, try to get away early.'

'Fine.' While she was talking Caitlin heard her message alert ping, and she hung up, and turned away from the window, adrenalin still speeding into her heart.

The text was from Lee. Caitlin stared at it for a moment; did she want to open this now? She'd swung between hoping he'd text and telling herself it was far too soon, she was reading too much into a casual night out. But now the text was there, she realised she was excited.

It's just a drink, she told herself. *A bit of fun, for me. The kids don't need to know. It's like it was before: I can have one evening a week, being me, and it can stay in that box. I don't owe anyone any explanations.*

She opened the message.

Just about recovered from the weekend. Great to see u. U around this week for a beer?

Lee's cheeky eyes and his smooth biceps; the small gap between his front teeth; the smell of his T-shirt: all flashed in her memory so vividly Caitlin could taste the cider in the pub. And alongside that, a memory of her own exhilaration, like being on the edge of a sharp drop, when he leaned forward to talk to her over the general bar racket and she inhaled his salty skin. It was so physical, it made her feel alive again.

All I Ever Wanted

Caitlin turned and saw Scarlett chatting to Joel and Nancy at the table inside. Nancy was smiling at her sketch pad and Joel – well, obviously Joel was singing. She could tell that from the slightly strained smile of the last remaining couple in the café. Scarlett liked kids, and she was always good for some babysitting.

I can look after my children, thought Caitlin. *And I can give them a fresh start.*

Chapter fourteen

May 21st, 2007

Took Cheryl's gladrags down to a charity shop in town this morning. Because I'm sick to the back teeth of seeing glittery tat, all unworn, flashing me every time I open the wardrobe to get a pair of trousers, but also because – three hail Marys for this, sorry, mam – it gave me tremendous pleasure to send Madam a postcard to whichever lentil-weavery she's now inhabiting with that teenage musician, informing her that the humble citizens of a backwater she hated are now swanning around in her best Dolce e Gabbana, which they've acquired for a pound or two. And that Longhampton's orphaned cats are eating salmon steaks, thanks to her inability to let a tarty bustier pass her by.

Well, no. Be serious. It was a Help the Aged shop, which I'm all for these days. It's an investment in my not-so-distant future.

Not that they'll be selling for a pound, either, thanks to the amazon who stepped in and brokered a better deal for the old dear running the place.

Rare that you see killer business acumen and legs like that round here – not since Cheryl bailed out. I was rather charmed. Don't think she knew who I was either, which was even more charming. We had tea, and she was as amusing to talk to as she was stunning to look at. A fellow escapee from London. Lavinia liked her too. Lavinia hates most women. She's a jealous old puggie.

Kim's put me in for another legal series in the States, which I simply can't face. I'm going to have to do it to pay for the legal fees Madam and I have managed to rack up getting shot of one another, which is, as my dear old mother would say, bloody ironic. Plan to tell Kim my liver's packed up again.

Eva stared at the diary in front of her on the study desk. That was the story of her and Mick's meeting. Their wonderful, romantic, life-changing meeting, and Cheryl got more lines than she did. She frowned, and felt a bit cheated. Was that just how perspective worked, looking back and seeing it for what it was in the bigger scheme of things? How would she have written it?

A thought occurred to her, and she opened up her emails. Eva didn't keep a diary but up until a few years ago, she'd kept in touch with a few of her old mates in London by email – it was easier than trying to co-ordinate their schedules to meet for drinks.

She scrolled down, down, down, watching the subjects change as the years went back. Vet reminders, sale reminders, gardening mailouts, through to emails from Mick, invitations from his old friends who never quite got the hang of emails, party photos, then back into her business mails, friends she hadn't spoken to in years . . .

There it was: to her friend Mel. Eva remembered writing it, rewriting it, half-scared to commit something so delicately amazing to the screen, in case it jinxed it.

> Mel, news – finally. I met the most amazing man at the
> weekend. He's not remotely my type, and I can't tell you
> who he is, because you won't believe me, but I felt The
> Tingle.

They'd all joked about The Tingle over wine when they first got jobs. One by one, her friends had felt it, and happily married the Tingle Giver, until only Eva was left, still protesting that The Tingle belonged in the same drawer as Santa and karma. Until she'd felt it herself.

I knew straight away, she thought, staring at Mick's handwriting, then back to her own email. *I knew. Did he? He said he did later . . . but was that the truth?*

She turned the page, curious to know how Mick described their first proper date – martinis in a hotel bar that she'd never even heard of, and dinner in Shepherd's Market, a hideaway corner of Mayfair that felt like stepping back into a more glamorous world.

The words 'fascinating', 'beautiful', 'too young' leaped out at her, but before she could read further, her phone rang.

It was Alex.

'Hello,' she said. It felt strange to hear his voice while looking at Mick's writing. As if she was being unfaithful somehow.

'If you're ringing about the diaries, I'm reading them right now.'

'Ha! No, well, glad to hear you're hard at work but actually it's about something else.'

'Go on.' Eva shut the diary so she could concentrate on Alex's voice.

'It's a bit last minute but I just thought . . .' He coughed, trying to sound nonchalant. 'I'm introducing a television drama day at a film festival in Birmingham at the weekend, a series of plays from the BBC in the seventies – crossover theatre experiments. Better than they sound, honest! Michael's not in them but quite a few of his contemporaries are. I wondered, do you fancy coming along? We could talk about . . . well, whatever you like.'

'If you mean the diaries . . .'

'Not necessarily. We can talk about other things,' said Alex. 'I have a range of conversational topics, not all of them directly related to mid-century filmstock.'

He was so easy to talk to. 'And I suppose this could be my chance to meet Becky, finally? Should I bring my parka? Or would that confuse you?'

Alex laughed. 'There'll be a fair few anoraks there, if you know what I mean. It wouldn't be inappropriate.'

'Let me check my diary and get back to you,' she said. 'It sounds . . . interesting.'

'Smashing!' said Alex, which was exactly the sort of word Eva had started to expect him to use.

It was hard to make herself go back to the diaries but once she'd started reading, it was hard to stop. Her own life unfolded in front of her, interwoven with worries and triumphs Mick had never shared with anyone else. Night fell as Eva sat at the desk and worked her way through the exercise books, turning page after old page until dawn started to break through the crack in the curtains.

Bumble and Bee kept her company. Bee clambered onto Mick's armchair and snored contentedly through the night. Bumble slept on and off, unsettled by the unannounced change to the usual sleeping arrangements, and by the occasional wave of sadness that rolled invisibly from Eva's hunched shoulders. And occasionally, a snort of laughter. Mick had always made her laugh; now was no exception.

She read through their year of dates and dinners, their glamorous holidays, Mick's genuine struggle not to fall in love with a woman so young and 'so much smarter than me', his sometimes painful observations about his colleagues and his hairline and the bottle of scotch he hid in the attic and thought about too often. He was funny, and honest. Eva relived the whirl of the wedding she'd thought was minimalist (Mick didn't), his admiration, bordering on pretend fear, of her 'Thatcher-esque planning abilities' and their romantic honey-moon in New York where he crept out before she woke to bring her bagels in bed, and they kissed on the Staten Island Ferry 'too much, and like bloody teenagers'.

Some of what Mick wrote brought tears to Eva's eyes – his simple expressions of love for her, jotted down for his eyes only, and his touching amazement that she didn't find him superficial or too wrinkly. Some of it reopened old irritations – Mick never talked to her about Una or Cheryl, but they were here all right, in nostalgic anecdotes and sometimes phone conversations he'd had while she was out. Roger, it turned out, had a code for sneaking off early to play golf with Mick: 'going over the VAT invoices'. Eva skimmed past some passages that were either too dull (detailed descriptions of golf courses, or bitching about people she didn't know) or too personal. She knew she'd have to come back to them later. She'd have to come back to all of it later. The main thing was to finish them, so she could tell Alex one way or another whether she could let these be edited.

Her eyes were sharpened for any more references to children, theirs or anyone else's, but there was nothing. Nothing that set off that dull ache of regret that his other comment had. Eva was relieved, but also strangely disappointed.

The last entry was just before they went off on what was their final holiday together: a trip to Italy. The last line Mick had written was: ***Note to self: sort out E's surprise***.

Eva stared at his handwriting.

And then he'd gone. Mick was gone. There was no more.

Eva had braced herself for that final line, assuming it would open another floodgate of grief, but instead a stillness settled over her. The memories of the days that followed their return were all hers, not Mick's. She was in control of them, she didn't need to hear those days relived through someone else's eyes. She didn't have to go back there.

Instead, what she'd just read was a happy, full life, spoken in a voice she knew so well. The only jarring thing was that the version of herself she read in it wasn't . . . quite her. Like a very good actress playing her, but still, not the woman she saw in the mirror.

She sat back in her chair. The more Eva thought about that, the odder it felt.

Bee got up, stretched and made the expectant face Eva had

come to recognise as 'feed me now'. Relieved that she'd dragged herself through a task she'd been dreading, and found it not quite as bad as she'd thought, Eva pushed herself away from the desk.

'Good morning! Time for breakfast,' she said, and the pugs wagged their tails to hear her voice.

Anna arrived while she was making coffee for herself in the kitchen.

'It's just a flying visit,' she said, handing Eva a stack of paperbacks, tied up with a bag of toffee swinging from the bow. 'I brought you a book bouquet.'

'Thank you!' Eva was overcome.

'Don't thank me until you've read them.'

Anna was kind, and tended to deliver tougher advice via the medium of her shop's speciality book bouquets, rather than in person. When Mick died and Eva was barely leaving the house, ribboned piles of novels and travel books and brisk 'pick yourself up, start again' guides found their way onto the doorstep, along with offers of pug-walking and fudge. It had been Anna's what-ho detective novels that got Eva through the long nights, not Roger's Harley Street doctor's sleeping pills.

'Have you time for a drink?' said Eva, taking the books from her. 'I've been wanting to talk to you about something.'

'The diaries?' Anna sounded hopeful.

'Sort of.'

While Anna settled herself on the barstool, Eva undid the ribbon and examined her gift. There were two self-help guides to 'enjoying a childfree life' which might as well have been subtitled 'Travelling is fun!', Prof. Alex Montagu's *History of British Comedy Films*, which Anna said had flown off the shelves, *Gangsta Granny* for Joel, a picture book about dancing dogs for Nancy, and on top, a little colouring book of fashion magazine covers and a tiny pack of pens.

'Colouring in's good for stress,' explained Anna. 'You can choose your own colours. All the reassurance of the lines, but with some creative input. Very restful.'

'Anna, can I ask you a personal question?' Eva hesitated. She and Anna were good friends, but there were some areas of their personal lives that they'd only skirted around so far.

'Um, yes?' said Anna bravely. 'As long as it's not about my weight. Everything you see before you, I blame on teenagers and their biscuits.'

Eva pressed her lips together, then took the plunge. 'When you and Phil got married ... Did you have a conversation about whether you'd have children?'

Anna had started to sip her camomile tea. She stopped, and put the mug down on the counter, but kept her hands wrapped around it. 'Yes. We did. Many conversations. I met him when the girls were quite small – Lily was only four – and he thought three kids was plenty. I was only twenty-seven, so ... yes. It was an issue. He really, really didn't want to smell another nappy again. I mean, *really* didn't.'

'And did you ever think . . .' Eva didn't want to push too far. She hated the thought of making Anna share more than she wanted to. 'Did you ever think Phil had changed his mind? Would he have told you if he had?'

Anna let out a long breath. 'I know he did. We agreed, after four years, when things were settled, we'd try for our own baby. Sarah, his ex, had gone off to the States to work, so I was doing all the parenting with him at home – three kids and a dog! From nothing! – so it wasn't like I wasn't prepared. And then Becca found she was pregnant with Finlay, and that was that. She was our daughter, she needed us. She was only eighteen. And I was proud to be part of that "us", if you know what I mean.'

Eva watched Anna's overly cheerful expression. She was trying to be positive, as she always was, but there was a flinch.

'That must have been hard,' she said. 'Looking after Becca's baby when you wanted your own.'

'I won't lie, it was,' Anna sighed. 'Because Phil was very different with Fin, much more relaxed than he had been with the girls, and we both felt . . .' She stared at her tea. 'Anyway, when Becca and Owen got their own place, and I wasn't looking after Fin for her, he changed his mind *again*, and we decided we'd throw caution to the winds and see what happened. With the cut-off point of his forty-fifth birthday.'

'Why then?' It was Eva's forty-fifth in a few weeks' time. She'd shocked herself by noticing; she kept forgetting she wasn't thirty-eight.

'You know what blokes are like. Came down to maths. He worked out that he'd be sixty-five by the time any baby graduated and he couldn't face drawing a pension *and* paying for uni fees. So that was the cut-off.' The smile turned a little rueful. 'And that was last March.'

Eva raised an eyebrow and Anna shook her head.

'No, it turned out the universe didn't have that plan for us. And I was heartbroken. Real grief, crying, sobbing, like someone had died. Well, I suppose someone had, in a way. And poor Phil – we went to Maui for his birthday and I cried the whole time. But then I woke up one morning in our five-star hotel and I realised I had three lovely stepdaughters, and a grand-child who's my little buddy, and a great bloke, and I could travel where I liked for the next twenty years. With my fully-functioning pelvic floor. And my tiny suitcase.' Anna turned her palms over in a 'hey . . .' gesture. 'There are upsides. But I needed to get past the sense that I was missing out, to a place where I realised I'm still me, regardless of what other roles I have. I still make a mean birthday cake. I'm still there for sports day and nativities.'

What Anna was saying made perfect sense but Eva had a sudden tumbling slideshow of all the birthday cakes she wouldn't ice, the wonky nativities she wouldn't fill up at, the plaits she'd never plait, the small hands that would never reach for hers, and the regret was so sharp she knew it was showing through. She gripped her mug tightly.

Anna stopped. Her big blue eyes examined Eva's face. 'I'm sorry. I should have said, *why do you ask*, before I dumped all that on you. Have I just put my foot in it?'

'No.' Eva managed a smile. 'No. It's just something I read in Mick's diaries. I thought he didn't want children. He thought I didn't. Maybe we both . . . kind of did. Deep down. And now it's too late.'

'Oh, Eva.' Anna stretched out a hand. 'Was I tactless?'

'No! You're never that. Was I tactless to ask you?'

'No! And it's not too late, you know. If you want a child . . .'

'I'm forty-five next month! That's the cut-off point, appar-ently,' Eva added, with an ironic raise of her eyebrows.

Anna looked mortified. 'Not necessarily! Just for men who've already been there, got the posset-stained T-shirt. There are options. Have you ever considered going it alone? Or adopting? Or fostering?'

Eva shook her head. 'No. And I don't know if that's for me. It's just the . . . finality of it. I feel too young to be old yet.'

'Forty-five's not old! And you're in an amazing position, Eva. You've got money, and no commitments. There are so many things you could start. Another degree, or a year off travelling, or . . . This book project!'

Her eyes were bright with encouragement, and Eva knew Anna meant it but she couldn't get past the dull pain of knowing she'd ended up here because she and Mick hadn't known each other quite as well as they'd thought. And she couldn't admit that. Not even to Anna.

'Is that your phone?' Anna asked.

It was. Eva looked at the screen: **Alex Montagu**.

'Why are you blushing?' Anna leaned forward as Eva dropped the call. 'You're blushing. Is that the very man my book group ladies are so keen on?' She pulled Alex's book off the pile and turned it round so they could admire his author photograph on the back.

Someone from Alex's publishers had stepped in and given him a smarter haircut and a sports jacket, Eva noted. With his messy quiff Brylcreemed down he looked almost like one of the matinee idols he was writing about. 'He wears a duffle coat in real life,' she told Anna. 'And says things like *berk* and *gosh*, and leaves a trail of bicycle clips behind him like *Carry On* calling cards.'

'He rides a bike? I'll tell them that. They'll swoon. Why's he phoning you?'

'Oh, he's asked me to a film festival he's speaking at this weekend.' Eva watched as a voicemail alert popped up. 'I assume he's going to use the opportunity to quiz me about Mick's diaries. Whether I've read them and can give him the nod.'

'Or . . . he might think you'd enjoy a film festival?' Anna looked pleased for her. 'Have you made plans? If Patrick and the children aren't here, why not go? I keep telling you, you've got to get out there. See people. Join the world again.'

'Hmm.' Anna's reaction was making Eva's more cynical mind tick. 'You think Roger put him up to it? Roger was asking me whether I was getting out and about when I saw him in London. Muttering about Mick not wanting me to stay in.'

'No,' said Anna. 'I don't think Roger put him up to it. I think this Alex seems rather thoughtful. And obviously enjoys your company. I think you should go. Have fun. I'll look after Bumble and Bee, before you use that as an excuse.'

Eva tipped her head to one side.

'Do it,' Anna urged her. 'You like him, don't you?'

How to answer that? Eva felt a shifty sort of excitement. Shifty for all sorts of reasons.

Anna didn't wait for a response. 'Great! I like him too, if he's taking you to the movies. Have you made a decision then? About the diaries?'

'I thought I had, but . . . I don't know. Alex swears he's most interested in the parts where Mick talks about acting and how directors work, and I believe him, but . . .' She thought about what she'd read, losing herself in Mick's distinctive written voice: their lakeside wedding, their courtship, their excited trip to collect Bumble and Bee from the breeder. Mick wrote beautifully about their love, their quietly dovetailing routine, two independent grown-ups learning to mesh their lives. Sweet, human moments an editor would want to keep in. And if she was being brutally honest, they were more interesting than the bits where he expounded at length about digital versus film cameras.

'I'm sure you can ask for private things to be taken out,' said Anna.

'The trouble is, Mick was more or less retired when we met,' she said. 'There'll be lots more work and celebrity gossip in Una and Cheryl's sections. If you take out our private life, there won't be much left.'

'There's Barney the Baker!'

'True.'

'Listen, Eva, I'm not an expert on these sorts of books,' said Anna, 'and neither are you. But you've got a chance to chat to a man who is, so why don't you grab the opportunity to sound him out? Go to this film festival with him!'

'You don't think there's an inherent problem with going on a date with your late husband's editor?'

'Did I say the word date?' Anna's eyes opened wide.

Eva shook her head. She hadn't meant it like that. 'No, but you were thinking it.'

Anna nudged her. 'All I'm saying is that you're too great to deprive the world of your company. You've got to go out there, meet people. Mick would *not* have wanted you staying in, being lonely for his sake. I know that.' She looked dreamy. 'Maybe it's part of the big plan. It would be a very romcom way to . . .'

'Stop it right there,' said Eva. 'If there's one thing I've learned, it's that life is *not* like the movies.'

Chapter fifteen

'**B**e good for Scarlett,' said Caitlin. She yanked open the fridge; just eggs and cheese. *Fine, scrambled eggs.* She slammed it shut and started to unpeel the Velcro rollers from her hair. Ten minutes wasn't long to create glamorous volume, but it was all she had. Thanks to Joel's missing bookbag, she was already running an hour late. But maybe that was a blessing in disguise; the longer she had to think about her first official date for six years, the more jittery she got. 'If she has to phone me, then I'm disconnecting Netflix. And I mean it this time.'

Joel pulled a face. He was already in his pyjamas, obligingly, although he did have his iPad with the film version of *Les Misérables* on it. 'As if.' He plugged his earbuds back in and vanished into his other world.

Caitlin turned back to Scarlett, who was helpfully running Sellotape over her black jacket to remove pug hair. 'God, look at that . . . I was only in the house ten minutes last weekend – those dogs are shedding machines. OK, so there's eggs, bread and cheese, make Joel some eggs on toast if he gets hungry again. He needs to turn that off and go to bed by nine. Latest. He'll probably take it up with him – I wouldn't fight it, to be honest,' she added in a low tone. 'It's the holidays.'

'No school for a fortnight, yaaaay!' Joel raised two fists in the air. 'Easter break!'

Caitlin spun round. 'Are you earwigging?'

'No,' said Joel.

'Nancy in bed already?' Scarlett handed the jacket over. She'd come prepared with several magazines and her manicure bag. Scarlett's nails were magnificent to behold. Both Nancy and Joel had shown an interest in her glittery gels, and she strongly suspected she'd come back to unicorn manicures all round. Still, Caitlin was relieved Scarlett had agreed to babysit at short notice, especially after last time when Joel had made her dress up as characters from *Brave* so he could 'serenate' her. For three hours.

'Yup. One story, then out like a light. She's had a long day – we went swimming.' Caitlin pulled on the jacket, and checked her bag: purse, with cash for taxi home; lipsticks, keys, breath mints . . . Breath mints! Her heart was beating far too fast. She couldn't remember the last time she'd felt so excited about leaving the house. About anything, frankly. It was like being a teenager again.

But she wasn't a teenager. Caitlin pulled herself back. She had responsibilities. Big ones.

'Scarlett,' she said under her breath, trying not to alert Joel.

Scarlett was admiring the ladybird mugs hanging from the hooks by the sink. Joel and Nancy were invited to so many pottery parties Caitlin had become a dab hand at sponge-printing insects. 'Hmm? These are gorgeous, Cait.'

'Thanks. Listen, if Nancy wakes up . . .' She hesitated. How much to tell Scarlett? She was a mate, but there really wasn't a lot to talk about at work apart from whose turn it was to clean the grill, and this could end up fodder for endless 'advice' and speculation . . .

Hang on, she thought, remembering how her own mother had 'filtered' the news about Joel from her colleagues. No. There was nothing wrong with Nancy. No child of hers was ever going to have something to feel ashamed of. 'If Nancy wakes up and she seems distressed, call me. Don't wait for her to tell you what's wrong.'

'Why?' Scarlett put the mug down.

Caitlin met her curious gaze and refused to feel bad. 'She finds it hard to speak in stressful situations. She might tell Joel, but if he's asleep . . . Call me.'

'Is she OK?'

'She's fine,' said Caitlin firmly. 'She's seeing a speech thera- pist, they think Nancy's fine. But in the meantime, it compli- cates things a bit, so just check on her.'

Scarlett looked sympathetic. 'Poor baby. No, that's not a problem. I'll keep popping up and looking in.'

'It'll give you a rest from this one,' said Caitlin, only half-joking.

'Mum, where are you going?' Joel pulled out an earbud. 'You're wearing a *lot* of make-up.'

'I'm going out. For a drink with a friend.'

'But Scarlett's *here*.' Dramatic sweep of the arm.

'I do have other friends. Plug yourself back into Misérables World, would you?'

Scarlett wagged a finger at him. 'Mum's allowed to have a social life too, you know. She's not just Mum. She's also a real person.'

Joel looked dubious, and Caitlin coughed to shut Scarlett up. She'd decided to keep Lee under wraps for the time being.

She didn't want to upset Nancy any more, although a small voice in her head did wonder if maybe knowing Mum and Dad were happy apart might be better than worrying that they missed each other. Plus, she didn't want Patrick to know. Not just yet. Not that it was any of his business, but she suspected he'd leap to conclusions and a tiny, tiny part of her didn't want him to be hurt. Even though he'd wanted the separation.

Pain in every direction, she thought. All the more reason to enjoy these small pockets of happiness where you could grab them.

'I can be Mum *and* a real person,' she said. 'I'll be back by midnight, like Cinderella.' She blew Joel a kiss, which he returned theatrically, then she steered Scarlett to the front door, and dropped her voice. 'We're only going for a drink, nothing fancy. The Apple, down on Welsh Back. I can be back in ten minutes.'

'I wouldn't care where that lad was taking me, so long as he wore a T-shirt. Those arms . . .' Scarlett mimed extreme jealousy. Caitlin had showed the café girls some photos she'd taken on her phone, and then Joanne had found more of Lee's band on the internet. The consensus at the café was that Caitlin should totally go for it. And if she got sick of going for it, she should pass Lee on to them. 'Back by midnight, my arse.'

'I will be!' She peered into the mirror by the door and added more hairspray to her bouncy curls. 'It's not a . . . well, this *is* a date. But it's just a date.'

And it was going to be gorgeous. The Apple was a pub-barge with great cider and a buzzy atmosphere: she was more or less guaranteed a moonlit stroll along the riverside, with Lee's strong arm around her shoulders and Bristol twinkling in the background. And then home by midnight, and back to Mum duty in the morning, but with her energy levels restored and the shiny new Caitlin back under wraps, like the Batmobile.

Caitlin ignored the memory of walking home with Patrick under the streetlights. This would be different.

'I wouldn't be back by midnight if I was going out with that guy,' sighed Scarlett. 'I will need *all* the details.'

'I'll make sure there are details to be had,' said Caitlin, and swished out in a cloud of hairspray and anticipation.

Lee was waiting for her down on the waterside, perched on an iron bollard near the floating Apple, wrapped up in a warm Army surplus parka. Caitlin allowed herself a moment to enjoy walking towards *her date*: Lee was already drawing approving glances from a passing hen night and she was pleased to see him waving the attention away.

'Hey, babe!' He beamed when he saw her, and levered himself up.

Great thighs, thought Caitlin, beaming back. Working in a gym in town – 'just to pay the bills' – certainly had its upsides.

There was a moment's one-hello-kiss, two-hello-kiss? awkwardness, but then they were in the bar, holding a pint of cider each and trying to find a table, and soon the conversation was flowing as easily as it had done on the first night.

'So,' said Caitlin, trying to sound cool. There were quite a lot of students from the university hanging around, making her feel ancient with their perfect skin and edgy piercings. 'How's the band? Any more gigs coming up?'

'Yeah, it's all good!' Lee drummed his index fingers on the table. 'We've got a spot at a Battle of the Bands night in Gloucester in a fortnight – fancy that? There's room in Danny's van if you don't mind travelling with a load of electrical cables on your knee. Not band stuff, to be fair,' he added, 'Dan's an electrical apprentice during the week.'

'Definitely.' Caitlin glowed inside. A tour bus! Of sorts. 'I'll see if I can arrange some childcare but that sounds amazing. I'd love to go.'

'Great! I'll put you down as reserve roadie.' He beamed his sunny smile. Caitlin liked the way Lee didn't react to her mention of childcare; it didn't seem to bother him that she had children. Nothing did. He had a very easy attitude to life that she found incredibly refreshing. 'You can stand next to Sam's girlfriend and stop her doing harmonies,' he went on. 'Man, she is the worst singer . . .'

'Is she called Jeanine?' Caitlin joked, immediately. *Spinal Tap* was one of her favourite films. Patrick hadn't got it at all; he spent the whole first half criticising the band's attitude, as if it was a real documentary, and then snapped, 'But that's ridiculous, Boston *is* a college town!' and refused to watch any more. Patrick could be very literal. Not getting *Spinal Tap* was the beginning of the end.

Lee seemed confused. 'No, she's called Ruby? Do you know her?'

'Er, no. Sorry, we're at cross purposes – I was referring to *Spinal Tap*? The film?'

Lee looked blank.

'Maybe it's a bit of a cult film,' said Caitlin, as he fiddled with a beer mat as an excuse to lean his arm a little closer to hers. She could feel the warmth of it, and the fine blonde hairs.

'So, tell me more about this Battle of the Bands thing,' she asked, just to get him talking again, 'who else is playing? Do you actually have to *battle* them?'

While Lee reeled off the line-up, enthusiasm animating his handsome face, Caitlin wondered not for the first time, how old he actually was. About the same age as her? Late twenties, definitely. Not younger. Not a *lot* younger, anyway. He couldn't think she was that ancient – and she wasn't, she reminded herself, she just felt it. And he'd asked her out. He was the one who kept accidentally brushing her hand as he moved the beer mat round the table and casting those flirty looks from under his lashes while he drank his pint.

The truth was, Caitlin thought, smiling back as his words blurred into a sexy '*yadda yadda* Danny's van *yadda* Snapchat story *yadda* banter' stream, he didn't need to try: there was a spark already burning slowly between them. It wasn't a meeting of minds so much as a physical familiarity. He was a song she already knew, and liked. Lee's body language spoke louder than their actual conversation, which was pretty normal, pub-chat stuff, and Caitlin had a funny calm certainty, under the excitement of flirting, that something would happen, if she wanted it to.

It was a giddying thought. She didn't have to be perfect, or witty, or live up to some impossible ideal of womanhood – Lee obviously thought she was just fine as she was. Two kids, wobbly tum, loud taste in music, and all.

'Another cider?' she asked, since the first cider had gone straight to her head in a good way. She got up, and without thinking, put her hand on his shoulder to steady herself.

Lee's shoulder was strong through the thin T-shirt material. Her hand lingered a second longer than it should on the solid curve of his muscle. She couldn't remember the last time she'd felt so uncomplicatedly attracted to someone.

Lee turned his head and smiled up at her. 'Why not?' he said, and Caitlin's stomach looped. And it was still only quarter past eight.

After another pint at The Apple, their undemanding conversation moved onto Surprising Facts, and the accidental brushes of his hand against her arm, or her shoulder against his, became less accidental. Caitlin revealed she'd been on her university ladies' darts team, something she'd never actually told anyone else, and Lee revealed he'd also played darts for his local pub, so the obvious next step was to find a pub with a dartboard, so they could settle who was the best.

They wandered up the old, uneven steps into the old city, in search of an unposhed-up pub, which turned out to be harder to find than Lee had confidently assumed, but it was so nice, strolling around Friday-night Bristol, chatting about places they'd been, and arguing about who was the best drummer of all time, that Caitlin was almost sorry when they found a side-street pub with a dartboard and no queue to play. She suspected Lee let her win the best of five sets, since he was doing the maths in his head, but he seemed impressed with her arrows.

'You know what we should do now?' he said, finishing the last chips. 'Drink up here, then go and find a pub with a pool table.'

'Pool?' Caitlin laughed. 'Why pool?'

He winked at her cheekily. 'You look like the kind of girl who plays a mean pool game.'

'You can tell that, how?' She tried not to look too delighted; that had always been the look she'd aspired to, in her pre-Joel days – the cool girl with the smart mouth and the big hair who could also do handbrake turns and trick shots. Not that she'd been able to do handbrake turns or trick shots, but she'd bought all Hole's albums and got quite good at roll-ups in between revising for her A-levels.

Lee tipped his head, pretending to examine her, and his blonde hair fell into his eyes. 'You look like the sort of person who likes to be good at things.' He smiled in a slow way that made a nostalgic rush of desire shimmer through Caitlin, carried on a wave of cider.

'I'm really not,' she said. 'I'm the least competitive person I know.'

He didn't reply, but the slow smile broadened. 'I find that quite hard to believe.'

'Fine.' Caitlin checked her watch. She still had ninety minutes before she turned back into a mum-pkin. With a flirty toss of her head, she threw back the last of her drink and smiled at Lee. 'Let's go find a pool table.'

It turned out that a pool table was even harder to locate than a dartboard, and Caitlin and Lee walked round the busy streets without finding very much, but chatting all the time. At some point, Caitlin wasn't sure when, their hands brushed and the next moment her middle fingers were entwined with Lee's. He said nothing, and nor did she, but his skin against hers felt like a hotspot burning between them.

Their wanderings eventually brought them past a stretch of railings where someone had woven a tin-foil river in between the uprights, on top of which knitted fish were fastened in a rainbow of wool, glimmering and shimmering in a silvery crochet net.

'Oh my God, yarn storming! I love things like this!' Caitlin was so excited that she even dropped Lee's hand so she could reach for her phone and take a photo of the delicate woolly shoal. 'Isn't it gorgeous?'

'Those are great fish,' agreed Lee. 'It's like they're moving in the streetlight.'

'Aren't they? It's *amazing* how creative people are in this city. I need to get myself back into making stuff again. It's so good for your mood.' She took a step back to get a better shot. 'I used to knit loads, when I was younger. My gran taught me, we'd sit and do it together. She knitted squares and I knitted miniature versions of rock stars . . .' She sighed, thinking of the hours spent with Granny Joan while Joel slept and their needles clicked. Creating things. Things that weren't gradeable, or checked against a pattern. Things that just *were*. It had helped so much, in those unformed days when Caitlin felt like she'd ruined everything – apart from her beautiful Joel. 'I always wanted to do an art degree,' she said.

'Why didn't you?'

'Parents wouldn't let me. They wanted me to get a qualification in something useful.' Caitlin touched a filigree crocheted fin in pearly aquamarine wool. It was lovely no one had nicked all this. 'Mum works in HR, she's very careers-focused. I only got to do History of Art on the understanding that I'd take a Law conversion course after. But then . . .' She shrugged, a small gesture for a massive drama. 'I had Joel after I graduated, and life took a different turn.'

'Why don't you do one now?'

'One what?' Caitlin glanced across at him. Tick: Lee hadn't asked if she'd regretted Joel (no), or if her parents had been disappointed (yes cubed). 'A Law conversion course?'

'No! An art degree. You could do Textile Design or something.' He raised his eyebrows, as if it was a perfectly normal thing to do. 'Does knitting count as sculpture?'

Caitlin held in the delicious moment of someone suggesting she did an art degree, believing that she was the sort of person who could, then breathed it out. 'Ha! No, I can't.'

'Why not?'

'Because I've got two kids? Because I've got to work? I haven't got enough hours in the day . . . to knit myself a degree. And anyway . . .' She was about to say, *what use would it be now?* then realised how sad that sounded, and stopped.

Lee was serious. 'Yeah, you have. Do it part time. Do it over four years or something. It's like me and the band. I work shifts at the gym so I can buy some time off for my music. I make time. One day, hopefully, the music'll make time for me.'

Caitlin gazed at Lee and felt herself falling into his seductive grey eyes. Maybe she could! Why not? Nancy would be at school soon and she'd have her daytimes free. Patrick would be paying some maintenance – she didn't have to go back to work full time . . .

'You're the only person I know who does anything creative. I mean, professionally. Well,' she corrected herself, 'apart from my sister-in-law's late husband. He was an actor. Quite famous, actually . . .'

Caitlin would have gone on, but Lee didn't seem interested in name-dropping. He was gazing at her underneath the street-light, and the shadows were making his eyes seem even darker and his wide mouth more sensual. 'It's not about time, anyway,' he said. 'It's about feeding your soul, being open to inspiration, everywhere you are, whatever you're doing. Like tonight. On the one hand we were having a drink, having a laugh, but it's the kind of experience you want to turn into music. You by the river, and the darts, and the moonlight . . .'

Lee leaned closer, and Caitlin found herself leaning closer too. They were leaning on the railings, side by side, and gazing right into each other's eyes.

Oh my God, thought Caitlin, *what if he's going to write a song about me? Seriously!*

'I've had a really great evening,' he said softly.

'Me, too.' Her heart was thumping hard in her chest, and she willed herself not to say anything stupid. *Don't talk about the fish, Caitlin. Don't mention knitting.*

'Thanks for sitting on that park bench all those weeks,' said Lee, in a half-whisper.

'Thanks for jogging past all those weeks. Then falling over.'

'I didn't fall over.' His eyes locked with hers. 'I was trying to catch your eye and I tripped on that stupid dog.'

'Thanks, dog.'

Lee tilted his head very slightly, and pulled her closer, and Caitlin could smell the cider and his warm skin and his after-shave, the taste of him in her nose.

He's going to kiss me, and I'm going to— she started to think, but before she could finish the thought, Lee's mouth was pressing against hers, warm but firm, his soft lips slightly parted and his taste unlike Patrick excitingly new. Caitlin angled her head up to fit better together with him – he wasn't a lot taller than her, in her heels – and just as the kiss was beginning to warm up from tentative to something more, she heard the familiar shrill peal of her phone.

Her phone. In her pocket.

The only people who ever called Caitlin on her mobile were her mother, Patrick or Joanne. Or whoever was babysitting.

Caitlin struggled to find it.

'Hey. Can't that wait two minutes?' Lee jokingly tried to stop her, but she pulled away.

'Can't, sorry. It could be the babysitter.' She didn't add, or my annoying ex.

Her heart sank when she saw the caller ID: **home**. 'Hello?'

'Mum, it's Joel.'

'Hello, Joel.' Caitlin stepped back, extricating herself from Lee's arms. Something in Joel's voice pulled her backwards, into her familiar self, as if she was on a bunjee rope. 'Is everything all right?'

'Um, yes and no.'

Caitlin's brain flipped anxiously through lurid scenarios and stopped with a sudden vision of Nancy, waking up, being scared, not being able to tell Scarlett what was wrong. But Joel was there. Nancy could talk to Joel. 'Are you all right? Is Nancy OK?'

'I'm fine. So's Nancy.'

The relief. 'So, what isn't all right?'

'Mum, there was an accident.'

Caitlin wanted to believe that this was just Joel's over-theatrical sensitivities taking over, but something told her it wasn't.

'What happened? No, actually, let me speak to Scarlett. Can you put her on, please?'

'She's with Nancy.'

'Where's Nancy?' She shook her head at Lee, who was

raising his eyebrows in query. 'Where are you? Just tell me what's going on, Joel, I won't be cross.'

'Nancy's outside with the firemen.'

Caitlin nearly dropped the phone. 'With the firemen?'

'It's fine, Mum, don't worry,' said Joel. 'The firemen are nearly done . . .'

'I'm coming home right now,' said Caitlin, already marching towards the road, her arm in the air for a taxi.

Chapter sixteen

Caitlin and Lee scrambled out of the taxi as near as the driver could get to her house – what with a fire engine, an ambulance and two police cars parked up in front of it – and stared at the scene in front of them.

Caitlin tried to speak, but white fear snatched the breath out of her bone-dry lungs.

Theirs was the final house in the terrace, and the kitchen window, which looked out onto the side road, had been flung wide open, the pineapple-print curtains soaked and flopping out like damp streamers. Blue emergency lights bounced off the white stucco paintwork, but there were no lights on inside, apart from an eerie glow in the hall. Firemen stood around packing up equipment while two ambulance crew were consulting with neighbours and a police officer.

She stumbled towards the front door, her mouth acid with fear. The house was her sanctuary, her safe place in the world, where she protected her little family. She felt violated herself, seeing it so broken. What the hell had happened here to need all three emergency services? She'd phoned Scarlett from the taxi but all Scarlett had said was, 'Just get back here, OK? It's not as bad as you think,' which immediately made Caitlin panic about how bad it was. Her chest felt as if it were full of frantic birds fighting to escape.

Lee whistled. 'Normal Friday night round at yours, is it?'

Oh, why – why – *do I end up screwing up every good thing I get?* she thought. It felt wrong now, to be tipsy and happy. 'Sorry, Lee,' she said over her shoulder, 'I need to get in and check the kids are OK. It's fine for you to go home. You don't have to stick around if you want to get back.'

'I don't mind, if there's anything I can help with?'

'No, honestly, it's ... Oh God, who's on the phone *now*?' Caitlin answered it without thinking, and the voice on the other end managed to send dual waves of despair and relief through her.

'Caitlin? What the hell's going on?'

'Hello, Patrick.' She carried on down the path, swinging her gaze around, trying to see the children.

He sounded agitated. 'I've just spoken to Joel! He says he's destroyed the house – is that right? Or is this something he's seen in a film?'

Caitlin pushed past the paramedics to get inside the house. Where were the kids? Upstairs? In the ambulance? 'It's not as bad as it sounds.' Except it was: the house smelled weird and there were big puddles of water in the hall. She looked round in horror – what had happened?

'There's no need to start stressing out,' she said, trying to hide the panic in her voice. 'It's all under control. Patrick ... hang on a second.' Caitlin pressed the phone to her neck, and turned round. Lee was still hovering by the front door, and she was torn between not wanting to seem rude, because it was decent of him not to do a runner on seeing all this, but not really wanting the kids to meet him. He was the reason she hadn't been there when they'd needed her.

'Lee, just go,' she whispered. 'I'm fine here.'

'Really! This place looks like a bomb's hit it.' He stepped gingerly into the hall. 'Can I make some tea, or . . . clean up? I feel bad this happened while you were out with me . . .'

'Who's that?' said Patrick on the end of the phone. She clamped it against her chest to muffle it properly.

'Chaos can happen here whether I'm in or not, believe me.' *Where were the kids?* The birds in her chest were fighting up to her throat now. 'It's sweet of you, but I can cope. Please. This isn't the best time . . . you know. To meet my children?'

Comprehension dawned belatedly on Lee's face. 'OK. I get it. But . . . I feel bad leaving you with this mess.'

'Good. Feel bad, but . . .' It had been such an amazing evening. But if felt like it had happened to someone else now. 'I'll call you later, OK?'

'OK,' he said, reluctantly, and turned to leave.

Without a backwards glance, Caitin rushed into the sitting room, where a policewoman was taking notes. The sitting room looked fine: just as she'd left it.

'Mrs Reardon?'

She could hear Patrick yelling, 'Caitlin, Caitlin!' into the phone.

'I'll call you back,' she said, and hung up on him.

'Where are the children?' she asked the policewoman, who pulled an 'oh dear' face and led her outside.

Nancy, Joel and Scarlett were sitting in the back of an ambulance round the corner from the house. Nancy and Joel were wrapped in blankets so only their faces were visible, and

Scarlett looked as if she'd been thrown into a swimming pool. Her wet hair was plastered to her head, and she seemed shell-shocked.

Caitlin threw her arms open and bundled Nancy and Joel into her body, smothering their heads with frantic kisses and hugging them tightly. Fierce love coursed through her, along with roaring guilt that she'd let this happen.

'I'm sorry, Mum—' Joel started, but she shushed him.

'Doesn't matter, doesn't matter.' Her heart was beating so hard she wondered if they could feel it. 'So long as my babies are safe.'

They stayed cuddled up until Caitlin felt able to speak calmly. The policewoman, she knew, was standing at a respectful distance waiting to talk to her, but they didn't have all night to hang around, not on a Friday. She wiped her nose with the back of her hand, hitched Nancy up onto her hip and stepped back, trying to look stern but understanding.

'So,' she said, 'what happened?'

'Oh my God, Mum, it was—' Joel started, then Scarlett glared at him.

'What happened,' said Scarlett, 'was that *someone* . . .'

'Was trying to help,' protested Joel.

'. . . decided that he wanted a bath before bedtime. But first he wanted some scrambled eggs.'

Caitlin kept her arms around Nancy, and swung her gaze between Joel and Scarlett. Something was going on here. Joel squirmed.

'But *someone* didn't tell me that he was running a bath for himself, or,' Scarlett drew her spine up, which was an effort while wrapped in a blanket, 'that we weren't supposed to use the toaster on the side in the kitchen.'

'Sorry, no, I should have said,' said Caitlin. 'It's faulty. I've been meaning to put it out for the skip for weeks now.'

It was one of Patrick's last instructions, before he left. 'Either get that toaster mended or throw it out, it's dangerous.' Caitlin pushed that to one side in her head.

'So while we were in the kitchen stirring the eggs in the pan, we smelled this disgusting smell from the toaster,' Joel butted in. 'Because Scarlett had put bread in it? And it was burning? And starting to catch fire? So we had to put that out, and then while we were doing that, we started to feel drops of water running down the light bulb, like it was raining inside . . .' He stretched out his hands, and squinted quizzically upwards, miming indoor rain. Caitlin suppressed the urge to throttle him.

'And then the kitchen ceiling fell in,' said Scarlett bluntly.

Joel spun round, disappointed with her lack of theatricality.

'What?' Caitlin's mouth dropped open.

'The fireman reckoned you must have had a bit of a leak already, but the water got under the floorboards in the bathroom, and that's above the kitchen, isn't it? Whole ceiling came down. Plasterboard, plaster, water. The lot. The fireman reckons it's a rebuild job because . . . something about the electrics?'

'Oh my God,' breathed Caitlin. 'You could have been killed!'

'And all the lights went off,' Joel added. 'Like that – pow!'

'Stop enjoying this,' she snapped. 'This is serious.'

'Thank God most of it missed me. No idea how we weren't hurt. I ran upstairs to get Nancy and I left him downstairs in the porch for safety.' Scarlett wiped her brow. Flakes of plasterboard clung to her dark hair. 'When I came down with Nancy, he'd phoned 999 and his dad.'

'But why are the police *and* the fire brigade *and* the ambulance here?'

'Because the lady asked which service I required and I said, all of them. I thought it was better than to ask for the wrong one?' Joel suddenly looked very small in his blanket. 'I thought that was the right thing to do. Then I phoned Dad. Dad can fix it, can't he?'

'*I* can fix it, Joel.' Caitlin made an effort to control herself. An awful thought was forming in her head: had Joel done this on purpose, to get Patrick back here? To shove his parents back together? After all, it worked in the movies.

'Did I do the wrong thing?' His lip was quivering. Sometimes the big-boy face slipped, and she remembered that it wasn't that long ago since Joel had left his last tooth under his pillow for the tooth fairy.

'No. Of course you didn't. I wouldn't know who to choose either.' She bounced Nancy on her hip and checked she was still OK. Nancy's thumb had gone back into her mouth, an old habit she'd stopped nearly a year ago. She hadn't spoken but she was staring around her with a haunted expression.

'You're all right, aren't you, Fancy Nancy?' she murmured into her hair. Nancy smelled of baby powder and warm biscuits. Caitlin didn't know where she was getting the strength to hold her for so long but she couldn't bear the thought of putting her down. She felt a powerful urge to make her speak.

'What an adventure! Seeing the policemen!'

'Just like your book!' said Joel, helpfully. 'Eh, Nancy? Like you were reading? Shall I go and get the book?'

Nancy shook her head, and hid her face in Caitlin's neck. Caitlin wondered if they were too far out of the house for her to feel safe talking, but even so, *she* was there, Mummy holding her safe in her arms. She was there with her. Her body ached to hear just one word. *Please God*, she prayed urgently, *don't let this have made our house unsafe for Nancy now. Please don't let her be too scared to speak at home.*

'Just tell me you're OK, sweetie pie,' she whispered in Nancy's ear, stroking the fine strands of strawberry blonde hair away from her ear. 'Just whisper, I'm OK, Mummy. I'm OK, Mummy. Can you say that for me? Please?'

In response, Nancy buried her face further, pressing her sharp nose into Caitlin's soft neck. She shook her head, and trembled.

A year ago, Caitlin thought, Nancy would have babbled excitedly about the firemen, about the hoses, about the rain inside. She'd have been sitting in the driving seat of the ambulance, pressing buttons. Caitlin had video of Nancy on her phone, doing just that, at a fete on holiday. It wouldn't have occurred to her to be scared with her big brother and her mummy around.

Now, she seemed frightened of her own voice, and what it might say. And Caitlin couldn't fix it. She couldn't even find out what it was that had stolen her baby's voice, and she'd have given up her own voice just to hear Nancy tell her what was wrong.

She stroked Nancy's hair and tried not to cry herself. 'Don't worry, darling, everything's going to be all right.' She knew she was babbling, but she couldn't bear the silence. 'It's all going to be fine.'

'Mum, your phone's ringing,' Joel pointed out. 'And that policeman wants to talk to you.'

Caitlin had only just persuaded the policeman that all was well, when her phone rang again.

'It's my other law enforcer,' she said, giddily.

The police officer gave her a strange look.

'Sorry, nervous hysteria,' she explained. Thank God he hadn't breathalysed her. Caitlin had never sobered up so quickly in her whole life, but even so there was still more cider than was strictly responsible swilling round her bloodstream.

'Hello, Patrick,' she said. 'It's fine, everything's under control.'

'What the hell happened?'

'I'm not entirely sure yet.' Might as well admit it, she thought. Get it over with. 'I was out.'

There it was. Said. Caitlin held her breath.

There was a small pause, then he asked, with audible tightness in his voice. 'Where?'

'Does it matter, Patrick?' Which Caitlin knew immediately was the wrong response.

'It wouldn't be any of my business if my children hadn't been left at risk, but they were. So I'm asking.'

'I was out having a drink with a friend. Scarlett's sat with them before, from work, remember? She's reliable. This was an accident.'

'Anyone I know?'

'Sorry?'

'Whoever you were out with?'

'Patrick! I don't have to answer that.'

There was a pause. 'I think you just did.'

Caitlin rolled her eyes. Patrick had a way of setting invisible traps in conversations that she always, *always*, walked right into. 'Can we talk about this later? I've got quite pressing issues right now. Like, what I'm supposed to do next.'

The fireman was standing talking to the police officers. And the paramedic. Were they already compiling a report for social services? Her heart thudded in her chest: all she really wanted was to tell the kids everything would be fine and slam the door on everyone. Patrick used to sort all this stuff out. The parking fines. The arguments with the neighbours about parking space. 'Patrick? It's not illegal to leave your kids with a babysitter, is it? Or is it?'

Her voice was dangerously high.

'Of course not. Calm down, Cait. First things first. Have you checked there's no danger from the electricity supply? Have you turned everything off at the fuse box?'

She gazed up at her blank-eyed house. A shudder ran through her body; she'd let it down. She'd let Granny Joan down, not maintaining it properly. 'The lights are off – the power must be out. There was some kind of emergency light in the hall. I think the firemen brought it.'

'Check the firemen have turned off the electricity at the main fuse box and then if there's a problem with the water, turn the stopcock off. You know where that is?' Patrick's tone was calming, and for once, Caitlin didn't hear any judgement in it.

'No!' It came out as a wail. The reality of what could have happened was beginning to sink in. Joel, dead under falling plaster. Nancy, in the bath as it collapsed. She felt sick.

'It's under the sink. Calm down, Caity. Just take deep breaths. You've had a shock.'

Patrick hadn't called her Caity in years. Not since Nancy was born. The nostalgia made her ache.

'If the fire engine's there then I'm sure they'll have done all that,' he went on in his reassuring voice. 'But check. Make sure you ask someone what precautions have been taken.'

Caitlin looked up and saw the main fire officer coming her way, with a female police officer. 'Oh God. They're coming to talk to me. They look really serious.'

'Do you want me to talk to the police?' asked Patrick, and Caitlin didn't want to feel the relief she did, but it flooded through her. 'I'll talk to the police, while you get the fire officer to show you the stopcock and everything.'

Caitlin felt a tug on her coat; it was Joel. He was trailing his blanket like a Superman cape. 'Is that Dad?' he whispered and his eyes were heartbreakingly bright. He needed to speak to him.

She didn't hesitate. For herself, yes. For the children, no.

'Yes, it's Dad. Do you want to say hello?'

'Yeah!'

The policewoman and the fire officer were watching as she handed the phone over, and the policewoman gave her a sympathetic smile.

'Always better when you've spoken to Dad, eh?' she said, and Caitlin nodded unhappily.

'Hi, Dad!' Joel sounded remarkably cheerful. 'Everything's under control! I did everything you said!' He listened intently as Patrick talked and the relief on his face, the sense of the world being right again, made Caitlin's chest hurt. 'OK, I'll tell her. Bye, Dad! Dad? Dad? Are we going to see you this weekend with Auntie Eva and Bumble and Bee?' There was another long pause. His face struggled to look brave; the smile was his drama club one. 'OK. OK, love you too Dad, bye.'

'Dad's going to sort everything,' he informed her as he handed the phone back, and even the fire officer looked like he might cry.

The next hour passed in a blur as Caitlin was marched around the house to examine the damage. There was a lot of it. The short version was the bathroom, and the kitchen, and very likely the entire wiring system would need to be replaced.

'Looks like it's never been done,' said the fire officer, who did a bit of DIY in his spare time. 'Very old system. Did you buy the house to renovate?'

'No, it was my granny's,' said Caitlin. She was holding Nancy's emergency services story book, which had miraculously escaped ruination in the kitchen. 'We knew we had some work to do on it, but it was always such a big project. Never enough time, or money . . .'

They gazed at the sodden remains of the kitchen ceiling, swept into piles against the ruined worktops. Bits of the bathroom above were visible in the half-light. Caitlin had no idea how you were supposed to fix things like this. Where did you start? How did you trust any of it not to fall apart again? Part of her wanted to walk away from the whole mess and pretend it hadn't happened, but she knew she couldn't. She'd been trusted to look after this.

Her safe place. And now there were strangers standing in the ruins of her kitchen. Something peeled away inside her soul.

'Well, at least you've been saved the cost of ripping it out,' said the fireman. 'I'd find somewhere else to stay for the next week or so – this isn't safe for curious kids.' He paused. 'I'd say you've got at least one of them. We nearly took him home on the fire engine!'

Caitlin didn't answer. She didn't know what to do next. None of the girls at the café had any space – and she felt like she'd taken advantage of Scarlett enough already – and her mother was a seriously last resort. At least the kids didn't have to be in school for a week or so, but she needed to get in to work . . .

Her phone rang and Caitlin indicated to the fire officer that she'd have to take it.

'Good luck,' he said, and waved goodbye.

It was Patrick. He didn't waste time. 'Get in a taxi and go to the Holiday Inn. I've booked you rooms for tonight.'

'What?' Out of habit, Caitlin started to protest, but Patrick talked over her. 'I don't want the kids spending the night in a damp house with no electricity. That's madness. Just get over there, and have some supper and put them to bed. Make it an adventure. I'm trying to rearrange my work schedule to come down tomorrow but obviously it's gone eleven on a Friday night so . . .'

'There's really no need, Patrick.' It was just words though. The sound of someone saying, 'It's all going to be fine' was falling on Caitlin's ears like angel song. She wanted to be able to sort this out, but she knew her limits.

'Of course there's a need. It's booked in my name and I've prepaid, so don't worry about the bill. Do you need me to call you a taxi too?'

'No! Listen, that's really kind but I think I'm going to have to take the kids to my mum's.' She gazed around the hall. One side was absolutely fine; the other was wrecked. It reminded her of photos of the Blitz – perfect sitting rooms with a wall torn off. 'It's not ideal, because I've got to be in work but maybe I should just take them there tonight?'

'What, to London?'

'Yes.'

'Why? Do you want to do that?' He sounded baffled. 'Why do you always go for the nuclear option? You plan to drive there now? You want to spend a week being career mentored by your mother while she gives the children secret literacy tests and rewrites your CV?'

Patrick knew her too well. And anyway, she couldn't drive, she was way over the limit. Caitlin didn't know why she'd even said it. She felt exhausted.

'Well, no, but where else can I go?'

He sighed. 'Eva would be happy to have you stay with her. You were taking the kids there for the Easter holiday anyway, weren't you? I'll give her a ring, let her know what's happened.'

'What?' Caitlin bolted upright. 'No, honestly, it's—'

'You can't stay in the house.' Patrick was in full practical mode. 'I'm not happy about the kids being in there with dodgy wiring, and it's going to need assessing for insurance. Maybe we can drive down for an hour or two this weekend to look at it together.'

'What about Eva? What if she has plans?'

'Caitlin, she'll want to see you if she's there, and if she's not, I'm sure she'll be happy to give you a bed in a crisis like this. She really enjoys seeing the kids. She told me so. And it'd be good for you to spend some time with her.'

Caitlin wasn't sure this was a hundred per cent true. Did she want to spend a week with Eva? Did she know her well enough to crash in that strange, quiet house for a week? Already the thought of it was making her tense up.

'Caitlin?'

Caitlin sank back against the hall wall and gazed around her. The damage felt like a physical pain. It was more than a house to her, more than the 'pretty fireplace' that Patrick thought she was so hung up on. The small rooms had comforted her when she'd woken up in someone else's life aged twenty-one – knitting with Granny Joan in the cosy sitting room, walking a sobbing Joel up and down the full length of the hall in the middle of the night, sitting on the front step watching him waving at pigeons with his chubby hands. Dramatic, even then.

She touched the striped wallpaper in the hall. It had been there since she'd moved in, nearly ten years ago. God knew when Granny Joan had put it up. It was damp now, and would all have to come off.

'Caitlin? Are you listening to me?'

It was changing, she thought. Everything was changing, whether she liked it or not.

'Yes,' she said. Joel and Nancy were sitting with a police-woman, and she could hear the sounds of 'I Dreamed a Dream' floating through the air. Not from Nancy, though.

'Good,' said Patrick. 'I'll see you tomorrow. Now get the kids to bed.'

'Thanks, Patrick,' said Caitlin, then added, because it was true, 'I appreciate this.'

There was a pause. 'I'm doing it for the children,' he said, and the stern voice was back. 'For God's sake, learn where your stopcock is, will you?'

Caitlin bit back a retort and hung up. She realised she was still holding Nancy's book. Jolly fireman, jolly ambulance crew and several jolly police officers were rescuing a selection of careless individuals from their own stupidity on the cover. Flames, floods, cats up trees – all manner of self-inflicted catastrophes, and none of the careless individuals looked anywhere near as wretched as Caitlin felt.

Chapter seventeen

'You know what the best part of that was?' Eva sat back on her bar stool as Alex returned from the bar with two cappuccinos.

'Was it my brief but informative introduction about the history of regional drama at the BBC Pebble Mill studios?' He put the coffee in front of her; he'd carried hers carefully so it hadn't spilled, although there was more froth in his own saucer than in the cup. Eva had saved seats in the window so they sat side by side, looking out at the weekend crowds strolling out of the venue. 'Or was it the way I'd primed my students to ask questions at the end, as if they were ordinary punters?'

'You mean those weren't ordinary punters?' She pretended to look surprised. 'You made nearly two hundred of your students turn up to an afternoon of television plays? On a Saturday? How big is your tutor group?'

Eva had been impressed at the turn-out for Alex's 'curated session', even more impressed by the knowledgeable programme notes he'd written about the drama commissions that crystallised an era. He spoke confidently in front of the audience at the beginning of the afternoon, took unruffled questions at the end along with a retired script editor, and raised some genuine laughs. The day had gone quickly, and yes, Eva was going to have to report to Anna that she'd had a very good time, although it was hardly a date, what with her sitting in the audience and Alex on stage in his professorial cord jacket, with a lectern and a retro microphone as a nod to the period pieces they were watching.

Or at least she assumed his cord jacket was a deliberate nod.

'There's only twenty or so. It was nice they all came.' Alex stirred four sugars into his coffee with a modest shrug. 'Mind you, it's part of their course, so they had to. They're a nice bunch, though – apparently they agreed to ask questions in case no one did, and I looked like Professor No-Mates.' He pushed his glasses up his nose and looked at her. 'And you met Becky!'

'That was the best bit I meant,' said Eva, solemnly. 'I'd started to worry she'd look just like me in her parka from behind, then she'd turn round and be like ET, under the hood. And it turns out she's . . . completely normal.'

Becky was actually very pretty, tall and barely thirty. Eva told her she'd been flattered to be mistaken for her, and when she'd explained why, Becky had giggled, nudged Alex and said, 'He's like his own *Carry On* film, he is!'

Alex's mouth twisted up at the side. 'There you go. So you had a good time?'

'I did. Thank you for inviting me along.'

'You're very welcome. And you're reassured that I'm a bona fide drama nerd who's really only interested in Mike Leigh's early work?' He waved his spoon at her. 'You notice I didn't say a single thing about anyone's private life there?'

'I did.' Eva looked down at her coffee. She didn't want to talk about that just yet. The real reason she was there. She was enjoying being out of the house, having a new experience – as herself, for a change, not Mick's wife or the pugs' owner. It had been a while since she'd flown solo like this.

It stung more than she expected to have it brought back to her that she was there for Mick. 'Is that why you invited me here? To convince me that I say yes to the diaries?' She looked up and met his eye. 'Am I the last wife to agree, then?'

'No!' Alex had been smiling affably but instantly his expression froze. 'No, not at all! I mean, I hoped it would set your mind at rest about my academic credentials, but . . . I wanted to ask you . . . I mean, no, sorry, came out wrong . . .' He took a deep breath. 'I thought you'd enjoy these films. That's all. No more than that.'

The programme was made up of dramas filmed before Eva was born. This was Mick's era. He'd assumed she'd be interested in today's programme because Mick would have enjoyed them. Or known the actors.

Eva pressed her lips together. She didn't know what to think.

'Well, since we're on the topic, I read them all the other night,' she said. Might as well deal with it. Get it out of the way.

'And?' Alex was peering at her, holding his cup in both hands. He was acting casual, but the level of coffee was dangerously close to spilling.

Eva drew a deep breath. It was like Mick was there, on the spare bar stool, watching them with his devilishly amused eyes. She'd struggled with the decision since she'd read the final line but kept coming back to what Alex had said the day he'd brought the diaries over: the diaries were Mick's voice, his own words after a lifetime of speaking other people's. He'd spent years crafting them, pouring his soul into the lines. What else could she do? It wasn't up to her to silence that beautiful voice because she didn't like some of what he said.

'If you can edit them the way you promised,' she said, slowly, 'taking out any very personal details, and making it Mick's conversation with the reader, then yes. Go ahead.'

To her surprise, it felt like a weight had lifted from her shoulders.

'Brilliant!' Alex reached over and grabbed her hand in thanks. 'Thank you! Thanks, Eva. Oh, buggeration . . .' The other hand that was holding the coffee cup spilled it, and they both lunged for napkins to mop the resulting slick of hot milk off the bar top before it slid over the side and onto Eva's bag.

'Sorry, sorry . . .'

His hand had felt warm on hers, and the instinctive gesture was so welcome Eva was glad of the fluster to distract her.

'I didn't want to pressure you,' he said, patting ineffectually at the spillage. 'But Una and Cheryl have both agreed this week, so this is wonderful news. Wonderful! I can pass your consent on to the publisher, and to Roger?'

'Yes. Yes, do that. I'll email.'

They stopped mopping and looked at each other, neither sure what to say next. It was a clear moment, thought Eva. A turning-point. A bit like putting the first of Mick's jackets into the charity-shop bag, or taking their message off the answering machine. She was Mick's past now, alongside Una and Cheryl, but still here, moving forward.

As whom, though? Who was she now?

'Eva . . .' Alex began.

'Ah ha!' There was a voice behind them and a hand clapped on her shoulder. Eva felt herself being pushed together with Alex, their heads smooshing together in an awkward embrace as their shoulders bumped. 'The love birds! I thought I'd find you in the bar!'

She struggled to turn round, but it meant turning her body even further into Alex's. The contact pushed her nose into his jacket; he smelled of aftershave and coffee and tweed. A massive man with a big black beard was standing behind them looking thoroughly pleased with himself. That seemed to be his default look, thought Eva. Pleased with himself.

'So this is the lovely Zoe?' he went on, extending a massive paw towards Eva. 'Fantastic to meet you at last! I'm Gerry Crowther. I've heard a lot about you!'

'Hello. Eva Quinn,' she said, calmly, shaking it. She could hear Alex's faint groan at her side, but she didn't turn around. 'Pleased to meet you.'

Alex had a girlfriend. Called Zoe. Eva realised the shimmering feeling in her stomach was disappointment. *Stop it,* she thought. *Of course he'd have a girlfriend, he's an interesting, intelligent man. And he's not bad-looking either.*

'Oops!' roared Gerry Crowther and looked between the two of them. 'Have I put my foot in it?'

'Not at all.' Alex seemed to recover more quickly than he had done from the coffee spill. 'Eva, Gerry is an old colleague of mine from Lancaster University – we haven't seen each other in a few years. He's an American Studies professor. Gerry, Eva is a ... friend of mine. She's here for the film festival.'

Maybe he was being discreet about their project. Maybe he'd picked up on her fledgling independence. Whatever, 'a friend of mine' was sweet and right, and Eva felt grateful for it.

'So where *is* the lovely Zoe?' enquired Gerry. He set his glass of wine down on the counter next to them and heaved his bulk up onto the stool with a sigh. 'If that's not a leading question?'

'In Manchester,' said Alex, at the same time as Eva said, 'Well, I should be getting back, it's a long drive.' She gathered her bag and coat; she didn't want to hang around and hear about the lovely Zoe, or indeed, talk about Mick. 'Sounds like you two have some catching up to do! Nice to meet you, Gerry.'

'Don't go yet,' said Alex. His eyes registered disappointment. He reached out and touched her arm and this time it was a very natural gesture. 'I haven't asked you to fill in a feedback form.'

'Send me one in the post. I'll tick all the "excellent" boxes.' It reminded her. 'Oh!' she said. 'I've got a present for you.' She reached into her bag and pulled out a small metal circle: his missing bicycle clip. 'I found this in my hallway.' Eva made her expression serious. 'I think it might have come off my hoover?'

Alex took it. 'Thanks,' he said, and his amiable smile reached up into his brown eyes. 'And thanks.'

Eva met his gaze and held it. 'You were right,' she said. 'When someone has a voice like that, you need to let them speak.'

Eva drove home to The Quarry listening to music but not really listening at all. When she let herself back into the dark house, it felt quiet without the pugs to welcome her. Bumble and Bee were still up at the dogsitter's being spoiled rotten. She didn't turn any lights on, but wandered slowly through to the study, circling round and round in her thoughts.

Have I done the right thing? she kept asking herself. *Give me a sign.*

The diaries were stacked on the desk, and she opened the top one at random, flicking on the task lamp so she could read.

'*Meeting at National Theatre re a possible Shakespeare this autumn. At least I won't need any padding if I get Falstaff. Bit the bullet, and*

**phoned clinic. Shorter stay than last time, which
will be good. Dinner with Eva at The Ivy on
Friday. Find it hard to believe I've had to wait
fifty-seven years to meet a woman who can look
like that, talk like that, listen like that – and still
want to come home with me. Worry she's the last
hallucination of an old soak.'**

She frowned. She hadn't noticed that first time round. *The
clinic.* What was that? They'd only been dating a few weeks at
that point. If Mick had had a medical, she wouldn't have asked.
And he did have regular check-ups.

That's the sort of thing Alex will edit out, she reassured
herself. What possible interest could that have to anyone? A
well man clinic.

*Just the vultures who'd wonder if it was a drying-out clinic. Or
journalists digging up dirt on Tyson. Or any other insinuations you
should be protecting him from.*

She closed the exercise book, and flipped over a few pages
in her own diary, which she'd dug out to check a date against
Mick's. It was a business diary, each day crammed with tiny
writing, dates and times. Eva hadn't trusted phones not to
crash. That whole week, the week of Mick's mysterious clinic
appointment, she'd been back in London: meeting with
Simeon and the venture capitalists to negotiate payouts from
the business, then she'd met her old PA for lunch, seen the
finance director for a gossip, then been to a shop launch, haircut, PR launch at a bar, gym, drinks, lunch, blow-dry, breakfast . . . She flipped back, marvelling at the amount she'd shoe-
horned into her life without realising. Every day up to the day
she moved to Longhampton was jammed with appointments

and phone numbers, the pages marked with business cards from long-forgotten networking meetings. And then it stopped.

But her life was so much fuller once she met Mick, Eva reminded herself, even if her diary was empty. Fuller, richer, busier in a better way.

She flipped forward again to find the dinner at The Ivy Mick had mentioned. There: *dinner with MQ, Ivy 7.30pm Fri*. That night was like a film sequence in her mind: the black cab back to his club, then an early flight from City Airport to Galway to stay with his friend McCarthy for the weekend. McCarthy had a castle, and a whiskey distillery.

Eva couldn't shake the word 'clinic' out of her head. You didn't book a rehab clinic on Friday, then fly to a whiskey distillery on Saturday, did you? No. Mick had said he was sober, and she'd believed him. And what did it matter now? It didn't.

She picked up both diaries and moved them to the in-tray, and as she did, a folded piece of paper with EVA written on it in uneven capitals slid out, from where it had been tucked under a book.

Carefully Eva unfolded it: it was two drawings of the pugs from the previous weekend. Joel's dynamic cartoon-version of Bee, complete with flying cape and fluttering Bambi eyelashes, and Nancy's balloon Bumble. His head was the same size as his body and he had a tail like a piglet, but something about the way Nancy had drawn his round, anxious eyes, surrounded by soft wrinkles, and the tilt of his ears made it definitely Bumble, not Bee.

Eva sat down in her chair, in the darkness, touched. Her mind went back to the quiet time Nancy had spent with her dogs while Joel was clattering around the house with Patrick. The little girl and the patient pug, not talking but communicating. Nancy had lain gazing into Bumble's eyes, running her small hand along the furrows of his head, stroking his dark ears. She was talking to him without words, and he was talking back, delicately tapping his narrow paws on her arm, making his strange happy purr. And then she'd drawn his love.

Patrick and the children weren't coming for another fortnight. That's a long time, thought Eva, and felt surprisingly sad.

The phone rang on the desk, and she jumped. Who would ring at this time? She checked her watch. Nearly midnight. For the last few years she'd expected a call from the home, saying her mother had finally slipped away, but now there was just her and Patrick left. And the children.

She grabbed the phone. 'Hello?'

'Eva, it's Patrick. I didn't get you out of bed, did I?'

'No, not at all. Is everything all right?'

'Um, yeah – quick question, I know it's your birthday next week, but are you going away for it?'

'Yes, I think so.' Eva's forty-fifth, the one that Anna had decreed was the End of Phil's Youth, was on Thursday. Patrick didn't usually remember, let alone book in a treat beforehand. She was pleased; maybe seeing her more often had jogged his memory. 'I was thinking about it but hadn't booked anything. It's weird – I was looking at a few places last week and I'm sure prices weren't this high . . .'

'It's the Easter holidays,' said Patrick, as if she should have known.

'Oh. I didn't realise.' Right, so this was about bringing the children over, not her birthday. Or maybe the two were connected, somehow? But Patrick was talking again and something in the tone of his voice set Eva's 'little brother concern' alarms ringing.

'Listen, I wonder if I could ask a massive favour?'

She looked down at the cartoon pugs. Super-Bee was yelling, 'I'm pugalicious!' at some cows. The cows were radiating excitement with wavy lines round their heads. 'Of course you can.'

'There's been an accident at home – don't ask, I'm still getting to the bottom of it – and I can't have the kids staying in the house until it's sorted out.'

'Oh no! What sort of accident?' Eva had got up to turn on the main light, but sat down with a thump as her mind filled with horrors.

'Overflowing bath. Collapsed ceiling. It's not safe, basically.' Patrick sighed and she could imagine him running his hand through his hair. 'I've booked them into a hotel for tonight, but I thought it'd make the situation less stressful for Joel and Nancy if we could turn it into a surprise holiday – coming to stay with you, doing some fun things – while the house is fixed. If it's not too much bother,' he added.

'Of course! It's no bother at all! When did you want to come?' A thought occurred to Eva: who *was* coming – Patrick, or Caitlin? She hadn't really had a chance to talk to Caitlin properly since all this had started, and she still didn't know exactly what had happened between her and her brother. That could be . . . awkward, over a whole week. 'Will it be you? Or Caitlin?'

'Caitlin,' he said. 'Is that a problem? I'm going to try to get down to Bristol next week to sort things out with the house. She hasn't the first idea about builders.'

'No, it's not a problem. It'll be nice to, um, spend some time with her.' Eva pulled a face at the phone. What else could she say?

'Thanks, it's only for a few days.' Patrick's voice was tired but he was good in a crisis; he went into a sort of work auto-pilot. 'It's better than dragging them to London to Caitlin's parents.' He paused. 'I don't know how much Cait's told her mum about Nancy's . . . Nancy's speech problem, but I can imagine Lynne deciding she needs to fix it then and there, and while I'm all for pushing for better specialist advice, I don't know if now's the time to be stressing Nancy out any more than is necessary.'

Eva couldn't remember much about Caitlin's mother, other than she'd spent half an hour at her wedding to Patrick, telling Eva and Mick that she still thought Caitlin would make an excellent solicitor, and maybe Roger could give her some work experience? Mick had said it made a change from people asking him what it was like working with Peter O'Toole.

She picked up Joel and Nancy's drawings. A tight, warm knot of emotion rose in her chest. 'I'd love to see them,' she said. 'It'd be my pleasure.'

'Great. That's so great. Thanks, Eva.'

As Patrick was talking an email popped into Eva's inbox. It was from Alex.

She clicked on it automatically.

Just checking you got home all right. Thanks so much for coming along today, and for putting your trust in me. I am beguiled by Mick's voice, and we'll make the diaries his Oscar-worthy performance. AJM

'. . . about lunchtime?'

Eva gazed at the short message. Was Alex at home? Was he still in the bar with Gerry Crowther? Was he thinking of her, wherever he was, or was he thinking of Mick, of his future contract? She shook her head.

'Yes! Yes, that's fine. I'll look forward to it.'

'Thanks, Eva. You're the best. Speak in the morning.'

Eva leaned on the back of her chair for a moment, trying to process that burst of information and what it meant for her weekend plans and her fridge, but her eye was drawn back to her laptop.

Leave it till the morning, she told herself. But there was so much to do before Caitlin and the kids turned up, and she wouldn't get a moment's peace . . . Her fingers were already moving.

Thanks! I enjoyed it. And yes, I'm trusting you to make the stress of these diaries worth it. Hope you had a good night too – Gerry doesn't look the sort of bloke who turns in early . . . EQ

She clicked send and started tidying the desk, but Alex replied at once.

He's a sterling chap but in small doses! I'm sorry you felt you had to rush off – I had many more pertinent observations to make about the BBC. I also wanted to ask your opinion about an idea I'd had for the diaries, involving your input? What you said about voices gave me an idea. Maybe we could discuss it over another coffee. I'd be delighted to show you round the faculty here, or I could spill hot liquids over you nearer to Longhampton.

Something about the speed of his reply, the jokey tone between the lines, made Eva feel unanchored: the thought of

Alex sitting in his own study at midnight, surrounded by books, turning Mick's exercise books of secrets into lines of book text, factualising it, filtering it, his sensitive mouth turned down as he made notes, listening to the rise and fall of Mick's voice, watching the characters move around like chess pieces across Mick's small stage . . .

She stopped herself, surprised at her uncharacteristic burst of imagination. She didn't even know if Alex had a study.

I don't want to be personally involved with these diaries, if you don't mind. Editing, yes – public association, no. But we can talk about your idea. Let me see what my diary's like – I've got some family commitments coming up.

Eva sent it, then closed the laptop before he could reply. She didn't want to reveal any more of herself, not tonight.

And there was something else she needed to do before she went to bed. She ran her gaze around the study until she found two framed photos of her and Mick – there were hundreds, all over the house, identical and now, not quite the same to Eva's eyes. In the half-light, she took out the prints, and replaced them with Nancy and Joel's drawings, then put them on the desk where the children would see them.

When they came to stay, in the morning.

Chapter eighteen

Caitlin had only been a temporary resident of Longhampton for just over twenty-four hours, but it felt like longer.

It wasn't the town. Longhampton was nice enough – if you liked statues of famous cows, and shops that sold cushions embroidered with humorous quotes about cocker spaniels. And it wasn't Eva, who'd welcomed them into her house with the sort of graceful hostessing that made Caitlin wish she'd had five more minutes to salvage matching underwear and some ironed clothes from the house before she left. The kids seemed at home in Eva's clutter-free ski lodge; they'd barged straight in, heading for the yapping dogs, waving hands still sticky from copious in-car snacks and, in Joel's case, trailing snotty tissues. Caitlin had wailed 'Don't touch that!' three times before her coat was off. Eva had just smiled her serene smile and told her not to worry.

The thick crop of framed photographs on every surface, however, had been noticeably stripped back since Caitlin's last visit.

At least Joel's holiday cold gave her and Eva something neutral to talk about. Eva was gamely playing along with Patrick's 'surprise holiday' idea, and was far too polite to come straight out and ask what Caitlin had done to wreck their house. Caitlin felt stupid enough about the whole thing (Eva had probably never even left a tap running) and she didn't want the messier details getting back to Patrick. She'd already briefed the kids on the drive over to leave any explanations to her.

Not that she felt very happy about telling the kids to keep quiet about anything right now. Caitlin gazed at Nancy across the table in the ice-cream parlour – one of the few Longhampton cafés not populated with dogs eyeing up the pastries. In between spoons of mint sundae, Nancy's little cowrie shell mouth was tightly shut. She hadn't spoken since they'd left the Holiday Inn yesterday morning, and her eyes were wary. The speech therapist's exercises hadn't had any impact at all on her ability to speak outside the house.

'I think Nancy wants another hot chocolate,' said Joel, with a meaningful nod at his sister.

Caitlin gave him a sharper look than she would have done, had she been in a less self-critical mood. The therapist had warned against letting Joel do Nancy's talking for her, but it wasn't easy to stop him without hurting his feelings. 'Does that mean *you* want another hot chocolate?'

He looked wounded. 'No? Why?'

'Nancy?' Her heart sank as Nancy said nothing.

Joel sucked the snot up his nose with a revolting squelch and coughed.

'Why don't we see if we can find a bakery and buy Auntie Eva something nice for tea?' she suggested.

'Oh, there's no need,' said Auntie Eva, who was sitting right next to her. She hadn't said much but Caitlin assumed that was because her ears had sealed over after six solid hours of Joel recounting the plots of all the major Disney musicals.

'It's the least we can do now we've eaten your croissants,' Caitlin said with a pointed look at Joel. On the table, her phone rang. She groaned, and sent it to voicemail.

'Patrick again?' Eva's eyes, above her raised coffee cup, were pleasant but sharp. Not much got past her, Caitlin could tell.

'No,' she lied, because it was Patrick, ringing to check something or to tell her something. 'Unknown number.'

And *that* was the problem. Patrick. Longhampton, Eva, the kids – all fine. It was Patrick, from a distance of two hundred miles, who was wearing Caitlin's patience.

Patrick had phoned every fifteen minutes with instruction and criticism while they were driving to Eva's, then again when they were unloading the bags, and after that Caitlin had stopped taking his calls, but that hadn't stopped him texting. Caitlin was grateful – *beyond* grateful – that he was sorting out the builders and the home insurers. Every time she thought about the ruined ceiling, and the exposed floorboards, she felt drained. She'd offered to help, but Patrick made her feel that if it was up to her, it just wouldn't be done properly and he'd taken over everything.

It wasn't fair, thought Caitlin. Patrick couldn't play the 'you love your fireplace more than me' card at mediation, and then make out she wouldn't deal with the repairs properly. Where did he get this idea that she couldn't cope? Why did he assume she needed help all the time?

Was it because Eva was so competent, Caitlin wondered? She looked at her sister-in-law over the table. From what Patrick said, she seemed to cope with everything, from widowhood to business to dog training, with the same quiet assurance. Eva was looking a lot better than she had done the first time Eva had brought the children over. She was still thin, but her face had lost its pinched quality and she was wearing a stripy Breton top and tiny diamond earrings.

The biggest difference was that she seemed far more relaxed with the kids, managing to look enthralled with Joel's rambling, politely ignoring the droplet of snot hanging off his nose. Although maybe that was a side effect of spending a lot of time around actors.

Nancy was dividing her attention between Joel, her hot chocolate and Eva. She and her aunt, Caitlin noted, had the same pointy nose, and the same faint crease in their chin. She hadn't noticed that before.

'Would you like a spoon for that last bit of cream?' Caitlin asked, hoping for a response while Nancy wasn't concentrating.

It didn't come. Nancy shook her head.

'She doesn't need a spoon,' said Joel, quick as a flash. 'She can have Auntie Eva's, look – here!'

'Well spotted, Joel,' said Eva, and Caitlin saw a nice pinkness warm her face.

She started to slip her phone back into her handbag but couldn't resist a look to see if Lee had texted. At the thought of sweet, keen, non-judgemental Lee, Caitlin suppressed a shiver that had nothing to do with the gelateria's stern air-conditioning.

He'd phoned on Saturday morning to check everything was fine, and Caitlin worried that she'd probably overshared in her explanation. She'd only had about an hour's sleep; it had all tumbled out. But he hadn't seemed too put off by the chaos: he'd sympathised, sent her three sad-face emojis later, and told her to call if she needed any help. His mate Danny was an electrician, after all – he knew people who could sort her out.

See, Patrick, she thought. *I can cope.*

Caitlin's phone vibrated in her hand, and her pulse skipped, in case it was him.

It wasn't. It was Patrick: **Have you cleared time off work with Joanne? No point losing job when you go back.**

'Oh, for God's sake!' she said aloud.

'Problem?' Eva's eyes flickered sideways towards the children but Joel was engrossed in explaining the exact division of a chocolate flake to Nancy and wasn't listening.

They were sitting too close for Caitlin to pretend otherwise.

'Just Patrick checking I haven't been sacked.' Caitlin's irritation, already simmering with exhaustion and post-date euphoria, bubbled out. 'Has he always been like this?'

'Like what?'

'A compulsive micromanager. Who doesn't believe anyone can do anything unless he's issued personal, specific instructions.'

'I suppose he can be a bit of a perfectionist.'

Caitlin laughed at Eva's careful understatement. 'And the rest. Was he one of those little boys who had very complicated Lego models no one was allowed to touch?'

'He had a train set, actually. Quite a big one, in the spare room.'

'That figures,' said Caitlin. Round and round, with Patrick in charge of the points and the tiny passengers.

Eva went on, 'It's just how we are in our family, I'm afraid. Terminally organised. Patrick and I are both chronic list-makers, always have been. You probably know Dad was a doctor, so he liked routines. And Mum was a planner too – we even had a diagram for our Christmas tree.'

'A what?' Caitlin stopped fiddling with her phone.

'A tree diagram. Mum worked out optimum distribution of baubles, tinsel placement – you know. So every year it was identical, no matter what size the tree was. I only remembered that the other day, when I was going through Mick's diaries. He mentioned it – he thought it was a hoot.' An ambiguous expression shadowed Eva's face. 'Funny how different things can look when you see them through someone else's eyes.'

'A tree diagram.' Caitlin was impressed and horrified. 'Now *that's* controlling.'

'Well . . . I think Mum found order reassuring after Dad died. She wanted everything to be just as it was. Paddy's the same. He shows how much he cares by looking after people. He cares a lot, you know. About everyone.' She smiled. 'He means well. Even if he can be a bit bossy with it.'

'I never knew that,' said Caitlin. 'About the tree diagram.' No wonder his nervous tic had appeared when Joel and Nancy hurled tinsel and coloured lights at theirs, and she insisted on bringing out the battered homemade decorations they'd lovingly bodged together at nursery.

'So,' she began, hoping for more mad detail of Patrick's murky childhood, but Eva obviously wanted to steer conversation in a different direction.

'Tell me,' she said, 'what's the latest on the house?'

There was a slurping noise as Nancy reached the end of the hot chocolate with a straw, and another one as Joel sucked the snot up his nose. They'd been in the ice-cream parlour for nearly half an hour, which was about their maximum non-fidgeting capacity. Caitlin automatically clicked off a 'one-minute to bad behaviour' countdown and began gathering their belongings together. 'The insurance company is sending an inspector round next week,' she said. 'Patrick's trying to get time off to meet him and get some builders round.'

'From Newcastle? Aren't you going?'

'No need, apparently.' Caitlin pushed Nancy's hat towards her and mimed putting it on. Brilliant. Now *she* was resorting to mime too. 'Did you say there was a bandstand, Eva? Shall we go and look at that, Nancy?'

'But it's your house.' Eva frowned. 'Isn't it?'

Caitlin reminded herself to be diplomatic. 'Yes, it is my house, but Patrick thinks if the builders see I'm a woman, they'll rip me off. And I won't know the right questions to ask.'

Eva seemed to be processing this, struggling with – Caitlin assumed – Caitlin's rights as a homeowner and a woman, and her little brother who could do no wrong.

'It's easier, Eva,' she said, breezily. 'I've offered to help but he won't have it. And you can only offer so many times before you start to feel a bit useless.'

'Oh. I'm sure Patrick's just trying to save you the stress. It must be very upsetting, a house flood. And you've got your hands full with the . . .'

Caitlin caught a glass just before Joel swept it to the floor, swishing his coat on, and Eva looked amazed. 'How do you do that? It's like you've got eyes in the back of your head.'

'What? The children? Practice,' said Caitlin, grimly. 'Joel! Cover your mouth when you cough.'

'Sorry.' He made a show of coughing into his hand, in the manner of a tuberculosis patient. An older couple on the next table shuffled their chairs further away.

'Are we all done?' Eva sounded like a children's television presenter from the nineteen eighties, bright, cheerful and in control. 'If you head outside, I'll—' This time her phone rang in her bag and when she pulled it out, Caitlin saw her expression change. 'Oh, for . . .'

There was a brief flash of a very different, much less composed Eva. Caitlin could have sworn she'd just spotted an eye roll, a glimpse of impatient steel under the calmness.

'We're going to the bandstand! We're going to the bandstand!' Joel chanted.

'Give it a rest, Joel. Problem?'

Eva struggled with herself, then gave in to her irritation.

'Oh, it's just Patrick. Two missed calls and a text to remind *me* to remind *you* to phone your boss. And also reminding me to follow up on Nancy's speech therapy guidelines. And to check my own house insurance.' She paused. 'As if I might have forgotten to get any.'

'What with you being a grown woman, and all,' said Caitlin drily.

'His older sister, in fact.' Eva tutted, then blurted out, 'I used to carry spare dinner money for that boy, you know. In case *he* forgot.'

They shared an eye-rolling look, and even though Eva was the exact opposite of Caitlin's usual friends, Caitlin had the sudden urge to be her mate. In The Quarry, Eva came across as the absent host's wife, welcoming but definitely a support act, even now, to the man in all the photographs. Here, in the café, Caitlin wondered if she was seeing Eva the boss. There was a wry sense of humour about Irritated Big Sister Eva she hadn't expected. 'No instructions for Joel?' she enquired.

'Apparently not. Should I text back?' Eva raised her phone. 'Hand washing? Times tables?'

'Tell him he's got a cold and he's sneezing everywhere,' said Caitlin. 'That's if you're keen to find out how to cough correctly.'

Eva half laughed, half gulped and when she put her hand to her mouth to hide her reaction from the children, Caitlin suddenly saw Nancy in her eyes. Her guilty mischief.

It sent a sensation through her that was somewhere between hot and cold.

Chapter nineteen

'Maybe we should go out?' Eva had to raise her voice over the sound of Joel bellowing an assertive version of 'Let's Call the Whole Thing Off' in the hall. From the sound of thumping on the wooden stairs, he was improvising a tap dance to go with it. He wasn't exactly Fred Astaire. 'What do you think? Bit of fresh air?'

Eva and Nancy were in the study with the dogs, listening from a safe distance. Or rather, Eva was checking her emails for more questions from Alex, and Nancy was drawing Bumble, who was huffing and snoring by her chair. It was only for a few hours – Caitlin had gone back to Bristol with Patrick to deal with the builders – but Eva felt honoured that Caitlin, not Patrick, had asked her if she wouldn't mind babysitting for a few hours. It felt like a gesture of trust, and she appreciated it.

'Nancy?' Eva prompted her. 'Or would you rather stay in?'

On the other side of the partner's desk, surrounded by colouring pens, Nancy looked up and quickly looked down again. She didn't want to be rude, but clearly she didn't want to speak either. Her pen scribbled faster.

Eva felt stupid. They'd been happy in their shared silence up to that point, with the occasional secret glance when Joel had two or three goes to hit the right note. Now the silence felt like a third person.

Eva reminded herself of her own quietness, as a child. And she'd turned out fine, hadn't she? But even as she thought it, a small voice reminded her that there had been reasons for that: she had no one to talk to. Was that the same for Nancy? It wasn't something Eva wanted to think about, but the longer she spent with Nancy, and the more the little girl burrowed into her heart, the more Eva saw her own complicated internal dialogue and she hoped, so much, it wasn't the same.

She gazed at Nancy's head, bent over her page, her face hidden by her angel-fine hair, and wondered what her voice sounded like.

'Potato!' yelled Joel.

'Potahto!' he yelled back to himself in an American accent.

'Tomayto!' he roared in his own voice.

'Tomahto!' roared American Joel, amidst a ricochet of tapping. 'Let's call the whole thing off!'

Eva saw what Nancy was drawing, and in a flash of inspiration, changed tack.

'Bumble, what would you prefer?' She gazed at the pug. 'A hot chocolate from the café in the park? Or a walk to the book-shop for a book? But you have to promise not to get hot choc-olate in your wrinkles because it's very hard to get out. And you mustn't eat any books.'

Nancy giggled and scribbled something on her paper.

'Nancy? Do you know what Bumble wants?' she asked. It was easier to talk to Nancy without Caitlin hovering, needling for a sound, or Joel, answering for her. Eva never knew what to say to children, even on a good day; being quiet with Nancy had its upsides.

Nancy didn't reply, but Eva could see that she had started to draw trees and flowers around the balloon pug. He was being

279

led by a stick-figure girl in a red dress. Nancy. Slowly, Nancy drew some more figures in the picture. A lady with wild black curls, and a boy, and ... another lady, with ... short brown hair. And they were all holding hands.

Eva's throat tightened up.

Tentatively, Nancy looked up at her, then down at her drawing, as if she wanted to be sure Eva had got the message.

'The park? Good choice, Bumble,' she said. Her voice felt croaky. 'Maybe your spotty friend will be there. Did Bumble tell you he has friends at the park, Nancy?'

Nancy shook her head and though her lips were pressed together, her eyes smiled.

Eva leaned over and hoisted the pug onto her knee so he could look over the desk at Nancy. His pink tongue lolled.

'Bumble and Bee have lots of friends. There's a spotty dog called Pongo, and a grey dog called Buzz. And a very clever dog called Gem – lots of friends.'

Nancy didn't respond. Eva wondered if she was talking in too babyish a way for a four-year-old. So much she didn't know.

'And,' Eva ploughed on, 'they have great old chats just by sniffing each other. And they leave messages by sniffing ...' She was going to say, sniffing each other's wee, but she wasn't sure that was appropriate.

Before Eva could find a better way of explaining pee-mail, Nancy pushed the chair away from the desk, got down and came round to Eva's side, where she wrapped her arms around the dog and leaned against Eva, so she could rest her head against Bumble's wrinkles.

The soft warmth of Nancy's small body melted something inside Eva's chest, but at the same time the hollowness opened up again, as if her heart had been scooped out and replaced with longing. She leaned forward and breathed in the soft powdery smell of Nancy's hair.

The three of them stayed like that until the singing and thumping finished in the hallway. Then Nancy went to the door, and held out her hand to her auntie, with a broad smile on her heart-shaped face, and Eva felt the empty space inside her fill with something sparkling and alive.

Back in Bristol, the builder had been all over Caitlin's damp house, sticking his fingers into damp walls, sniffing damp air, making resigned noises. Now, in the ruined kitchen, he stopped walking, put his hands on his hips to stare at the ceiling, and pulled his lower lip over his top one in a manner that indicated a diagnosis was imminent.

Caitlin tried to catch Patrick's eye. She knew what was going to happen next: he was going to make that sucky-in air noise, and ask them which cowboys had done the last job in this house. Three different builders had looked at their kitchen when they'd first thought about extending it – Patrick was the only person Caitlin had ever met who had actually got three quotes instead of just going with the first one – and all of them had done the hands on hips/air-sucking/cowboys routine. It had become their running joke, to the point where any bodged job in the house got the same response, sometimes with a semi-obscene trouser hitch.

Once upon a time. Not now.

Patrick refused to look around. He knew Caitlin was trying to catch his eye, but his face was stony. It had been stony since she'd arrived at the house, half an hour late.

'You didn't reply to my text,' he'd hissed, while the builder and the bloke from the insurance company were exchanging details. 'You could at least have let me know you were going to be late, and not involved in an accident.'

'*Which* text?' Caitlin had tried to keep her voice down. 'There were so many! And I was driving.'

He'd glared, that dark, you've-disappointed-me look, the one that made her feel simultaneously bolshie and guilty. 'You know what I mean.'

'I'm here now. The traffic was insane. Anyway, you always told me not to text and drive.'

Patrick's phone had rung at that point, which gave Caitlin a moment's moral respite. Clearly, it was work, as ever. When he'd checked it, grimacing, he'd slid it back into his back pocket, and said, 'I don't suppose it matters what I think any more. But I worry. I can't help it. I worry, Caitlin.'

'Why? Are you suggesting I can't look after the kids on my own?'

He'd gazed at her, said nothing, and Caitlin had stomped into her ruined kitchen, where the insurance man stood with the builder, waiting for her and Patrick to finish their domestic and get on with the inspection.

'So, what's the verdict?' she asked, to get at least one question in before the men started talking over her head. It was her house, as Eva had reminded her. It *deserved* her responsibility.

The builder yanked down a frond of peeling wallpaper, three redecorations thick, and a chunk of plaster came down with it. Caitlin's spirit sagged.

'Mice?' she suggested, trying to lighten the atmosphere.

'No, water damage,' said the insurance man, patiently.

The builder at least had the grace to look amused. 'Upstairs it's not as bad as it looks,' he said, at which Caitlin's heart lifted, only to plunge again when he added, 'but you're going to need to dry out and replaster this ceiling here, plus you've got water in your electrics, and that's going to need going over properly.'

'How long are we talking?' Patrick butted in.

The builder sucked his teeth – finally! – but Caitlin didn't have the energy to check if Patrick had seen. 'Depends on how soon we can start, how many men I can get on it.'

'Roughly?' Patrick persisted. 'Our kids need to be back in for the new school term starting.'

'It just has to be safe,' Caitlin interrupted, keen to stay in the conversation. 'Don't worry about decorating, or anything. I just don't want them electrocuted.'

The insurance man's eyebrows rose into his comb-over.

The builder sucked his teeth. 'Ten days? If we get dehumidifiers in and—'

'Great. Ten days. Does that work for you?' Patrick turned to her.

Something in his business-like manner made Caitlin suddenly sad, not angry. 'Yes,' she said. 'As long as we're here for the eleventh.'

'Good. Fine. So, Steven, can you run me through the claims process again?' He turned to the insurance man and the two of them began discussing forms with all the passion of men who really enjoyed admin.

Caitlin wandered into the hallway. Nancy's bike was leaning up against the wall, silver tassels dangling from the handlebars, and Caitlin was swamped by a bitter longing to turn the clock back to last year, when Nancy never stopped chatting and

Patrick still *liked* her and Joel was her happy, sunny boy, and she could love them all with her uncomplicated motherly love. How had that gone?

Caitlin closed her eyes. Seeing Patrick today was weird. She'd forgotten how he could look handsome one minute, then she'd do something without knowing what, half the time, and his eyes would go so cold the handsomeness vanished.

She took her phone out to check everything was fine with the kids. She didn't want to make Eva feel useless, the way Patrick's constant checking did to her, but Nancy not talking made everything so much more stressful. She'd told Joel to ask regularly if Nancy needed the loo, and she now wore a special ID necklace, but Caitlin still had nightmares about her wandering off. Plus, she didn't know how Eva would react if something went wrong.

There were no texts, much to her relief.

She started a quick hello to Eva, but as she was typing a text from Lee popped up.

Half day at work just finished now dont suppose ur around for a cheeky drink? J

Caitlin's face flushed as a clandestine heat swept through her.

Yes, she thought. *Yes, I would like a cheeky drink. That would take the sting out of today nicely.*

Yes! She typed. **Where do you fancy? Got to be quick though, need to get back for the kids' tea. Cxx**

'Caitlin?' Patrick coughed. 'Can you run through the flood again for Steven?'

'Of course.' She slid her phone into her back pocket. Granny Joan would approve of her getting on with her life. That's what

she'd said, right here in this kitchen, many times. She just
hadn't realised that 'getting on with her life' would be a repeat
activity.

'So, which one of my favourite literary aunties have you turned
into then? Aunt March? Aunt Em? Or just a Wodehouse
general-issue bonkers old aunt?'

On the other side of the bookshop counter, Anna leaned on
her elbows and looked conspiratorial.

'Less of the old, thanks,' said Eva. 'Or I'll take my two
customers away.'

Nancy was perched on a toadstool in the children's section
with Bumble and Bee, carefully blowing bubbles towards the
open windows so Bee could slam her paw against them; Joel
was in the television and film section, looking at books about
the West End stage.

'It must be going well,' Anna observed, 'if you're being left
in charge on your own.'

'Only until six. Caitlin promised she'd be back in time for
supper and bed. I just have to keep them amused and alive
until then.' Eva cupped her hands around the mug of tea Anna
had offered. She felt warm inside. Tired – after being woken at
6 a.m. by Joel's discovery of an old hunting-horn left by a long-
forgotten partygoer – but warm.

'She didn't want them to see the house in a bad state,' she
added. 'And Patrick will be there, and I guess that might not be
ideal . . . so I'm in charge. By default.'

'They're not fighting, and they're not covered in Ribena.
Take it from me, that's a win so far.'

'Thanks,' said Eva and grinned. 'Caitlin told me to keep

moving on the hour, to stop them getting bored. Seems to be working so far.'

'And how's the house-sharing going?' Anna hooked an eyebrow.

'It's fine. No, not fine – good.' Eva surprised herself. 'I mean, yes, it's a bit of an adjustment being woken at all hours, and I have to lock myself in my study now and again to escape Joel – do ten-year-olds ever stop asking questions? I mean, ever? – but it's quite nice having someone around in the evenings. Caitlin really isn't how I remember. I supposed I expected her to be much more . . . angry about Patrick but she seems pretty zen. That's her, really. Pretty zen about everything.'

What had she expected? An angry child-woman in stripy tights? A sobbing divorcee? The bouncing, tipsy bride from their kooky homemade wedding? This new Caitlin was none of those: if anything, she was like one of the interns in Eva's old office – smarter than she made out, less confident than she dressed.

'Has she thrown any light on why she and Patrick are splitting up?' asked Anna.

'Nope. They're more in touch than ever. Patrick calls Caitlin all the time, with reminders. And he calls me to remind me to remind her. And then he reminds me to remind myself about things I've already done. It's actually quite irritating. I'm sure he never used to be like this.'

'Maybe he thinks you need looking after too?'

Eva shook her head, mock-sadly. 'And to think I used to live in London, and fly on big aeroplanes three times a week.'

In the Film and Entertainment section, Joel was now explaining tap dancing in some detail to a bemused pensioner holding a book about Fred Astaire. Eva made a mental note to remove him in five minutes.

'So, yes,' she said, raising her palms. 'Everything seems to be . . . fine.'

'Good.' Anna patted her affectionately on the arm. 'I knew it'd work out,' she said. 'People come into your life for a reason. Joel and Nancy . . . they're here to remind you that you're very much part of a family. And maybe . . .' She tilted her head.

'Maybe what?' said Eva.

'Maybe they're here to help you decide what the next stage of your life is going to be.'

'Meaning?'

'You know.' Anna gave her a significant look. 'Your own family. Have you thought any more about . . . what we were talking about?'

Bumble grumbled, and Eva's attention was drawn to the children's section; Nancy whispered into Bumble's ear, then sat back and picked up the bottle of soap bubbles again. Something tugged deep inside her. 'It's too late for that,' she said, as much to herself as to Anna.

'You know that for definite?'

'I'm being realistic.' Eva couldn't take her eyes off Nancy, and the delicate way she was concentrating on the bubble hoop. 'I'm forty-five next week, I'm not going to meet anyone in time now. My eggs are probably powdered.'

'Well, you don't need to *meet* anyone, necessarily. Why don't you get a check-up? Then you'll know one way or another.'

Eva turned her head. Anna's expression was serious.

'I've been thinking about it since I last saw you – it stirred up a lot of memories for me. The way you talk about children, it feels as if you need permission one way or another, so why not ask your body? What's to lose? If it's too late, you can accept it's out of your hands and if it's not . . .' Anna shrugged. 'You'd be a fantastic mum. And you'd cope.'

'I don't think I'm cut out for early mornings,' said Eva, but the truth was, after the experience over the past few days of the house ringing with children's laughter and excitement, now she suddenly didn't know if she cared about early mornings. Without warning, something had flicked on inside her, watching Caitlin supervise the children's slapdash toothbrushing, or when she sat on the edge of Nancy's bed, reading her stories. Eva suddenly felt acutely aware of the experiences about to slip through her fingers, experiences she hadn't known even existed, really, until now. The door was closing fast but there might still be time, just, to squeeze past it, if she made up her mind now. Right now. Today. In the next seventy-two hours. To flip the rest of her life in a totally new direction, or lose that chance forever.

And that went against every single rational instinct in Eva's body.

'But I'm on my own,' said those rational instincts, for her. 'And I'd get mistaken for their granny, and . . .' Her voice trailed off as Nancy looked over from the children's area and blew her a stream of perfect soapy bubbles. She waved, and Eva sensed the imaginary child in her head pummelling on the inside of her mind, desperate to be heard.

I can't ignore it, she thought. *I can't ignore this.*

'Don't rule it out because it's not going to unfold in exactly the way you expected it would,' said Anna. 'Life isn't like that. It doesn't care whether you had a plan. You've got money, time, your health – lots more than most people. And you've got support. So many people who want to see you happy.'

She smiled, and Eva suddenly felt disorientated with the options open to her. It was only now Mick had gone that she'd started to realise how much their life had revolved around his choices: when they got up, what they ate, who they spent time with. She hadn't minded, because she'd wanted what he'd wanted anyway, but now the world stretched out in front of her like the magic-kingdom map on the wall of the children's section: options, all of them hers to pick, spiralling off into the distance. But every choice led her away from where she was now.

'Oh, just do it,' said Anna. 'Stop caring about how to be perfect, and see what's possible. And if it is too late, you've always got these two to lavish all that love on.' She slipped out from the counter, nudging Eva with her hip, and marched over to Nancy on her toadstool.

'Ooh, Nancy!' she exclaimed. 'You've found our magic bubbles! Do you know the secret?'

Eva saw Nancy's head instantly drop at being asked a direct question by an unfamiliar adult, and without thinking, she crouched down to her level to support her.

Her knees clicked ominously but she ignored them.

'Does Bumble know the secret?' she asked. 'Can you whisper to him, then he can whisper to Anna?'

Nancy shook her head, still clutching the bubble tube, but when Eva rested her hand lightly on her back for reassurance, she raised her head, heavy like a flower on a stem, enough to look up at Anna.

Anna crouched down too; she was easy around children, and had much younger knees. 'The secret is . . . you can blow your wishes into the bubbles! Shall I show you how?'

Nancy hesitated, and looked across at Eva for reassurance. She nodded, encouragingly, and Nancy offered Anna the tube.

'Thank you!' Anna dipped the wand and looked mysterious. 'You just make a wish, and blow very gently into the bubble so your wish goes into the magic and you let it go . . . There!' A stream of pearlescent soap bubbles cascaded into the air.

Nancy's eyes widened then she smiled, delighted at the prettiness, and for a breath-catching second, Eva thought she might speak. She didn't, but the toothy grin she gave Eva made her heart swell and lift and spin like one of the magic bubbles. And it said more than words could.

It said she was there as Nancy's trusted adult. She was her auntie, her protector, and they'd just shared a special moment: a moment of magic they both believed in.

'Are you going to have a go now, Nancy?' she asked.

'Go on,' said Anna. 'Put a wish inside one.'

Nancy blew a fat bubble, very carefully, and it floated up towards the shelves. The three of them watched it, until it popped. Nancy's face was serious, and her eyes, Eva thought, suddenly lost their giggliness and seemed sad.

What had she wished for? Her parents back together? To be home again? For everything to be normal?

She laid her hand on Nancy's head and wished she could pull the sadness out, like a thorn from Bee's paw.

'Do you want to take this home?' Anna offered Nancy the tube with great solemnity, and then winked at Eva over her head. 'I think we might have some more, to give to Auntie Eva. She has some birthday wishes to get practising.'

In the pub with the pool table, Caitlin closed her eyes and let the cool cider slide down her throat. 'I needed that,' she said, with a sigh.

'You've nearly finished it,' Lee pointed out. 'You sure you can't stay for a whole pint? What good's a half?'

They were in a corner table; he'd kissed her cheek when she arrived, and they were sitting close enough for their knees to be brushing, but the ghost of a more passionate kiss hovered between them, as touchable as a third person.

'No, I've got to get going in a minute.' Caitlin checked her watch. Time with Lee sped past, unlike the minutes she'd waded through with Patrick. 'I said I'd be home by six, so Eva doesn't have to get stressed about tea. I'm surprised she hasn't called already, actually.'

'Sounds like she's coping fine.' Lee grinned. 'Why don't you stay? We're playing a gig tonight in town – I can get you an Access All Areas pass.'

'Tempting.'

'Then be tempted!'

'No, I've got to make a move.' Caitlin wanted to stay but she also needed to get home to make sure the kids really *were* fine this time. 'This was a lovely bonus to my day. Wish I could stay longer.'

'I do too.' Lee met her gaze, and the attraction in them made her shiver. 'When are you next back?'

'Joel and Nancy have got to be in school for the eleventh, so that weekend,' she said. 'Although . . .' A thought occurred to her. 'I'll have to come back before then to sign off some building work, and Patrick will be starting his weekend with the kids so . . .'

The children would be safe with Patrick. Meanwhile, she didn't have to report anywhere or to anyone. She could stay out as long as she liked. With whoever she liked. 'Friday? I'll have to call in at the house but we could have lunch, and . . .'

She trailed off. A cheeky glint appeared in Lee's eyes and Caitlin's stomach flipped.

'And . . . ?' he prompted. He curled a finger around hers, finally, and electricity tingled up her hand.

Caitlin hadn't felt so weightless since she was a student. Blood rushed to her head, then zipped round other parts of her body.

'And . . . it's Friday.' A seductive smile curled round her lips. 'Who knows?'

Chapter twenty

'It's like we're in a restaurant. But . . . we're on a train!'

Joel spread a hand towards the white napkins and silver cutlery, then picked up a cup and displayed it on his palm: next to him, Caitlin fought the urge to grab it before it flew off in the direction of the businessmen dispatching a full English in steely silence.

'Put. It. Down,' she hissed.

'Yes, it's a dining car, it's both.' Eva glanced at the menu. First Class Pullman breakfasting clearly wasn't the new experience for her that it was for Caitlin, Joel and Nancy. 'What are you going to have?'

'Can I have different kinds of eggs?' said Joel, in wonderment. 'Like . . . scrambled *and* fried *and* poached?'

'Of course. If you ask the waiter nicely.' Eva shook out her napkin, then turned to Nancy, even tinier than normal in the big leather seat next to her. To Caitlin's surprise, Eva shook out Nancy's napkin and tucked it into her T-shirt. Nancy beamed shyly, enjoying the ceremony.

'What would you like, Nancy?' Eva pointed at the menu. 'What about eggs? Or some cereal?' She pulled an outraged face and said, 'Or kippers? Eurgh! Bee likes kippers.'

Caitlin watched as Nancy leaned in to study the menu, unselfconsciously twisting Eva's fine gold chain in her fingers.

It so wasn't what she'd expected just weeks ago – Eva chatting to her kids in such a relaxed way. Not that she'd turned into a playgroup helper overnight – that morning she'd already used the words 'inconsequential', and 'de trop', and she never got down on the floor with them without flinching and doing that odd, apologetic smile. But Caitlin could see a bond forming between Nancy and her auntie, and it was because Eva talked to Nancy the way she talked to her ridiculous dogs.

Caitlin could see Eva employed the same narrative ramble she directed at the pugs, with gaps for Nancy to nod or point or smile. It had bugged her at first, that Eva put her daughter and her dogs on the same level, but slowly she realised that the lack of real pauses and the silliness made it easy for Nancy to communicate. Eva was guarded with adults, but when she spoke to her pugs, her face softened with an unexpected tenderness; she was the same with Nancy. She caught every flicker and shadow of Nancy's expressions, just like she watched her dogs' squashed faces speaking wordlessly to her – and she understood.

A year ago, Caitlin knew she'd have sniggered at that kind of crazy. Now, she didn't. The speech therapist had warned her it might be a long haul to coax Nancy to speak in public, and with Big School looming in September, every adult that Nancy could communicate with was beyond precious to her.

'Look at me!' Joel had made his napkin into a hat and was balancing it on his head. The businessman opposite unfolded his newspaper with a cross flick of the wrist.

'Joel, calm down.' Caitlin made a mental note to spend some proper time with Joel during the day. He was getting louder and louder, and her mother had mouthed 'ADHD' at her the last time they met – on one of his 'quiet' days.

They were heading to London to meet Lynne for her regular Easter Day Out with her grandchildren. It was always educational, and not just for Nancy and Joel. Caitlin hadn't slept a wink: her mind flip-flopped between all the things that could go wrong, and how best to handle the revelation that Joel had nearly destroyed Gran's house. On top of that, Caitlin was worried about how Nancy would react, going back to London. She'd gone over and over the weeks leading up to Nancy's refusal to talk and her instinct was that it had started then, just after their holiday. Caitlin couldn't shake the feeling that maybe there was something there that had scared her. Maybe she wasn't doing the right thing in taking her back, even if it was for a special treat.

The waiter reappeared with pots of coffee and trays of food, and Joel dived enthusiastically into his many eggs.

'So, Eva! What time's your appointment with the publishers?' Caitlin asked, leaning over to cut Nancy's toast into strips.

Eva had a date in town too, and she was an entirely different person in her 'going to London' clothes: a plain but clearly expensive pencil skirt, a heavy silk shirt in a colour that made her skin glow, and that long gold chain. She suddenly seemed more in focus. Even her hair, blow-dried sleek, made her hazel eyes smoulder above her strong cheekbones. Today, unexpectedly, Eva looked like the wife of a film star, the director of a business, and Caitlin was a bit in awe.

'We're meeting at eleven,' she said. 'The publishers want to run through their plans for Mick's book – publicity and so on. Cheryl and Una will be there. And Roger will be coming along too, Michael's solicitor.' She smiled, bleakly. 'I don't think I've got much to contribute, but Cheryl and Una will have some ideas, I'm sure.'

So Cheryl Murray would be there. That explained the uprated outfit. 'How about your editor? Is he going?'

'Yes, he's just emailed me to say he's on his way – quite a funny email, actually. Alex doesn't know whether or not to tell Cheryl he used to have a poster of her on his bedroom wall when he was at school.'

'How long ago was that?'

'Long enough for it to be a definite *don't* tell her,' said Eva, drily.

'Good advice,' said Caitlin. 'That's why you're going, to offer *him* advice.'

'Thanks.' The corners of Eva's eyes were creased under the concealer, Caitlin noticed. As if she hadn't slept much either. 'I hope it won't take too long. I just want to make sure they're not planning anything tacky.'

'Well, you can always go shopping when you're done!' She sat back, pushing another couple of pieces of toast at Nancy. She wasn't showing any outward signs of panic about going to London but Nancy was now heartbreakingly good at hiding things. 'You must miss the clothes shops, stuck out here in the sticks. After being part of that scene.'

'Funnily enough, the clothes were the least interesting part of my job.' Eva changed the subject. 'So you'll meet your mum, have the day with her, and I'll see you back in Paddington when? Five? Are you sure that gives you enough time?'

'Plenty,' said Caitlin. 'They'll be looking forward to whatever they get to eat in First Class on the way back. Thank you, by the way.'

Breakfast on the train had been Eva's treat, along with their First Class tickets, and taxis at each end. Caitlin was grateful; cash always seemed to evaporate in the holidays, and although she could ask Patrick for a top-up, it would come with a lecture about budgeting. And that would lead to another conversation about the house and right now, Caitlin wanted to blot it all out of her mind until she had to go back to Bristol to see how it was all going.

'The pleasure's all mine.' Eva smiled. 'I'm glad we could share an adventure. It'll be nice to see your granny, won't it?' she added to Joel.

He shot a swift glance at Caitlin. 'I think so,' he said, but didn't sound too sure about it.

'Yes, it will,' said Caitlin, but she wasn't sure either.

Two hours later, Eva perched gingerly on a low sofa in the reception area of Mick's publishers, and eyed her reflection in the masses of plate glass. Her plastic security pass was hanging askew on her lapel. She tweaked it straight.

It read: **Mrs Eva Quinn**. Mrs Michael Quinn III, she thought, ironically. There was no sign of the first two Mrs Quinns – no hairspray on the air, no squeak of distant airkissing. Eva wondered if someone should have co-ordinated them. Was it odd that she didn't know? Was there some kind of etiquette about keeping in touch with your late husband's other ex-wives?

The receptionist smiled blandly. 'Hannah won't be long.'

Eva made a 'no problem' noise, and glanced around the reception walls, lined with glossy celebrity autobiographies; familiar, comfortable faces smiling from under gold lettering. In nine months' time, Mick would be up there with them. Which version of him would they choose for the cover? she wondered. The sexy young rebel with the bad-boy quiff? The tanned prime-time soap star? Not Barney the Baker Mick, that was a small relief.

Not her Mick. Their Mick.

Eva smoothed her skirt. It had arrived in a Net-a-Porter box over the weekend: she didn't want a repeat of her last trip to London when her frumpy outfit had said everything she was trying to hide inside. Today, her nerves were covered up in MaxMara. Eva had always embraced the potential of the right clothes to blend her into her surroundings, or act like armour. Her mind slid back, despite itself, to the last time she'd seen Cheryl and Una, standing at Mick's graveside, the surreal highpoint of the most surreal day of her life. All those strangers, grieving for a different man from the one she'd lost. That had been when Mick had started to slip away from her, she thought, her eyes fixed unseeing on a biography of Sir Terry Wogan. When the anecdotes in the eulogy could have been about someone she hadn't met, but they had. She'd sat in her pew feeling that waking-up-from-a-dream feeling, sensing details already slipping away.

'Mrs Quinn? Hello, I'm Hannah, Trudy's assistant?' A friendly woman appeared from nowhere, dressed in polka dots. Eva guessed her age at about twelve. Hannah pushed open another glass door, waved Eva through and set off ahead of her, clumping along in the same flat brogues Caitlin wore. The ones that made Eva feel about a hundred.

The meeting was in a glass-sided room. Even before Hannah knocked and entered, Eva could see that Una was in full flow: everyone around the table was smiling and nodding and looking faintly windswept.

One solitary butterfly of panic fluttered up her chest. Roger wasn't there. He'd promised. Alex was though, cleaning his horn-rimmed glasses. He raised a hand of welcome and Eva felt relieved to see him.

Then he made a tiny wink towards Una, and she had to press back a smile as she followed Hannah in.

'. . . and the real success story for us has been blow-dry bars, walk-in no-appointment bars where clients can pamper themselves before a big night out, for a set price. The stand-out success in that has been my signature cut . . .' Una's diamond rings sparkled under the office lights as she waved her fingers around her signature pixie cut. Eva had to admit it looked fabulous. Una must have been at least sixty-five and looked younger than she did.

'Eva!' A woman Eva didn't recognise leaped up from the table. 'We haven't met but I'm Trudy Hastings, I'm looking after Michael's diaries. Thank you so much for coming! You know Una here, of course, and Alex . . .'

'Hello, darling,' said Una, and clasped Eva's upper arms with small, strong hands. She delivered a kiss to each cheek, in a cloud of Opium edged with cigarettes. 'Nice to see you again.'

Eva was aware of glances being exchanged just out of their field of vision.

'Hello, Una,' she said. Eva had nothing bad to say about Una. What was there to say? She'd have ended up running a chain of salons with or without Mick's divorce settlement. Una was smart, sartorially and financially. She'd probably negotiated a different royalty rate from hers and Cheryl's.

And this was the woman Mick chose first, thought Eva. *This was what my husband initially thought the rest of his life would be like. What do she and I have in common – apart from him?*

The doubts she'd managed to reason away began to rise again, slowly, in the back of her mind. Another butterfly flapping around her chest, and another, and another.

'Sophie's our Marketing Director, and Bryony, our Publicity Director . . .' Trudy ran through the other names and Eva pinned them mentally to each chest like gameshow stars. An old work trick. Publicity, Marketing . . . this wasn't giving her a good feeling.

'And of course you know Alex . . .'

'Hello!' Alex rose from his seat, moved round and gave her a quick peck on the cheek. It took her by surprise, but it didn't feel wrong. 'You look very elegant today. Are you going on somewhere else?'

'No, I . . .' Eva started, and realised he was teasing. 'Maybe,' she said instead. 'Keep your coffee away from me, please.'

'Hannah, can you check reception again?' Trudy checked her watch. 'Cheryl's assistant phoned to say she was running late,' she explained. 'She has to get here from Heathrow.'

'I have to leave by one.' Una tapped her pen on the table. '*I've* got to get to a product meeting in Clerkenwell – we're launching a multi-tasking styler,' she added. 'It's called The Una-versal.'

Everyone smiled politely. An assistant reached out for a pastry from the selection, felt the silent scrutiny of the room, and withdrew her hand.

After twenty minutes' polite waiting, with no sign of Cheryl, Una insisted on the meeting starting, and so Trudy began.

'Right, let me run you through our initial plans for making *Quinn* the celebrity biography event of the year.' She smiled, and a prickle of foreboding ran across Eva's skin. Celebrity? Not theatre? Or arts?

She glanced over at Alex and saw his face was diplomatically blank.

'Let me hand over to Bryony, who's already got some plans fixed . . .'

'Hi, everyone!' Bryony raised her hand in welcome, and her bracelets jingled down her wrist. 'So. OK. Everyone loved Michael Quinn. He was my mum's first crush, he was the voice of my kids' babyhood, he's one of those national treasures everyone feels they knew, but!' Her eyes sparkled. '*These* diaries will be revealing a very different side to him. One everyone's going to want to read. And we have a wonderful secret weapon in the form of you guys!'

Eva made herself smile back, even though she could feel herself pulling away. 'When you say *very different* . . . How do you mean? His humour? His observations – I mean, about the way theatre was changing, or television?'

Bryony stopped passing out pages. 'Yes! Um, sort of . . .'

That was a no.

'If you just let Bryony explain I'm sure she'll put your mind at rest,' said Trudy, quickly.

That was a double no. Eva opened her mouth to speak, but didn't know how to phrase her protest, and Bryony carried on.

'To break it down – Una, we felt it would be most impactful to focus on the iconic seventies style that you two created in your early years. I'm thinking of that amazing photograph of you in the sheepskin gilet and Mick wearing your jeans – we want that, in a nutshell.'

Una nodded. It was a seam she'd mined often enough in her own publicity. 'We're going to talk more about picture rights, aren't we? Because, you know, inspired by Mick's daft diaries, I was looking through my drawers the other day and I found a whole box of photos from our first house . . .'

Bryony clapped her hands together. 'Amazing! Perfect!'

Trudy smiled reassuringly at Eva. Alex didn't look up.

'Cheryl's the LA years, obviously. I've been working with her publicist to secure some spots on key talk shows, e.g., Loose Women, Graham Norton, etc. She's happy to talk about the effect of fame on their marriage, as that comes up a lot in the diaries. I think that's going to be very exciting and really emotional.'

Exciting and emotional. Coke-fuelled and messy, in other words. Eva shrank from the mental images. Not her Mick. Not her man.

Oblivious to her discomfort, Bryony turned to her. 'And finally Eva, the theme of your "years" of the diaries is of a happy retirement, a focus on the next generation, even. The "grandad" years.'

The word caught her off-guard, grazing against a raw nerve.

'What? He didn't *have* grandchildren.' Or did he? She glanced over at Una, who was checking her phone, unconcerned. 'I don't think, um, Tyson . . .'

'Tyson's not having kids any time soon,' said Una, without breaking text. 'If you know what I mean.'

'Speaking figuratively,' said Bryony. 'I mean all those children Michael entertained with his Barney the Baker programmes – he was a sort of surrogate grandfather! It's a wonderful full-circle end to the story.'

'Yes, actually I think this is a period a lot of people will be interested in,' interjected Trudy. 'You've got the readers who know Michael Quinn as a hell-raiser curious about his retirement, and the people who only knew him as Barney the Baker curious about his rock'n'roll past. It's perfect.'

'You make him sound like two different people.' Eva's voice sounded stiff, even to her.

'Well, in a way he was, wasn't he?'

She looked round the room, at the faces watching her reaction, waiting for her to offer up some anecdotes too. Una's were well-practised: Hamlet, Harrogate and hairspray. Cheryl probably had an assistant checking her PR spreadsheet, deciding which stories of LA excess to wheel out this time. But Eva's memories felt too precious to share like that. She didn't have enough to spare. And all these things made her seven years with Mick feel like . . . like nothing.

She looked over at Alex; he was staring down at his agenda. On purpose. She felt betrayed – by him, by Roger, by Mick, by everyone. This wasn't what she'd agreed. The disappointment felt like acid in her stomach.

Eva opened her mouth to speak, but closed it again, afraid of what might come out. But then why was she so afraid, a voice asked her. Who is there left to protect?

I don't want to be here, she thought. *I don't want to agree to any of this. I can't.*

Eva had never walked out of a meeting before, even bad meetings, but now she had a powerful physical need to leave. Mick would have said, *this is bollocks, I'm off*, but then he was Mick and you could get away with that kind of twinkly-eyed rudeness when you were a man. She had to leave on a good note. One that didn't make her look obstructive or rude, but which gave her time to think. But she had to leave.

'Sorry,' she said. 'I'm very sorry, but this isn't what I agreed to. I need to reconsider my position.'

A ripple of surprise went round the table but Eva wasn't listening. She pushed back her chair, and walked out.

'Eva!'

She turned. Alex was jogging down the corridor. His hair flopped over his face but his flushed cheeks were more down to self-consciousness than lack of fitness.

'Wait!' He held out a hand. 'Don't run off. I've got something for you.'

'I don't think I want it,' she said. 'Whatever it is.'

'Don't be like that.' He seemed genuinely upset. 'I'm just as disappointed as you with that meeting. It's not what I thought it was going to be at all.'

'No?' She gazed at him shrewdly.

'No,' he said. 'It isn't.' He tried to smile but failed. 'Look, can we go somewhere more private?'

'Why? So you can spin me more bollocks about your serious intentions but really check to see if I've got any photos of me and Mick on a celebrity cruise?'

'You're angry, and I understand, but please . . .' He paused. 'Then you can tell me to sod off, if you want.'

Eva wanted to tell him to sod off then and there, but somehow she couldn't.

'Fine,' she said. 'You can buy me a latte in that coffee shop over there. But if you spill it, I'm leaving.'

As they left the building, a taxi pulled up and a tall woman in a short skirt stepped out. Eva watched her adjust her flowing hair, then pull a pair of shades over creased eyes, before she let an assistant open the door for her.

It was her husband's second wife. And she hadn't even recognised her successor.

'I just don't see why I have to be involved at all. None of this has anything to do with me – I'm not a "celebrity wife" like Cheryl. Or even Una.'

They were in the Starbucks over the road, at a table for two. Alex looked straight at Eva. His eyes, behind the glasses, were intelligent. Deep brown, flecked with gold; she'd never looked so closely at them before, but the table was very small. Their elbows were nearly touching.

'Tell them you don't want to be involved in that side of things. But you know what? The irony is that you're the wife readers will identify with.'

She groaned. 'Come on.'

'No one knows you made a million quid on your dotcom sale. To your average reader, you're a normal woman who met a famous heartbreaker and changed his life. And it was real. You didn't sell your wedding to *Hello!*, you didn't have a trashy divorce.'

'And?' She looked straight back. 'Whose business is that?'

He lifted his hands. 'People who want to believe in love. You can tell from the way Mick writes about you that he adored you. And you were the one who finally understood him.' Alex lifted his hands – carefully, so as not to knock anything over. 'That's a happy ending.'

'You don't need a happy ending in a serious memoir.' Eva scrutinised him. 'Is that what this meeting was about? To break it to me gently that it's going to be full-on rehab and alimony and . . . oh, for God's sake. No, Alex. Why are you even trying to sell this to me?'

Alex rubbed his nose. 'Trudy seems to have a rather different emphasis at the moment but we're working on it.'

'Well, you keep working,' said Eva. 'Because I'm not going on Loose Women to talk about Mick's imaginary grandchildren.' Just saying it made something wrench inside her. Surrogate grandfather. He could have been a real grandfather. If they'd . . .

Stop it, Eva.

She let her gaze travel across the café, to a table where a little girl was eating a cupcake, accompanied by her mother and granny. She had hair like Nancy, in thin bunches. But unlike Nancy, she was chattering away, her face alive and her voice bubbling without a pause.

Was Nancy all right in London? Was she coping? Was she whispering in Caitlin's ear? She envied Caitlin that. The precious words Nancy hid in Caitlin's ear, instead of blowing them into silent bubbles.

'Eva?' Alex was looking at her, curious.

'Sorry?'

'Are you all right?' he asked. 'You look like you're crying.'

Across the room, the girl giggled – a pretty sound – and the words came out of Eva's mouth before she had time to think about whether Alex was the right person to tell.

'Nancy – my niece – can't talk.' Saying it made her realise how normal it had become and how horrific it was. 'Well, she *can* but only to her brother and her mum, and not always then, if she's stressed.'

'Why's that?'

Eva shook her head. 'They don't know. She's been referred to a speech therapist – there's nothing physically stopping her, no traumatic event they can identify, apart from her parents' separation but they've handled that as well as anyone can.'

Alex looked sympathetic. 'Poor kid. How does she cope?'

'Surprisingly well, actually. She points, and she smiles. And she talks to the pugs.'

He didn't laugh. 'They're great listeners, cats and dogs.'

'Caitlin left them with me for a few hours last week while she went back to Bristol. I took Nancy and Joel to a bookshop, and my friend gave her some bubble mix. She told Nancy it was magic bubble mix, and you could blow your secrets into it.' Eva felt her throat closing up. 'Nancy takes it everywhere with her. She's got it today, in her little travel bag.'

'Cute.'

Eva started to say yes, then changed her mind. 'No, it's heart-breaking. I keep finding her hidden away in corners, with Bumble and her bubbles.' She dug her nails into her palms. 'She sits there, blowing bubbles so carefully, watching them float away. And when they burst, it's like her little heart's breaking, then she blows more. So carefully. I want to ask her what she's wishing for, what secrets she's blowing into those bubbles, but she can't tell me.'

'She might not tell you even if she could speak,' said Alex. 'Secrets are secrets.'

Eva looked up at him. 'Four-year-olds shouldn't have secrets, should they?'

'No. But we all did, didn't we? Didn't you?'

Yes, she'd had secrets. And that was why she worried about Nancy. Little girls shouldn't have secrets.

'You obviously care a lot for your niece.' Alex stirred sugar into his coffee.

'I do. She's a sweet girl. I didn't realise how funny a kid could be, without even speaking. And her brother's a treat.'

'You never wanted children of your own?' He asked lightly, but asked all the same.

Eva twisted her face. 'Funny how no one ever asks parents whether they ever thought about *not* having kids.'

'Hey, I'm not a parent. I get the same question.'

'Then you know how annoying it is.'

'True. But I'm nosy.'

She laughed. 'You are. I don't know why you're asking me when you've got my husband's diaries in front of you.'

'That's him. I'm asking *you*. Did you want children?' Alex looked at her over his coffee cup, and she felt an edge to his curiosity – was she betraying Mick by saying this?

Again, the words slipped out. Maybe it was being asked about her own opinion that caught Eva off guard. 'Yes, I would have liked a child. But maybe not enough. Mick was straight with me about not wanting more, I appreciated that. We *chose* not to. It's a different decision from not being able to have them.' Eva felt the effort in keeping her voice bright.

Alex was gazing at her, and she knew he was seeing through her nonchalance to the complicated layers of emotion underneath. He'd read that telltale line in the diaries; did he think, like Mick had done, that she lacked a natural maternal yearning? Was he judging?

'And you?' Eva jabbed back, to deflect attention. 'Any family plans? It's different for men, though. You've got another twenty years to decide.'

'Not really. I'm thirty-eight. Apparently men have got a sell-by date too.'

'And what does . . . was it Zoe, think?' Her cheeks heated.

'As you heard me tell Gerry, Zoe moved to Manchester for work last year, so I literally have no idea what her family plans are,' he said, evenly. 'For what it's worth, I'm like you. I'd like a family but I don't think my world would feel incomplete if I met someone who didn't want children.'

'I suppose it's less easy for men to go it alone,' said Eva. 'You don't need the turkey baster but . . .'

'We don't have the oven.' He looked wry. 'Back to nicking them from outside supermarkets, I guess.'

Eva started to laugh, guiltily, then stopped. 'Or being a godfather.'

'Yup.' He looked as if he was going to carry on, then said, 'Sorry, I didn't mean to get too personal. I think it was your niece . . . What a sad situation.'

'We'll get through it. Silver lining is that I'm getting to know her. We just have to find our own way.' She smiled.

'Good. Anyway, I've got something for you.' He pushed a flat parcel across the table. 'Don't get excited, it's just a token.'

'What for?'

'Your birthday. It's this week, isn't it?'

Eva felt warm. 'Thank you. How did you know?'

Alex pulled a 'doh!' face. 'Because I've been reading about your birthday celebrations every year?'

'Oh yeah.' Eva unwrapped it: it was a slim book of modern sonnets, by Michael Symmons Roberts.

'I don't want to sound like a stalker,' he said, 'but you did tell me you read English at university. I thought you'd enjoy these. You told me that, by the way,' he added, 'I didn't read it in the diaries.'

'Thank you,' she said. She had told him. They'd talked about habits they'd got out of; hers had been reading poems. His had been listening to albums all the way through. 'That's . . . very thoughtful of you.' She squinted at him. 'It's pointless to pretend it's my fortieth, isn't it? You know me better than I know myself.'

'I think you know yourself pretty well,' said Alex. And he smiled, in a way that made Eva wonder, suddenly, if she did.

Chapter twenty-one

Lynne was waiting for Caitlin at the entrance to the London Transport Museum, in the middle of Covent Garden. She was deep in conversation with a pair of American tourists, and from the brisk way she was pointing at the South Bank, and then towards the City, then getting out her own Oyster card and waving it, Caitlin guessed she was restructuring their day's sightseeing activities into a more efficient schedule.

It was a big concession that her mother had agreed to meet them in Covent Garden, and not at the Science Museum or the National History Museum, her first choices. Like Piccadilly Circus and Oxford Street, Covent Garden wound Lynne up. It was full of unfocused students on gap years and tourists not making the most of their limited time in London. Caitlin also wondered, gloomily, if Lynne saw the student Caitlin in every young girl with stripy tights and Docs, and felt the urge to remind them about contraception, and the negative effect gastro-enteritis could have on its efficacy.

'What's Granny saying to those people?' Joel tugged her sleeve. 'And do we have to go to the museum? Can't we watch the robot man? He's amazing.'

'No, the museum will be fun! There are old buses. And old carriages from the Underground.'

'But we've been on those in real life. Why do we have to go on old ones?' He pulled his glum face. 'Will Granny test us again? Like she did on the dinosaurs?'

'Just use your imagination and pretend you're there in Victorian times.' Caitlin squeezed Nancy's hand. It was more to reassure herself than Nancy; she needed to know she was there, safe, by her side. Since she'd stopped chattering outside the house, Caitlin found herself reaching for physical contact more.

'I'll do my best.' Joel heaved a sigh.

'Try, for me.' Caitlin found a quiet spot, out of Lynne's line of sight, and bent down to Nancy's level so their noses were nearly touching. 'Fancy Nancy, are you all right?'

Nancy nodded. She'd been sparkly on the train, eating welsh cakes with marmalade *and* jam, but now her expression was watchful, like a baby owl.

'She's fine,' said Joel. 'She's wearing her special shoes.'

They all looked down, and admired Nancy's shoes with the sequinned flower on the toe.

'I know you're feeling shy,' Caitlin went on, softly, 'but it would really, really make Granny's day if you could try to say hello to her, maybe when we're somewhere quiet? Just hello. That's all.'

She hated herself for asking, and for the flicker of panic that went across Nancy's face, but Caitlin knew the alternative would be her mother needling all day, trying to trick a word out of her. Not from one-upmanship, but to prove they weren't trying hard enough, and that the speech therapist and Caitlin and Patrick and the other internet experts Caitlin had read up on were wrong. With Lynne, there were *always* solutions. Always.

'You don't have to if you don't want to,' she went on. 'But it would make me very proud, and it would make Joel happy too.'

'Yes,' said Joel, 'and if you don't want to, you can tell me and I'll tell Granny.'

'No,' said Caitlin, with a quick glance. 'We want Nancy to talk to Granny on her own.'

'But why? If Nancy can't talk to Auntie Eva, why would she talk to Granny?'

'Because she knows Granny much better than Auntie Eva,' Caitlin started then realised that was a conversation she didn't want to get into.

'That's silly,' said Joel. 'Auntie Eva's much easier to talk to than Granny. She doesn't ask stupid questions like "What do you want to be when you grow up?" and "What was the last book you read?" Granny asks me that every time I see her. She never remembers what I said last time.'

'Joel,' warned Caitlin. 'Not now.'

'I'm just saying.'

'Well, some things are better if you just say them in your head.' Caitlin stood up.

Nancy was already staring at her flowery toes, silent.

Come on, Nancy, she thought. *For me.* The American tourists were marching off in the direction of the Royal Opera House, and Lynne Hardy was heading their way.

Lynne saved her first pep talk until the children were running round the piazza after lunch, chasing pigeons and running off their chocolate brownies. Her first pep talk for Caitlin, anyway; she'd already told Joel what a great career civil engineering would be, to his polite bemusement. Nancy hadn't yet said, hello. To be fair, thought Caitlin, she hadn't had a chance to get a word in.

Lynne leaned forward on the metal café table. It wobbled on the cobbles and annoyance crossed her face briefly. 'Is this a good time to have a chat?'

'It depends on what you want to chat about,' said Caitlin, warily.

'I've been speaking to . . .' Lynne started, the table tipped again, she frowned. 'I've been speaking to a friend of mine about your situation.'

'Mum, it's really . . .'

'Your dad and I are concerned that you haven't taken any legal advice about protecting your interests during this separation.' Lynne clasped Caitlin's hands. 'I admire you for wanting to keep things amicable with Patrick, but he has every right to half of Gran's house. He could force you to sell it. I don't want to scare you, but I'm not sure you realise how vulnerable your position would be if Patrick decides to get an aggressive lawyer on the case.'

Caitlin took a deep breath. 'Why on earth would he want to get an aggressive lawyer? The mediator worked fine. We're working on a financial settlement.'

Lynne's eyes, dark and sharp behind her glasses, darted between the children and Caitlin. She obviously wanted to spit it all out before they returned; she knew what big ears Joel had. 'Yes, but from what I know about Patrick, I'd say he's going along with this because he hopes you'll get back together.'

'If he thought that, he'd be looking for a job nearer home, Mum. And he was the one who wanted a separation!' Caitlin remembered that cool, cool look of disappointment Patrick had given her back in January when he'd informed her it was over, and a shiver ran over her heart. He wouldn't tell her why. Just that 'she ought to know'.

No, Patrick might be keeping things amicable but he wasn't coming back. She'd ruined whatever vision he had of her, and that, as far as he was concerned, was that.

'What exactly did he say when you went round the house with the builders?' Lynne went on.

'What do you mean? He was . . . fine. Got them on the case straight away. We're supposed to be able to move back in a week's time.'

'Great news!' Lynne patted her hand, then she said, 'Did he blame you, though? Was he angry?'

'No! How could he blame me? I told you, I wasn't there. Scarlett was babysitting. Neither of us blamed her either – it was just one of those things. I've told Joel about running baths, but he gets distracted so easily . . .'

'Exactly.' Lynne regarded her over her glasses. A piercing, knowing look.

'What?' Was this about Joel now?

'You weren't there.'

'Mum, I'm allowed a night out now and again.' Caitlin could feel herself blushing. She didn't have to explain herself to her mother; she was thirty-one years old.

'Have you met someone else? I'm not prying, love, but you must realise that that might change things for Patrick, if he felt you were moving on. That's when a lot of divorces start to get nasty, when new people are brought into the equation – especially if there hasn't been a third party involved up until now?' She paused to let the implications sink in.

Caitlin swallowed. For the first time Lynne had said something that actually rang alarm bells. Lee was everything Patrick actively disliked: he played in a band, he didn't have a full-time job, he had no savings and he enjoyed living life as it came. All he needed was a motorbike and Patrick would be drawing salt rings around the house.

'Have you met someone else?' Like Joel, Lynne didn't shy away from direct questions.

'No,' said Caitlin automatically.

'Really? You can tell me, Caitlin, I won't judge you.'

'No!' Lynne totally *would* judge, and anyway, she hadn't: Lee was a friend. It was far too early to call it anything other than that. She'd met someone she enjoyed going out with, and she was just having some fun. Some very, very long overdue *fun*.

Lynne misread Caitlin's hesitation for sadness. 'Caitlin, you mustn't sell yourself short. You're a beautiful, vivacious woman, with your whole life still ahead of you.'

'I know, Mum,' said Caitlin. 'But . . .'

'Mum! Mum! Look at me!' Joel was hopping over bollards, and doing an on-off pavement jump into invisible puddles. 'I'm siiiiiiinging in the rain!'

Caitlin mimed a standing ovation, and Nancy clapped too, but with none of the squeals of approval she'd have let rip with a year ago. Caitlin fought down a desire to run over there and hug them both up.

Lynne saw her reaction. 'How's my favourite granddaughter getting on with the speech therapist?'

'Fine.' Caitlin leaned on the table and it tipped to the side again. 'She's having weekly meetings but apparently it's a case of— Oh, for God's sake!' She grabbed a napkin from the stand and folded it crossly into a wedge. 'A case of being creative and looking for other ways to help her communicate until what-ever's causing this is worked out in her head.'

'And you're absolutely sure there's . . .'

Caitlin had been jamming the napkin under the table's foot. She looked up, red-faced. 'Absolutely sure there's nothing what?'

Lynne's face set firm. 'Someone has to say it. Are you absolutely sure she isn't hiding some sort of secret? There. I'm sorry, Caitlin.'

Caitlin sat up. She eyed her mother squarely. 'Nancy has seen nothing, or heard nothing to have upset her. I know that for a fact. I've been with her almost every waking hour since she was born.'

'I'm just saying.'

'Well, don't. We've been over everything with the therapist. Patrick and I are both heartbroken about it. Equally. It's one of things we absolutely agree on.'

They regarded each other, as adults not mother and daughter. *I'm nothing like her*, thought Caitlin, noting Lynne's determined chin and controlled hair. *I'm just like Dad. Dad's a bit of a pushover too. I wonder if she finds us both a bit frustrating.*

The pause grew, and in it, Caitlin watched a series of expressions cross her mother's face. She refused to break the silence. If living with Patrick had taught her one thing it was that nothing was as unsettling as a long pause in which the other person could hear all their worst fears.

'So, shall we engage a solicitor?' Lynne pressed on. 'Since we've now established that there's a chance things may not remain as cordial as they are now?'

'I understand what you're saying, and I appreciate your concern.' Caitlin reminded herself that she had a degree, and two children, and a house. She was no longer a teenager who would let everyone down if not sufficiently supervised. 'But you know what? I'm proud of the way Patrick and I have handled our separation so far. The children know they're loved, he's managing his weekend contact better than I expected, and one good thing is that they've got to spend time with Eva. So in actual fact their family experience has *broadened* as a result of our decision to separate.'

Saying that made her feel unexpectedly emotional. And it was true. Caitlin wouldn't necessarily have said so a few months back, but a couple of times in the last week she'd spotted the emotion that warmed Eva's face when Joel broke out an impromptu song for her, or when Nancy leaned into her shoulder. And she'd started to think maybe she'd found a friend too. Maybe not someone you'd go to Vegas with on the spur of the moment, but a friend who'd give you smart advice about buying cashmere. Or pay for your kids to travel First Class to distract them from a trip you were worried about, then let them fall asleep on your designer jacket.

Eva, Caitlin suspected, was probably quite a laugh when she'd had a glass of wine.

Lynne stirred her coffee without looking up. 'Oh.' It was a very loaded 'oh'. 'And how is that going? You staying with Eva?'

'Brilliantly, thanks. The kids love her house, they've got their own room, and there's a huge garden to play in. And she's been great.' *Beyond family-duty great*, Caitlin thought. 'She didn't hesitate in asking us to stay at such short notice – I feel like I'm getting to understand her a lot better.'

Lynne sipped her coffee. 'How do you mean, understand her?'

'Well, I always assumed from things Patrick said that Eva didn't like children, or that she was more into her career, but I don't think that's true.' Caitlin paused. 'I just think she's been unlucky, timing-wise. She's great with the kids. Shame she and Michael met so late on.'

'Hmm,' said Lynne, and tilted her head.

'Mum! Muuuum!' Joel was swinging around a lamppost, while Nancy stared in awed admiration at his agility.

'That's great, Joel – be careful! Stay where I can see you.' Caitlin turned back to Lynne. 'What? Spit it out, Mum.'

'It's just that . . .' Lynne seemed to be choosing her words carefully. Not that it would stop her saying whatever it was she had to say, Caitlin knew that. You didn't end up running the HR department without learning nice ways to say horrible things. 'I understand where you're coming from, Caitlin, and it's good that you're building family networks for the kids, but I think you need to be careful with Eva.'

'What on earth do you mean by that?'

'Well. Joel and Nancy . . . They're probably the one chance she'll have to experience parenting, aren't they? She's going to form attachments to them – naturally, of course, and how lovely – but—' Her head tilted, as if she didn't want to articulate her next thought.

Caitlin felt a stone form in her chest. 'Do you want to stop right there, Mum?' she warned. 'Because it sounds a lot like you're about to say something pretty crappy.'

'I'm sorry, but again, someone has to say it. Just be careful. Eva's unlikely to have her own family, she's seeing yours in very emotional circumstances – you need to make sure everyone understands where the boundaries are. Especially when the children are staying in her house, but following your rules. She has no experience of parenting children – how on earth is she managing with Nancy, for instance?'

'She and Nancy communicate very well. In fact, Nancy finds Eva's dogs particularly helpful.'

'What?' Lynne sounded shocked. 'Is that a good idea? How can Nancy call for help if they bite her? How can she tell them to go away?'

'She doesn't need to – they're very gentle and loving towards her. They're fine, Mum. And she talks to them.' Caitlin couldn't believe she, of all people, was saying this but there it was, coming out of her mouth. *Dogs are fine*.

Lynne was silent for a moment. 'Nancy talks to dogs, but she won't talk to her teachers, or to her granny?'

'Yup. She doesn't talk to Eva either, if it makes you feel better.'

'How would that make me feel better?' It clearly made Lynne feel better; Caitlin could see it in her face. 'I think that makes the situation even more complex.'

'No, it doesn't. The speech therapist said it's normal. Children with mutism often find animals a useful communication tool. And anyway,' Caitlin simmered with annoyance. Why was she even having to say this? 'Children can never have too many people to love them. They've only got you and dad on my side, and I happen to think that the kids get as much from Eva as she gets from them. I didn't like dogs but these ones . . . are OK.'

'Caitlin, I think you're being a bit obtuse.' Lynne pinched her nose. 'I'm just telling you, from personal experience of *many* of my close friends, that menopause does funny things to women. Your whole sense of what it means to be a woman changes overnight, you realise certain options are shut to you, certain parts of your life are *over* . . . And Eva's been widowed on top of that.'

'Are you trying to make out Eva's some sort of menopausal nut job who's going to run off with my babies?'

'I'm doing nothing of the sort. I feel for the poor woman, she's been through the mill. But my instinct, *as a mother*, is to make sure you, and my grandchildren, are legally protected. She might side with Patrick if he decides to go for custody. Then see how happy you'd be with her looking after them.'

Joel and Nancy were running back towards the table, and Caitlin knew their attention span was officially now into the red. She spoke rapidly and the words came out hard. 'I've been living in Eva's house for ten days, Mum. I can assure you she's far from crazy, she adores the kids and I don't think for one second she's about to start interfering in their lives in anything other than a good way.'

Lynne smiled but it didn't quite reach her eyes. Caitlin felt her grip on her adulthood slipping. 'Fine. You know best. You always know best, Caitlin. But I'm a crisis manager, and I put strategies in place where I see crises happening. Nice people do odd things, I would know. It would make me and your father much happier, if only for the children's sake, if you spent a few hours with a competent solicitor ringfencing their inheritance a bit more securely. That house is worth a lot of money.' She tried a smile, a more natural one this time. 'Even without a bathroom floor!'

I knew it, thought Caitlin, *this was about the house*. She'd never forgiven her for ending up with Gran's house. The irony was, if Joan was here now, she'd have nipped all that bitching about menopausal babynapping in the bud, just like she'd dismissed Lynne's handwringing about Caitlin's 'lost opportunities' and got on with teaching her how to settle a teething baby.

'Fine,' she said. 'I'll look online and find someone.'

'No need.' Lynne was already smiling at Joel, who was running over with a tiny cupcake some freebie distributer had handed him. 'A colleague gave me the name of an excellent Family Law solicitor. I've already spoken to them.'

'You've what?'

'I wanted to check they could take your case on. And before you say anything, we'll cover the first lot of fees for you.'

'Mum . . .'

'Mum! Mum! Look! I got a cake! And Nancy got one too!' Joel threw himself at her, while Lynne extended her arm to Nancy. 'Can I eat it?'

'Did you get a cake too, Nancy?' Lynne cuddled Nancy nearer. 'What flavour is it? Is it pink? Are you going to eat it now or save it for later?'

Nancy glanced at Caitlin, then turned her head away, staring at her shoes rather than nuzzling into Lynne's neck the way she did to Eva.

Lynne caught Caitlin's eye over the top of Nancy's head and pulled an 'oh dear' face.

No, thought Caitlin. She's just doing what I wish I could.

Eva was already on the train when Caitlin herded Joel and Nancy down the busy platform at Paddington. She was sitting at their reserved table, a newspaper folded at the crossword in front of her, staring into space.

Caitlin thought she looked rather regal, sitting there with her gold chain. Something about Eva's smooth brow, with the hair pushed back off it like that, and the frown that indicated her mind was working through something. Then, unexpectedly, she smiled at something in front of her – a book? – and it was like the sun coming out from behind the clouds.

Eva's resting face, she realised, was quite fierce. But she wasn't fierce. Not really.

'There's Auntie Eva!' roared Joel and she must have heard through the glass because she looked round and the smile changed into a welcoming one.

Caitlin glanced down at Nancy, clinging to her hand with a determination that told her she was worn out. 'Can you see Auntie Eva?' she asked, but she knew the answer from the broad beam that split Nancy's tired face.

Once the train got moving, Joel nudged her and muttered until Caitlin produced the box of stupidly overpriced cupcakes the children had chosen in Covent Garden.

'For you,' she said. 'From us. To say thank you for a lovely day out.'

'Oh! That's so kind.' Maybe it was the light in the train but Caitlin thought Eva's eyes seemed to fill. 'You didn't need to do that!'

'Nancy picked a blue one for you.' Joel pointed at the box, nearly dislodging a fondant rose. 'And I picked this one with a Superman logo on it.' He looked longingly at it. 'It's got a special filling.'

'We'll share.' Eva had a knife and plates brought over and they ate cake, and drank tea from silver pots, and somewhere around Evesham the children fell asleep: Joel with his mouth wide open, dribbling on Caitlin, and Nancy tucked sideways against Eva's armrest.

The carriage had emptied of businessmen by Oxford, and Eva and Caitlin were left alone in companionable silence, as the train rocked and the children breathed in the heavy animal way Caitlin never got tired of. Nancy snuffled in her sleep, and for a moment, opened her mouth and murmured, as if she was about to talk.

Caitlin froze and met Eva's equally breath-caught gaze: their shared glance went through Caitlin like an electric shock.

Was Nancy going to say something?

Eva seemed on edge, but Caitlin's whole body was tingling. *Please,* she begged silently, *please speak to me, Nancy.* Her arms ached to reach over to take her baby, making a safe place where she could be that happy little girl again.

Nancy didn't speak. She snuffled and her forehead creased, then she curled further into Eva with a worried grunt. Eva wrapped her jacket around Nancy's shoulders and Caitlin fought the urge to make them swap places. *It would wake Nancy up,* she told herself. *Just leave her.*

And Eva looked so proud, she thought. *Surprised, and protective. It'd be mean to take that little thing away from her. I'm here. I'm the first person Nancy will see when she wakes.*

The train steward passed, and Caitlin stopped him. 'Do you fancy a glass of wine?' she asked Eva. 'I'm having one. We're getting a taxi back, right?'

Eva hesitated, then nodded, rather shyly. 'Yes. Yes, please.' And then she smiled, the first proper 'friends' smile Caitlin had seen from her. It gave Caitlin what Joel called a smile inside his chest as well as on his face.

When the wine came, Caitlin reached forward and chinked her glass with Eva's. 'So, tell me, now we're on our own,' she said, confidentially. 'Was Patrick always such a nightmare to play Monopoly with as he is now?'

It was a long time since Caitlin had talked so much. Eva was a good listener; she made exactly the right noises at the right time, and asked thoughtful questions. Caitlin knew she'd probably overshared, one too many grumbles about Patrick's impossible standards, and how she felt they'd always come second to his work, but Eva didn't pull her up on it. Instead she offered tiny snippets of a Patrick Caitlin wished she'd known before.

'The thing you have to remember is that he idolised our dad, and Dad was a workaholic,' Eva said in a low voice, over the sleeping heads of the children. 'Paddy only had Mum's version of Dad to go on, once he was old enough to ask about him. He's always been harder on himself than he is on everyone else.' She stopped and glanced down at a slumbering Joel, then looked back up at Caitlin. 'They're angelic,' she whispered, in awe.

'When they're asleep.' The love in Eva's voice made Caitlin want to share a private treasure she'd kept to herself lately. She pulled her phone out of her bag, carefully so as not wake either of them. 'Do you want to see something?'

Eva leaned forward over the table and Caitlin pressed play on a video she'd watched so many times it was imprinted on her brain. It was Patrick and Nancy, pretending to do their *Strictly Come Dancing* routine at a friend's wedding.

'That is adorable!' whispered Eva, as Nancy in her birthday tutu swayed and stretched out one arm at a time, copied from the dancers on television, her toes balanced on Patrick's toes. Caitlin had turned the sound off, but she could see Nancy's upturned face bright with love for her daddy, and it looked as if Patrick was singing down to her.

'That looks adorable but he's actually singing "My Heart Will Go On" like a man trapped down a well,' whispered Caitlin. 'Listen.' She turned up the sound a few notches, just loud enough for Patrick's tortured bellowings to be heard. 'No wonder they cleared the dance floor.'

'We had to make him stand at the back when we went carol singing,' Eva confided. 'Don't ever tell him I told you. Have you got any more?' She looked up, tentatively, and her eyes locked with Caitlin's. 'Have you got any of Nancy . . . before she stopped speaking?'

Tenderness was written all over Eva's face. Caitlin nodded, silently, and found the clip she'd watched over and over again. She turned up the sound as loud as she dared, and they both leaned over the phone on the table to catch it.

There was Nancy, singing and dancing with Joel, for Caitlin's last birthday. In the back garden at home, before that familiar world had been lost forever.

'Happy birthday, dear Mumm-eeeee!' Nancy was spinning round in her Flower Fairy skirt, smiling directly into the lens, into Caitlin's face. 'Happy birthday to you! See my wand, Mummy. I'm making a spell. An I love you spell!' She twirled and skipped, her face alive with the pleasure of communicating. Then she blew a loud kiss and giggled uproariously, her head thrown back in delight.

'I love you, Fancy Nancy,' said Caitlin's voice off-camera and the blissful ignorance in it made Caitlin cry. The thought of never hearing that sound again, that sheer joy, made her want to die inside.

She looked up and saw Eva's eyes were full of tears too. Without speaking, Eva – her chilly sister-in-law with the child-unfriendly carpets – reached out a hand and squeezed her fingers. Neither of them said a word, but each understood something that was too powerful and indefinable for words in any case.

When they arrived at Longhampton station, the car Eva had arranged was waiting for them. Joel was only half-awake as Caitlin got him into his jacket and levered him to his feet.

Nancy was still fast asleep on Eva's shoulder. She'd dribbled on her jacket again. 'If you slide out,' Caitlin whispered, 'I can lift her off you.'

'It's fine.' Eva carefully hoisted Nancy onto her hip. 'Let's not wake her up. If you don't mind?'

There was a new – if cautious – confidence in the way Eva's arms supported Nancy's slumped body, Caitlin thought. Not a secret desire to take her away, like her mother assumed. Just a natural wish to share in something precious and special. What kind of mean-spirited cow would she have to be to deny Eva that? Nancy and Joel both had so much love to give.

'No,' said Caitlin, as the warmth of a new friendship spread through her. 'I don't mind at all.'

Chapter twenty-two

'OK, big man, so Dad'll be here about six, just like a normal Friday and then I'll come back and collect you all on Sunday night. Or maybe Dad will bring you back, we haven't decided yet.' Caitlin hugged Joel to her and gave him the special loud raspberry kiss on the top of his head. While she still could. He wriggled a bit harder every time now. 'You'll be good for Auntie Eva, won't you?'

Joel looked outraged. Or as outraged as a ten-year-old wearing a jumper and a gold lamé tie, 'borrowed' from the charity bag by the stairs, could. 'Of *course* I will. I'm not *three*.'

'I know. But this is the first time she's looked after you all day on her own, and she's not used to your shenanigans. Break her in gently. No dramatics, please. And you'll make sure Nancy's got everything she needs? You'll keep an eye on her if you go out?'

'*Yes*, Mum. Obviously.'

Don't turn into a teenager just yet, Caitlin begged silently. Big school was only one term away now. That'd speed up the process, whether she liked it or not.

Joel squirmed out of her arms. 'We'll be fine, Mum. Stop being weird.'

'I can't, weird is how I am.' Caitlin let him go. 'It's how you are too, that's the magic of genetics. Where's Nancy?'

327

'Dunno. Probably in Bumble's room with him.' Joel gestured upstairs with his phone. It never seemed to be out of his hand these days, thought Caitlin. She was beginning to regret ever showing him how to film things on it. She didn't know which was worse: the probability that Joel would end up immortalising her doing something embarrassing, or the fact that there'd be isolated moments over the weekend that she'd miss him trying.

'Nancy!' she yelled up the stairs. No reply. 'Where's Bumble's room?' she asked, as an afterthought. 'I thought that was the conservatory.'

Joel was filming Bee marching out of the kitchen, her tail circling moodily as she approached. She and Joel were kindred silent-movie spirits. 'No, it's in Auntie Eva's dressing room. Bee, come here, Bee . . .'

Caitlin set off up the stairs. She was still technically ahead of schedule but she wanted to make the most of every free moment she had in Bristol. The builders – who were terrified of Patrick and his demands for perfection – wanted her to make some final decisions about the repair work before they packed up, but after that the weekend could commence, kicking off with an afternoon pint with Lee in the pub round the corner from her house. Plans were a little fluid after that, but the main event was that The Glebes had a gig at The Fleece – the biggest venue they'd played yet and something Lee was really excited about.

Caitlin was excited too. For him, and for her.

Upstairs, Eva was in her room, standing by Mick's rapidly emptying wardrobe with two big Harvey Nichols bags and a pile of shirts. She was folding briskly; since they'd come back from London two days ago, she'd taken four bags to the charity shop and emptied the wardrobe in the spare room Caitlin was sleeping in of its assorted evening wear and old coats.

'You need hanging space,' she'd explained, but to Caitlin it looked like the action of a woman who'd finally started to move on. Someone who also wanted people to stay in her spare rooms.

'Want me to drop those off when I go past?' she asked.

'No, you get going.' Eva checked her watch. 'You'll have missed the morning rush hour now. We'll be going into town tomorrow, when Patrick's here.'

'You're sure about looking after them?' Caitlin hesitated. It was only until Patrick arrived after work – so, about nine hours – but she knew from experience what could happen in that time. It had only taken Joel twenty minutes to render an entire house uninhabitable. 'Give them a list of stuff to find in the garden, Nancy loves that. And if all else fails, ask Joel to make up a play – it's not quiet but he can do it in another room.'

Eva waved a hand. 'Honestly, it's fine! I'm looking forward to it.'

It had been Eva who'd suggested looking after the children, and the shy way she'd offered, with something in her eyes that expected Caitlin to say no, had made Caitlin's heart melt. She didn't want to say no now, in case it looked like she didn't trust her. Because she *did* trust her. Talking to Eva on the train about Patrick, about her fear of letting people down (they'd had a second, large glass of wine each), about how much the kids had changed her life – it had given them both a new angle on each other. A nice one.

'Is Nancy in with Bumble?' she asked, instead.

'She certainly is.' Eva nodded towards the corner of the bedroom where the roof sloped to a point. 'They're chatting. You can hear them.'

Caitlin concentrated; yes, she could hear a very soft whisper. She crept into the room, and saw Nancy lying with her front half hidden in the alcove, while her pale legs swung back and forth outside. Eva had been keeping an eye on her the whole time, guarding her without crowding her, like one of the pugs.

Caitlin got on her knees and crawled towards the space. Bumble was by the triangular shard of window, curled in a basket, next to Nancy's pink bag, which bulged with her magic secret bubbles and the toy pug Eva had given her to stand in for Bumble and Bee when she wasn't in Longhampton.

Her heart stopped to hear even the faintest traces of Nancy's voice, so soft it was more like wind in the trees, or the tide ruffling the shingle on the shore.

'. . . only you know, because you are my friend, Bumble . . .' Nancy's face was pressed into Bumble's soft black ear. When she heard her mother, she stopped suddenly and looked guilty.

Caitlin pretended not to have noticed. 'Hey! I'm off to see our house, Fancy Nancy,' she whispered. 'The builders have fixed everything! You'll be back in your own bed on Monday.'

Nancy squinted at her solemnly, and Caitlin could tell she was applying one of the secret rules she used to judge whether she could speak or not. She inched further forward into the space, and beckoned Caitlin in.

Caitlin wriggled on her elbows; there wasn't much room for the three of them.

Nancy climbed up her side until she was speaking right into her ear. The sudden warm gust of Nancy's baby smell wrapped itself round Caitlin's heart. 'Be careful, Mummy.'

The bittersweet relief of hearing Nancy's voice, whatever words she said, spread through Caitlin like warm chocolate. But 'be careful'? What did she think would happen?

'I will, sweetheart,' she whispered back. 'I'll make sure your room's all ready for you. Let Auntie Eva and Joel know if there's anything you need, and Dad'll be here by tea time.'

Nancy said nothing but pushed her soft face into Caitlin's neck and whispered, 'I love you, Mummy.'

'I love you, Nancy,' said Caitlin. 'I love you to the moon and back.'

'And Bumble.'

'And Bumble.'

Bumble gazed at them both with boggly eyes as they stroked his suede coat. So this was a new safe space, thought Caitlin. Nancy can speak to me in here, and in her room. But nowhere else in this house, and in no one else's earshot. It was a tiny improvement.

She wondered if Bumble knew how honoured he was. Then she realised that it was because of the two dogs that Nancy was speaking in this house at all. He probably thought *she* should feel honoured.

Doubt gripped her. Was this right? Leaving Nancy and Joel here with Eva so soon? On her own? What if something happened? What if Nancy needed to speak?

Caitlin shook herself. Joel was here. Nothing was going to happen. And Eva would be watching them with eagle eyes, out of pure nerves. The real worry should be how spoiled they'd be in her absence.

Builders in Bristol, Caitlin thought, worked fast. There was no trace of the flooding in the house, apart from a lingering smell of plaster dust, and the cables snaking over the plastic sheeting that stretched from the front door down to the narrow hall. The kitchen ceiling was replastered and two units replaced, and the bathroom floor had been dried out, reboarded and repaired with black and white tiles.

In fact, thank God for the flood, because it was a massive improvement on the tired old lino that had been there before, Caitlin reflected. She and Patrick had talked about redoing the nasty floor in the bathroom for ages, and now, in the space of a week, they had.

'Obviously we haven't had time to paint your walls,' said the builder assigned to show her round the various repairs. He wasn't the foreman; his polo shirt had Tommy embroidered over the name of the building firm. The thread was still shiny new. 'The boss said he needed you to choose some colours so the decorators can come in next week. When it's all dry, like.'

'No problem,' said Caitlin. Her phone pinged in her pocket with the text she'd been on pins for all morning. It was Lee.

There yet? Leaving work now – will be at the pub in 15. x

Spiders of guilty excitement skittered in her chest. Caitlin still wasn't sure if she was wearing the right thing. All the way down to Bristol she'd been running through the contents of her wardrobe in her mind and what she really wanted to do was to slip into her bedroom and grab the off-the-shoulder jumper that would be just long enough to cover her arse if she could zip up her skinny jeans, which would go with the boots that . . .

'. . . for the boss to come back?'

She blinked. Tommy was clearly waiting for an answer. 'Sorry?'

'Can you hang on for a bit till the boss comes back? He's gone to another job in Westbury. He won't be long.'

'How long is long?'

Tommy's eyes shifted from one side to another. 'Dunno? Half an hour?'

Half an hour in builder terms meant an hour, Caitlin knew that much. Maybe two. Maybe mid-afternoon. And she had a date to get to. What exactly would she be hanging around for? To have this conversation again, with the same pretend-understanding nods from her, but this time to a more senior bloke?

She swept a hand round the bathroom. 'It all looks great to me. I mean, the ceiling's done downstairs, and you've sorted out the electrics, and this floor is much nicer than the old one.' She grinned. 'I'm sure we'll find out soon enough if it's not right.'

'He's got a checklist to go through . . .'

Patrick's checklist. Of course. 'OK, I can wait half an hour,' Caitlin conceded, because Tommy looked so panicky and she needed to rifle through her wardrobe before she left. 'But I've got another appointment I need to get to. So maybe if he's not back, he can ring me? Let me give you my number.'

'OK,' said Tommy doubtfully as Caitlin reeled off her number.

The sun came out and washed the bathroom with an unexpected warm spring light.

In an hour's time, thought Caitlin, with a tingle, it'll be the weekend, and I'll be drinking cider with a hot bloke, with somewhere to go and a house to come back to. My kids are happy with my sister-in-law, the sun is out, and Patrick's off my case. This really is Spring.

Caitlin had left Eva with an emergency pile of DVDs that Nancy would apparently watch on repeat (and another, larger, pile for Joel) but after half an hour in which Nancy had hovered anxiously in the hall, in case Caitlin returned, she settled down again with Bumble, half in, half out of his alcove, while Eva worked her way through Mick's old clothes, sorting them into piles for – at Anna's suggestion – the charity shop, the homeless shelter, and the Longhampton Amateur Dramatics Society.

Joel came up after a while, followed by Bee, and rolled ties round his hand, firing out questions about the clothes, about the house, about Mick. Questions which were much more direct than the ones Caitlin had skirted around.

'Auntie Eva, why didn't you have children?' he asked. 'Don't you like children?'

'Of course I like children.' Eva hesitated over the shirt Mick had worn on their first anniversary trip to New York, then folded it and put it in a bag before she could think about the cocktails in the Rainbow Room. 'I love spending time with you two.'

'So why didn't you have any? We could have had cousins.' He looked sad. 'We don't have *any* cousins. Everyone else at school does.'

Eva bit her lip. How to explain to a child? 'A lot of things have to be in the right place to have a baby. And I had some of the right things, but not at the right time.'

It sounded simple: no one to blame. But as every day took her further away from her marriage, Eva was starting to see herself standing in the distance, next to Mick in the diaries, an Eva she didn't always recognise. It *had* been a series of choices. Or choices not to make choices. How had it taken her so long to see that? She'd chosen to stay quiet, to ignore the voice in her head. To let other people, other circumstances, decide for her.

'It would have been nice to have cousins,' she heard herself say, in a strange, cheerful tone. 'But you don't always get everything you want. Sometimes you get different things instead.'

'Like when I wanted a Komodo dragon for Christmas and I got a guinea pig.'

'Something like that.'

Eva reached for the next jacket. The black Hugo Boss jacket Mick had been wearing the day they'd come back from holiday. Just looking at it made the panicky smell of that day come back, and she quickly emptied the pockets, to give herself something to think about, dumping the contents onto the dressing table. Coins, cards, folded paper, old envelopes, the usual.

'So what did you get instead?' Joel's question was innocent, and quite cheerful. 'Bumble and Bee? They're *almost* as good as cousins, I suppose.'

Eva looked at him, with a lump in her throat.

She was saved from having to find an answer by her mobile ringing. It was Patrick.

'It's your dad,' she informed Joel. 'I wonder what he wants.'

'To tell you to do something, probably,' said Joel. 'Can we make cappuccinos now, please?'

'Hi, Eva, sorry to bother you.' Patrick was in his car. 'Have you spoken to Caitlin this morning?'

'Not since she left. Why?'

'Because she was supposed to liaise with the builder to go through a list of queries I emailed to him last night, and he can't get hold of her. She hasn't checked in with you?'

'She hasn't needed to. We've been fine.'

'Sorry. Of course. I'm glad you're having a nice day. So there's no reason Caitlin isn't answering her phone?'

'Not that I know of. Maybe it's run out. Maybe it's at the bottom of her bag.'

There was a pause, then a huff. 'Right, I'm going there myself.'

'What? You're meant to be coming here for six.' Eva modified her voice; she didn't want to sound as if she needed reinforcements. 'We're looking forward to seeing you for tea!'

'With my cake,' said Joel.

Eva hadn't realised he was listening in. She moved a few steps away.

'I'll still be there for tea. I'll move my afternoon appointment – it's not that important. I can make some calls from the car.' The sat nav was being reprogrammed as he spoke. 'Fine, there. I only need half an hour with the builders. Then if there's anything that needs sorting I can get them to do it before they vanish.'

'Don't you think you should let Caitlin sort this out for herself?' Eva had a sudden memory of Caitlin's dejected expression on the train the other night, staring out of the window while she rambled, two glasses of wine down, about never meeting Patrick's standards. 'It's her house.'

'It's *our* house. And I want to know everything's safe. For the children. Cait doesn't know what she's looking for, and even if it's not been done properly, she'll say it's fine, so as not to upset them. You can't just say fine when safety's at stake.'

Eva had a flash of sympathy for Caitlin. Their mum had been the same; never letting anything go until she'd checked it. 'Caitlin's a perfectly able woman,' she said. 'Don't treat her like a baby just to make a point.'

'I'm not doing this to prove a point. I'm doing it because Caitlin told the builder she'd be available and she's not. If you speak to her,' he went on, 'tell her I'll be calling in there about half two.'

'Fine.' *Well, I tried,* she thought.

'And tell the kids I'm looking forward to seeing them!' Patrick's voice softened. 'Don't start tea without me.'

'I'll see you about six then.'

When he'd hung up, Eva was about to put the phone back on the charger, then changed her mind and dialled Caitlin's mobile. Caitlin deserved a warning that Hurricane Patrick was heading her way.

The phone rang out, and out, then went to voicemail.

Caitlin's effervescent voice pealed in her ear. 'Hi, this is Caitlin, I can't take your call, please leave a message! Byeeeeee!'

Should I say something? Eva wondered. *Why do I feel like I'm warning her of something bad? That's weird, isn't it?*

No, she thought. *It's just my brother. I've had thirty-seven years of this. She's only had seven.*

'Caitlin,' she said, 'Patrick's on his way to the house. He'll be there about two thirty. All's great here, in case you were worried!'

As she hung up, another thought occurred to her: Caitlin hadn't rung to check on the children. Shouldn't she at least be phoning to make sure the morning had gone all right?

Was everything OK with Caitlin?

You're getting as bad as Patrick, she thought, and went to supervise Joel making cappuccinos like the out-of-work actor he was already in training to be.

After lunch, Nancy carried on playing with Bumble in the kitchen, and Joel politely refused Eva's offer of a treasure hunt in favour of watching Netflix on his tablet at the breakfast bar.

'I've got a lot to catch up on,' he informed her. 'Mum only lets me have thirty minutes' screen time a day. It's bad for my eyes, but it's going to take me forever to get to the end of *Night at the Museum Two.*'

'So shouldn't I . . . ?'

'No!' He covered his tablet protectively and grinned. 'I won't tell her Bee ate off Nancy's plate if you don't.'

Eva knew when she was being played. 'Another half hour,' she said. 'Then it's off.'

'Deal,' said Joel.

When the phone rang soon after, Eva assumed it would be Caitlin calling back to check in, but it wasn't. The voice on the other end of the line was Alex's, and something made Eva say, 'I'll take this in the study, OK, Joel? Just stay in the kitchen with Nancy and come and get me if you need anything.'

He raised a thumb without looking up, and she stepped quickly into the privacy of the study.

'So how are you?' said Alex. 'Recovered from London?'

'Just about.' Eva moved some things round the desk; she hadn't read either of the emails Trudy had sent her about Mick's diaries after their meeting. She had, however, read the book of poetry Alex had given her. Twice. It had reminded her how much she'd enjoyed reading poetry, a long time ago. 'I'm on auntie duty today.'

'Hmm. Sounds very quiet for babysitting.'

'I know. Their mother said to worry if there's a sudden racket, but worry more if it's too peaceful.'

Alex laughed. 'Listen, I hate to draw things back to your least favourite topic, but when I was going through my own notes, I realised that we never spoke about that idea I mentioned on email the other day.'

'Which idea?'

'I was going to raise it at the meeting, but I wanted to speak to you first. You weren't the only one who felt that there were some . . . issues arising from Mick's diaries. Cheryl, in particular, has a whole list of what she calls discrepancies, and what Una calls . . . well, I won't say what she called them.'

'I can imagine.' Eva sat down.

'You talked about voices in these diaries. Mick's voice is very strong and one of the great strengths is the way he reports conversations, but I wonder if maybe we need to hear your voices too. His wives. There's a wonderful kind of Greek chorus image to you three.'

Eva didn't reply. There had been times, in her marriage, when she'd listened to Mick telling a story she was involved in, and he did 'her' voice, the way he did the pugs. She'd never really enjoyed it. It hadn't sounded like her, even though he always got a laugh.

'So would you consider writing something yourself?' Alex was saying. 'Either a letter to Mick, or your version of a particular event . . . I don't know. It's only an idea. I just felt the way you told me that story of your meeting, over the bag of clothes – there was something so immediate about it. While I've been

339

reading the diaries, I have to confess I've often wanted to pick up the phone and ask you how you remember it.'

'I don't know,' she said. 'It'll be different though. I'll be remembering it, from here, and Mick . . . was writing as it happened.'

'But you'll think about it?' He laughed, and there was a nervousness in Alex's voice she hadn't heard in a while. 'It's not just an excuse to keep phoning you up and . . . well, it is, actually, but . . . Ha ha! I'm not putting this very well . . .'

Silence fell on the line but it wasn't an empty silence. It was a very full one.

'Alex, that poetry you gave me—' she started but was interrupted by Joel bursting into the room.

'Auntie Eva!' Joel rushed into the study and leaned on the desk, swinging his legs. 'There are cows in the garden!'

'Sorry, Alex, hold on a moment.' She pressed the phone to her chest. 'No, they're on the other side of the fence, sweetheart. I know it *looks* like they're closer but that's because the fence is hidden by the hedge and . . .'

'No! There are cows! In the actual garden!' His expression was somewhere between delight and horror. 'And there's a *massive* one! Doing huge cowpats on the grass!'

'Really?' She wasn't sure whether Joel was serious, or whether this was part of some imaginary play. Caitlin would know instinctively how to respond, in a fun, encouraging manner. She didn't.

'Yes, really! Come quick!' He was hopping from foot to foot. 'Now!'

Eva weighed up the situation. There was no way the cows would be in the garden; although the calves sometimes came up to the hedge for a nibble of something more interesting, they couldn't actually get through the wire fence in the hedge. It was more likely that this was one of Joel's dramatic moments. She'd probably find Nancy and the pugs dressed up as cows in the garden, waiting for Joel to come back and perform some sort of cow-related song and dance. And she'd look mean if she refused to play along.

Joel let out an urgent squeak, and Eva put the phone back to her ear.

'I've got to go. There's an incident unfolding here,' she said.

'So I hear. That kid's got great projection. You should get him signed up for drama classes.'

'Ha! I'll tell him. It'll make his day.'

'Glad I've made someone's,' said Alex. 'And good luck with the incident.'

Eva gabbled out a goodbye, hung up, and turned to Joel. She hoped he wouldn't notice the tell-tale flush in her cheeks. 'Right, now you've got my attention, shall we go and see these cows?'

'They're round the back!' Joel's face was alive, and he pulled her hand as he went through, grabbing it with surprisingly strong fingers.

He must have made a cow costume, she thought. Or else he's going to be filming my reaction for *You've Been Framed*. And she felt proud: it'd be a nice story to tell for her first official day as Auntie In Charge. The Day We All Pretended to Be Cows.

Caitlin would be amazed. And so would Mick, if he'd been here to see it.

Chapter twenty-three

'Wow,' said Eva, struggling to suppress her initial, less child-friendly reaction. 'You weren't kidding.'

There was definitely a large bovine presence in her back garden.

'There!' Joel stood on the glass table in the conservatory and waved his arm towards the rose bushes at the end of the garden, which were now hidden from view by about two tons of solid beef. 'There! That really huge cow! Is it going to try to get in the house? Can it barge through the French windows?'

'That's not a cow, that's a bull,' said Eva automatically, and realised that probably wasn't going to set Joel's mind at rest.

'Bloody hell,' said Joel, but she was too stunned to tell him off. A bit of light swearing seemed like the lesser of many evils, right at that moment.

One, there was a bloody great bull standing in her rose garden. How it had got there was obvious: the wire fence had been pushed to one side like a net curtain, presumably by the prize specimen currently browsing in her beds.

Two, a couple of his lady friends had taken the opportunity to broaden their horizons by following him into Eva's garden – two doe-eyed brown cows the size of small cars, with their own calves following behind. Their angular haunches made the picnic table look tiny as they munched at her hedges and flicked their tails flirtily at the bull.

And several other cows were heading towards this exciting development at the end of the pasture. It would only take five minutes of minimal cow curiosity before the place looked like a milking shed. Eva had no idea how you went about holding back a tide of cattle. Or even if it was advisable. She had a vague memory – getting less vague by the second – of a local news report about a walker who'd been trampled to death by a herd of cows only that summer. Even after nearly ten years in the countryside, cows still scared Eva. They were so much bigger than you expected, somehow.

Still, they couldn't get into the house. But they could make a real mess of her lawn with their hooves and . . .

'He's done another poo,' observed Joel.

'It's good for the roses,' said Eva, as calmly as she could. And then as if things couldn't get worse, the bull turned and eyed the two cows that had joined him in the garden. Its tackle swung . . . well, *bullishly* between its mighty legs, as it made to amble over to them.

No, thought Eva, panic rising. Joel didn't need to see *that*.

'Joel, what a good job you noticed this.' She swallowed; her throat was bone dry. She'd just remembered something else, about cows with calves at foot being 'unpredictable'. 'We need to call the farmer. Ken'll come and get them back.'

'Will he shoot them with a stungun? Or poison darts?' Joel looked hopeful.

'No. He'll probably have a sheepdog.'

'What, for cows? Don't they just know how to talk to sheep? What will the sheepdog do with a herd of cows? Will it run up to the cows and nip their legs?'

343

'Maybe.'

'Or will it just bark and bounce up and down at them? Like Bee was doing?'

Eva had started to go inside, already trying to remember if she had contact details for Ken Thomas, but Joel's words stopped her in her tracks. 'What?'

'Like Bee was doing just now? She was running around telling them to go home. She's a sheep-pug! No! A cow-pug!'

The blood drained from Eva's face. Bee was out there? Ken had only reminded her a few weeks ago about not letting the dogs out around cattle; he'd recounted in grisly detail the plight of a couple of townie dogs that had got in with his herd – one had been despatched by a single kick to the head (the vet thought) and the other had been trampled in the process. It hadn't been quick.

'Bee was so cross,' Joel went on. 'She was all, "Oi didn't say yow could come in here!"' He had Bee's furious Brummie drawl off perfectly. '"Yow've got to go back home at once! Bugger off. The lot of yow!"'

Eva felt sick. She could see it now – Bee's furious face, the powerful hoof . . . One cow moved nearer, and the size of it frightened her, even through the glass.

'Where are Bumble and Bee now?'

'Dunno. Nancy took them out in the garden for a wee.'

'What? Where's Nancy?'

'I don't know. I think she went to pick some flowers for you.' Reality dawned abruptly on Joel's face. 'What if she's out there too?'

Eva's breakfast coffee surged back up her throat. Now she really did feel sick. Nancy was in the garden with at least three enormous cows, which could kick her or stamp on her or crush her . . .

A frantic yapping started from nowhere, and Eva rushed to the side door of the conservatory. The cows stared back at her but didn't move. The bull didn't even turn his head.

Both dogs were outside. Bee was barking at one of the cows from the rosebeds, but Bumble was standing, frozen to the spot, trapped between the bull and the nearest cow. He looked petrified, his black eyes bulging so wide with fear that she could see white all around them.

Eva felt as if her brain had gone into slow motion while her heart had sped up.

What should she do? Joel was hopping from foot to foot, waving his arms, and she had a sudden, horrible image of him running out and frightening the cows into a stampede. She had to keep at least one of the children in her care safe.

Where was Nancy? Oh God, Nancy. Nancy couldn't call for help. She couldn't even shout at the bulls. She'd be locked in her own silence.

The bull took one ominous step towards Bee, and in a flash, Joel's dramatic bravado deserted him. His face crumpled with fear and suddenly he looked much younger.

'Are they going to come in the house?' he whimpered, unable to tear his eyes from the cows. 'Don't let them come in!'

Eva crouched down and held his arms. 'They're not coming in,' she said. 'The farmer will come and get them. Go and call 999, ask for the police, and tell them that there are some cows loose. Give them our address. You're good at calling the police, Joel. I'm going to call the farmer myself.'

Her mobile? Where was her mobile? She needed to get Joel away but she still had to call Ken.

Joel had his phone in his hand, ever ready to film. Not now, though.

'Can I borrow that?' she asked, and he thrust it at her.

The bull had turned its attention from the cows to Bumble, who was still frozen. From a distance, Bee started yapping again. The bull lifted one massive hoof and dropped it to the ground. Small divots of earth flew up. Bumble seemed to be in a trance, his eyes popping and glistening with panic. He was so small. So pathetically defenceless with his wrinkles and friendly lolling tongue.

'Is the bull going to stamp on Bumble?' Joel was trying to be brave but it wasn't working. Eva could feel him shaking as he leaned into her.

'No. Absolutely not. Call the police.' She gave him a push. 'When you've done that, go inside, find Nancy and stay upstairs till I shout for you.'

'What if she's outside?' Joel's eyes were almost as huge as Bumble's. 'She can't talk! She can't tell the bull to leave her alone! I need to help her.' He made a lunge for the door but Eva grabbed him.

'No, Joel,' she said firmly. 'You've got the most important job. Quickly! Nancy's probably upstairs, perfectly safe. Now, off you go!' She gave him a push towards the door, and didn't turn until she heard his feet clattering on the hall floor.

Eva fumbled with Joel's mobile, and stared out at the cows in the garden, her mind racing while she tried to Google Ken Thomas's number with fingers that wobbled across the screen. After what felt like an hour, she found it, and dialled, but it rang out and out at his end.

No answering machine. Typical.

She pressed redial and redial, in case he walked in, and took a careful step nearer the door. She remembered someone telling her that cows moved slowly but when they got together, it was like being trapped inside a machine of bones and knives and sheer tonnage. So far they were still, but that could all change, in a dog-stamping instant.

Where was Nancy? There was no sign of her in the garden; it extended around both sides of the house so maybe she'd run round to the front. As long as she was out of sight of the cows – there was no way she'd try to run through them. Eva took a tentative step out, and scanned the lawn but all she could see were the cows, the hulking bull and her two soft-skinned, clueless pugs.

Bumble looked so vulnerable. It took every ounce of Eva's willpower not to rush out and grab him, even if it meant risking both their lives.

'Bumble,' she whispered, trying to catch his eye. 'Bumble!'

Nothing.

Then suddenly there was movement. Bored with the foliage she'd been chewing so far, one of the cows marched towards the rose bushes, provoking the other cows to follow her more quickly than Eva thought possible. The warm, sour smell filled her nostrils; she couldn't remember ever being so close to cows before. Their distended udders swung, the veins a pale blue on the bulging skin. Even the calves were bigger than they'd seemed, safely on the other side of the hedge.

Bee started yapping again, wilder this time, and the bull turned its attention to her, whipping its long tail from side to side. She was dancing around its back legs, and the thick end of the tail smacked her hard on the face, sending her off-balance, and flying into the rosebed with an agonised yowl.

Her eyes, Eva thought, horrified. Bee's bulbous pug eyes were so exposed and the tail had got her right between them. The bull began to turn around to finish the job off, as the pug

347

scrabbled to get upright again amongst the bark chips. She seemed disorientated, as if she couldn't see properly, and there were red scratches along her smooth side.

Without thinking, Eva took a step forward to grab her, and the movement only made the bull shift faster. With a nasty look in his eye, he let out a raspy breath and dropped his head towards Bumble, still frozen. It was pretty clear what he intended to do next; the only question was how fast it was going to be, and just how hard he could kick the help-less dog.

Adrenalin surged through Eva's veins; Bumble was small enough and fast enough to get out of the bull's way, if he wanted to, but right now he was so paralysed she wondered if maybe he'd had a heart attack.

'Bumble!' Pain ripped up Eva's dry throat as she tried to shout but nothing came out. 'Bumble!'

He stood there, staring at the bull while Bee grunted and howled, backing herself under the shelter of a rose bush.

Which do I get first? Eva thought. Please don't let Nancy be watching this from upstairs. Because one or both of these dogs is about to get trampled to death.

Then suddenly Eva heard something she thought was impossible.

'Bumble, come!'

A small, clear child's voice rang out across the garden, and for a weird second Eva had no idea who it was. Then she realised. It was Nancy. It was the first time she'd heard Nancy speak in real life. The first words. It was a beautiful, beautiful sound.

'Bumble, come!' Nancy called again, from somewhere Eva couldn't see. Precise and delicate, but very clear, with an unmistakeable urgency. She was using the same up and down tone she'd heard Eva using when she recalled the pugs with nuggets of cheese.

Bumble appeared to break out of his trance at the sound of Nancy's voice. He turned his flat head in her direction, his face frantic with panic as he took in his perilous position for the first time: huge bull to one side, and two large cows approaching him, their heads down.

Eva forgot about her own safety and lurched into the garden to find Nancy, her eyes frantically searching the horizon. She spotted her on the other side of the lawn, standing on a bench by the long stretch of paving where Mick had set up his enormous barbecue.

'Nancy!' she yelled. 'Don't move! Don't get down!'

There was a sudden flash of pale fur, and Bee raced down the flowerbeds, through the flowers and in between the cows, to Nancy's side and scrambled onto the bench with an athleticism that Eva wouldn't have believed if she hadn't seen it.

There were still a couple of cows between Bumble and Nancy, but if Bumble could somehow run between the cows' legs . . .

Up on the bench, Nancy was bending down and patting her knees encouragingly as she'd seen Eva do when she was calling the dogs in from the garden. 'Bumble, come here! Oh!'

The cows had started to move towards her, thinking Nancy was offering some form of lunch, and as Bumble made a break for it, the bull also decided enough was enough. He stamped a hoof down so hard it smashed through the surface of the lawn, pushing deep enough into the soft earth below to force it to stumble. It bellowed in confusion – a furious, deafening sound – and in that second, Bumble bolted towards Nancy, and Eva charged after him.

She didn't know how she covered the ground as fast as she did, but somehow she was there, and Nancy was clinging to her hip, her legs wrapped tightly around her waist, and Bee's collar was in one hand, and a howling, shivering Bumble was clamped under the arm that wasn't supporting Nancy, and then, with a white-hot pain scouring her throat and chest, Eva was running and running round the side of the house, until she fell into the porch and slammed the door shut.

Joel stood there, his eyes round, holding the phone.

Eva struggled to control her ragged breathing, to reassure them a sensible adult was in control, but thoughts of what might have happened – to the children, to the dogs, to her – flashed gorily through her head.

'I called everyone again,' he said. 'Sorry. They're all coming.'

'S'fine.' Eva closed her eyes. 'It's fine.'

'Is it?' Joel sounded uncertain, and Eva held out her arms.

'Yes. It is. Come here,' she said, and felt two small bodies leaning into her, then clinging on to her. The smell of their baby hair filled her nose, and she could feel their hearts thumping through their skin.

Only one thought flashed in her head, though. One thought above everything else.

Nancy spoke. Nancy spoke here, in her house, for the first time. For her. And Eva had never felt more elated or emotional in her entire life.

Chapter twenty-four

'And there aren't that many bands round here who are equally influenced by Metallica and Carole King.' Lee leaned forward on his elbows on the outdoor table and his cheeky smile twinkled in his grey eyes. 'I'd say we're quite unique, to be fair.'

Nine, thought Caitlin. That's the ninth time you've said 'to be fair'.

She smiled back, and tried to make herself stop counting, but she knew she couldn't. Not now she'd started.

The ironic thing was that Lee was looking gorgeous. Even more so than normal. He was wearing a navy hoodie under an old leather jacket, and the glimpse of soft skin at his throat was doing funny things to her. He'd obviously showered before he left work because his hair glinted damply in the sunshine, and the hand that held his pint of Doom Bar had three leather bracelets wrapped round the wrist – Caitlin had a fatal weakness for Man Jewellery. More than that, he seemed to be very excited about their date. He kept shooting her flirty looks, looks that said, *this is great, isn't it?*

But he kept saying, 'to be fair', to the point where Caitlin was struggling not to yell, 'You don't have to be fair all the time, you're not Judge Judy.'

Stop it, she told herself, firmly, because she knew it wasn't a good sign.

Then she thought, *I hope Nancy's managed to show Eva what she wants for lunch.* Would Joel have remembered to explain she didn't like any sort of sauce touching her food?

'So tell me about the gig tonight,' she said instead, forcing herself to concentrate on Lee's positives. The way he kissed. His drumming. His Scottish accent. The way this was all about fun, and physical pleasure and . . .

'Yeah, it's a bit of a dream come true for us, to be fair.'

Ten.

'Danny was talking to the promoter and if it goes OK, he's thinking of booking us for a festival he's running in the summer?'

'That would be amazing!' Caitlin sipped her cider. Maybe he was nervous. Third date, big gig, come-back-to-mine? nervous. 'I love festivals.'

'Do you mind camping?' Lee leaned forward again, with a grin, and Caitlin shoved her misgivings to one side as his knees touched hers under the table. 'It's a good laugh, and to be fair, we do need a hot backing singer . . .'

'Nngggh!' It burst out of her.

'What?' He sat back, confused.

'Nothing,' said Caitlin. 'Just . . . demonstrating my backing vocals!' She shook her head. 'I'm not a great singer, to be f—. To be honest with you.'

'No worries. We usually have everything turned up so loud we can barely hear Noah even. Another cider?' He indicated her empty glass.

'Um, maybe a diet coke this time?' she said, and picked up her phone. 'Just need to . . . You know. Make a call.'

'Sure. Be right back.' Lee grinned and slid out of the picnic table seat, giving her a flash of his runner's thighs, long and strong under his jeans.

Caitlin felt very conflicted.

She watched him stroll back into the bar and sank her head into her hands with a groan. It wasn't that she didn't fancy Lee – she did – but something had definitely unclicked.

The truth was, she had to acknowledge, the *idea* of Lee was just that bit more appealing than actual Lee. Daydream Lee had lived in her imagination for months, while he ran round the park and she imagined what it would be like to snog him, and, really, it was incredible that Actual Lee had come so close to her fantasy. But she couldn't ignore the fact that if he was really right, if there really *was* a connection between them, it wouldn't matter that he said 'to be fair' so much. She'd probably think it was adorable.

The sun went behind a cloud and some of the shine left Caitlin's day too.

But he was so good-looking, protested the other, bewildered, voice in her head. Why pass up the chance for some excitement after all these years? And he was a drummer! All her life she'd wanted to date a drummer. She didn't have to *marry* him.

Caitlin reached into her bag for her phone, to text Scarlett the dilemma, then realised that wasn't very mature either. Checking what your opinions were by asking someone else.

Another shock.

She rested her chin on her hands. It was the house. Facing up to the house had spoiled everything. That and the shadow of 'what would Eva do?' which had subtly inveigled itself in her head. Eva wouldn't have a fuck buddy. She had university professors giving her books of poetry.

But then I'm not like Eva, thought Caitlin, and felt a squirm inside she didn't enjoy.

Just see how it goes, she told herself, as Lee returned with the drinks. *Have fun. He's keen. Isn't that worth something?*

They had another drink, some crisps and talked more. Caitlin focused hard on the marathon Lee was running for Macmillan, and mentally superimposed the word 'gym' every time he mentioned his job at the 'leisure centre'. By the time the work crowd were starting to fill the outdoor tables around them, Caitlin knew the moment of truth was fast approaching: move on to the next phase of the date, or bail out.

'So.' Lee raised an eyebrow. 'Fancy something to eat? I've got to be at Danny's for five thirty to get ready.'

Caitlin steeled herself to say no but heard herself say, 'Why not?'

'Great!' He seemed delighted. 'Let's get some falafels on the way over.'

He stood up, and she stood up and in doing so stumbled against the table. Lee caught her, and it brought them into a semi-clinch. His face was very close to hers, so close she could feel his warm breath, and desire rushed over her as his fingers stroked the soft flesh of her arm. He smelled like sex and summer and leather and everything else Caitlin had a weakness for. All the hormones in her body raced in circles and made starburst patterns in her groin.

Lee's eyes locked with hers, and she hesitated. But when he leaned forward and started to kiss her, Caitlin's common sense kicked in. She had to stop this, before the date got any further.

'Lee,' she said, and turned her head at the last second. His soft lips brushed against her cheekbone, caressing the bone around her eye.

And then she saw something over Lee's shoulder that made her jerk away in shock.

It was Patrick. Patrick, standing on the pavement outside the pub, staring at them both.

He was wearing his best suit, the navy one, and his hair was fluffy from an early morning wash. And his face was grim with disapproval.

'What are you doing here?' she managed, her brain struggling to catch up. 'Shouldn't you be in Longhampton? With the kids?'

'No!' A deep furrow had appeared between his dark eyebrows. 'I drove down this morning. My car's parked down this street, it's as near as I could get to the house – bloody parking's worse than ever. How long have you been here?'

'About an hour?' It was more like two. Caitlin glanced at her watch. Wow, three. Time had sped past. 'And why are you at the house anyway?'

Patrick looked fit to spit. 'Because I've been with the builders! The builders you were supposed to liaise with hours ago, if you'd answered your phone.'

The builders. The foreman. Bollocks. 'It's in my bag,' she said. 'I'm not ignoring it, I just didn't hear it ring.'

'What if Eva had tried to call you? You can't just abdicate responsibility like that. You're their mother.' Patrick raised his hands. 'Oh, and by the way, thanks for letting me know you were dumping the kids on my sister all day. I didn't realise you'd roped Eva into babysitting so you could have an afternoon down the pub.'

'I didn't! I came back to sort out the house. Anyway, Eva *wanted* to babysit. They love her and she wants to spend time with them.'

Lee was still standing by the table, next to her. He took a step forward, to show he was with her, then looked from Patrick to Caitlin and raised a cocky eyebrow.

Oh, please don't say, Aren't you going to introduce us, thought Caitlin. Please *don't*.

'So . . . aren't you going to introduce us?' asked Lee, with enough of a chippy tone to get Patrick's back up.

'I'm sorry, I forgot my manners.' Patrick reached forward with his hand; for a mad moment, Caitlin wondered if he was going to smack Lee. But he didn't. He was in super-polite nuclear disapproval mode. 'I'm Patrick Reardon. Caitlin's husband.'

'To be fair, you're the ex-husband,' said Lee – again, chippily.

'Yes, the ex who has just detoured two hundred miles to sort out the marital home. That kind of ex.'

'Still an ex, pal.'

'And you are?'

'Lee Turnbull. Pleased to meet you.' He was making his accent a couple of degrees more Scottish than normal, Caitlin noticed. Was that deliberate? Did he think she wanted someone to defend her? Because she didn't. She was very done with white knights now.

'Oh, pack it in, both of you,' said Caitlin. The last thing she wanted – it turned out – was to be squabbled over like someone in a soap opera. Especially when Patrick was firmly in the right. She knew he'd be adding this to his mental spreadsheets, making it into something it wasn't. Dropping her even further down in his opinion. 'Lee's a friend. We're having a drink. Before his gig.'

Now Lee turned to her, with surprised eyes. 'I'm sorry?'

'Don't,' she said, and felt stupid about that too. *Brilliant, Caitlin,* she thought, *you're pissing* everyone *off now.* 'Just . . . we'll talk about this later.'

'Why aren't you answering your phone?' Patrick ignored Lee completely. 'Do you have any idea why the builder needed to talk to you?'

'To sign it off. It looked fine.' Caitlin pulled her spine tall. She really, really wished she hadn't had that last pint of cider. It had gone straight to her head. 'I have to pick some colours for the kitchen and we're done.'

Patrick leaned forward over the table, and carefully placed a computer print-out in front of her. 'No, Caitlin. They've forgotten to put the ventilation fan in. And a few other things.' There were red scribbles on every column. To her horror, Caitlin felt the old obstinacy rising up in her; the annoying urge to dig in her heels even though she knew she was in the wrong, rather than be told what to do. What her mother called her kamikaze streak.

'So you've put them right. That's great. Well done. Thank you.' She meant it, but it came out sarcastic.

Patrick eyed her. He was obviously seething. About the builders, or about Lee, or about her own shortcomings she couldn't tell.

'Don't be like that,' she said, and hunted for her phone in her bag. 'I was waiting for him to— Oh no, look, I must have put it on silent by mistake. There's only . . . three missed calls, and they're all from you. And . . . four from Eva.'

As if the phone could hear while they were all staring at it, it began ringing. Eva again. Caitlin disentangled herself from the table and stood up.

'Hi, Eva!' said Caitlin self-consciously. 'Everything all right?'

'Yes!' She sounded breathless. 'Something amazing's happened! I've been trying to call you!'

'What?' Caitlin glanced sideways at Patrick. He was standing very close to her, while glaring at Lee. She took a step away, but he followed her.

'Nancy's spoken! Nancy's actually spoken out loud!'

The words reverberated around Caitlin's head. 'What?'

'We were in the garden and she called Bumble over and he came! She was so clear! I couldn't believe it.' Eva made a noise that might have been a sob. 'She has such a beautiful voice, Caitlin. And it's all because of Bumble! I'm so proud of them both!'

Caitlin's stomach dropped like a stone down a well, falling and falling until it landed somewhere dark. Nancy had spoken? Without her there? To Eva?

But that's great, she told herself. *That's progress! It's great. It's* great.

'What's going on?' Patrick mouthed. Caitlin mouthed back 'nothing' and turned her shoulder. His words about her abdicating responsibility were still stinging.

'That's fantastic,' she managed. 'But she does speak to Bumble, doesn't she? Inside?'

'Yes, but this was different!' Eva's voice was jubilant, and Caitlin felt a weird, unwelcome irritation creeping over her. 'I'm just amazed she had such presence of mind – I thought she'd be far too scared, what with the size of the cows, but she just shouted right out and he came and . . .'

The dread solidified. 'Cows? What cows? What do you mean, scared?'

'Well, that's the other part of it. Don't panic, everything's under control now but . . .'

'Of course I'm panicking, Eva.' She wasn't joking. Alarm

bells jangled in her head. Cows? They were meant to be staying in and reading, or watching DVDs. 'Don't ever say don't panic to a parent.'

'No, no, don't worry, all that happened was that some cows got out of the field and came into the garden. Um, and a bull. The pugs managed to get caught up in the middle of them, and I was so scared for poor Bumble. He was literally about a second away from getting trampled, but Nancy was such a hero! She stood on the bench by the barbecue, and she shouted for him, and—'

'Stop.' Caitlin had gone completely cold. She knew her face was white; the blood had drained into her stomach. 'Go back. Nancy was *outside* with a loose bull? How did that happen? You didn't let her go out there, did you?'

Finally Eva paused. Caitlin turned and saw Patrick too was staring intently at her. He looked horrified, even though he'd just been proved right: her ignoring the phone *had* been stupid. And dangerous.

'No, of course not. She went out on her own.' Eva's voice faltered. 'I think . . . she went to pick some flowers. Obviously I wouldn't have let her if we'd known about the cows . . .'

'Why weren't you watching her?' It came out as a screech. 'Nancy can't talk! She can't shout for help! You have to keep an eye on her *the entire time*! What were *you* doing when she wandered off like that?'

She felt Patrick's hand on her arm but she shrugged it off. Fiery emotions were powering through her, spiked by her own guilt that she'd left Nancy alone, and shame that Patrick had caught her with Lee, and embarrassment that Lee was witnessing all this. What a bloody mess. What a bloody mess she'd made of everything.

'That is the first rule of parenting!' she hissed, hating herself. 'Anyone knows that. You don't let kids out of your sight. How could you not know that?'

'I was with Joel. Caitlin, don't overreact, please—'

'Don't tell me how to react – you can't imagine what I'm feeling.' She squeezed her eyes closed but could only see her tiny, silent, terrified baby girl in a field full of massive cows. Hooves, bones, whippy tails, those huge gummy jaws. Caitlin felt as if her insides were being torn out of her chest. 'How could you even *think* about your dogs when you knew Nancy was out there. That's . . . I'm sorry, but that's *not normal*.'

'Well, of course I was worried about Nancy! It goes without saying! But Bee was already injured, and the bull was turning on Bumble and—'

'No! Don't say another word about your bloody dogs. Not in the same breath as my daughter! Please!'

Eva fell silent.

'I trusted you, Eva. I trusted you to look after my children!' Caitlin was shivering. 'And you let this happen. That's the last time you ever, ever look after them on your own again. *Ever.* From now on, Patrick has to be there too.'

'Caitlin!' Eva's voice was faint with hurt, but it only fuelled Caitlin's anger – with herself, far more than with Eva.

'If anything had happened to Nancy . . .' she started but felt too sick to continue.

'Give me the mobile.' Patrick was by her side.

'No!' She turned away, hiding the phone. 'Stop telling me what to do, Patrick!'

'You're in shock and you're being offensive. Give it here.' She struggled, but Patrick firmly removed the phone from her shaking hand.

'Eva, it's me,' he said tersely. 'Where's Nancy now? Is she all right?' He listened, then said, 'OK, that's good. Fine. I know . . . I know . . . Calm down and tell me exactly what happened.'

Caitlin sank to the seat, numb. Lee sat on the other side of the table, glaring at her. He looked like he was going off her pretty fast, too.

Awkwardness hung over them like wet clothes.

'Should I go?' he mouthed.

'Yeah.' Caitlin tried to smile but failed. Her face wouldn't work. The only image in her head was Nancy. She hadn't been there when Nancy needed her. *No one* had been there for Nancy. What kind of shit human beings were they? 'Sorry, I'm going to have to go back tonight. I need to make sure everything's all right.'

'Sure.' Lee looked uncomfortable. 'It sounds pretty bad. I hope your little girl's OK.' He raised an eyebrow. 'Are you . . . all right with him?'

For a second Caitlin didn't know what he meant. 'Who? Oh, you mean Patrick? Er, yeah. He's just . . . He's her dad. Look, I'll text you later. Hope it goes well. Good luck.'

'Cheers.' He went to kiss her cheek, then pulled back. Suddenly it felt wrong. Everything felt wrong. 'I'll let you know how it goes. The gig.'

Caitlin smiled but her ear was sharpened to Patrick's voice. He was still talking, issuing instructions about hot sugary tea, and duvets, and CBBC. Reassuring, and calm. She simmered. How dare he *reassure* Eva? Why wasn't he raging with her, for putting their daughter in danger like that? Was he on her side now?

Caitlin clenched her fists until her nails dug into her palms. The holiday mood had gone, as if it had never been there. How could life flip so quickly? But then it always did. She never got any warning of any of the disasters that happened to her.

She turned back to wave goodbye to Lee but he was walking away, his long loping strides covering the pavement until he turned the corner, and was gone.

A suffocating weight descended on her chest.

Patrick had stopped talking. He handed the phone back to her and sat down at the table, leaning forward to examine her expression. He'd always done that. It always made Caitlin wonder what she looked like to him.

'Tea? Do you need some tea?' he asked brusquely. 'Or something stronger? You've gone pale.'

'I'm fine,' said Caitlin, automatically.

And then he started. 'I know you're shocked, so am I, but there was no need to say that to Eva. You've got no right to lecture her about not taking proper care of our children when you dumped them with her to meet up with your new boyfriend.'

'Hello? I came here to deal with the builders and what I do in my spare time is none of your business any more. She was looking after them. She *wanted* to. She . . .'

'Don't start that.' Usually when Patrick was angry he went quiet and still but now there was a fury about him that Caitlin had never seen. 'You act as if there's one rule for you, and another for everyone else. You never think of anyone apart from yourself, Caitlin. You don't even realise you're doing it.'

'Bollocks.' She narrowed her eyes. 'I spend my entire waking life looking after my children. I barely think of myself *at all*, and then when I get half a day off, someone I trusted to care for them, their own relative, is stupid enough to put them in real danger!'

'Eva made a mistake. We all make mistakes.'

'You can't make mistakes when it comes to safety. And you can't worry about your *dogs* more than children – that's absolutely crazy. Seriously, Patrick, don't tell me you don't find that outrageous?'

Stop it, Caitlin, warned the voice in her head, *don't push yourself into a corner out of bloodymindedness.*

Patrick wrinkled his nose. 'No, of course I'm shocked by that, but it's a bit rich of you to talk about Eva making mistakes when this isn't the first mistake *you've* made.'

'Meaning?'

'Meaning you let Nancy get lost on her own just a few weeks ago, and you told Joel not to tell me. And then the time you wanted to go out partying with Loverboy there you left them with' – Patrick curled his lip – '"Scarlett from work", and Joel flooded the house and Nancy ended up petrified of her book about fire engines.'

'What? She isn't petrified of it. Don't make stuff up, Patrick. You haven't even seen her since we went to Eva's.'

'No? Stupid, careless Eva told me the other night, when I phoned to see how they were getting on. She tried to read it to Nancy one afternoon while you were busy, but Nancy started crying. Clearly that whole incident's traumatised her.'

Caitlin felt empty. 'I didn't know that.' Why hadn't Eva said? Was she hoarding up details like that? Had her mother been right – was Eva trying to build herself a role in Nancy's life that Caitlin wasn't part of? 'She should have told me. That's weird, not to tell me.'

'Maybe she didn't want you to know your carelessness had had such a distressing effect.' Patrick's tone was cutting. 'Either you trust people to look after our children while you go out, or you don't. You can't decide after the event that they weren't up to the job and blame them for the consequences.'

She pressed her mouth tight shut, because she knew he was right. And it scorched her soul with humiliation.

'I just don't get why you're behaving like this,' Patrick went on. 'Leaving everything up to other people. Like today, not dealing with the foreman. It's just so *irresponsible* – he waited for two hours for you. They've got other jobs to go to. I had to cancel meetings to come and sort it. But no, *you* had to get to the pub, so you just swanned off. And then you have the nerve to have a go at everyone else?' He shook his head. 'Seriously.'

'Then don't bother doing it,' she snapped back, stung. 'Leave us to get on with things. Oh. I forgot. You have. You decided we were too messy to live with. So you got a job so far away from us that you wouldn't have to.'

'You know, that's so far from the truth that . . .' Patrick stopped, then stared at Caitlin as if he was seeing her for the first time.

Then he shrugged. The anger left him, and what was left in his eyes was disappointment. Caitlin felt small. Small and stupid, but still angry.

'What happened?' he said. 'You were never like this.'

'*You* happened,' said Caitlin, spitefully. 'You sucked the joy and fun out of my life so I had to find it where I could.'

Patrick stiffened as if she'd slapped him, and she knew she'd gone too far. But she couldn't stop. She hated herself more than she hated him, and he was easier to get at.

'Don't lecture me about neglecting our children when you're the one who barely saw them from one end of the week to the next,' she said bitterly. 'You put your job way, *way* before any of us. I had to do half the dad stuff as well as all the mum things.' Caitlin was speaking so fast she barely knew what she was saying; it was pouring out from a place in her head she hadn't wanted to go, not while they were keeping everything amicable. 'You've got no idea about what makes a fun family life.'

'What's that supposed to mean?'

'It's . . .' Caitlin shoved her hands in her hair. 'It's impossible, Patrick. We were never ever going to make this work, purely because you're . . .'

She stopped. Patrick looked stunned, and more handsome that she remembered. His eyes were confused, and she couldn't say it. Something was stopping her from delivering the coup de grace.

'Because I'm what?' he repeated.

She stared at him, unable to speak.

Just like Nancy, she thought, in a moment of awful clarity. The power of that Reardon silence. They know exactly what they're doing. He's only holding those questions in so I'll wonder what he's thinking. And there's no point me doing it because he can read me like a book.

'Don't look at me like that,' she said, unable to stand it any more. 'Just say whatever it is. Go on. Say it.'

Patrick waited another long second. Caitlin jutted her jaw defiantly, and braced herself for the worst.

You're a terrible mother and a useless adult.

I never loved you.

It's your fault Nancy's not talking.

It's nothing I haven't told myself, she wanted to yell.

His voice, when it came, was cracked, but he didn't drop his gaze. His eyes still burned into hers.

'Was that him?' Patrick was trying to be steely but he licked the dry skin on his lip nervously. 'Is that the guy you were seeing . . . before?'

'Before?'

'Don't play dumb, Caitlin. I know. Was that him?'

The question hung in the air. Caitlin knew whatever she said would change everything from this point. If she said yes, Patrick would be devastated; if she said no . . . then her face would give her away and he could add *liar* to that list.

'It's not what you think,' she blurted out, and knew immediately it was the worst thing. It was yes and no and I'm a liar, all at once.

Patrick's expression wavered, as a ripple of pain passed across his face like a bomb blast, and Caitlin instinctively wanted to reach out to soothe his shattered dignity, and to explain. But then just as quickly his eyes hardened and she felt the cold chill of his disapproval.

'I thought so,' he said, then smiled the bleakest smile she'd ever seen. 'You think I always want to be right. Well, I don't. Not always.'

They sat silently, two miserable people in a sea of cheerful Friday afternoon drinkers, and Caitlin knew the 'amicable separation' phase of their divorce had just come to an end. And it scared her, not knowing what would follow.

Chapter twenty-five

'I can't stop thinking about what Caitlin said. I wake up in the middle of the night, thinking, God, she must think I'm a terrible person. That I care more about the dogs than I do about Joel and Nancy. I mean, how can she think that?'

'Eva, don't.' Anna stopped walking and pointed at the bench, motioning her to sit down. They were in the park, and Bumble and Bee had done their lap of the flowerbeds, finishing up by the coffee stand where Pongo, while still closely attached to Anna, had managed to steal a doughnut. 'We all say awful things in the heat of the moment. That doesn't mean they're true, or even that you really feel that way once you've calmed down. Have you seen Caitlin since? Or the kids?'

Eva shook her head, sorrowfully. 'That was their weekend. They're not due back till the end of the month.'

'And how was Caitlin when she collected them?'

She sat down with a sigh, making a bubble of coffee froth out of the plastic lid. 'She didn't. Patrick took them home to Bristol. He was in a weird mood too. Barely speaking.' The thought of the happy, easy weekends changing into something tense and monitored made Eva's heart shrivel. Joel and Nancy's confused faces, thinking she couldn't take care of them. Caitlin's mistrust and anger. 'I keep expecting a call to say Caitlin's changed the arrangements.'

'She won't do that. Come on, it was an accident. It happens to everyone at some point. My dad once left me in the ballpit at IKEA. Came home with a flat-pack wardrobe, a ton of meatballs and an empty carseat. Mum went berserk. *Anyone could have taken her!*' Anna pretended to tear out her hair. 'Dad pointed out I didn't come with instructions, so it was unlikely.'

Eva forced a smile. Anna was trying so hard to cheer her up. But she knew she'd never been careless with Lily, Becca or Chloe. You couldn't be, when they weren't yours.

'And have I turned out damaged?' Anna went on. 'Course not. Dad told that story at our wedding! Phil admitted he'd done the same thing, but at the gym crèche. We had people coming up to us all night, with some horrendous stories. I'm sure your parents were the same, you just don't remember.'

Eva twisted the plastic lid, round and round. There was a pale beige lip print where her mouth had been. 'That's the point, I do remember. My dad was . . . he was emotionally illiterate. Not on purpose, he just didn't have that parenting instinct. It wasn't nice. I'd never want to put Joel and Nancy in a situation where they didn't feel safe. I hated it.'

And I don't want to be like my dad. Someone who should never have had children. It filled Eva with a chilly sensation. Another thing she'd thought about in the middle of the night: maybe some subconscious instinct had subtly steered her away from disaster? Choosing the wrong men, staying later and later at work, avoiding the possibilities. Maybe her body had known a truth about herself she didn't. And Caitlin's voice, distorted down the phone. *How can you imagine how I'm feeling? You're . . . bizarre.*

'Caitlin said I couldn't understand how she felt – well, maybe I can't.' It was hard to hear herself say such mad things; she couldn't imagine saying them to anyone but Anna. 'Maybe I'll never be able to look after them properly if I don't have that parenting gene.'

'Look.' Anna turned on the bench, tucking one leg underneath herself. 'You and I have been through all this. Parenthood – it's not some kind of moral verdict. It's just biology. This isn't about what you'd have been like as a parent – this is about being a babysitter. Caitlin's last babysitter wrecked the house, for God's sake. No harm done with you. Next time, you keep all the doors locked, and never take your eyes off them. You've learned your lesson. Move on.'

'OK,' said Eva. 'Thanks. You always make things feel so normal.'

'And there's something else I wanted to tell you.' Anna chewed her lip. 'I'm not sure this is the best time now.'

'Go on.' Eva felt her stomach scoop out, a dark hole forming just under her ribs. She had a feeling she knew what Anna was going to say next. 'What is it? And don't make up something about Becca getting a new job.'

'I'm . . . Oh dear. My timing is rubbish.' She put her empty coffee cup carefully on the bench, then looked straight into Eva's face. Anna had truthful eyes, deep blue and open. She never bothered lying; it showed. 'I'm having a baby.'

It was so Anna, thought Eva, as her lips formed a smile: not the bald 'I'm pregnant' or, worse, the twee 'we're pregnant' that they'd both scoffed at. 'I'm having a baby.' It was all she'd ever wanted: a baby of her own. She already had a family.

'It's really early days,' she went on, hurriedly, searching

369

Eva's face for signs of distress. She grabbed her hands. 'You're literally the only person who knows apart from Phil, and I wouldn't normally tell anyone, but . . . I remember how I felt. And I wanted you to know because not telling you would feel, I don't know, insulting somehow. To us. To you. Maybe that's just me being selfish, wanting to tell you, I'm sorry.'

And now there's just me. The words formed in Eva's head, behind her eyes. *Just me, standing on the harbourside as the last of my friends sails away to a place I can't follow.* She felt the loneliness reach up and swallow her heart.

'Don't be sorry,' she said. 'I'm really happy for you! I am, honestly.'

'Are you? You don't have to pretend. You can tell me to shut up and never mention it again if you want.'

Eva managed a half-laugh. 'And how's that going to work? Are you going to pretend you've just had a really big lunch for nine months?'

'Sorry. I'm sorry. I just didn't want you to find out from Lily or someone at the shop. I . . . I don't want it to spoil things between us. I'm not going to turn into one of those baby bores, I promise. Or at least I won't be any worse than I am now. Oh God, this wasn't how I planned to tell you.'

'Anna, stop apologising, I'm thrilled.' Eva squeezed her hands back. Was that why Anna had urged her to go to the doctor? That 'not too late' chat – had she known then? There was a lump in her throat but it wasn't all for herself – it was for Anna and the joy she couldn't hide. As the initial shock faded, Eva realised she *was* happy for Anna. It ran a sharp nail down her own conflicted soul, but she was still happy for her friend.

'Is Phil excited?'

'He is. Well, he is now. It was a surprise. Definitely not

planned. He'd been talking about going for the snip, and I suppose it must have shocked his swimmers into some kind of last-ditch efficiency drive. But as I say, it's very early days. And that's another reason I wanted to tell you. In case something went . . .' A shadow crossed her face.

'Don't,' said Eva. 'Nothing's going to go wrong.'

They sat on the bench, their dogs lying by their feet. Across the park, two women were walking with baby buggies, matching black Labradors walking obediently alongside. The classic yummy mummies Eva and Anna had always raised their eyebrows at when they hogged the best tables in the open-air park café, creating a wall of giggling toddlers.

Their laughter drifted across the flowerbeds to Eva and Anna's bench, but neither of them said anything.

On the way back to The Quarry, Eva dropped the last three bags of Mick's clothes into one of the charity shops. That was it. The final wardrobe cleared.

Well, apart from the few items she couldn't bear to think of being worn by someone else. His old jumper that he wore for pottering in the garden. His battered cords. His favourite shirt. All hidden in a chest of drawers, still smelling of him. His real clothes, not the costumes that made him famous Michael Quinn, everyone's favourite 'whatever'.

'Oh, Mrs Quinn, you've been so generous to us.' The charity shop manager rushed out of the back room as she was leaving. 'I wanted to say thank you. We must have raised hundreds from your donations.'

'No need.' Eva felt awkward. She'd shared out the clothes

between random shops, not wanting to see a whole window display of Mick in stiff dummy poses. 'I met Michael in a charity shop, so it seems . . . appropriate that we're giving it back.'

'Oh! I thought you met in a bookshop?'

She hesitated, then shook her head. It seemed pointless to keep up the lie now. 'No. The Help the Aged shop, in fact. On the high street.'

The lady smiled. 'Ah, well, that's even better. Anyway, I'm glad you called in, we were just about to post this to you.' She held out a large envelope. 'A few personal things we found in some jackets. All those inner pockets in men's jackets, they're a nightmare! We haven't looked,' she added, as Eva took the envelope from her.

It felt as if it had the usual Mick detritus: coins, cards, phone numbers. Eva folded it in half and shoved it in her bag. She didn't want to look at it now. Just another thing to look over, then throw away.

'I read you've got a book coming out?' the lady went on, conversationally. 'That'll be interesting – will there be much about Longhampton in it? We like to think of Mr Quinn as our most famous resident . . .'

Fortunately, Eva's phone began to ring before she had to answer. She excused herself and stepped outside to take the call.

It was Patrick.

'Do you mind if I stay this evening?' he asked. 'I've got a meeting in Worcester in the morning and I need to be fresh.'

'Worcester? Um, yes, of course.' Was that a funny note in his voice? 'Is everything OK, Paddy?'

He left a pause, then said, 'I'll tell you when I see you.'

Patrick arrived at ten, with his overnight bag and a suit carrier. He also had a bunch of flowers for Eva.

'They're to say thanks for letting me stay at short notice,' he said, as the pugs sniffed around his ankles. 'And also sorry for what happened last Friday.'

'I'm the one who should apologise . . .' Eva started, but he shook his head.

'No, I'm sorry. These things happen. Caitlin had no right to talk to you the way she did. But she'd have reacted exactly the same way if it had been me looking after them. Or her mother, or anyone. If it's any consolation.' He looked bleak.

'She had every reason to be angry and panicky . . .'

'She acted like that because she knew she was in the wrong. If she was that worried, she wouldn't have left Nancy alone in the first place.' Patrick ran a hand through his hair. 'Look, I've got . . . I've got something I need to talk to you about. Let's make a cup of tea.'

Eva followed him down the hall into the kitchen. The dogs trailed behind her, without their usual chirrupy barks, as if they sensed something serious was unfolding and wanted to listen.

'Please tell me you haven't made up a meeting in Worcester to come here to apologise to me,' she said, lightly. He seemed to want something to occupy himself, so she let him get the teapot, put the kettle on. 'A phone call would have been fine.'

'It's not that.' Eva watched as Patrick poured the hot water into the teapot, fitted the lid and leaned back against the kitchen cabinet. His usual small, meticulous movements. He

stared at it for a moment, then said, 'I've got an informal inter-
view for a position in Worcester. Someone I used to work with
is setting up a new business, and he's looking for a regional
manager for the West Midlands.'

'But you've only been in your new job a few months!'

'I know.'

'Will they let you move? Aren't you meant to be rolling out
some new sales push?' Eva's mind searched for a reason. It was
out of character for Patrick to make snap decisions like this. 'Is
there a problem there?'

'There's no problem.' Patrick leaned back against the counter. 'I just . . . I had a conversation with Caitlin when I took the
kids back last weekend. She said some things that I don't
accept, about my care of the children, but she blames me for
moving away. And she's right about that. I hate being so far
away from them. And at the same time, I don't like the way
she's behaving, so I want to be nearer, in case . . .' His mouth
closed, into a tight line. Eva didn't like what it said.

'In case what?'

'In case they need me.'

'Oh, Patrick. Caitlin's not going to do anything silly.'

'It doesn't need to be silly. It just needs her to be careless,
and she's more than capable of that. I used to think she was
spontaneous, but now I think she's incapable of thinking about
anyone other than herself. Joel's got more common sense.'

Eva stared at him. Whenever Patrick talked about Caitlin's
failings, he never sounded bitter, more disappointed. The
same way he'd doggedly stuck with his first car, a red Alfa
Romeo that spent more time in the garage than it did on his
drive, lavishing money and time on it, even though it was
clearly a lemon. She'd thought then it was weird, his

insistence that its perpetual unreliability could be fixed, since he didn't take the same attitude with under-performing stores. But he'd loved it. He'd only sold it the year before he met Caitlin.

'I know this is a stupid question, but why did you let them send you to Newcastle in the first place?' she asked. Was Caitlin telling the truth? Did he honestly put his job before them all?

'It wasn't a choice – I was more or less sent up there. And I genuinely thought it would be good for us – a fresh start.' He turned his hands upwards. 'We could have got a fantastic house up there, big bedrooms for the kids, a garden. But no. Caitlin made up some bollocks about needing to stay in Bristol. Not wanting to leave her house, the kids' schools. I think she just didn't want to come.'

'The house is full of memories for her, you know.' Eva reached over for the teapot and poured. 'She was telling me about being there with her gran, when Joel was a baby. It's her safe place.'

'I get that. We didn't have to sell, we could have rented it out. But Caitlin never wanted to move on. It's hard, knowing that you're competing with the past and losing. And . . .' He blew out his cheeks, self-consciously. 'Cait didn't tell you?'

'Tell me what?'

'I thought you two were all pally now.'

'I thought we were too.' Eva picked up her mug. 'But I'm not a mindreader either. Tell me.'

Patrick paused, struggling with the confidence. The effort in his face made Eva's heart sink; this was something he'd bottled up. 'There was someone else.'

'What?' She froze, tea halfway to her lips.

'She'd been lying about where she was going, nights when

she supposedly went out to Zumba but never washed her kit afterwards. Always on her phone, always going on about needing space. She even said I was spying on her, I said I needed to know where she was. I don't think that's unreasonable. She swore there was nothing going on, but . . . that's who she was seeing in Bristol on Friday. A bloke. So it wasn't just the house, it was me she didn't want.'

'She never told me that.' Eva was shocked; she wouldn't have guessed Caitlin had been cheating, not from the way she had talked about Patrick. Frustrated and angry, yes, but not casual, the way you'd expect from someone whose heart was elsewhere. She'd known friends of Mick's who'd turned out to be having affairs, and it had been obvious a mile off to her, from the boredom in their eyes, the coldness.

Patrick's shoulders slumped, and Eva was about to lean forward and console him but before she could, his face closed up again. His jaw was hard, clenched like Superman's.

'Which is fine, that's her choice. But the children didn't choose not to be with me, I was wrong to walk away from them, and I need to find a way to get back. So I put out some feelers and this opportunity came up.' He took his mug from the tray. 'It's a sideways move, a step down actually, but I'll be closer to the kids. Caitlin can do what she wants.'

'Are you sure?'

'I couldn't go back, even if I wanted to,' said Patrick. 'I know how people should behave. And I can't live with someone who lies to me, and lies to themselves.' The old Patrick was back, furious and judgemental. Eva saw her mother in his face, and knew anything she said would be a waste of breath. Patrick had made up his mind. And she felt sorry for Caitlin.

'Have you eaten?' she asked. 'Can I make you something?'

He shook his head. 'I don't feel much like eating right now.'

Eva couldn't sleep. Her mind flickered behind her closed eyes, as if she'd drunk too much coffee, and Caitlin, and Patrick, and her mum, and her dad went round and round in her mind. Especially her mum and dad. If Patrick was judging Caitlin against their relationship, he wasn't being fair.

She stared into the semi-darkness, leaning forward to see into the dogs' sleeping area – just to reassure herself – and saw only Bee sprawled out on the luxury bed. Where was Bumble? Was that why she'd woken?

Eva threw back the duvet and slid her feet into her slippers, slipping quietly out onto the landing. There was no light under Patrick's bedroom door; good, she thought, at least he's getting some sleep.

But as she turned to go down the stairs to the kitchen, Eva caught a tiny movement out of the corner of her eye. The door to the bedroom where Joel and Nancy slept was ajar, and as she moved closer, she saw a shape on the bed.

Her heart quickened. She moved closer and heard a faint noise, like a sigh. The moonlight spread a pearly grey light over the pale carpet of the landing as she stepped closer, her heart hammering. And then she saw inside the room.

The shape on Nancy's single bed was Bumble, curled into a tight fawn egg on her Hello Kitty duvet cover. He was snuffling gently, rolled against her pillow, as close as he could to his missing friend.

Eva smiled and went into the room to stroke him. She nearly

377

jumped out of her skin when she saw Patrick sitting on the edge of Joel's bed, hunched up, holding something.

'Patrick? What are you doing in here?' As her eyes adjusted to the light, she could see he was holding a bear – Joel's teddy bear, worn at the ears and missing an eye. Caitlin had never got round to replacing the glass button.

Patrick nodded. He was still in his clothes, his tie pulled loose under an unbuttoned collar. His eyes were bleary.

'Couldn't sleep.'

'Well, go downstairs, I'll make you some cocoa.'

He shook his head. 'Just wanted to sit here. My favourite bit of the day, watching Joel and Nancy sleep. I used to ask Cait if she could put them to bed later, so I could read bedtime stories but she wouldn't. Had to keep them to a routine.'

Eva sat down on the bed next to him. 'I'm sorry, Paddy.'

He shrugged. 'It's just little things you miss. Bathtime. Bedtime. Feeling you're part of their memories. Sometimes I'd come home late and, and just sit on the floor, by their beds. Listening to them sleeping.' He tugged at the teddy's ear. 'I hate thinking they might wake up scared, and not have anyone there to make the bad men go away. Especially Joel. What kind of sad bloke does that, though?'

Eva saw Patrick's eyes glistening in the half-light, and her heart contracted at the image of her little brother, sitting like a loyal guard dog at the feet of his sleeping children's beds. A demonstration of his love that they'd probably never even see.

This is what it means, she thought, that tidal wave of parental love that you can't understand until it's consuming you. And her heart shrank again, for herself, it would only ever be something she could guess at.

'It's what Dad would have done,' he said, and finally Eva couldn't bear it any more.

'No,' she said. 'It's exactly what Dad wouldn't have done.'

He turned to her, but she stared straight ahead. 'You're a million times more of a dad than he was, Patrick. Mum might have wanted you to think he was loving and decent and all that, but . . . he wasn't. She wished he was, but he wasn't.'

She felt Patrick turn to her and when he started to speak, to defend their father, she said, calmly, 'You know what one of my earliest memories is? Coming downstairs when you were a baby, and hearing Dad telling Mum that he never wanted us. They weren't even having a row. I think she'd asked him to make my lunch while she fed you, and he just said it. "You were the one who wanted these kids, Barbara, not me."'

She could hear his voice now, bitter and matter-of-fact, and remembered the shock of hearing something so un-Dad-like coming out of her adored father's mouth. The sunflower pattern of the wallpaper on the stairs, the up-and-down wail from Patrick that she felt she had to stop, so Daddy wouldn't say that again.

'He said that?'

She nodded. 'Once I knew that, I could see it. Why he was always at the surgery, for a start. He just didn't like being around children. Mum preferred to say Dad was so wonderful, supporting her so she could be at home with us, but it was actually so *he* didn't have to be at home. With us. That's not why *you* work so hard. It upsets me when I hear you say that.'

Patrick seemed to be struggling to process it. 'Did Dad know you heard him?'

Eva shook her head. 'I'm not saying he was abusive, he just . . . clearly hated parenthood. I can see that now. It took

379

me a long time to separate that from him just not liking *us*! I wondered for a long time if we were even his kids, if they'd adopted us. Seriously, Paddy, he wasn't a great dad, and Mum gave you a totally unrealistic role model to live up to, because that's the father she wanted him to be. She *knew* he wasn't like that. But when Dad died, and Mum clung on to her version of him, for herself as well as for you . . .' Her voice trailed off.

That's what she saw in Nancy, the little girl with the big secret she couldn't tell.

'I worry about Nancy,' she said, quietly. 'I worry about all of you.'

Patrick did something he hadn't done since he was a boy: he put an arm around his sister's shoulders. It was a gesture that swept Eva straight back to their childhood, when sometimes he'd have nightmares and she'd slip into his room to comfort him, only to have him pretend he was fine. And then he'd put his arm around her, as if being in charge of the comforting made the fear go away.

They sat next to each other on the single bed, and Eva felt her breath slow, in and out, in and out, until she and Patrick were matching breaths, and the room felt smaller and smaller, and darker. An unexpected calm love filled Eva's whole body, and in her mind she pulled them all in to her – her brother, her niece, her nephew, her dogs – protecting them with her whole soul, wrapping her arms around them, holding them tight.

'It's going to be OK,' she whispered.

She felt his nod. He didn't speak. Couldn't, maybe. Was he crying? She couldn't remember ever seeing the grown-up Patrick cry.

'You've made this house come alive,' she whispered. 'You, and Nancy, and Joel. It feels like such a happy place now.'

He said nothing, but squeezed her.

Eva went on, feeling she could say anything into the darkness, 'The dogs were so lonely after Mick died. Even lonelier than me. And now Joel makes Bee speak again, and Bumble adores Nancy. Please don't stop coming. I'll never let anything like that happen again, I promise.' She swallowed, unsure of whether she was asking too much. 'I know I can't understand a parent's love, but—' she began, but he stopped her.

'No,' he said. Patrick spoke in fits and starts. 'When I first met Joel, I knew as much about parenting as you do – less, probably. It didn't stop me loving him. And it didn't stop him loving me, I know that. I loved Joel first because he was Caitlin's, then I loved him for himself. Because he's a great kid. He's funny, and he's caring, and he's just . . . kind. And I made mistakes, because I was trying too hard, and Joel forgave me, because he knew how much I wanted it to work.'

Eva's throat tightened. She'd always known her brother cared deeply about his adopted son, even though they were poles apart, but she'd never heard him express it so plainly. Every syllable ached with love.

'When Nancy came along, I knew a bit more about parenting, but I didn't love them differently. Nancy was mine, but Joel had chosen to be mine, and I'd chosen to be his. We both had to learn, together.'

Patrick leaned his head against hers. 'Don't tell me you don't understand about love, Eva.' The words were gruff, coming from a deep part of him, a place he rarely brought out for inspection. 'You do. You understand love just fine.'

The moon moved behind the curtains and let a pale finger of light fall between the two single beds. Bumble stirred on Nancy's duvet, snuggling into her pillow, and the tears that had been pooling in Eva's eyes slid down her cheeks. She cried, even though she didn't, strangely, feel sad.

Chapter twenty-six

Caitlin stood at the café counter, wiping the same spot over and over again, with harder and harder strokes. She was vaguely aware that Scarlett and Mary were watching her from the kitchen, but she didn't care. She had too much else to care about right now.

The letter from Patrick's solicitor was still in the pocket of her jacket, waiting for her like a finger-tapping bailiff, heavy with polite menace. It was on thick paper, which somehow indicated how very serious this now was, and though it only ran to a few brief paragraphs, each one of them made her feel sick. Sick, guilty, scared.

Her mum had been right: Patrick had changed his tune once he'd realised she was moving on, and the tune was a very angry one.

She wiped the counter until her own unhappy face reflected back at her from the black Formica. Patrick wanted residency split between them; he was 'concerned' with Caitlin's 'parenting choices', particularly around Nancy's continuing speech disorder; he wanted to revisit the financial agreement. All couched in that faux-polite but still aggressive legalese that made it clear that this was now way beyond the capacity of that nice mediator in the cardigan.

Caitlin stopped wiping and leaned on the counter, sinking her head in her hands.

She didn't know what to do next. That was what it came down to. First she'd been furious at Patrick's questioning of her parenting, then she'd been panicked at the abrupt escalation of hostilities, which she knew was partly her fault after the way she'd taken her self-loathing out on Eva, then she'd felt cornered. Caitlin knew she couldn't waste time engaging the wrong solicitor, and she couldn't face doing it alone. It went against every instinct in her body, but she needed help.

It was time to take her mum up on the offer of that lawyer. And she knew she had to do it now, before she talked herself out of it.

The café was in its post-lunch, pre-tea lull, with only a few tables occupied. It was nearly twenty to three, ten minutes before Caitlin usually left to walk up to the school for Nancy, so she didn't have long. This wasn't a call she wanted to make with the sonar-like bat hearing of her children around.

Scarlett emerged from the kitchen, clearly on a gossip-gathering mission. Before she could speak, Caitlin pulled off her spotted pinny and handed it to her. 'I need to make a call,' she said. 'Can you cover for me for a bit?'

'But Joanne wants to talk to us before you go.' Scarlett frowned. 'She's on her way back from the wholesalers. She says she's got a big announcement.'

'It's urgent. Two minutes.'

'Cait, I think it's about a new café.' Scarlett dropped her voice. 'I just *happened* to overhear her talking to someone in the back office, and . . .'

Caitlin would have been agog for the craic last week, but that was last week. Now she didn't care if Joanne was about to open a Sadie's Kitchen on Mars.

'Scarlett, I've got to make this call. I'm sorry. I'll be back in a tick.'

She weaved around the gingham tables, narrowly avoiding bumping into Joanne herself, who was marching in with an armful of files. As Caitlin turned back to apologise with a wave of her hand, and saw the dismal selection of regulars, eking out half a carrot cake and removing the nuts as if they were radioactive, she thought, what in the name of God am I doing here?

She had no answer. But her mother would definitely have at least one. That was the price she'd have to pay for asking for assistance.

Lynne picked up on the third ring, and answered with the brisk professionality that made Caitlin feel simultaneously reassured and on the back foot.

'Mum, it's me,' she said. 'I'm really sorry to ring you at work, but I need your advice.'

'You need my advice? Stop the press!' Lynne pretended to sound amazed. 'Is this April Fool's day?'

'No. I've had a letter from Patrick's solicitor.' Caitlin swallowed. She'd ducked into an alleyway near the café, and it smelled of dirty water and seagulls, which didn't help. 'You were right. He's decided to fight. He's talking about going for fifty-fifty residency, and wants to go back to mediation. I think he's hinting that if the mediator doesn't make it happen he'll go to court and get a judge to decide. Can he do that? Can he make Joel and Nancy stand up in court and say who they want to live with?'

It made her sick. Nancy in court, scared and silent, being pressured to speak. Joel overcompensating, trying to pretend he was fine. Caitlin clenched her fist.

'Oh.' Lynne's tone changed. 'Oh, dear.'

'And he wants to review the financial agreement too. There's something about the house and him investing money in repairs – he can't make me sell Gran's house, can he? He can't . . . kick us out?'

Her chest felt like someone was standing on it. She could hardly breathe. The dank alleyway seemed to be closing in on her, and when she shut her eyes, the letter rose in front of her, each little paragraph a bombshell. Patrick never started things he couldn't finish. She knew this meant he'd go as far as he possibly could, maybe even taking the children off her if he could . . .

'I don't know why he's being like this, Mum.' It came out as a wail.

'Has something happened?' asked Lynne. 'Tell me, Caitlin.'

Mum knew. She was smart. There was no point pretending, but even as she spoke Caitlin could hear herself modifying events.

'I saw him last week in Bristol. I came home to sort out the house and he bumped into me having lunch with a friend. He . . . he jumped to conclusions. And then Eva was supposed to be looking after the children and she let Nancy wander off into a *herd of cows*, and I . . . I gave her a bollocking and told her she couldn't see them again. In front of Patrick.' Caitlin ground to a halt.

'Don't say I told you so,' she said. 'Please.'

Further down the alleyway, a cat leaped silently from a high wall and two birds fluttered upwards in panic, their wings catching on the bricks.

And there were other things, things Caitlin wasn't saying because they made her feel stupid. The overflowing recycling bin of wine bottles that she'd forgotten to put out for a few weeks; Patrick had clocked it. He'd always nagged her about her wine intake, now she looked like an alkie. And her best underwear scattered over her bed, where she'd put it out in preparation for that non-starter of a date. All so much worse than it looked, to a man who had an eagle eye for details and pieced every shred together to make sure he knew exactly where she was, what she was doing. He called it caring, she called it borderline surveillance.

I've made this mess for myself, she thought, unhappily. *That's what Mum's going to say. It's about time I started acting like an adult and fixed my own problems. And she's right.*

Then Lynne spoke. Her tone wasn't smug, it was sad, and caring. 'Don't worry, Caitlin. Leave it with me, and I'll call you back in five minutes.'

The relief was immediate, like cool water down a parched throat. 'Thanks, Mum.' Caitlin knew she sounded tearful. She felt about ten years old again.

There was a pause, and Lynne's voice, when it came, was unexpectedly tender. 'It's what mums are for,' she said.

Lynne didn't mess around. Two days later, Caitlin was sitting in the sunlit offices of a top Bristol family law specialist, her mother in the leather chair next to her, asking the questions Caitlin was too shell-shocked to ask and, more importantly, taking notes.

At the end of the hour, Lynne and Sheila Marlow, Caitlin's new solicitor, shook hands over Sheila's Scandinavian pine desk, and Caitlin allowed herself to be steered out of the building, across the car park, and towards Lynne's company car.

Inside, Lynne checked her emails from work while Caitlin mentally surveyed the wreckage of her old life, as revealed by the questioning she'd just experienced. It was like a bombed city: recognisable in parts, but with heartbreaking details exposed in the rubble. Little moments of her old life that she'd never get back.

Finally Lynne hooked her phone up to the charger and turned to her daughter in the passenger seat. 'I think that was very productive. Sheila's handled hundreds of these cases. It's like she said, mostly posturing. One letter from her, and that'll be the last you hear from Patrick's solicitor.'

'I'm not so sure,' said Caitlin. 'The letter said he's reviewing his employment arrangements to be closer to the children. Patrick wouldn't move jobs unless he felt it was absolutely vital.'

It hurt in an unexpected way. He'd move back for Joel and Nancy, but he wouldn't stay for her. What did that say?

'Don't be so sure. Maybe things aren't working out for him up there.' Lynne checked her make-up in the sun visor. 'This might be quite the convenient excuse to slide away. He looks like a daddy martyr and he gets to leave without any awkward questions.'

'Patrick's not like that,' said Caitlin and Lynne shot her a look.

'Isn't he? He's suddenly remembered he invested all that money in your kitchen. He wasn't doing that a few weeks ago. You've got to toughen up, Caitlin. You can't let him dictate terms. They're your children.'

'No, Mum, they're ours. He adopted Joel. And Nancy's his.'

'So? You're their mother.'

Caitlin stared into the car park. Who did she have to talk about this with? Last week she'd have said Eva. Now she'd comprehensively bombed that relationship.

'What's up, Caitlin? Come on, tell me.' Lynne's voice was soothing.

Caitlin rested her head on the cold window, and spoke towards the dashboard, not looking round.

'I'm scared,' she said. 'I'm scared Nancy won't ever speak again outside the house. I'm scared Joel's going to think he's been abandoned by his dad again. I'm scared I can't protect them from all the unhappiness that's coming their way.'

There was movement across the car park. A woman about her age was striding confidently towards the door, swinging a briefcase, followed by two trainees who were scurrying to keep up. She wore sensible mid-heeled shoes, and seemed to be delivering a series of commands with a pleasant, neutral-toned lipstick smile.

That could be me, thought Caitlin. In a parallel universe that probably is me.

And that was another peak on the Iceberg of Fear. She was also scared she'd never get a proper job, now she'd been making paninis for ten years. She was scared she'd never meet a decent man, now she had two kids by two different fathers. She was scared of falling into this pattern of the wrong men, the wrong actions.

She didn't want to tell her mum that. Caitlin already knew they were her mum's fears for her too.

'Do you remember the last time you and I were on our own in a car together?' said Lynne.

'No,' said Caitlin.

'I do. I was driving you to your final term at university.'

Oh yes. Their old Volvo rammed to the roof with Caitlin's books and terrible posters. It had taken ages for Lynne to park it and in the end Caitlin had got out and hidden in shame while Lynne asked two students to help her. 'Where was Dad? He couldn't do it for some reason, could he?'

'He had a conference, you're right.' Lynne turned to her, her face warm with nostalgia. 'You know something? I always wanted to take you back, but your father loved that drive. He never got to spend much time with you once you were grown-up. I rather envied it.'

'We didn't talk a lot,' said Caitlin. 'We just sat and listened to Radio Four mostly.'

'I know but . . . You miss that time when it's gone. It goes very quickly. One minute you were a bossy little thing in OshKosh, the next you're arguing about politics and dyeing your hair.'

'Well, if that was the worst thing I did as a teen . . .'

Lynne sighed. 'Anyway, I remember driving along with you in the passenger seat, thinking we might never be alone like this again, mum and daughter. You'd come back from university grown-up. Independent. And I wanted to tell you how excited I was for you. I wanted to say how I knew you'd be fine in your Finals, and how they didn't matter so much anyway, but in a few months you'd be flying out into the world, and I couldn't wait to see where you'd go. I was so proud. So proud I didn't know how to put it, without making you feel burdened.'

Caitlin had been about to make a point about her 2:1, but she fell silent, hearing the sorrow in her mother's voice. And then she was back in that car too. She remembered how exhilarated *she'd* been. And then . . . and then . . . Glastonbury, the pregnancy, the one-instant wiping out of all those hopes. Brilliant girls don't drift from job to job to fit in with childcare. Brilliant girls don't waste their lives, hiding in the park drinking pre-mixed gin and tonic.

'And then I let you down,' she said dully.

'No.' Lynne turned to her in the seat, and her eyes were bright with tears. 'Then you flew in a different direction. It was hard for me to see you struggle. I didn't handle it the way I wanted. But what broke my heart was that you didn't come home. And every night when I knew you were turning to *my* mum for help, I wished I'd told you just how proud I was of you. Not your grades, but your spirit. And your questions, and the way you charmed everyone around you. You will always be my beautiful, brilliant girl. You *never* let me down, and if I made you feel like that, then I failed – as a mother.'

Lynne looked so crestfallen. Caitlin couldn't bear to see it.

'Mum, you didn't fail me. Why have you never said any of this?'

'I tried. I wanted to help you, but you didn't want my help. Your dad's the same, hard to help.' A watery smile that touched the corners of Lynne's eyes. 'Do you remember how it was only me who could shake the bad dreams out of your pillow when you were small? That's all I wanted to do, when you were struggling with Joel. Shake your pillow. It doesn't matter how old you get, Caitlin. I'm never going to stop wanting to make the bad things go away.'

Caitlin looked at her mother, and saw her for the first time as a woman just like her, scared of the impact her mistakes could have on a fragile life. There was a vulnerability in Lynne's face that she'd never seen before – or had she never wanted to see it?

She had a sudden flash of a teenage Nancy turning away from her, preferring to take her broken heart to Lynne, or to Eva, to piece together instead of her, and a pain ripped through her.

'Mum,' she said, and leaned over the car to bury her head in her mother's shoulder. 'I'm sorry I disappointed you.'

She felt Lynne's hand stroking her head, as if she was a little girl again. 'No,' she heard her murmur into her hair, 'you've never ever done that, Caitlin.'

Joel and Nancy were excited to see Caitlin arrive with Granny in tow, but they weren't so stupid not to twig that something was up. Not least because both Granny and Mum had red eyes, and weren't sniping at each other.

'Look who's here! Granny wanted to surprise us!' said Caitlin.

'Why?' said Joel.

'Because . . . it's a surprise!'

'I've brought cake!' Lynne swung a bag from the nice bakery in town. 'Cupcakes for everyone!'

Nancy regarded the cake suspiciously. They'd had cake the afternoon she came back from the first appointment with the speech therapist. Thinking about it, Caitlin wondered if maybe cake had been a mistake.

But they walked home with Joel talking constantly and Caitlin's attempts to draw Nancy into the conversation failing. She clutched Caitlin's hand, tightly, and smiled up at Lynne, but Caitlin couldn't get her to do more than wave at some cats and a dog that 'looked like Bee' according to Joel.

As usual, Joel had his phone out.

'Isn't he quite young to have such a posh phone?' asked Lynne mildly.

'It's Patrick's old one. He wanted him to be able to get in touch.' Caitlin made a 'what can you do?' face. 'He mainly uses the camera – I'm hoping there'll be footage we can sell to the television one day.' She turned down to Nancy. 'And maybe we can record you dancing on it? Like your dog in the book? The one who doesn't do ballet?'

Nancy wriggled and turned her head away.

'Mum, Mum, Mum! Noah's mum put our world record attempt on YouTube! Do you want to see?' Joel shoved between her and Lynne.

'Not now,' said Caitlin. 'When we get home.'

'Your school? On YouTube?' Lynne looked concerned. 'Is that a good idea?'

'It's an *amazing* idea,' said Joel. 'It's got a hundred likes already. Someone might see me singing and ask me for an audition!'

Caitlin wondered whether this was the moment to remind Joel that he'd actually left before the record attempt started.

'Joel, sweetie, you've got to be careful, there are plenty of not-so-nice people out there,' Lynne said.

'But if someone saw me singing on YouTube, you wouldn't need to take me to the audition, would you? I could do it from home!'

'No, no and no,' said Caitlin, and for once, she got a look of approval from her mother. That was a novelty.

Lynne stayed for tea and cake, and was given the tour of the house repairs by Joel, complete with dramatic re-enactment of the flood.

'This is where the bath overflowed,' he told her, with a flourish. 'And if you look out there, that's where the ambulance was parked, and the fire engine . . .'

'You're making it sound a lot more dramatic than it really was,' said Caitlin, breezily, thinking of Patrick's solicitor. 'Why not show Granny Lynne the new colours we're going to paint the bathroom? And then Nancy, it'll nearly be time for your bed!'

'And maybe Granny can read a story?' Lynne glanced at Caitlin. 'Will there be time?'

'Yes.' Caitlin smiled. 'Yes, I think we'd all like that, wouldn't we?'

To her relief, Nancy nodded enthusiastically, and a warm glow filled Caitlin's chest.

Later on, once Nancy was asleep, and Lynne had left, Caitlin let Joel have an extra half-hour over his bedtime. She wanted to spend some time alone with him, just him and her, the way it had been for those years before Patrick, and she had something to say to him that needed space and quietness, so she could read his face. The solicitor had warned her that other children might talk about divorce, laced with their own distorted versions of overheard adult gossip. 'It's best to prepare them with facts about what happens next,' she'd said. 'Don't leave it to their imaginations.'

They curled up together on the sofa, Joel in his Spiderman pyjamas, Caitlin in her onesie to watch 'just one' episode of Doctor Who. Since no one was watching, he snuggled into her while she sipped her coffee, and Caitlin made herself note every tiny memory: the nut brown of his hair, his warm bedtime smell, the mole on his neck, just under his ear.

When the credits rolled she said, as casually as she could, 'Joel, there's something we need to have a chat about.'

She felt his body stiffen against hers. 'Is it about the cows? Because that wasn't anyone's fault. I was watching Nancy, and so was Auntie Eva but we got distracted.'

'Sweetheart, it's not about the cows. I'm not cross about the cows. That was an accident.'

'Is it about Nancy, then? Is she all right?' Joel looked up, his brow heartbreakingly furrowed. 'Is it about school next year?'

Caitlin drew a deep breath. He worried about so much. 'It's nothing like that. It's a . . . good thing! Dad's going to get a new job so he can see you and Nancy more often.'

It made her ache how brightly Joel's eyes lit up. 'Really?'

'Really.'

'Yay!' He lifted his fists in triumph. 'So when's he coming home?'

'I'm sorry, Joely. He's not moving back in.' Caitlin struggled to find the right words. She wasn't sure she knew what they were herself. 'But he does want to spend a lot more time with you and Nancy. He misses you.'

Joel couldn't hide his disappointment. He searched her face for clues as to how he should react. 'But not you?' His voice cracked.

So did Caitlin's heart. She made her voice stronger than she felt. 'Dad and I are going to try living in different houses for a while. We'll get on better like that.'

'So where will we live? With you, or with Dad?'

'With both of us. We're all going to talk it over with a special advisor to make sure everyone's happy.' Caitlin hadn't wanted even to raise the possibility, but Lynne had insisted that she prepared him, just in case.

'Who's going to talk it over?' His expression clouded. 'Just me? Or me and Nancy?'

'Well,' Caitlin was getting in deeper now than she'd wanted to, but he'd asked, and she had to answer. 'Nancy's a bit too young to explain what she wants, so it might just be you, but don't look so worried, it won't be scary. There's no right or wrong answers, it's just a chat. Like when we chatted to the speech therapist about Nancy, and what we'd all been up to, in case it gave her any clues that might help Nancy talk more.'

That had been fun. A casual chat with a professional about any traumatic events that might have slipped under the family radar. Joel had seen through it at once – he had Lynne's bullshit detector.

Joel looked close to tears. 'But . . . what if I say the wrong thing?'

'There's no wrong thing to say.' Caitlin grabbed his bare foot and held it, like she had done when he was little. He'd always loved that, her cycling his chubby legs. 'You just say what you want, and if you're happy with what we suggest. You won't have to choose. Maybe you won't need to talk to anyone – I just want you to know exactly what's going on with me and Dad, so you don't have to worry that we're not telling you stuff.'

'Will we still see Auntie Eva?'

'Yes, of course. But if Dad's moving nearer Bristol, you won't have to go all the way to Longhampton to see him. He'll be in his own place.'

'So we won't see her every other weekend?'

'It depends. She might come down to stay . . . Listen, Joely, there are no firm arrangements yet. I'll let you know when I know more. But in the meantime, let's focus on the fun stuff coming up.' Caitlin cuddled him. 'There's the summer fayre at school, then that play you're in, and then Nancy's end-of-term concert . . .'

'Hmm.'

They both knew a year ago, Nancy would have been taking a starring role in her end-of-term concert. Singing, dancing, right at the front with a big smile and an even bigger fairy tutu. This year, Caitlin wasn't even confident Nancy would be persuaded onto the stage. She was dreading it.

She stroked Joel's cowlick. It was thickening into proper boy hair now. 'Have you been helping Nancy practise?' she asked.

'Yup.' He fiddled with his phone. 'She does the steps with me, and I sing, and she sings a bit but it's mainly miming.'

'Do you think she'll do it with the others? On the stage?'

He glanced up. 'I don't know, Mum. I'm trying to help her, and she's really good, but when we tried to do it in the park the other day, she couldn't. It was like . . .' He screwed up his face. '. . . her legs were moving and she was singing in her head, but it wasn't coming out.' Joel blinked. 'But her eyes were dancing. Do you know what I mean? It's like she *wants* to. But she can't. Not when we're not there. I wish I could help her.'

An acid misery washed through Caitlin's whole body; she tried to hide it from Joel. 'Maybe if we're in the front row, encouraging her? Where she can see us?' She nudged him.

'What if we got up on the stage with her and sang? Would she do it then?'

He squirmed, horrified at the thought of Caitlin on stage, delighted at performing himself. 'Maybe.' Joel let Caitlin cuddle him for a moment, then he turned round, so he could look straight at her. 'Mum? Is Nancy going to get better? Like, ever?'

'Yes,' said Caitlin, even though she'd promised herself she'd never lie to her kids. 'Of course she is. And we're going to get tickets to the *Sing Along a Sound of Music* at Christmas, and we're all going to sing. OK? Even me.'

Joel gazed at her, with his solemn, half-child, half-boy eyes, and she caught a glimpse of his grown-up face. Caitlin rarely thought about Joel's father but this was one of those occasions: she wondered what that tanned surfer boy was doing now, whether he was looking at his kids with that gaze, whether he still had the long hair, the only thing she really remembered apart from the inky dolphin leaping the bone of his hip, or whether he was now bald, in a suit, ageing comfortably in an Australian suburb. What kind of dad would he have been? Would her life have worked out differently if she'd bothered to get his number?

But Joel's gaze wasn't that stranger's – it was Patrick's. And Caitlin's. The calm scrutiny of two people who wanted to believe you were the person they hoped you were inside.

Caitlin felt her defences rise automatically, then stopped. *I've got to be that best version of me from now on*, she thought. *For them. Patrick and me – that doesn't matter. I've got to get a grip, for Joel and Nancy. I might have screwed up the life I could have had, but I can't fail at being a mother. I can't let them down.*

As she thought it, she wobbled. Deep down it was her worst fear. That she had already failed. Nancy, silent; Joel, a hyperactive worry machine. The teen years still to come. Mum, she thought. She thought she'd got it cracked with her Grade-A student and then look what happened.

But Joel slowly reached out his hand and touched her face. His trusting eyes, believing she could make everything better.

'Love you, Mum,' he said.

And Caitlin's heart exploded in a fierce fireball of joy, pride, protectiveness and helpless adoration. There was nothing, in that instant – no sacrifice, no terror, no wall of flame to leap across – that she wouldn't have done for her boy without even thinking.

'I love you, Joely,' she whispered back, and when he threw himself into her arms, Caitlin finally started to understand her own mother.

Chapter twenty-seven

Joel and Nancy's weekend with Patrick in Longhampton was coming up, and Eva still hadn't heard from Patrick whether it was on or not. She very much hoped it was. Caitlin hadn't replied to her long text of apology, and she wondered if she ought to send a written note. But what if Caitlin didn't reply to that? Would she have to keep on apologising by carrier pigeon? By telegram?

Eva found herself fiddling with her phone even more than Joel, and when she came out of Longhampton surgery, after the fertility check-up Anna had finally nudged her into having, the voicemail messages on the screen made her pulse race.

She walked quickly across the car park, mentally preparing herself for more recrimination, but the message was from Alex. 'Hello, Eva, it's Alex.' He sounded on edge. 'I need a quick word with you. I'll try you at home. Sorry. Bye.'

He'd rung again, half an hour later. 'Eva, Alex again. Can you call me when you get this? There's something I need to discuss with you, about the diaries. Thanks.'

Eva stopped by the car. The pugs lolled at her from the back seat. They liked a run out, even if they had to sit in the car for a bit. Bee bounced in her harness, wanting to be let out. Bumble sprawled sadly. He missed Nancy.

'Yow just wait there,' Eva told Bee, in Mick's old Bumble voice, and called Alex's mobile.

'Eva!' He picked up on the first ring, and seemed relieved to hear her. 'Did you get my garbled messages? I'm so sorry to leave so many.'

'It's fine. What's happened? Is it something to do with that publicity? Have you taken a stand?' She was joking but could tell he wasn't.

'Sort of.' He paused, awkwardly. 'Um, it's not something I want to discuss over the phone. Are you around today? I'm on campus till lunchtime, but I can meet you somewhere.'

'No problem. Do you want to come here?'

'Er, no. How about we meet somewhere in town? Somewhere we can talk.'

'Let's go to Queenswood Forest Park,' said Eva. 'I'll bring the dogs. They'd love to see you, and there's a café. I'll pick you up at the station.'

'Um, OK,' said Alex, and for once he didn't add a single 'jolly good', or even a 'super'. In fact, he sounded glumly modern.

At the park entrance, under the canopies of oak trees, Eva took Bee's lead, since she was the less predictable of the two, and offered Alex Bumble's. They eyed each other; Bumble in his harness, Alex in his tweed jacket. Their round brown eyes weren't dissimilar.

'Are you sure?' He pretended to be nervous. 'Quite a responsibility.'

'Just beware of his many fans,' Eva replied, tucking extra treats into her pocket, to be safe.

They set off around the easiest trail, and Eva made conversation flow about the dogs, about Alex's lecture series. There were few other walkers about, with it being mid-week, and the spring leaves on the trees, and blossom floating down, made it feel like one of Nancy's story book forests. Eva's mood surprised her: she felt buoyed by her doctor's appointment, not depressed. It wasn't so much what Dr Kingsley had said about the low chances of conceiving in your forties, but that she'd taken charge. So she only had a tiny window left to act – there was still a window. She could be true to the decision she'd made with Mick, not to bring children into their marriage, and still, maybe, have time to be a mother.

It thrilled her. It wasn't an either/or, any more. She hadn't had to choose Mick or children. She wasn't shackled to that choice for the rest of her life.

'Come on,' she said eventually, watching Bumble bury his flat face in some bluebells. They'd paused on a bench, dedicated to an old couple called Ida and Stanley. It looked out over an intricate monkey-puzzle tree. Eva relaxed, stretching out her long legs, until she realised it was quite an intimate gesture, bringing her head very close to Alex's shoulder, and she sat up again. 'What is it you wanted to tell me?'

'I don't know how to start this,' he said, covering his face with his hands and wiping them slowly down. 'It feels . . .'

'Just tell me,' said Eva. 'I think we know each other well enough now? I mean, you've read my husband's views on my breasts. You know all our pet names. I have no secrets.'

'True.' Alex managed a hunted smile. He slid down too, nearly touched her arm, and sat up again too, surprised by the intimacy. It was easy. Too easy. 'Look, can we walk? I feel better in motion. I spend so much time sitting on my rear end.'

'Rear end' was much more like the usual Alex. Eva nodded and began walking again. Bumble and Bee immediately trotted out ahead of them, prancing in tandem.

'I was talking to Cheryl Murray yesterday,' he began.

'Ah! You were granted an audience.'

'Only on Skype. I needed to clear up some details with her. You remember I asked you all to write something for me? Well, she wrote screeds and screeds of axe-grinding gossip about their marriage and her career . . . it was surprisingly funny but totally libellous. She's extremely indiscreet, Cheryl.'

'They'll be pleased about that, the publicity girls?'

'Oh, very. So, we ended up talking about her children – she's in some custody battle with that rock star she was married to.'

'The one before the royal?'

'Indeed.' He shot her a sideways glance, his eyes flirty with amusement. 'There's some kind of husband full house she's going for. I don't know what's next after the actor, the bass player and now the duke.'

'An oligarch?'

'Bit long in the tooth for that now, I'm afraid. And I'm not sure Cheryl's got the discretion for a politician.'

'Should *you* be telling me any of this?'

'Not really, no.'

This was very pleasant, Eva thought, strolling through the empty paths between the tall trees and chatting away, but Alex was clearly going round the houses and the longer he did it, the harder the knot in her stomach tightened.

Then he took an audible breath, and said, in one go, 'I was interested, you know, after what you'd said about Mick and you deciding not to have children, whether he and Cheryl had had a similar discussion, since they didn't have children either.

I know that sounds nosy, but from a biographer's perspective, the different marriages . . . When you talked about it, it felt like two adults reaching a mature decision, based on honesty, love, wanting the same future. Whereas Cheryl and Mick were younger – I was curious, I guess, about which one of them was driving that decision at that time. Obviously she changed her mind when she met Ove the rock star. And the duke.'

Bumble turned and gazed at Eva, face quivering to check she was all right. She smiled back, and he carried on.

'Not sure where this is going,' she said. 'But go on.'

'One of the things Cheryl wrote about was honesty in her marriage. All the ways she and Mick were never honest with each other. It's very funny, and Bryony at the publishers is ecstatic – once the libel lawyers have cleared it, she's got some auction going on between which paper gets to splash their Sunday edition with the details but . . .'

Alex stopped walking and turned to face Eva. His expression was taut, as if he was choosing his words carefully. 'One of the things she talks about is how she had a miscarriage, about a year before they broke up.'

Something flickered in the pit of Eva's stomach. An ominous sensation, like the first little flames of a fire.

'And how . . . how Michael's reaction was to go out and have a vasectomy which he didn't tell her about until it was done.' Alex's eyes were sympathetic. 'I think that's what that reference to the clinic was in the diaries. I think he had a check-up just after he met you. And I assumed, from what you said, that you didn't know. And I really, really didn't want the first time you heard about it to be from the papers.'

Blood banged in Eva's ears. She could hear her own heartbeat in her temples, in her throat.

Mick had had a vasectomy? And he'd never told her?

'I . . . I didn't know that,' she said. It didn't change anything, yet it changed everything. If she'd known, from the start, that he couldn't have kids . . .

She blinked, surprised at the flames taking hold inside her, burning up her memories. What weird vanity had led Mick to say he didn't *want* children, rather than admit he couldn't have them? What if she'd known? Why couldn't he tell her?

Eva thought of the leaflet Dr Kingsley had given her, charting the dramatic fall in fertility between forty and forty-four. If she'd known this three years ago when those last broody yearnings had gripped her, lying in bed watching Mick sleep and imagining his genes mingled with hers, what would she have done?

The realisation took a while to reach the bottom of her heart, but when it did, it spread through Eva in powerful waves, tingling out to her fingers. It was a shock, suddenly not knowing yourself, feeling that invisible gap between your head and your heart.

Even Bee now circled unhappily, feeling Eva's tension through the lead.

Alex's head drooped. 'I didn't know what to do when I read that. Part of me thought it was fascinating, that Mick was such a different husband to each of his wives, as if they were different roles he was taking on, with different leading ladies, but the other part of me . . . I was furious. For you. I guessed you didn't know, from the way you spoke about it being a choice. And you put so much faith in his honesty – you're the only one who cares about Michael's reputation as this straight-talking, down-the-line bloke. And there was no way of stopping it coming out, once Cheryl started publicity for the book. I felt responsible. If I hadn't persuaded you to go ahead with this project, you might never have known.'

Eva couldn't speak. She didn't know what to say. Everything seemed to be happening behind a thick pane of glass.

Alex looked stricken. 'Eva, please say something. Have I done the wrong thing?' He touched her arm.

She pulled herself back. 'No. No, Alex, I appreciate you telling me . . .'

But did she? What else had Mick lied about? What other secrets might Una drop on her, or Cheryl?

Already it was starting to feel as if her marriage had happened to someone else, just like her old single life – a skyline receding into the distance in a rear view mirror. The diaries had started to prise Eva's memories away from her heart, pulling away the glue between her and Mick with insinuating doubts, tiny contradictions here and there. And now this. This changed everything. She'd been married to an actor.

They were standing in the middle of the wood, where several trails crossed. One down to the observation look-out, others into the arboretum, another into a big field where two dogs were bouncing around with a ball.

'So I don't know whether I can carry on with this.' Alex rubbed his face. 'This isn't the project I agreed to work on. When I initially spoke to Roger, he insisted it was going to be a serious publication. Memoirs. A Life in Acting. That's not where it's heading now.'

'Have you spoken to him? Should I?'

Roger, she thought. Did he know about Mick's vasectomy? Of course not, why would he?

'I've tried. He's not happy either, but there's not much we can do now contracts have been signed. The publishers have editorial control, not him. And we can make a case for privacy, but when Roger looked at the contracts I think he was relying on everyone being kind to one another. Which isn't generally how this works, sadly.'

Was it even fair to reshape Cheryl's story to make her own more palatable? No, it wasn't. She had to face the truth as much as anyone else.

'I was already considering going on a long holiday when it's published,' said Eva bitterly. 'But I don't recognise half of what you're telling me about my own husband, so I'm beginning to wonder if I should even care.'

'And the other thing . . .' Alex frowned, looked away, then looked back at her. He seemed to be pushing the words out. 'Why not get all the uncomfortable conversations out of the way, eh? When I spoke to Cheryl, my first thought wasn't an academic reaction. It wasn't about the work at all. It was about you. How *you* would feel. I couldn't stand the thought of you being hurt like this. I wanted to protect you.'

Eva stared at him. His eyes were shining behind his glasses, and when he pushed his hair off his face, she felt a strange tug deep inside her chest.

'I have thought so much about you,' he went on, 'and lately, not in the context of these diaries. You're an extraordinary woman, a real dame, if you don't mind an old expression. You gave Mick support, and inspiration, and love during your marriage – and you come out of this with dignity.' He shook his head, as if trying to shake away words lining up inside his mind. 'I don't think he deserved it, to be honest with you, Eva. I think . . .'

He stopped.

'What?'

'It's not up to me to think things like that.' Alex met her gaze. 'I'm just supposed to be thinking about the footnotes and the source material.'

They stood, their eyes locked together, wordlessly. Bee sat down on Eva's foot. She didn't notice. She was staring at the soft curve of Alex's lip, the intensity in his perceptive eyes. *Wrong*, she thought. *Stop it.*

Eventually, he broke the silence, and she was grateful, because she didn't know how.

'So what it boils down to,' he said, 'is that I feel the same as you do about these diaries right now. I'd quite happily walk away from the wretched things. I've got to admit, I normally leave biography projects feeling like the subject's an old friend but that's not the case here. I admire Michael Quinn professionally as much as I ever did, but I'm not sure I like him as a man.'

'Please don't leave us,' said Eva. 'You've done so much work, and they're nearly there, aren't they?' She twisted her mouth into a broken smile. 'I don't know if I could go through all this again with anyone else but you.'

Her words hung on the air, and as she realised what she'd said, another meaning unfurled, the sense of it drifting between them like falling leaves.

'The diaries, I mean,' she added.

'Um, of course.' Alex shifted. 'Obviously.'

And then, because Eva felt awkward, she heard herself say, 'I'm not sure I'd want to go through a marriage like that again either!' and immediately wished she hadn't. For so many reasons.

Alex's shoulders stiffened, and Eva desperately wanted to rewind time and say it differently, but you couldn't do that. You only got one chance to say things, which is why, she told herself, it was often better to say nothing at all. Life only had one take, unlike the movies.

Eva hugged her jacket closer. The sun was shining, but it wasn't as warm it looked. Had he just said he felt something for her? Or had she got it very wrong? 'Alex, I'm going to stop talking. I've had a lot to take in today. I'm going to say something stupid, I know it. I'm sorry.'

He touched her arm and she didn't pull away. 'Please tell me I haven't offended you?'

'No.' Eva shook her head. 'You haven't offended me whatsoever. I'm grateful for your honesty. It was my turn to be clumsy.' She turned and gave him a smile. Even their smiles felt different now. 'Thank you for thinking of me.'

Alex smiled sadly, and they turned to take the path that led back to the car park.

Chapter twenty-eight

Caitlin stepped through the door that Patrick was holding open for her, and thought, *that's bloody typical.*

He could sit in that mediation meeting, letting her do all the talking and just adding the smallest detail to make the mediator think she was useless . . . and then he'd hold the door open for her. As if courtesy meant *anything* any more.

'Thanks,' she said sarcastically.

'My pleasure,' he replied, as if they hadn't just spent an hour fighting over who should look after their children, and for how many hours per week. 'How are you getting back to work? Do you need a lift?'

Caitlin turned to him. Lynne – and Sheila the solicitor – had advised her in the strongest terms to remain as calm and courteous as possible with Patrick to stop mediation escalating into court procedures. Both of them pointed out how generous it was of Patrick to detour halfway round the country to sort out the builders, something that Caitlin had sort of taken for granted. But that morning, Patrick's solicitor had sent a new proposal for the financial settlement, pointing out that her client would have to find accommodation nearer to Bristol and that there was a significant amount of equity in the family home. It would make sense, the solicitor wrote, to release a portion of that. In other words, Caitlin could buy out a portion of Patrick's share, or she'd have to put it on the market.

The ramifications had sent Caitlin into a red mist.

'How can you offer me a lift when your solicitor wants me to sell the only place our daughter isn't scared to speak?' she demanded. 'Are you mad? Or just a total—'

'Caitlin, that's not what's being discussed.'

'Isn't it?' Her eyes flashed. 'Where else am I going to magic up that money from? Don't you care about Nancy? She literally – listen to me, Patrick, I've only told you this about a million times – she *only* feels safe in that house. If we move . . . who knows? She might never speak again. Are you happy with that?'

'Of course I'm not. But then I don't think we've worked through all the treatment options for Nancy.' He fiddled with his cuffs. Patrick was wearing his best work suit, and Caitlin knew he'd impressed the mediator with his file of information and his UN negotiator attitude. She hated him for being so reasonable. She hated herself for not being able to make Nancy feel safe enough to talk, and dance, and sing the way she used to.

'In any case,' Patrick added, 'she speaks at Eva's house . . . in certain situations.'

'Don't even start,' Caitlin warned. 'Don't even start me on all that.'

He sighed. 'Caitlin, the point of going to mediation is to try to talk about this in a constructive fashion. If you're going to be so defensive . . . It's not a criticism. I'm doing everything I can to make this work.'

'You're doing this to get back at me,' she said, without thinking, and immediately Patrick's head jerked up.

'I beg your pardon?'

'This is because you think I'm seeing someone, isn't it?' Caitlin lifted her chin now. 'It's just your way of getting back at me because I'm not under your control any more.'

Shut up, *Caitlin,* yelled a voice in her head. This was everything her mother and Sheila had told her not to do. Not just press the self-destruct button but mash it good.

'I honestly don't give a damn,' said Patrick. 'I've finally stopped caring about the mad way you insist on sabotaging your life. I thought I could help you, but you can do what you like from now on – tell yourself lies, be in X when you swear you're in Y, whatever – I just want the children to be happy. I'm prepared to do whatever it takes to ensure that happens.'

She stared at him. The dismissal in his voice was harder than any snipey insult. But then Patrick had never gone in for snipey insults. He just laid down evidence of her own stupidity, stuff she couldn't explain even to herself, and then looked at her, like a cat presenting its owner with a disembowelled pigeon.

He checked his watch. 'It's nearly three. Do you want me to pick the kids up from school and take them straight to Longhampton? What time does Joel finish?'

'He's got drama club.'

'Is that a new thing?'

'Yes. It's to do with this audition he wants to go for. Extra singing.'

'You didn't mention it.'

'This is the first week.'

They stared at each other.

'How come,' said Caitlin, 'that you could find a new job in Worcester just like that, for the kids? But you wouldn't find one when it was about staying with me?'

She knew she sounded hurt. She felt hurt. The hour in mediation had popped the question out of her, the mediator's determined examination of their marriage pushing all the toxins to the surface.

Patrick's eyes creased. 'That's not a straight comparison.'

'Isn't it?'

'No. I could say, how come you chose staying in your house over having a fresh start with me? Your past over your future?'

'Don't start. You know it wasn't like that.'

'Fine.' He beeped open his car. 'If we didn't get anywhere in mediation we're hardly likely to make headway here. I'll go and get the kids, shall I? Do you have to phone to get permission? Are their bags packed? Do you want me to drop you at home so you can get them ready?'

As he was speaking, his phone started to ring. It had rung throughout the mediation hour and Caitlin snapped, 'Can't you turn that off?'

'No.' Patrick answered it. 'Patrick Reardon? Oh, hello.' He glanced at her. 'Have you? I think she perhaps has her phone off. Is there a problem?'

A shadow passed over his face, and instinctively Caitlin reached for her own phone.

Four missed calls. All from the school. Her stomach dropped.

'Right. No, he's not. No. Definitely not, I've been with her all afternoon. No, I don't think Joel had a dental appointment?'

He caught Caitlin's eye, and she shook her head.

'No, no dental appointment. OK, we'll be right there.'

He hung up and when he looked at Caitlin the earlier antagonism had left his expression. He looked like the old, worried Patrick she remembered.

'What is it?' Her hands were gripping her bag strap hard, even though she didn't know what he was about to say.

'Joel apparently left school for a dental appointment this lunchtime.' Patrick's face was ashen. 'And he hasn't come back.'

The Friday afternoon traffic in Bristol was compounded by serious roadworks in two different places, and within five minutes, Patrick's car was stuck in a jam.

'Can't you turn round?' Caitlin was on the verge of getting out and walking. They were on the wrong side of town for the school but she couldn't bear sitting there, doing nothing. 'Can't your fancy sat nav find us a different route?'

'No. Caitlin, I want to get there as much as you do, but—'

Patrick's phone rang and the hands-free showed **Steve Gayle; Head Office** on the screen. He groaned, then caught himself.

'I'm sorry, I've got to take this. I won't be a second.' He pressed a button. 'Hello, Steve, what's the problem?'

Steve's voice boomed out of the radio speaker. 'Patrick, I've had Brian Norman on about the figures for the last quarter. Apparently they're missing a whole section.'

'Right. I'll get onto that.'

'No, he needs to run some details by you so if you could action that within the next hour, that'd keep that on track . . .'

Caitlin stared out of the window at the wall of cars around them as Patrick dealt with the problem, then hung up.

'Right,' he said. 'So what can we do while we're here? Do you want to phone the school again, see if he's turned up? Or check with your mother? Would Joel have gone there?'

'To London?' Caitlin frowned. 'No! Why would he do that?'

Patrick's brow was furrowed in practical thought. 'Did he know we were coming to mediation today? What have you told him about me moving back?'

'I said you were moving nearer, but not back in with us.' She swivelled in her seat. 'Before you say anything, I didn't want to – I think it's something we need to do together. I don't even want to think about how Nancy will take it.'

Before Patrick could respond to that, his phone rang again, and he answered it without even asking her.

'Hi, Steve again, sorry Patrick, while you're talking to Brian can you ask him where he is with the budget? I'm getting some push-back from regional sales about some of the projections . . .'

'Will do,' said Patrick. He sounded efficient, but at the same time, not in control. 'Sorry, Steve, I'm on another call, I'll get back to you asap. Cheers.'

Caitlin glared at him. 'Can you stop answering work calls, please? This is more important than some budget.'

'I don't have a choice.' He glared back at her. 'I'm not even supposed to be here today – they think I'm in York doing some site visits.'

'Fine. Whatever. But what did you mean by, did Joel know we were coming here today?' she persisted. 'Why are you assuming that's an issue?'

'I mean, is this something he's worried about?'

'He knew we were meeting today, yes. Not in a scary way, though. I've made it really clear, everything's going to be fine.' But the idea lodged in her head and she felt sick. 'I don't think we should start at the worst place. Maybe he's just decided to bunk off school this afternoon. Maybe he's gone for a wander. Maybe he's at home eating cornflakes.'

'Definitely not at home. The teacher said the truancy officer was in the area and went round to check. No one in.'

Caitlin stared sightlessly out of the car window. Where was Joel? And how come Patrick seemed to think he could second-guess her son better than she could?

Because he's Patrick's son too, she thought. And suddenly she had an image of him with Patrick's old phone, filming himself dancing and singing, his constant chat about YouTube that she'd tuned out, posting his videos online, for any weirdo to see. Any weirdo promising a ten-year-old show-off a chance to be on stage . . .

'Phone the school,' he said, but this time when his mobile rang Caitlin leaned over and smacked the hands-free button, hanging up the call.

'For fuck's sake, Patrick. Our son is missing! And you're taking phone calls about sales quarters! What is *wrong* with you?' She tried to pull his phone out of the hands-free cradle.

Patrick grabbed her wrist. 'Stop it! Is that going to help?'

'I'm trying to help you get a grip. I'm trying to make you realise that your *job* is the least important thing here!' Caitlin could hear her voice getting higher and higher. 'It's always been like this. I've always been the fourth, fifth priority on your list and this just proves it! There's something wrong with you. Something *wrong*.'

While she was speaking, his phone bleeped with a text. It bleeped again the second she stopped. Then vibrated with a call, and again **Steve Gayle; Head Office** appeared on the screen.

'Oh my God. Don't even look at that,' she snapped.

'I wasn't going to.'

An ambulance, followed by two police cars zoomed up the stationary lane next to them and they stared in horror, as they passed in a distorted ribbon of sirens.

'They'd have called us,' said Patrick. His voice wobbled. 'Someone would have called us.'

Caitlin said nothing. He grabbed her hand, squeezed, then let go, and she leaned her head back on the headrest.

She closed her eyes and thought about the first time she'd met Patrick. She remembered the darkness she'd felt closing in on her, for herself and the little boy in the back of her unreliable Peugeot, hating herself for the slipshod way she'd let the breakdown cover expire. It was raining. Her phone was dead. She didn't feel ready for this adult life. Please let someone turn up, she'd prayed. Please.

Then there'd been a knock on the window, and she'd turned her head to see the kindest eyes under a knitted hat. They were frowning with concern, offering her help. 'Why on earth don't you have a car charger for your phone?' Those had been Patrick's first words to her. Then he'd given her his spare.

Caitlin's heart rushed back to that moment. It had felt like the final act of a film: her life falling into place, all the bad stuff merely a rocky road to lead her to this wonderful man. And Patrick had been wonderful. She just hadn't been as wonderful as he'd thought she was, but it wasn't like she hadn't tried to warn him.

That's the story of my life, she thought. Never quite as wonderful as people hope.

'Is that what you think?' He spoke so quietly that Caitlin barely caught his words.

'What?'

417

'Is that what you think? That I put you fourth or fifth?'

She flushed, but her anger wouldn't let her apologise. She wasn't sure she wanted to apologise.

'You know I don't. My family means everything to me. But this is my working life, Cait. It's like this all the time. Call after call after call.' He sounded shattered.

'Our son is missing.' As she said 'our' Caitlin heard her mother's voice, but Joel was Patrick's son – he'd given him his honesty, and his determination. Better than genes. *He's a good bloke,* said a voice in her head. *A* really *good bloke.*

'I know, but the problems don't stop. It's what I have to do – sorting out stupid problems, being the man who finds the lost keys, stopping the wrong results going up to the exec board, and making sure the bloody fire extinguishers are working and . . .' Patrick let out a long breath. 'I don't *want* to take these calls. Of course I don't. But the quicker I deal with them . . .'

'The more you'll get.' Caitlin turned in her seat to face him. 'That's how it goes, Patrick. The more efficient you are, the more shit gets dumped on you. It's like a tide. You're battling against a tide of . . . pointless management bollocks.'

'Which is what I do to pay the bills,' said Patrick with deliberate patience.

The sympathy she'd started to feel for him began to recede. The *martyrdom.* 'Is it, though? Or do you just enjoy this sensation of being indispensable? I know you think I've got no idea what proper jobs are like,' Caitlin retorted, 'but I do know the difference between being busy, and getting so addicted to feeling needed that you're prepared to neglect your family duties.'

'You honestly think I care more about sales quarters than about Joel?'

'Why are you so shocked by that? You've always put work before us.'

Patrick wiped a hand over his face. 'No, Caitlin. I put work ahead of myself. So you could stay at home, and be with the kids, and not worry.'

'And you think that's better than you being at home with me? Sharing some of our family life? This isn't the nineteenth century.'

They stared at each other. They were being far more honest than they'd been in mediation, thought Caitlin. More honest than they'd been ever, because now there was nothing to lose.

'I don't know,' said Patrick. 'I could never get a handle on what you wanted because I don't think you knew yourself.'

The traffic began to move, and they made the rest of the journey to Joel's school in silence.

The student teacher who'd let Joel leave the classroom was sobbing in the head teacher's office when they arrived. It was her first week of teaching practice, and already it was turning into her worst nightmare.

'I'm so sorry,' she kept saying. 'I was covering the class for ten minutes while Mrs Clough popped out, and Joel told me he had a note, and that you were just outside and couldn't find a parking space.'

'We have Joel on CCTV leaving the school gates,' said Mrs Douglas. She looked grim. 'We've informed the police and they're looking out for him. He won't have gone far.'

'How do you know?' Caitlin said. She wasn't being aggressive. She just wanted to hear her say, 'Because this has happened before and they were found safe and well in McDonalds.'

But Mrs Douglas didn't say that. She started to talk about ring-rounds.

The next stop was to collect Nancy and already Caitlin could see the dangers of presenting it the wrong way. Because they were late, she was waiting on her own with Shelley, reading a book, and when she saw both Mummy and Daddy coming towards her, at first her face lit up with the spontaneous joy Caitlin remembered.

Then she must have read their expressions because it vanished like sun behind a cloud and she smacked the book shut on her lap.

Patrick had phoned Shelley in advance, and she was only just hiding her concern under her usual cheerfulness. 'Hello, folks!' she said. 'Do you want to take over here? We've got some great reading going on!'

'Hey, Nancy!' Caitlin stretched out her arms. 'What book is it? Can we read together?' She tucked herself on the floor behind her little girl and hoped Nancy couldn't feel the adrenalin shivering through her.

Patrick took off his jacket, and hitched up his trousers so he could sit on the floor too.

Nancy eyed him, then reached out and touched his cheek with her hand. It was her hello.

Patrick touched her small hand on his face, then gently laid his hand on her pink cheek. Caitlin could tell he was making a massive effort to control his emotions.

She cuddled up, putting her mouth right next to Nancy's ear. 'Nancy,' she whispered. 'Do you know where Joel is?' She tried to make it sound like a game.

Nancy shook her head, sending soft baby hair into Caitlin's face.

'Don't you? Would you tell Mummy if you did?' She glanced over at Patrick; normally Nancy would manage an imperceptible whisper in her ear outside of their house if it was really, really urgent, like an emergency loo stop.

'I bet you do know where Joel is,' said Patrick conversationally. 'Is he . . . here?' He hunted around for the first book that came to hand: about farms.

Nancy shook her head.

'He's not on a farm?' Patrick looked surprised.

Caitlin gave him a 'why would he be on a farm?' look, but he carried on. 'What about . . . here?'

This book was about schools. It was the book they'd been reading to prepare them for going up to proper school in the autumn. She held her breath; if Nancy knew Joel was somewhere other than school then . . .

Nancy stared at the book, and then shook her head, and buried it in Caitlin's chest. She could feel Nancy's heart beating inside her like a frightened bird.

Caitlin's gaze met Patrick's over the top of her head, and the world seemed to fall away from her. The only thing holding her up was the determined look in his eyes. A look that said, *I'm here*. And she was so, so grateful he was.

The Quarry had felt different yet again when Eva returned from her walk in the forest with Alex. She'd come in and with her coat still on, she'd taken down most of the photographs of her and Mick – three from the hall alone, and the big one in the kitchen. There were so many. She couldn't bear to look at some of them. They could have been of two strangers.

Two happy strangers, Eva reminded herself, standing there staring at her own smiling face under a sunhat in the Med. She'd changed too since they were taken: her face had thinned, and fine lines traced around her eyes. But the Eva she saw in those photos had options she no longer had, and she couldn't stop the burn of resentment creeping in.

Mick was gone. And for the first time ever, she realised she didn't yearn to turn back the clock. Or if she did, it was only so she could yell and demand some answers.

Eva distracted herself from her furious thoughts by cleaning. She spent the rest of the day getting Joel and Nancy's room ready for their weekend visit. She attacked it thoroughly, hoovering and airing the duvets; putting fresh flowers from the garden on the chest of drawers by the big window, and finally moving Bumble's spare basket to the foot of Nancy's bed. So Nancy would know he was welcome to sleep in with her.

After a shower that didn't make her feel much better, she went in to Longhampton to tell Anna about Alex's revelation about Mick, but she wasn't in the bookshop.

'She's got an appointment at the hospital,' Chloe informed her. 'She left you these?' There was a large book bouquet for Joel and Nancy on the counter, mostly bedtime story books, but even they sent a splinter of sadness into Eva's heart.

Longhampton's pretty spring colours did nothing to lift Eva's mood either, even though she trailed round the town, trying to find reasons to cheer herself up. When she came back, the post had been, and a parcel for her had been left on the doorstep.

Curious, Eva took it into the kitchen and slit open the Sellotape with scissors, while Bumble and Bee watched her from the floor, anticipating food.

'What do you think it is?' she asked Bumble, in Joel's Bee voice. 'Is it a cake?'

Bumble's ears turned over at the word 'cake'. It was one of the few he recognised, along with 'bed' and 'snuggle'; 'walk' was a non-starter.

Whatever was in the box was well-packed in bubble wrap and it took Eva a few moments to unravel it. What dropped into her hand was a tube of bubble mixture, with a note wrapped around it.

It's from Nancy, she thought, pleased. Then her chest filled with hope: was it a peace offering arranged by Caitlin? She unwound the note to find out.

The handwriting was grown up, and it wasn't Caitlin's. It was from Alex, and the message was very short.

Here are some bubbles for you to blow your own secret wishes into. Whatever they are, I hope they come true. A

She stared at the note. Was that a goodbye? Did that mean he was handing over the diaries to someone else?

The thought of never speaking to Alex again pierced Eva with a loneliness she didn't expect. No more funny emails in the small hours, no more snippets of ancient celebrity gossip, no more film festivals or spilled coffee or in-jokes about bicycle clips.

I really like him, she thought, but she knew she was lying to herself. There was more than that. Alex was the first man who'd listened to her. Listened to her properly and encouraged her to listen to herself. And he made her feel like someone she wanted to listen to.

Her phone rang on the table and Eva grabbed it, hoping it would be him.

'Eva? It's Caitlin.' Caitlin sounded strained.

Eva fought down disappointment and made her voice cheery. *Pretend everything was normal.* 'Caitlin, hi! Is this about tonight? Are you dropping Joel and Nancy off as usual?'

Please say yes, please say yes, she thought.

'Please say yes!' she added, half-jokily, because why not?

She had started to move towards the kettle but stopped suddenly when what sounded like a sob echoed down the line.

Eva froze. 'Caitlin? Are you all right?'

'No.' Caitlin was fighting back tears. 'Joel's gone missing and Nancy can't talk at all, not even to me. Not even at home.' This time she did sob, and Eva could barely make out the words.

'Please will you help me?'

Chapter twenty-nine

Eva had never talked to the pugs properly. That was Mick's job and she'd happily let Joel take over.

She didn't have the same crazy imagination Mick and Joel had. They both used the pugs' expressive eyes and mannerisms to lead the conversation into more and more absurd avenues. It was a two-way thing – she could tell Bumble and Bee loved being the centre of human attention, purring and hopping to the giggles of their ventriloquists.

Eva wasn't imaginative, she knew that, and she couldn't keep up the accents either. Bumble was supposed to sound like Alan Bennett but Mick always said, 'Why's Bumble gone Welsh?'

Today though, she found their voices. It was the only thing keeping her from hyperventilating as she drove from Longhampton all the way to Bristol, on a Friday rush hour, waiting for her phone to ring with news of Joel.

'Are yow comfy back there, bab?' she asked Bee, in Bee's chewy Brummie accent. 'Is Bumble giving yow enough room to see out?'

The pugs stared back at her. They were strapped into their car harnesses on the back seat, next to her overnight bag.

It wasn't really she who had been summoned to see Nancy, it was Bumble and Bee.

'Nancy's obviously upset about something. She won't talk to us,' Patrick had explained, once he'd got a distressed Caitlin off the phone. 'We're worried she knows where Joel is, and doesn't want to get him into trouble by telling us, so we were hoping, maybe, she might . . . Oh God, this sounds insane. We were hoping she might tell Bumble?'

It didn't sound insane to Eva. She'd told Bumble and Bee plenty of secrets in the years they'd been together.

'Haven't I?' she added to Bumble, as if he could read her thoughts. 'We've had some good old chats.'

Bumble boggled his eyes at her and lolled out his tongue.

'I'd say you're the better listener, Bumble,' she went on, slipping into his Alan Bennett voice. Mick was right. It did sound a bit Welsh. Still. 'Are you going to help our little friend?'

Bee barked, and she jumped in surprise. That was definitely the first time they'd joined in.

Eva focused on the road, just in case she was finally going mad.

Patrick was waiting for her outside the house when the sat nav finally brought her to a stop in their street.

'Still no sign?' she asked as she unclipped the pugs to lift them out.

'No.' He looked distraught. His hair was sticking up, from his constantly running his hands through it, and there were dark shadows under his cheekbones. 'We've had everyone out searching. The police haven't come up with anything. His phone's either out of range or out of battery.'

'How's Caitlin?'

'Hysterical, obviously. Blaming herself.'

'Oh no. It's not her fault.'

'She says it is. She told Joel we were seeing the mediator to discuss where the kids lived and that he might have to talk to them about what he and Nancy wanted.' Patrick's expression was desperate. 'It's not exactly a huge leap to assume he thought he'd be called in to court, in front of a judge . . . you know how dramatic Joel is. He watches a lot of that court television.'

Eva grimaced.

'I'm not blaming her.' He sighed. 'I should have made time to be there too. We should have told him together. Caitlin was only doing what she thought was right. She's only ever done the very best for the kids.'

In an instant, Eva's wariness of raging tiger-mother Caitlin disappeared, under a surge of concern. 'Where is she?'

'With Nancy. Upstairs. Come in, I'll get your bag.'

Caitlin and Nancy were sitting in Nancy's room at the top of the house. It was very pink, and full of dolls and toys, lined up in order against the wall.

Nancy was on the bed, in her *Frozen* T-shirt that she wore every time she visited Eva, and some stripey leggings. She looked very still, as if a lot was going on inside her head and she didn't want to move in case it spilled out.

Caitlin, hugging her, was a version of herself with all the colour drained out. When she saw Eva at the door, a strange expression crossed her face: relief, and awkwardness.

Don't be awkward, Eva wanted to say. *It was nothing, compared with this.*

She stretched out a hand and tried to smile. 'Hello, Caitlin. Hello, Nancy! Is this your room? Daddy said I could come and see.'

There was no response from Nancy, and a wan smile from Caitlin. Eva took that as encouragement.

'I've brought two friends to see you,' she went on. 'I just wanted to check Mum was happy about them coming upstairs?'

'Ooh!' Caitlin squeezed Nancy. 'Is that who I think it might be?'

'Shall I go and see if they want to come up? OK, you stay there and I'll be right back.'

Patrick was waiting on the landing, with Bumble and Bee on their leads next to him. Bumble was already straining on his harness, wanting to see his friend. Bee was sniffing out next door's cat, who sometimes came in through the dormer window.

'I put the little cameras on the harnesses,' Eva whispered, taking the leads. 'Mick got me these ages ago, when we wanted to see what the pugs were up to while we were out. You get a video stream, and some sound.'

'OK, but how does that help?' Patrick's gaze didn't leave Caitlin and Nancy. They were playing with her doll's house now, moving the dolls from one room to another.

'You download the app . . . look, here's my phone, it's all set up, but basically you can listen in. If there's something maybe Nancy feels she can't say in front of us, a secret Joel's asked her not to tell, then I can get her to tell Bumble, and you can . . . listen. If you leave us alone together with the pugs.'

Patrick frowned, then beckoned Caitlin over. She hurried out, casting glances backwards as Nancy listlessly played with her dolls.

'Eva, tell Caitlin what you've just told me while I distract Nancy,' he whispered, and Eva did.

'I only want to help get Joel home,' she said. She wondered if that was going too far. It had seemed like a brainwave at the time but maybe it was intrusive. Maybe Caitlin thought it was spying? Or her trying to take over again? 'I'll be super careful with the dogs, I promise. Super careful.'

Caitlin gazed at Eva, with glassy brown eyes, and suddenly reached out and hugged her. 'Thank you,' she mumbled. The words were hard to make out. 'I'm sorry.'

'It's fine.' Eva hugged her, then put her firmly at arm's length. 'Come on. Make out this is normal. Take Patrick downstairs for tea.'

Caitlin blinked, wiped her eyes quickly with the side of her finger, then said, brightly, 'Nancy? Shall I ask Daddy to make his special pancakes for tea?'

Nancy was kneeling by the doll's house, while Patrick patiently made two dolls eat supper. She wasn't playing, just passively watching him. He turned to her, and said, 'How about it? I think Joel would like pancakes when he gets home. I'm going to do that. Do you need two more helpers? Because I know two friends who've come to help you . . .'

Eva let Bumble and Bee off their leads, and they went charging over to Nancy. Tears sprang into Eva's eyes when a proper smile broke out over Nancy's face as they butted their wrinkly heads against her for kisses, letting her small hands scratch behind their ears, just where they liked it.

Patrick glanced over the top of the pug-hugging melee and nodded to Eva. Without a fuss, he led Caitlin out of the room, and she was left on her own with her niece.

The enormity of the situation weighed down on Eva. How was she going to do this? How was she going to find the right words for a little girl with no words at all?

Nancy emerged from the pugs and beckoned her over to the doll's house. It had been set up in a sloping corner of the room so it was almost an alcove, like the dogs' hideaway at The Quarry. Eva sat cross-legged as Patrick had been, with Nancy in the horseshoe of her legs, her arms around her. Nancy leaned back against Eva's chest and Bumble scrambled up too. The tiny camera on his harness – the one that had made Mick and Eva rush back from town because its total immobility suggested Bumble had died – would now be broadcasting a good view up Nancy's nose.

How to start, she wondered, but her rational brain was distracted by the trusting way Nancy was relaxing against her, and the baby smell of her hair, the soft strength of her feet braced against Eva's calves.

How could I have wanted this so much and never heard it in my heart? Eva wondered. She shook herself.

'Look what I've got!' She reached into her bag and brought out the bubble mix Alex had given her. 'I thought you might have run out of magic bubbles so I brought my own. We can share if you want?'

Nancy didn't stop stroking Bumble. She didn't take the tube when Eva offered.

'No? Well, shall I start?' Eva dipped the wand into the mix and thought about what she did wish for. Nothing she could say in front of Nancy. She wished to turn the clock back, to find Joel, to be honest with herself, to say things that should have been said, to be herself, instead of the person someone else wanted her to be.

You could only wish for things that could happen. Those were the rules.

'I wish . . .' Eva blew the bubbles. 'I wish that in exactly one hour, you and me, and Joel and Mummy and Daddy will be having fish and chips in your kitchen! How about that?'

Nancy inclined her head. She didn't look convinced.

'Let me do another.' Eva jiggled the wand. 'I wish . . . that you and Joel will come and stay with me and the pugs and Daddy this weekend!' She blew and this time Nancy smiled, a fraction.

'I wish you and Joel and Daddy *and* Mummy will always come and stay with me,' said Eva. 'It makes me very happy, to see you running around my house. And Bumble and Bee love their big cousins too.'

Nancy wriggled closer.

'I wish . . .' The nearness of Nancy, her simple affection, made the hollowness inside Eva's chest fill with something lighter. Something warmer, like eiderdown or apple blossom. Or soap bubbles. 'I wish we could tell Joel all this too. I wonder where he is? Do you know, my darling?'

Nancy froze and her hand stopped moving on Bumble's back.

'Is it a secret? Because if it is, you can put it in a bubble and blow it away.'

As Eva said that, she realised her mistake: she didn't want Nancy to blow it away, she wanted her to tell her it. *Damn.*

But Nancy took the wand and closed her eyes. Then she blew a stream of very determined bubbles, opened her eyes to check they were good, and closed them again.

So there was a secret. She did know where Joel was. That was a start.

Eva cuddled Nancy. She could feel her heart beating and her ribs expanding as she breathed. She felt small in her arms, fragile and strong at the same time.

She lifted a surprised Bumble up so he was sitting on Nancy's knee, but his weight was on Eva's lap. 'You know who's a really good listener? Bumble. I talk to Bumble a lot, don't I, Mr Bumble?'

Bumble gazed back, startled, and licked Nancy's arm with his pink tongue. She smiled – was that a ghost of a giggle?

'Bumble loves you, Nancy. He does. What's that?' Eva pretended to duck her head to Bumble's muzzle, and overcame her natural low embarrassment threshold. 'He says, I'm very fond of you, Nancy Reardon.'

It was a terrible Yorkshire accent for someone who'd been married to a Yorkshireman for seven years but it made Nancy smile.

'And you know who else loves you? Bee. Yow're luvly,' she added, in her Bee voice. 'And me. I love you, Nancy. Like sunshine. When you and Joel come into our house, it's as if all the flowers open up in the garden. And all the birds sing in the trees.'

She hugged her tight. 'I tell Bumble my secrets. I told him how sad I was when Uncle Michael died. I told him how sorry I was that you had to rescue him from the big cows. But how proud I was that you were so brave, and shouted out for him. He was proud of you too, weren't you, Bumble?'

Nancy rewarded her with a big smile, and Eva's heart flipped over. She kissed the top of Nancy's head. It smelled of shampoo. 'So if you've got a secret you need to tell someone and it won't fit in a magic bubble, then why don't you tell Bumble?'

Eva chewed her thumb and hoped hard. Nancy seemed to think; then, to Eva's amazement, she leaned forward and pulled Bumble close. Eva had to strain her ears to hear what she was saying because her whisper was so quiet only a dog could hear. A dog, or someone listening into a microphone on a dog.

'I wish Daddy would come home,' whispered Nancy then looked up bravely at Eva, as if the sky was about to fall in but she was ready for it.

Patrick and Caitlin were crouched just behind the door to Nancy's room, their heads close together over Eva's phone. They had one headphone each shoved in their ears, which was keeping them closer than Caitlin would have liked. She was finding it hard not to pull Patrick's arm around her for comfort.

'I talk to Bumble a lot,' Eva was wittering. The view was of Nancy's chest, which wasn't very helpful – one dog seemed to be sitting on Nancy's lap and the other was pressed up against Eva's leg, giving a close up view of the doll's house kitchen.

It had taken all of Caitlin's newfound resolve to put the children first to ask Eva to bring the dogs. She wasn't sure she could bear to see the pugs without imagining the danger they'd put Nancy in, but she desperately needed to find Joel and if Nancy knew something, and couldn't tell her without the aid of Eva's stupid pugs, Caitlin would have walked across hot coals to get them herself.

'Stop wriggling,' Patrick hissed.

'I'm not.'

Caitlin had to concede that Patrick had been amazing this afternoon. His best side had returned on its old white charger.

433

She'd started to get frantic, when the head started talking about stranger danger and the internet, but Patrick had scooped her up, dealt with the police, and then carried Nancy out to the car on his shoulders, as if it was an extra-fun day. Caitlin's heart had melted at the sight of him pushing down his own fear to make things normal for Nancy.

She glanced at him. He was staring at the screen, watching the non-action in the doll's house, a hank of hair falling over his forehead. And that hour in the car had been weird. Caitlin had had no idea how annoying Patrick's job was. A whole day of that? Constant phone calls, constant monitoring – she'd go crazy. It did explain why he was a bit of a control freak. And why he'd made lists at home instead of wanting to chat. How did you switch off from that?

Poor Patrick. It zipped across her heart very quickly, the flash of regret, illuminating her own lack of understanding. Was it too late? Had she got everything so wrong?

Patrick nudged her. The view was moving away from the doll's house to Eva's leg.

'Nancy said something,' he whispered.

'What?'

'I couldn't make it out.' He fiddled with the volume control until it was up to maximum.

Eva was talking again, half in that stupid accent, and half in her own when she forgot. 'And you know who loves you most in the whole wide world? Your mummy and daddy. You and Joel are the most special things they could ever imagine. More special than diamonds and pearls and sunshine and rainbows and . . .'

There was a muffled sound.

'Yes, and pugs.'

434

Caitlin looked at Patrick in shock. Nancy spoke?

He nodded, equally shocked.

The camera moved; the pug was rubbing its ear against Nancy, as if comforting her. 'You could have the most beautiful house, or the most beautiful clothes, or the biggest pile of money in the world, and it wouldn't be as precious as you are to your mummy and daddy,' said Eva's cracked voice. 'So don't think for one second that your daddy would ever leave you because he didn't love you any more.'

The camera was still for a long moment and she wondered if maybe it had broken, then she saw a lock of pale hair fall in front of the camera and heard Nancy's voice. Very very quiet, like a whisper into a dog's ear.

'Bumble. I wished Daddy would go away. And he did.'

A cold hand clamped down on Caitlin's soul. She looked at Patrick. He looked stricken too.

'When did you wish that, Miss Nancy?' It was the dog voice. Eva was getting her to talk to the dog.

'In London. We were playing the wish game. Mummy gave us wishes if we saw things out of my book.' There was a deep breath. 'Daddy was being cross. He shouted at Joel, and he was cross with Mummy. I wished he would go away . . . and he did.'

The heartbreaking logic of it. Poor Nancy! She thought that?

Caitlin got up to run to her but Patrick put a hand on her arm to stop her. Eva was talking again in her dog voice.

'There's nothing in this world you could say to make him do that. You know, we can remember the day you were born, can't we, Eva? We can. And what did your daddy do?'

Another pause. This time Eva stayed in her own voice. 'He phoned me up and told me that he had a tiny star. And that she

435

was absolutely perfect from her pink toes to her golden hair. And he could never imagine being sad again now he had his beautiful girl, and his lovely boy. He said their hearts were safe in his pocket now, for ever and ever, and his heart was safe in theirs.'

Tears were streaming down Caitlin's cheeks. She looked across at Patrick. He was staring at the screen, his eyes flooded too. He'd said that? To Eva? He'd been so emotional the night Nancy was born, tipsy drunk on his own happiness. She'd never felt more in love with Patrick, standing there in the delivery room, her buttoned-up man swept away with wonderment and adoration. But he'd buttoned it all back up again. Why? Because that's what he thought dads did?

'I wished I could see a fire engine like in my book, and one came!' Nancy's voice was quiet but distinct. 'And I wished I could have a dog, and you came, Bumble.'

'Was that why you didn't like reading that book together? Did you think the book was listening to you?'

The hair in front of the screen moved – a nod.

'And is that . . . Is that why you don't like talking outside the house, in case someone hears you wishing and it comes true?'

Caitlin's breath was bursting in her chest, burning like bonfire smoke. Her hand ached and she realised Patrick was gripping it tightly in his.

There was a sniff and a nod. 'I was scared. So I didn't talk. And now I can't.'

Caitlin scrambled up. This time she had to go to her baby. She had to. But Patrick pulled her down again.

'One more second,' he whispered. 'Eva's telling her something. Let her.'

'Do you know about wishes, Miss Nancy?' Eva's voice was

very soft. 'Only the ones that are *meant* to come true do. That's why those magic bubbles pop. It's because we've wished for the wrong thing! When you wished for a fire engine, one was coming anyway. And when you wished for a dog, Mr Bumble was already planning to meet you.'

'Really?' Nancy's voice was small but not on the edge of tears any more.

'I make lots of wishes,' Eva was whispering. 'I wished for a little boy, just like Joel. Kind and clever, with blue eyes and a big laugh. But that wish didn't come true. Maybe it wasn't meant to. But I'm not sad, because what I wanted was a *family*, Nancy, and here you all are. You and Joel, and Mummy and Daddy.'

'And Bumble and Bee.'

'And Bumble and Bee. My family. Our family.'

Caitlin's heart ached now for Eva. She remembered the conflict in her face as she carried Nancy from the train. As if she had her arms full of the most precious thing, but just for one moment. The pride and the longing, and the care. Knowing that she'd never have it for herself. That she could never take it for granted

She glanced at Patrick, stricken with sudden realisation. How hard had they made it for Eva, opening her house to Joel and Nancy and expecting her to cope? Expecting her to be grateful? Eva wasn't stand-offish – she was struggling with more than grief.

He looked back, unhappily, as if he hadn't realised either.

The hair moved across the camera. Nancy was hugging her auntie. 'Don't cry, Auntie Eva,' she said. 'Don't cry.'

'I'm not crying, sweetie pie. I'm just sad that you were sad all that time when you didn't need to be. We'd rather hear you singing and dancing and shouting and playing . . .'

The microphone rustled as the dogs climbed up onto Eva's lap. Caitlin assumed there was a mass hug-in going on.

And then, very casually, Eva whispered, 'Can you tell Mr Bumble where Joel is? He'd like to invite him to tea tonight. Will Daddy have to get him in his car?'

Clever Eva. Not making a big thing about it.

Nancy forgot she was supposed to be keeping a secret, and whispered into the dog's ear, 'He's gone to the railway station to wait until Mummy's come back from the place where Joel has to choose where we live.'

'Oh, he doesn't have to do that . . .' Eva started, but Caitlin had heard enough.

She ripped the earphone out of her ear and got up, running through to the bedroom where Eva and Nancy and the dogs were sitting by the doll's house. Nancy looked surprised to see her mother bursting out of nowhere but held out her arms urgently to be picked up, the way she did when she was a baby.

Eva looked up too and Caitlin smiled at her through her tears. She wanted to say thank you, for doing something no one else had managed to do, for giving her little girl her voice back, but her throat was choked.

Eva lifted Nancy up so Caitlin could swing her into her arms, and then Patrick was in the room too, jangling his car keys as if that had been the plan all along. His face was wet but he was pretending everything was normal.

'We ready to go, Fancy Nancy?' he asked.

He had never looked more *right*, thought Caitlin, than when he held out his arms to hold his little girl and his wife. Patrick was a good dad. A kind man. They had their problems, but wasn't it worth working through them for this? Wasn't it worth trying to be the best version of themselves, rather than trying to be something they weren't?

'Shall we go to the station and get Joel?' he said, and Nancy nodded.

They held their breath as she screwed up her face and whispered, 'Yes!' Then hid it in her mummy's hair, smiling and gasping with the effort.

Chapter thirty

If Eva hadn't been emptying the spare room to start painting it Nancy's selected shade of sunshine yellow, she might never have found the letter.

It was in an envelope the charity shop had given back to her months previously – a collection of odds and ends she'd forgotten to take out of Mick's clothes when she'd donated them. Later Eva worked out that the letter, in its unaddressed envelope, had been in his navy blazer, the one he'd been wearing the night he gave her the eternity ring on holiday in St Tropez.

She didn't need to open it to know it was for her.

Eva sat on the bed and read it through, and Mick's voice was as clear in her head as if he'd been standing there, even though, three years after his death, she couldn't quite remember what his nose was like without checking on a photo.

My darling Little Eva (how that dates me!)

I'm writing you this letter instead of sitting there with your hands in mine, telling you to your face, because I'm a coward. A coward, and a tongue-tied fool. I always do better with other writers' lines in my head, especially when it comes to matters of the heart. So forgive me. It's only because I want to get this right.

All I Ever Wanted

We talked a while back about babies, and I said that if you wanted them, I'd set you free to find a man who'd make you the fine mam you would be. I said I didn't want any more. That was only partly true. Here's why, in inelegant bullet points.

* Eva, I'll be honest; Una and I ruined Tyson. We fucked him up, as the great poet would say, with our dodgy genes, our bad parenting and our best intentions. I cannot, will not, do that again. My genes are alcoholic, they're selfish, they're short in the leg. And I'm not cut out for responsible shaping of a human life. I couldn't inflict the misery Una and I went through, the heartache, the worry, the rows . . . on your sweet self. Because I know you, Eva. I know you worry you'd be a bad parent because your cold fish of a dad laid that appalling burden on your little shoulders, and you'd drive yourself into the ground to prove him wrong.

* I'm too old. My darling, I'm already sixty-one, with a liver you could make paté from, and an aversion to exercise. I don't want to bring death into a child's life before he's old enough to drink a toast at my wake. I had plenty of friends in my youth who'd lost their dads too young, and it never ends well.

* I must steel myself here, and say all the above is just table decoration because I can't have children. Physically can't. I had the snip exactly two weeks before I met you in that charity shop. I was still achey, if you must know. I'm vain enough to hope you didn't think I was decrepit, with that limp. I made that rather radical decision because the reasons I've just given were true, and a million times more so, with my second (and penultimate) wife – who would have not been a millionth of the mother you could be. It's a decision I will regret and grieve for my whole life, and I am so very sorry. I did go back to the clinic

441

to enquire about reversals but alas, the first specialist had done too good a job.

And now the biggest honesty of all. I can't tell you this because I am terrified of losing you. There is nothing in the world I want more than to be three feet away from you at all times. I feel as if my life has been moving slowly to this point, like a great planet rotating into position. I don't want to share you, I don't want to risk losing you, I don't want anything other than to spend the rest of my days listening to you talk, looking at your beautiful face, watching you make my house a home. I know, to the outside world, we don't have a lot in common, but something about your soul, Eva, chimes with mine, and that is so rare in this world of discord and pissy little squabbles.

So you see my choice? Tell you, and risk losing you, or not tell you, and risk losing you because you're so disgusted by my cowardice. It's no choice, and I don't mind telling you, I'm yellow-bellied. Whatever you make of this letter, my beautiful woman, please forgive me. Because I am yours, forever.

M

Eva sat on the bed and read it three times. Tears blurred her eyes the second and third time round, but she wiped them away. Then she walked into the study and took out the note pad she'd been using to make notes for Alex, for her essay about living with a man who belonged to everyone, that was going to make up the forward to her late husband's diaries.

Dear Mick, [she wrote]
Thank you for your honesty. Bit late, but better late than never. Thank you for the time you gave me, and the mirror

you held up to me. I don't know if I know a lot more about myself ten years down the line from the woman you met, but I know what I'm not, and sometimes that's a better starting point.

Who knows? Maybe my planets are about to align with the love of this life too. I hope so. They certainly never stop turning. I'm glad I met you. I'm glad we only ever created happiness together.

With love, E

She read it back to herself, folded it up, and tucked it into the inside pocket of the one jacket of Mick's she'd kept: an old cord one he'd worn for pottering around the garden. One day that jacket would go out too. Maybe not quite yet. But soon.

Then Eva closed the door of the spare-room wardrobe, went downstairs to the hall, and picked up the phone, all without thinking. She dialled on autopilot, as if her brain had assumed control of her body, but at the same time, she had a strange certainty she was doing the right thing.

'Hello!' she said, when it was answered. 'Is this a good time to talk?'

'Eva? It's always a good time to talk to you. How's tricks?'

Alex's voice made her calm inside. Calm but filled with a rising excitement, the same way she felt on a plane, sitting on the runway before it was due to take off.

'Busy. I've finished your homework, for a start.' Out of habit, Eva turned away from the hall mirror and its unforgiving lighting, then made herself turn back and faced her reflection. Yes, there were lines around her eyes, and yes, her neck was starting to look like her mum's, but there was a glow about her. A warmth and a sparkle in her eyes, and she knew now where it had come from.

'Very good homework it is too,' said Alex. 'I might get you to edit Una's? There's a woman who's a stranger to a comma. Or tact. What else have you been doing?'

'I've booked a holiday,' Eva went on, her brain still running ahead of her. 'I wanted to go somewhere I've never been, and do something I've never done, so I put a pin in a list and I'm going pony-trekking in the Brecon Beacons.'

'What?' Alex laughed, his surprising rich giggle. 'I thought you were going to say swimming with turtles in Goa. Actually, are there turtles in Goa? I don't know. I've only ever been as far as Cannes.'

'No idea. Anyway, I've done turtles,' said Eva. 'And dolphins and, regrettably, sharks. My wet-suit days are behind me. I was wondering . . .' And now for something else she'd never done, the big one. 'Do you fancy coming with me?'

'To Brecon? What if I've already been pony-trekking?'

'Then you can help me with my bridle.' Her throat was dry but she tried to keep her tone light. 'Or whatever it is ponies have.'

Alex laughed again. 'If you can imagine me on a pony and you're not horrified at the idea of the carnage I could cause, then what can I say but yes? I'd love to. When?'

'The second weekend of next month. I've got a few meetings in London about a business idea I've had, and Joel and Nancy are coming to stay for a couple of nights, but I can change it if you're lecturing or something?'

There was a pause and Eva imagined Alex pushing his glasses up his nose, squinting mischievously through them at her. Seeing her, as she was, right now.

'Eva, you mind reader,' he said, 'how did you know a pony-trekking holiday in Wales was exactly what I'd wished for?'

She started to speak but when Alex added, more softly, 'With you,' Eva found she couldn't speak through her smile.

Patrick was waiting for Caitlin by the entrance when she walked into Eastville Park. She knew it was him from the upright way he was standing reading the noticeboard, his hands jammed into his pockets, his eyes fixed on the notices, oblivious to the other people wandering in with ice creams and pushchairs.

She wondered if Patrick remembered that it was the park where he'd asked her to marry him. They'd been watching Joel pirouette ahead along the path by the lake, swishing his imaginary épée at invisible swordsmen – it had been Robin Hood term – and he'd turned to her and blurted it out. He hadn't got a ring, or a prepared speech. It was very unlike Patrick.

'I just want us to spend the rest of our lives doing this,' he'd said, and then apologised for not planning an elaborate proposal with candles and a tiny Tiffany box.

Caitlin had accepted at once, specifically because he hadn't planned one. She knew then that he'd meant it from his heart.

'Thanks for coming,' he said, when she approached. His face was tired, and tense. 'Joanne didn't mind you swapping your shift?'

Caitlin almost said, 'When I told her you'd taken the day off work to talk to me she nearly gave us *all* a holiday,' but she didn't want it to come out wrong. Since she and Patrick had rescued Joel from his short exile in the railway station (not the scariest ordeal for him in the end, given that he'd spent most of it in the Pumpkin Café, struggling not to talk to strangers) they'd been communicating in a deliberately kind manner. It felt so different that Caitlin realised belatedly – and sorrowfully – what a strain it had been before.

'No, it was fine,' she said. 'And it's only a shift. You must have taken a whole day's holiday?'

Her tone must have come off a bit 'surprised' because Patrick shuffled awkwardly. 'Well, it's important. I wanted to talk to you properly. Now . . . the dust's settled a bit.'

'The dust's been settled a while,' Caitlin pointed out. 'Joel's pestering Eva to take her up on that crazy offer of meeting Mick's old agent. Nancy's wrecked a pair of shoes doing spins on her toes. I'm back to being driven insane by the laundry. It's about as normal as it ever gets.'

'I meant *your* dust.' Patrick looked straight into her eyes, his gaze honest and searching. 'With you. I need us to be straight with each other. I don't want this to get mixed up in your gratitude for being rescued. You always did have a bit of a thing about being rescued.'

Caitlin flushed. 'And you've got a bit of a rescuer complex.' She returned his gaze, and they stood staring at each other, on the edge of another argument.

One more word, one wrong step and this would end up where every other conversation had in the past. She couldn't bear another. Something had to change.

'I'm not—' Caitlin stopped herself, checking her instinct to argue back rather than look at the hard truth she was trying to ignore. She took a deep breath. 'Patrick, I'm so glad you were there for us all. We needed you. But *I* don't need to be *saved* from anything any more. I'm a mother, and an adult, and when I mess things up, from now on I deal with the fallout myself.'

She meant it. 'For your information,' she went on, since he was always so keen on evidence, 'last night, there was a bit of a domestic . . . incident, and I went online and found out how to unscrew a U-bend. And I did it.'

That was the very abridged version but Caitlin had rarely felt prouder. Nancy had clapped. Joel had sworn never to wash anyone's jewellery in the sink, and then clapped too.

'Which sink was blocked? Who blocked it?' Patrick's brow furrowed and he started to look annoyed, then he checked himself too. 'Good. That's really . . . great. Well done.'

'Thanks.'

They both fell silent, then Patrick said, 'Should we walk?'

'Yes,' said Caitlin. This was going to be hard, but they had to do it. 'That might be easier.'

They walked some way without speaking, past the bowling greens, and then Patrick said, 'Cait, I wanted to tell you that I've got that job I applied for, nearer home. I've got to work some notice, but the plan is to be back by August.'

Caitlin was surprised by how happy that made her. Not relieved, but genuinely happy. 'That's great news. The kids will be thrilled.'

'Good. I've missed them so much.' He waited for a second, then added, as if he wasn't confident of the answer, 'And you?'

She held his question carefully in her mind. Caitlin didn't want to get this wrong; she'd thought about it pretty much every moment since Joel had come home, running possible conversations through until she was prepared for all eventualities.

What rushed out of her mouth surprised her. 'Patrick, why did you decide to break up?' It wasn't the line she'd rehearsed;

447

that was much classier, and a lot longer. 'What did I do? Did you think I was seeing someone else? Because I wasn't.'

He looked at her, long and hard, as if he didn't quite believe her, then said, 'Look, it wasn't working any more, was it? Everything I tried to do to make things better seemed to make you want to be around me less. And we'd been so good together. I knew how good it *could* be, and it wasn't any more.'

'It was a rocky patch,' said Caitlin. 'I told you things would get deranged with two kids. I needed more space, you needed more attention, the kids eat up energy like vampires ... No one's fault. We should have cut ourselves a bit more slack.'

'Was it only that, though?' He gave her a piercing look, the one that used to make Caitlin throw up defensive walls. 'You looked unhappy all the time.'

'I was unhappy with myself,' confessed Caitlin. 'I just didn't see it as clearly as I do now. But I'm dealing with it. Mum's got me seeing some woman who makes me put figures in a sandbox and talk about my fear of failure. Which, to be honest, I thought I'd been talking about for years but still . . .'

'Well, it felt like I was causing it,' he said bluntly. 'I hated making you miserable. Trapping you in a dead marriage. Whenever we talked, we argued. You avoided me. I thought I was doing you a favour, setting you free to find something better.'

'You thought it was better *for the kids* that we broke up?' She stopped, staring at him in disbelief. 'Where's the logic in that?'

Patrick stopped walking. He looked heartbroken and ashamed. 'I thought we could work something out,' he admitted. 'I'd read about couples who'd managed to live apart but parent . . .' He shook his head. 'I got it wrong. I was *so* wrong. I can't stop thinking about Nancy. Our poor baby, thinking it was her fault I left.'

'At least we know now why she wasn't talking,' said Caitlin. She didn't want to rub it in but that last meeting with the speech therapist hadn't been easy for her either. At least she and Patrick had put on a united front for the guilt trip. 'It could have turned into a much harder thing to break if it had gone on longer.'

'But Joel too. Making him feel he had no choice but to run away. I'm a terrible father. Really . . . shit. All I ever wanted was a family and I destroyed it.'

Caitlin turned, surprised by the anguish in his voice, and saw Patrick was on the verge of tears. She'd never heard him sound so despairing. She'd never heard him admit that he'd got anything wrong, come to think of it.

'I was trying to give Joel and Nancy a perfect, happy childhood.' His voice cracked with the effort of forcing out the words. 'I couldn't believe how lucky I was to have met a woman like you, then to have had our beautiful children. And I tried so hard to . . .'

'Stop.' Caitlin grabbed his arms. 'Patrick, no one is perfect. Nothing is perfect. If that's what you're aiming for in life, you will go mad. We are what we are, and we do the best we can, and we love each other for trying. Right?'

This part at least was the message Caitlin had wanted to get over, but Patrick's reaction was sending her off course. She gazed up into his face, so open and easy to read. Even now, through the hurt in his red-rimmed eyes, when he looked at her, there was a simple love burning there, telling her what was in his heart. Nancy's eyes, clear and expressive.

And I love him, Caitlin thought, emotion sweeping through her like forest fire. *I love this determined, patient, kind-hearted man. If I let him go, I'll be making the biggest mistake of my mistake-strewn life.*

'I am *not* perfect,' she said emphatically. 'But I'm willing to be the best version of me I can manage. For you. With you.'

Patrick opened his mouth to speak, and nothing came out. He cupped her cheek in his hand and looked at her for a few long seconds; for a horrible moment, Caitlin was scared he was working out how to say goodbye.

'You are perfect *for me*, Caity,' he said at last. 'With all your flaws, and all my flaws – we make something more incredible than both of us. And I know that because life without you is . . .' He shook his head, as if he didn't know a word strong enough.

'Come back,' said Caitlin. 'Come home, Patrick.'

The word *home* sent a shiver of something inexpressibly tender across Patrick's face and impulsively, Caitlin flung her arms around him, and kissed him. She breathed deep, taking in the citrusy smell of Patrick's skin, and his clean shirt, and the familiar, yet exciting, taste of his lips, his mouth, his arms around her back, pulling her closer, closer, into the strong solidness of his body. They fitted so perfectly together, her heart and her soul wrapping around him with the same intensity – the same sensation of a key turning in a lock. Two broken shards of pottery fitting back together, fixed with golden glue to make something beautiful and new – and secure in the knowledge that it could always be fixed.

We rescued each other, thought Caitlin. *And that makes us equal.*

They stood, kissing and holding each other, until the tears had dried on their faces, and the sunshine felt warm on Caitlin's back.

'Cup of tea?' said Patrick, stepping back with a wonky smile. He gestured at the café at the bottom of the park.

Caitlin nodded. She knew her mascara had run. She didn't care. She wanted to dance and spin and sing, just like Nancy.

'I'll make it,' she said. 'Back home.'

Nancy stood two steps from the middle of the stage in her pink fairy tutu. She wasn't the main dancer in the routine but she had one line to sing which had to be louder than everyone else.

She was a bit fluttery in the tummy because there were quite a lot of people in the big room, lots of mummies and daddies. But they were all smiling and clapping so Nancy was trying not to be nervous. It was the last concert she would do before she went to big school, and she wanted it to be amaaaaazing, like Joel would say.

Nancy ignored what Shelley had said about singing to the back of the room, and stared happily at the front row which was filled with faces she knew. Mummy was sitting in the middle seat next to Daddy. They were holding hands. Joel was next to Daddy, and he was filming her on his camera, even though it wasn't strictly allowed. Next to Joel was Auntie Eva and her friend Alex in his funny glasses, and Nancy could see – even though Mummy and Daddy couldn't – that he kept smiling at Auntie Eva when she wasn't looking, and she kept smiling at him, secret smiles.

I will tell Bumble that later, Nancy thought. *I will ask what he thinks about Auntie Eva's friend.* She and Joel were going to stay with Bumble and Bee again, while Mummy and Daddy moved into their new house in Worcester. She and Joel had a bedroom each and Daddy had promised they could get a dog of their own.

Nancy smiled inside. And she smiled on the outside.

And when the music started for her song, Nancy stepped forward with the other flower fairies, opened her mouth and sang so loud she thought her heart would burst out of her chest.

Acknowledgements

Here's a confession: I live in Longhampton in my head half the time. Luckily for me, there are people around me who not only encourage this mad behaviour but also drop in themselves now and again. (Or so they say.) My inspirational agent, Lizzy Kremer, can see the town as clearly as I can, particularly the shops, as does her magical colleague, Harriet Moore. I've taken extended walks around the municipal gardens during the course of writing this story with Francesca Best, Sara Kinsella and Kate Howard, who all steered me firmly away from the bandstand, and back onto the right path. Thanks, genius editors! And Naomi Berwin, Veronique Norton, Sharan Matharu, and the fantastic team at Hodder who have willingly moved (mentally) into Longhampton too, and make ideal imaginary neighbours. They always have brilliant ideas, and cake. I'm grateful to you all. In my head, I'm taking the lot of you to Ferrari's for cocktails.

But the person who understood Longhampton best was my mother, Patricia, who died this summer while I was deep in the middle of this story of parents, children, language and silence. Mum taught me to read, but more than that, she taught me to love words and the infinite worlds they open up for you like golden keys. (She also taught thousands of other children to unpick Shakespeare, knit their own metaphors, and spell 'necessary'. Good teachers aren't just for exams, they're for life.) We talked on the phone nearly every lunchtime while I was walking the dogs, chatting about plots, people, stories we'd heard, books we recommended to each other. Longhampton sprang to life from the warm-hearted places we both grew up, from gossip and family secrets, from advice given and 'what would you do?' dilemmas, and the kaleidoscope of human behaviour. I will miss my beautiful, witty mother for ever, but part of her lovely soul will always be in the town she and I discussed as if it was our own in the quiet kindness Longhampton locals show each other, and the funny, some-times wise, things they say, and the book-hungry way their footsteps inevitably head towards Anna's bookshop.

Lucy Dillon

grew up in Cumbria and read English
at Cambridge, then read a lot of
magazines as a press assistant
in London, then read other people's
manuscripts as a junior fiction editor.
She now lives in a village outside
Hereford with an old red Range
Rover, and too many books.

All I Ever Wanted
is Lucy Dillon's seventh novel
for Hodder & Stoughton.

🐦 @lucy_dillon
f /LucyDillonBooks

LUCY DILLON

One Small Act of Kindness

Shortlisted for the RoNA Contemporary
Romantic Novel Award

What can you do to make the world a better place?

Libby and her husband Jason have moved back to his home-town to turn the family B&B into a boutique hotel. They have left London behind and all the memories – good and bad – that went with it.

The injured woman Libby finds lying in the remote country road has lost her memory. She doesn't know why she came to be there, and no one seems to be looking for her. When Libby offers to take her in, this one small act of kindness sets in motion a chain of events that will change many people's lives . . .

'A book you'll read into the wee hours, full of warmth, love
and bravery.'
Lucy Robinson

HODDER

LUCY DILLON

A Hundred Pieces of Me

Shortlisted for the RoNA Contemporary
Romantic Novel Award

**Letters from the only man she's ever truly loved.
A keepsake of the father she never really knew.
A blue glass vase that catches the light on a grey day.**

Gina Bellamy is starting again, after a few years she'd rather
forget. But the belongings she's treasured for so long don't
seem to fit who she is now.

So Gina makes a resolution. She'll keep just a hundred special
items – the rest can go.

But that means coming to terms with her past and learning
to embrace the future, whatever it might bring.

'Bittersweet, lovely and ultimately redemptive; the kind of
book that makes you want to live your own life better.'
Jojo Moyes

HODDER

LUCY DILLON

The Secret of Happy Ever After

When **Anna** takes over Longhampton's bookshop, it's her dream come true. And not just because it gets her away from her rowdy stepchildren and their hyperactive Dalmatian.

As she unpacks boxes of childhood classics, Anna can't shake the feeling that maybe her own fairytale ending isn't all that she'd hoped for. But as the stories of love, adventure, secret gardens and giant peaches breathe new life into the neglected shop, Anna and her customers get swept up in the magic too.

Even Anna's best friend **Michelle** – who categorically doesn't believe in true love and handsome princes – isn't immune.

But when secrets from Michelle's own childhood come back to haunt her, and disaster threatens Anna's home, will the wisdom and charm of the stories in the bookshop help the two friends – and those they love – find their own happy ever after?

'Lucy Dillon's voice is gentle and kind throughout . . . perceptive and well handled. A heart-warming piece of escapism for long winter nights.'
Red

HODDER